The Other Side

J. D. Robb

Mary Blayney

Patricia Gaffney

Ruth Ryan Langan

Mary Kay McComas

JOVE BOOKS, NEW YORK

THE BERKLEY PUBLISHING GROUP
Published by the Penguin Group
Penguin Group (USA) Inc.
375 Hudson Street, New York, New York 10014, USA
Penguin Group (Canada), 90 Eglinton Avenue East, Suite 700, Toronto, Ontario M4P 2Y3, Canada
(a division of Pearson Penguin Canada Inc.)
Penguin Books Ltd., 80 Strand, London WC2R 0RL, England
Penguin Group Ireland, 25 St. Stephen's Green, Dublin 2, Ireland (a division of Penguin Books Ltd.)
Penguin Group (Australia), 250 Camberwell Road, Camberwell, Victoria 3124, Australia
(a division of Pearson Australia Group Pty. Ltd.)
Penguin Books India Pvt. Ltd., 11 Community Centre, Panchsheel Park, New Delhi—110 017, India
Penguin Group (NZ), 67 Apollo Drive, Rosedale, North Shore 0632, New Zealand
(a division of Pearson New Zealand Ltd.)
Penguin Books (South Africa) (Pty.) Ltd., 24 Sturdee Avenue, Rosebank, Johannesburg 2196,
South Africa

Penguin Books Ltd., Registered Offices: 80 Strand, London WC2R 0RL, England

This is a work of fiction. Names, characters, places, and incidents either are the product of the authors' imaginations or are used fictitiously, and any resemblance to actual persons, living or dead, business establishments, events, or locales is entirely coincidental. The publisher does not have control over and does not have any responsibility for author or third-party websites or their content.

THE OTHER SIDE

A Jove Book / published by arrangement with the authors

PRINTING HISTORY

ISBN: 978-1-61129-130-8

JOVE®
Jove Books are published by The Berkley Publishing Group,
a division of Penguin Group (USA) Inc.,
375 Hudson Street, New York, New York 10014.
JOVE® is a registered trademark of Penguin Group (USA) Inc.
The "J" design is a trademark of Penguin Group (USA) Inc.

PRINTED IN THE UNITED STATES OF AMERICA

Contents

Possession in Death

J. D. Robb

Love is strong as death.

SONG OF SOLOMON

Whence and what art thou, execrable shape?

JOHN MILTON

One

She spent the morning with a murderer.

He'd been under guard in a hospital bed recovering from a near-fatal wound—courtesy of a misstep by his partner in crime—but she'd had no sympathy.

She was glad he'd lived, wished him a long, long life—in an off-planet concrete cage. She believed the case she and her team had built to be solid—as did the nearly gleeful prosecuting attorney. The sprinkles on the icing of this particular cupcake was the confession she'd finessed out of him as he'd sneered at her.

Given that he'd tried to kill her less than twenty-four hours before, the sneer was small change.

Sylvester Moriarity would receive the best medical care New York could provide, then he'd join his friend Winston Dudley behind bars until what promised to be a sensational, media-soaked trial, given their family fortunes and names.

Case closed, she told herself as she pushed her way through the heat-soaked Saturday afternoon traffic toward home. The dead now had the only justice she could offer, and their families and friends the comfort—if comfort it was—that those responsible would pay.

But it haunted her: the waste, the cruelty, the utter selfish-

ness of two men who were so puffed up by their own impor-
tance, their *station*, that they'd considered murder a form of
entertainment, a twisted sort of indulgence.

She manuevered through New York traffic, barely hearing the blasts of horns, the annoyingly cheerful hype of the ad
blimps heralding midsummer sales at the Sky Mall. Tourists
swarmed the city—and likely the Sky Mall as well—chowing
down on soy dogs from the smoking glide-carts, looking for
souvies and bargains among the shops and street vendors.

A boiling stew, she thought, in the heat and humidity of
summer 2060.

She caught the lightning move of a nimble-fingered street
thief, bumping through a couple of tourists more intent on
gawking at the buildings and their ringing people glides than
their own security. He had the wallet in the goody slit of his
baggy cargos in half a finger snap and slithered like a snake
through the forest of people lumbering across the crosswalk.

If she'd been on foot, or at least headed in the same direction, she'd have pursued—and the chase might've lifted her
mood. But he and his booty smoked away, and he'd no doubt
continue to score well on today's target shoot.

Life went on.

When Lieutenant Eve Dallas finally drove through the
stately gates of home, she reminded herself of that again. Life
went on—and in her case, today, that included a cookout, a
horde of cops, and her odd assortment of friends. A couple
years before, it would've been the last way she'd have spent a
Saturday, but things had changed.

Her living arrangements certainly had, from a sparsely furnished apartment to the palace-fortress Roarke had built. Her
husband—and *that* was a change, even if they'd just celebrated
their second year of marriage—had the vision, the need, and,
God knew, the means to create the gorgeous home with its myr-
iad rooms filled with style and function. Here the grass was rich
summer green, the trees and flowers plentiful.

Here was peace and warmth and welcome. And she needed
them, maybe just a little desperately at the moment.

She left her vehicle at the front entrance, knowing Summerset, Roarke's majordomo, would send it to its place in the
garage. And hoped, just this once, he wasn't looming like a
scarecrow in the foyer.

She wanted the cool and quiet of the bedroom she shared with Roarke, a few minutes of solitude. Time, she thought as she strode toward the doors, to shake off this mood before the invasion.

Halfway to the doors, she stopped. The front wasn't the only way in, for Christ's sake—and why hadn't she ever thought of that before? On impulse, she jogged around—long legs eating up ground—crossed one of the patios, turned through a small, walled garden, and went in through a side door. Into a parlor or sitting room or morning room—who knew? she thought with a roll of tired brown eyes—and made her way as sneakily as the street thief across the hallway, down and into the more familiar territory of the game room, where she knew the lay of the land.

She called the elevator and considered it a small, personal victory when the doors shut her in. "Master bedroom," she ordered, then just leaned back against the wall, shut her eyes, while the unit navigated its way.

When she stepped into the bedroom, she raked a hand through her messy cap of brown hair, stripped the jacket off her lanky frame, and tossed it at the handiest chair. She stepped onto the platform and sat on the side of the lake-sized bed. If she'd believed she could escape into sleep, she'd have stretched out, but there was too much in her head, in her belly, for rest.

So she simply sat, veteran cop, Homicide lieutenant who'd walked through blood and death more times than she could count, and mourned a little.

Roarke found her there.

He could gauge her state of mind by the slump of her shoulders, by the way she sat, staring out the window. He walked to her, sat beside her, took her hand.

"I should've gone with you."

She shook her head but leaned against him. "No place for civilians in Interview, and nothing you could've done anyway if I'd stretched it and brought you in as expert consultant. I had him cold and cut through his battalion of expensive lawyers like a fucking machete. I thought the PA was going to kiss me on the mouth."

He brought the hand he held to his lips. "And still you're sad."

She closed her eyes, comforted a little by the solidity of him beside her, by that whisper of Ireland in his voice, even by the scent so uniquely him. "Not sad, or . . . I don't know what the hell I am. I should be buzzed. I did the job; I slammed it shut—and I got to look them both in the face and let them know it."

She shoved up, paced to the window, away again, and realized it wasn't peace and comfort she wanted after all. Not quite yet. It was a place to let it go, let it out, spew the rage.

"He was pissed. Moriarity. Lying there with that hole in his chest his pal put into him with his freaking antique Italian foil."

"The one meant for you," Roarke reminded her.

"Yeah. And he's pissed, seriously pissed, Dudley missed and it wasn't me on a slab at the morgue."

"I expect he was," Roarke said coolly. "But that's not what's got you going."

She paused a minute, just looked at him. Stunning blue eyes in a stunning face, the mane of thick black hair, that poet's mouth set firm now because she'd made him think of her on that slab at the morgue.

"You know they never had a chance to take me. You were there."

"And still he drew blood, didn't he?" Roarke nodded at the healing wound on her arm.

She tapped it. "And this helped sew them up. Attempted murder of a police officer just trowels on the icing. They didn't make their next score. Now they have to end their competition with a tie, which oddly enough is what I think they always wanted. They just planned for the contest to go on a lot longer. And you know what the prize was at the end? Do you know what the purse for this goddamn tournament was?"

"I don't, no, but I see you got it out of Moriarity today."

"Yeah, I wound him up so tight he had to let it spring out. A dollar. A fucking dollar, Roarke—just one big joke between them. And it makes me sick."

It shocked, even appalled her a little, that her eyes stung, that she felt tears pressing hard. "It makes me sick," she repeated. "All those people dead, all those lives broken and shattered, and *this* makes me sick? I don't know why, I just don't know why it churns my stomach. I've seen worse. God, we've both seen worse."

"But rarely more futile." He stood, took her arms, gently rubbing. "No reason, no mad vendetta or fevered dream, no vengeance or greed or fury. Just a cruel game. Why shouldn't it make you sick? It does me as well."

"I contacted the next of kin," she began. "Even the ones we found from before they started this matchup in New York. That's why I'm late getting back. I thought I needed to, and thought if I closed it all the way, I'd feel better. I got gratitude. I got anger and tears, everything you expect. And every one of them asked me why. Why had these men killed their daughter, their husband, their mother?"

"And what did you tell them?"

"Sometimes there's no why, or not one we can understand." She squeezed her eyes tight. "I want to be pissed."

"You are, under it. And under that, you know you did good work. And you're alive, darling Eve." He drew her in to kiss her brow. "Which, to take this to their level, makes them losers."

"I guess it does. I guess that's going to have to be enough."

She took his face in her hands, smiled a little. "And there's the added bonus that they hate us both. Really hate us. That adds a boost."

"I can't think of anyone I'd rather be hated by, or anyone I'd rather be hated with."

Now the smile moved into her eyes. "Me either. If I keep that front and center, I could be in the mood to party. I guess we should go down and do whatever we're supposed to do before everybody gets here."

"Change first. You'll feel more in the party mode without your boots and weapon."

By the time she'd changed trousers for cotton pants, boots for skids, and made it downstairs, she heard voices in the foyer. She spotted her partner, Peabody, her short, dark ponytail bouncing, summery dress swirling. Peabody's cohab, e-detective and premier geek McNab, stood beside her in a skin tank crisscrossed with more colors than an atomic rainbow paired with baggy, hot pink knee shorts and gel flips.

He turned, the forest of silver rings on his left earlobe shimmering, and shot Eve a wide grin. "Hey, Dallas. We brought you something."

"My granny's homemade wine." Peabody held up the bottle. "I know you've got a wine cellar the size of California, but we thought you'd get a charge. It's good stuff."

"Let's go out and open it up. I'm ready for some good stuff."
Peabody kept eye contact, quirked her brows. "All okay?"

"The PA's probably still doing his happy dance. Case closed,"
she said, and left out the rest. No point in adding the details now
that would leave her partner as troubled as she'd been.

"We'll have the first drink with a toast to the NYPSD's
Homicide—and Electronic Detectives divisions," Roarke said
with a wink for McNab.

The wide stone terrace held tables already loaded with food
and shaded by umbrellas, and the gardens exploded with color
and scent. The monster grill Roarke had conquered—mostly—
looked formidable, and the wine was indeed good stuff.

Within thirty minutes, the scent of grilling meat mixed with
the perfume of summer flowers. The terrace, the chairs around
the tables, the gardens filled with people. It still amazed her
she'd somehow collected so many.

Her cops—everyone who'd worked the Dudley-Moriarity
case—along with Cher Reo, the ADA, newlyweds Dr. Louise DiMatto and retired licensed companion Charles Monroe
stood, sat, lounged, or stuffed their faces.

Morris, the ME who'd inspired the impulse for her to arrange this shindig to help with his lingering grief over his murdered love, shared a brew with Father Lopez, who'd become his
friend and counselor.

Sort of weird having a priest at a party—even one she liked
and respected—but at least he wasn't wearing the getup.

Nadine Furst, bestselling author and ace reporter, chatted
happily with Dr. Mira, department shrink, and Mira's adorable
husband, Dennis.

It was good, she decided, to blow off steam this way, to
gather together to do it, even if gathering together wasn't as
natural for her as for some. It was good to watch Feeney kib-
itz Roarke's grill technique, and watch Trueheart show off his
pretty, shy-eyed girlfriend.

Hell, she might just have another glass of Granny Peabody's
wine and—

The thought winged away when she heard the bright laugh.

Mavis Freestone rushed out on silver sandals that laced past
the hem of her flippy, thigh-baring lavender skirt. Her hair,
perched in a crowning tail, matched the skirt. In her arms she
carried baby Bella. Leonardo, beaming at his girls, followed.

"Dallas!"

"I thought you were in London," Eve said when she was enveloped in color and scent and joy.

"We couldn't miss a party! We'll go back tomorrow. Trina stopped off to talk to Summerset."

Eve felt her skin chill. "Trina . . . "

"Don't worry, she's here to party, not to give you a treatment. She did Bella's hair—isn't it mag?"

A half a zillion sunny curls surrounded the baby's happy face. Every single one bounced with tiny pink bows.

"Yeah, it's—"

"Oh, everybody who counts is here! I've got to give out squeezes. Here, hold Bellamisa a minute."

"I'll get us a drink." Leonardo patted Eve's head with his huge hand, then glided away in his calf-baring red crops.

"I—" As Eve's arms were immediately loaded with bouncing, gooing baby, the protest ended on a strangled gulp.

"Got some weight to you these days," Eve managed, then scanned the crowd for a sucker to pass the load to. Bella squealed, sending Eve's heart rate soaring, then grabbed a fistful of Eve's hair, tugged with surprising force.

And planted a wet, openmouthed kiss on Eve's cheek. "Slooch!" said Bella.

"What does that mean? Oh God."

"Smooch," Mavis called out, gesturing with a frothy pink drink. "She wants you to kiss her back."

"Man. Okay, fine." Gingerly, Eve pecked her lips at Bella's cheek.

Obviously pleased, Bella let out a laugh so like Mavis's, Eve grinned. "Okay, kid, let's go find someone else for you to slooch."

Two

Nobody ate like cops. Priests didn't do half bad, Eve observed, and doctors held their own, she decided as Louise, Morris, and Mira chowed down on burgers. But against a horde of cops, a ravaging pack of hyenas would fall short.

Maybe it was all the missed meals, the clichéd donut grabbed on the fly. But when cops sat down to free food, they did so with single-minded focus.

"This is nice." Nadine stepped over, tapped her wineglass to Eve's beer bottle. "A nice day, a nice group, a nice chance to just relax and hang. Which is why I'm waiting until Monday to nag you into coming on *Now* to discuss the Dudley-Moriarity murders."

"It's wrapped."

"I know it's wrapped—I have my sources. If I hadn't been out of town doing publicity for the book, I'd have been in your face before this."

Nadine smiled. She wore her sun-streaked hair longer and looser and had chosen a sleeveless, floating tank over pants cropped short to show off an ankle chain—but the camera-ready reporter was still in there.

"But I'll stay out of it today," Nadine added, and took another sip of wine. "You know what I like when you have one of these gatherings, Dallas?"

"The food and alcohol?"

"It's always first-rate, but beyond that. It's always such an interesting mix of people. I know I can sit down next to anyone here and not be bored. You've got a talent for collecting the diverse and the interesting. I was just talking with Crack," she added, referring to the six and a half foot, tattooed sex club owner. "Now I think I'm going to sit down next to the shy and strapping Officer Trueheart and the pretty young thing he's with."

"Cassie from Records."

"Cassie from Records," Nadine repeated. "I think I'd like to find out just what's going on between those two."

Eve wandered toward the grill, where Roarke had passed the torch to Feeney, under the supervision of Dennis Mira. They were sort of an odd pair—diverse, as Nadine had said—the lanky, dreamy-eyed professor and the rumpled cop with his explosion of ginger hair.

"How's it going?" she asked.

"Got another couple orders for cow burgers, and these kabob deals." Feeney flipped a patty.

"I don't know where they put it." Dennis shook his head.

"Cop stomachs." Feeney winked at Eve. "We eat what's in front of us, and plenty of it when we get the chance."

"Somebody ought to save room for lemon meringue pie and strawberry shortcake."

Feeney stopped with a burger on his flipper. "We got lemon meringue pie and strawberry shortcake?"

"That's the word on the street."

"Where's it at?"

"I don't know. Ask Summerset."

"Don't think I won't." He flipped the burger then shoved the spatula at Dennis. "Take over. I'm getting my share before these vultures get wind."

As Feeney rushed off, Dennis's eyes went even softer. "Is there whipped cream?"

"Probably."

"Ah." He handed her the spatula. "Would you mind?" he asked, adding a fatherly pat on the head. "I have a weakness for shortcake and whipped cream."

"Um—" But he was already strolling off.

Eve looked down at the sizzling patties, the skewered vegetables. It wasn't quite as terrifying as having a drooling baby dumped in her arms, but . . . How the hell did you know when they were done? Did something signal? Should she poke at them or leave them alone?

Everything sizzled and smoked, and there were countless dials and gauges. When she cautiously lifted another shiny lid, she found fat dogs—probably actual pig meat—cooking away like hot, engorged penises.

She closed the lid again, then let out a huff of relief when Roarke joined her.

"They deserted the field, seduced by rumors of cake and pie. You handle this." She surrendered the spatula. "I might do something that puts Louise and her doctor's bag to work."

He looked at the sizzle and smoke as she'd often seen him look at some thorny computer code. With the light of challenge in his eyes.

"It's actually satisfying, the grilling business." He offered the spatula. "I could teach you."

"No thanks. Eating it's satisfying, and I've already done that."

He slid the burgers from grill to platter, then used some sort of tongs to transfer the kabobs.

"If I'd known they were done, I could've done that."

"You have other talents." He leaned down, the platter of food between them, and kissed her.

A good moment, she thought—the scents, the voices, the hot summer sun. Eve started to smile, then saw Lopez crossing in their direction. He walked like the boxer he'd been, she thought, the compact body light on the feet.

"Ready for another round, Chale?" Roarke asked him.

"The first was more than enough. I want to thank you both for having me. You have a beautiful home, beautiful friends."

"You're not leaving already?"

"I'm afraid I have to. I have the evening Mass, with a baptism. The family requested me, so I have to get back to St. Cristóbal's and prepare. But I can't think of a nicer way to have spent the afternoon."

"I'll drive you," Eve said.

"That's kind of you." He looked at her—warm brown eyes

that to her mind always held a lingering hint of sadness. "But I couldn't take you away from your guests."

"No problem. They're focused on food, and dessert's coming up."

He continued to look at her, to search, and she knew he saw something as he nodded. "I'd appreciate it."

"Why don't you take this?" Roarke handed Eve the platter. "Set it out, and I'll have Summerset box up some of the desserts for Chale."

"You'd make me a hero in the rectory tonight. I'll just say my good-byes then."

"Thanks," Eve said when Lopez moved back to the party. "There's just a couple of things I wanted his take on. It won't take long."

"Go ahead then. I'll have your vehicle brought around."

She wasn't sure how to approach it, or even why she felt the need to. But he made it easy for her—maybe that's what men like Lopez did.

"You want to ask me about Li," he began as she passed through the gates.

"Yeah, for one thing. I see Morris mostly over dead bodies, but I can get a sense of where he is. Just by wardrobe for a start. I know he's coming through it, but . . . "

"It's hard to watch a friend grieve. I can't tell you specifics, as some of what we've talked about was in confidence. He's a strong and spiritual man, one who—like you—lives with death."

"It helps—the work. I can see it," Eve said, "and he's said it does."

"Yes, tending to those whose lives have been taken, like his Amaryllis. It centers him. He misses her, misses the potential of what they might have made together. I can tell you most of his anger has passed. It's a start."

"I don't know how people get rid of the anger. I don't know if I'd want to in his place."

"You gave him justice—earthly justice. From there he needed to find acceptance, and then the faith that Amaryllis is in the hands of God. Or, if not God, the belief that she, too, has moved on to the next phase."

"If the next phase is so great, why do we work so hard to stay in this one? Why does death seem so *useless* and hurt so damn much? All those people, just going along, living their lives, until somebody decides to end it for them. We should be pissed off. The dead should be pissed off. Maybe they are, because sometimes they just won't let go."

"Murder breaks both God's law and man's, and it requires—demands—punishment."

"So I put them in a cage and the next stop is a fiery hell? Maybe. I don't know. But what about the murdered? Some of them are innocent, just living their lives. But others? Others are as bad, or nearly, as the one who ended them. In this phase, I have to treat them all the same, do the job, close the case. I can do that. I have to do that. But maybe I wonder, sometimes, if it's enough for the innocent, and for the ones—like Morris—who get left behind."

"You've had a difficult week," he murmured.

"And then some."

"If closing cases was all that mattered to you, if it began and ended there, you would never have suggested your friend meet with me. You and I wouldn't be having this conversation. And you wouldn't, couldn't, maintain your passion for the work I believe you were born to do."

"Sometimes I wish I could see, or feel . . . No, I wish I could know, even once, that it's enough."

He reached out, touched her hand briefly. "Our work isn't the same, but some of the questions we ask ourselves are."

She glanced at him. Out of the side window she caught the movement. For a moment it seemed the streets, the sidewalks, were empty. Except for the old woman who staggered, who lifted an already bloodied hand to her chest an instant before she tumbled off the curb and into the street.

Eve slammed the brakes, flicked on her flashers. Even as she leaped out of the car, she yanked her 'link from her pocket. "Emergency sequence, Dallas, Lieutenant Eve. I need MTs, I need a bus, six hundred block of 120 Street. First aid kit in the trunk," she shouted at Lopez. "Code's two-five-six-zero-Baker-Zulu. Female victim," she continued, dropping down beside the woman. "Multiple stab wounds. Hold on," she muttered. "Hold on." And dropping the 'link, she pressed her hands to the chest wound. "Help's coming."

"Beata." The woman's eyelids flickered, opened to reveal

eyes so dark Eve could barely gauge the pupils. "Trapped. The red door. Help her."

"Help's coming. Give me your name," Eve said as Lopez pulled padding from the first aid kit. "What's your name?"

"She is Beata. My beauty. She can't get out."

"Who did this to you?"

"He is the devil." Those black eyes bore into Eve's. The words she pushed out held an accent thick as the heat.

Eastern European, Eve thought, filing it in her mind.

"You . . . you are the warrior. Find Beata. Save Beata."

"Okay. Don't worry." Eve glanced at Lopez, who shook his head. He began to murmur in Latin as he crossed himself and made the sign on the woman's forehead.

"The devil killed my body. I cannot fight, I cannot find. I cannot free her. You must. You are the one. We speak to the dead."

Eve heard the sirens, knew they would be too late. The pads, her own hands, the street was soaked with blood. "Okay. Don't worry about her. I'll find her. Tell me your name."

"I am Gizi. I am the promise. You must let me in and keep your promise."

"Okay, okay. Don't worry. I'll take care of it." Hurry, her mind shouted at the sirens. For God's sake, hurry.

"My blood, your blood." The woman gripped the hand Eve pressed to her chest wound with surprising strength, scoring the flesh with her fingernails. "My heart, your heart. My soul, your soul. Take me in."

Eve ignored the quick pain from the little cuts in her palm. "Sure. All right. Here they come." She looked up as the ambulance screamed around the corner, then back into those fierce, depthless black eyes.

Something burned in her hand, up her arm, until the shocking blow to her chest stole her breath. The light flashed, blinding her, then went to utter dark.

In the dark were voices and deeper shadows and the bright form of a young woman—slim in build, a waterfall of black hair and eyes of deep, velvet brown.

She is Beata. I am the promise, and the promise is in you. You are the warrior, and the warrior holds me. We are together until the promise is kept and the fight is done.

* * *

"Eve. Eve. Lieutenant Dallas!"

She jerked, sucked in air like a diver surfacing, and found herself staring at Lopez's face. "What?"

"Thank God. You're all right?"

"Yeah." She raked a bloodied hand through her hair. "What the hell happened?"

"I honestly don't know." He glanced over to where, a foot away, two MTs worked on the woman. "She's gone. There was a light—such a light. I've never seen . . . Then she was gone, and you were . . . " He struggled for words. "Not unconscious, but blank. Just not there for a moment. I had to pull you away so they could get to her. You saw the light?"

"I saw something." Felt something, she thought. Heard something.

Now she saw only an old woman whose blood stained the street. "I have to call this in. I think you're going to be late for Mass. I need you to give a statement."

She pushed to her feet as one of the MTs stepped over.

"Nothing we can do for her," he said. "She's cold. Must've been lying there for a couple hours before you found her. Fucking New York. People had to walk right by her."

"No." There were people now, crowding the sidewalk, ranged like a chorus for the dead. But there hadn't been . . . "No," Eve repeated. "We saw her fall."

"Body's cold," he repeated. "She's ninety if she's a day, and probably more than that. I don't see how she could've walked two feet with all those slices in her."

"I guess we'd better find out." She picked up her 'link, called it in.

Three

After cleaning the blood from her hands, she secured the scene, retrieved her field kit from the trunk. She was running the victim's prints when the first black and white rolled up.

"She's not in the database." Frustrated, Eve pushed to her feet, turned to the uniforms. "Keep these people back. Talk to them. Find out if anybody knew her, if anybody saw anything. There's a blood trail, and I don't want these people trampling all over it."

And where the hell were they, she wondered, when the woman was staggering down the street, bleeding to death? The street had been empty as the desert.

"What can I do?" Lopez asked her.

"Peabody's on her way—small slice of luck having a bunch of murder cops a few minutes away. I want you to give her a statement. Tell her everything you saw, everything you heard."

"She had an accent. Thick. Polish or Hungarian, maybe Romanian."

"Yeah, tell Peabody. Once you've done that, I can have one of the cops drive you where you need to go."

"If you need me to stay—"

"There's nothing more you can do here. I'll be in touch."

"I'd like to finish giving her Last Rites. I started, but . . . She's wearing a crucifix around her neck."

She debated. He'd already had his hands all over the body, and his clothes were stained, as hers were, with the old woman's blood. "Okay. You can do that while I start on her. Try to keep contact to a minimum."

"Your hand's bleeding a little."

"She dug in pretty hard with her nails. It's just a couple scratches."

Lopez knelt at the woman's head while Eve got gauges and tools out of her kit.

"Victim is Caucasian or possibly mixed race female of undetermined origin, age approximately ninety. Before expiring, she gave her name as Gizi. Multiple stab wounds," Eve continued, "chest, torso, arms. Looks like defensive wounds on the arms, the hands. She didn't just stand there and take it."

"She should have died at home, in her bed, surrounded by her children, grandchildren. I'm sorry," Lopez said when Eve glanced up. "I interrupted your record."

"Doesn't matter. And you're right."

"That's the difference between death and murder."

"It's the big one. Do her clothes look homemade to you?" As she asked, Eve turned up the hem on the long skirt with its wide stripes of color. "This looks handmade to me, and carefully done. She's wearing sandals—sturdy ones with some miles on them. Got a tattoo, inside left ankle. Peacock feathers? I think they're peacock feathers."

"She's wearing a wedding ring. Sorry," Lopez said again.

"Yeah, wedding ring, or in any case a plain gold band, the cross pendant along with a second pendant, starburst pattern with a pale blue center stone, gold earrings. No bag, no purse, but if it were a violent mugging, why not take the jewelry?"

She slid her sealed hand into the pocket on the side of the skirt, closed her fingers over a little bag. It was snowy white, felt like silk, and tied precisely with silver cord in three knots.

She knew what it was even before she untied it and examined the contents. She'd seen this sort of thing before. "Woo-woo," she said to Lopez.

"What?"

"Magic stuff. Witchcraft or whatever. We got herbs, little

crystals. I'd say she hedged her bets. Amulet and crucifix—and a spell deal in her pocket. Didn't help her."

Though she'd already noted time of death, she used her gauge to confirm. "Damn it, this thing must be broken. It's given me TOD at just past thirteen hundred. She died right here in front of us at sixteen-forty-two."

"Her skin's cold," Lopez murmured.

"We watched her die." Eve pushed to her feet, turning as Peabody jogged up, Morris in her wake.

"This wasn't on the party schedule," Peabody said as she looked at the body.

"I bet it wasn't on hers either." Eve took the weapon and harness she'd asked Peabody to bring, and after strapping it on covered it with the jacket her partner held out.

She sat on the curb, changed her skids for her boots.

"You need to get a statement from Father Lopez so we can spring him. Have one of the uniforms drive him back when you're done. You didn't have to come," she said to Morris. "I notified your people."

"I called them off. I'm right here, after all."

"Actually, I can use the head guy. My gauge is wonky. I recorded TOD as the damn TOD, since she died in front of me. But my gauge is putting it almost four hours earlier. Cause is pretty clear, but you might find something else. If you can take over on the body, I want to get on this blood trail, find the kill spot."

"Go ahead."

She followed the blood west.

The neighborhood was quiet. Maybe the heat kept people inside, she thought, or maybe most of them were at the sale at the Sky Mall or at the beach. But there was some pedestrian and street traffic.

Had no one seen a staggering, bleeding old woman and tried to help? Even for New York, that was too cold to believe. But the trail continued west for two blocks, right over crosswalks—as if the dying had felt obliged not to jaywalk. Then it headed north.

Buildings older here, she noted, squat towers of apartments and day flops, tiny markets and delis, the 24/7s, coffee shops, bakeries, and bodegas—and more people out and about on their Saturday business.

She continued another three blocks, then jogged north where the trail led into the mouth of a narrow alley between buildings.

And there, without question, was the kill spot.

Deep in the narrow trench, shadowed by overhangs, stinking of garbage from an overfilled recycler, blood splattered the pocked concrete walls, drenched the filthy ground.

She hitched open her field kit for a flashlight and played it over the walls, the ground, the neatly tied bag of trash beside the recycler.

"Did you tie that, Gizi? Bringing out the trash? Do you work here, live here? What were you doing in the alley otherwise? And how the hell did you walk better than six blocks after he sliced you to pieces? And why? Help would have been right around the corner."

Crouching, she unknotted the trash bag. Fruit and vegetable peelings, she noted, packaging from a small loaf of bread, an empty box of powdered milk, a long, slim bottle that had held some sort of wine . . .

She retied the bag, tagged it for evidence, and shifting it, found the key.

Old, heavy, she noted as she studied it. But then there were old buildings here that might still run to straight lock and key. She turned to the alley door and its keypad. Entrance digitally secured, but inside?

She'd have to see.

She bagged the key, labeled it, then walked back to the alley door and tried to see it.

Wants to take her trash out, comes out with her little bag, walked to the recycler.

Was he waiting for her? Why? Did she walk into an illegals deal?

Puts her bag down, turns—spatter says she'd turned, about three-quarters away from the wall when she was attacked. So he came from behind her, most likely. From the mouth of the alley or through the door behind her.

Eve positioned herself, started the turn from the wall. The first slice ripped the back of her right shoulder with a shock of pain that knocked her against the recycler. She grabbed for her weapon, swung to defend, but somehow the knife plunged into her back, once, twice. Dimly she heard something clink onto the ground, and thought: My key.

Then she was sliding down toward that filthy ground. But hands grabbed her, wrenched her around, shoved her hard against the wall. Through eyes glazed with shock and pain she saw the face of a demon—curling horns piercing the forehead, skin red as hellfire slashed with black and dirty gold. It bared its fierce teeth as the knife tore through her chest.

She put up her hands to fight, and the blade sliced them. She opened her mouth to scream, to curse, but had no voice.

As she fell, the only thought in her mind was Beata.

She came to coated with sweat. The hand holding her weapon shook as she slapped the other over her body looking for blood.

But she stood, unharmed, just as she'd been before she'd felt the first blow.

"What the hell was that?" Dizzy, she bent over, head between her knees until she got her breath back.

"Dallas? Hey!" Peabody rushed forward. "Are you okay?"

"Fine."

"Jeez, you're white as a ghost."

"I'm fine," she insisted. "It's the heat." To prove it, maybe to assure herself of it, she swiped the back of her hand over her sweaty brow. "Who's on scene?"

"Five uniforms, Morris. Crime scene got there before I left to follow you in." Peabody scanned the alley floor, the walls, the stinking recycler. "That's a hell of a lot of blood. How'd she manage to walk all that way after this?"

"Good question. It looks like she came down to take out her trash. The contents of the bag I tagged look like basic garbage from a single. And there was a key between it and the recycler. Could be hers, as it's about the only clean thing in here. Contact crime scene. We need them down here. Stick with the bag until they get here. I'm going to check the buildings. If that's her trash, she had to come from one of these two buildings."

She didn't draw a clean breath until she'd stepped out of the alley—and the instant she did, the shakes and dizziness vanished as if they'd never been.

She tried the ground-floor market first, moving past the displays of summer fruit and sleeves of flowers into the relative cool of the shop.

She walked to the counter where the woman sitting on a

stool behind it greeted her with a wide smile. "Good afternoon. Can I help you find something?"

"NYPSD." Eve badged her. "Do you know a woman, in her nineties, gray hair—long, probably worn in a bun, dark eyes, olive complexion, five feet four, about a hundred and twenty pounds? Weathered face. Shows its miles. Heavy East European accent. Might wear a cross and an amulet with a blue stone."

"That sure sounds like Madam Szabo." The woman's smile faded. "Is she okay? She was just in this morning."

"Do you know where she lives?"

"In one of the weekly units above. On three, I think."

"Do you know her full name?"

"Ah, it's Gizi, Gizi Szabo. She's from Hungary. Is she in trouble?"

"She was attacked and killed this afternoon."

"Oh my God. Oh no. Wait." She pushed up, opened a door to what looked to be a tiny office/storeroom. "Zach. Zach, come out here. Somebody killed Madam Szabo."

"What are you talking about?" The man who stepped out wore an expression of annoyance along with a short-sleeved, collared shirt and knee shorts. "She's fine. We just saw her this morning."

"This is the police."

"Lieutenant Dallas, Homicide."

Annoyance dropped away into quick concern. "What the hell happened? Did somebody break into her place?"

"I'd like to check her unit, if you know the number. And I'll need your names."

"Karrie and Zach Morgenstern," the woman told her. "This is our place. Oh, Zach." Karrie curled a hand around his arm. "She stopped in here almost every day since she came."

"How long is that?"

"About a month maybe. She came to find her great-granddaughter. This is terrible; I can hardly take it in. I really liked her. She had such interesting stories—and she told my fortune once. She's—what is it, Zach?"

"Romany. A Gypsy. The real deal, too. She's in four D, Lieutenant. I carried some stuff up for her a couple times. Man, this is crap, you know that? Just crap. She was a sweetheart. Do you want me to take you up?"

"No, I'll find it. The alley between the buildings. This building uses that recycler?"

"Yeah. Damn thing's been broken for nearly a week, and we can't get them to come and . . . " Zach trailed off. "Is that where she was killed? In the alley? You mean we were right in here when . . . "

"Nothing you could've done. Is there anyone you know who gave her any trouble? Anyone who'd want to cause her harm?"

"I really don't." Zach looked at Karrie, got a shake of the head. "She was nice. Colorful. Did some fortune-telling out of her place."

"You said she was here to look for her great-granddaughter."

"Yes." Karrie sniffled, blinked at tears. "God, it's really hitting me. She came over—the granddaughter—about a year ago. She didn't live far from here, and she came in a couple times. That's why Madam rented the place upstairs. Anyway, the granddaughter came to work, wanted to dance—on Broadway, like they all do, you know? Then about three months ago her family stopped hearing from her, couldn't reach her. And the place she worked waitressing said how she just stopped showing up. They contacted the police, but the cops didn't do much, I guess . . . Sorry."

"No need. Do you know the granddaughter's name?"

"Sure. Madam Szabo talked to everybody about her, put out flyers." Karrie continued as she reached under the counter, "She worked at Goulash—Hungarian restaurant a block west. We hand out flyers for her. You can have this. She's beautiful, isn't she? I think that's what her name means."

"Beata," Eve murmured, and felt as if her heart cracked in her chest. Such grief, such sorrow it almost took her to her knees as she studied the photo on the flyer.

The face that had been the light in the black.

"Ma'am? Um, Lieutenant? Are you okay?"

"Yeah. Thanks for your help. I may need to speak to you again."

"If we're not here, we live up on six. Six A, front of the building," Karrie told her. "Anything we can do."

"If you think of anything, you can contact me at Cop Central." Eve dug into her field kit for a card. "Anything strikes you."

Eve walked out just as Peabody approached. "Sweepers have the alley," she said.

"Vic was Gizi Szabo, and had a weekly unit on four. Claimed to be a Gypsy from Hungary."

"Wow. A real one?"

"Nobody claims to be a fake one," Eve returned, and felt herself steady a little. "Been here about three months, looking for a great-granddaughter who went missing." Eve used her master to access the apartment building's entrance. "Did some fortune-telling out of her place."

One glance at the ancient elevator had Eve choosing the stairs. She handed Peabody the flyer. "Run them both," she said. "Had Morris confirmed TOD before you left?"

"His TOD jibed with your gauge. Around one this afternoon."

"That's just bogus." And it infuriated her more than it should have. "I know when somebody dies when I've got my hands on their fricking heart, and I'm *talking* to them."

"Hungarian Gypsy fortune-teller. Maybe it's some sort of—"

"Don't even start with that voodoo, woo-woo, Free-Ager shit. She was alive, bleeding, and talking until about an hour ago."

At the door of 4 D, Eve took the key she'd found out of the evidence bag, slid it into the lock. And turned the knob.

Four

It reminded her of her first apartment—the size, the age. That's what she told herself when struck, just for an instant, with a sharp sense of recognition.

The single room had no doubt been rented furnished, with a couple of cheap chairs and a daybed with a cracker-thin mattress, a chest—newly and brightly painted—that served as dresser and table.

Boldly patterned material had been fashioned into curtains for the single window, and with these and scarves and shawls draped over the faded chairs, spread over the narrow bed, the room took on a hopeful cheer.

One corner held a sink, AutoChef, friggie, all small-scale, along with a single cupboard. Another table stood there, painted a deep, glossy red under its fringed scarf. For seating, there were two backless stools.

Eve saw the old woman there, telling fortunes to those who sought to know their future.

"She made it nice," Peabody commented. "She didn't have a lot to work with, but she made it nice."

Eve opened the single, skinny closet, studied Szabo's neatly hung clothing, a single pair of sturdy walking shoes. Kneeling, she pulled two storage boxes out of the closet.

"Beata's things. Clothes, shoes, ballet gear, I'd say. A few pieces of jewelry, face and hair stuff. The landlord must have boxed it up when she didn't come back, didn't pay the rent."

It hurt, hurt to look through, to touch, to *feel* Beata as she dug through pretty blouses, skimmed over worn slippers.

She knew better, she reminded herself, knew better than to become personally involved. Beata Varga wasn't her victim, not directly.

The promise is in you.

The voice spoke insistently inside her head, inside her heart.

"Tag these," Eve ordered, shoving to her feet. She crossed over to the chest, studied the photo of Beata propped there and fronted by three scribed candles. Beside the photo a handful of colored crystals glittered in a small dish along with an ornate silver bell and a silver-backed hand mirror.

"What do we have on the granddaughter?" Eve asked.

"Beata Varga, age twenty-two. She's here on a work visa, and employed—until she went missing three months ago—at Goulash. No criminal. The family filed a report. A Detective Lloyd is listed as investigating officer. Missing Persons Division out of the One-three-six."

"Reach out there," Eve told her. "Have him meet us at the restaurant. Thirty minutes."

She opened the first drawer of the chest, found neatly folded underwear and nightclothes, and a box of carved wood. She lifted the lid, studied the pack of tarot cards, the peacock feather, the small crystal ball and stand.

Tools of her trade, Eve thought, started to set the box aside. Then, following impulse, pressed her thumbs over the carved flowers on the sides. Left, left, right. And a narrow drawer slid out of the base.

"Wow." Peabody leaned over her shoulder. "A secret drawer. Frosty. How did you open it?"

"Just . . . luck," Eve said, even as the hairs on the back of her neck stood up.

Inside lay a lock of dark hair tied with gold cord, a wand-shaped crystal on a chain, and a heart of white stone.

"They're hers." Eve's throat went dry and achy. "Beata's. Her hair, something she wore, something she touched."

"You're probably right. Szabo probably used them, along

with the cards and crystals, maybe the bell and the mirror in locator spells. I'm not saying you can find people with spells," Peabody added when Eve just stared at her. "But that she thought she could. Anyway, Detective Lloyd's going to meet us."

"Then let's see what else we can find here first."

The old woman lived simply, neatly, and cautiously. In the cloth bag in the bottom of the chest Eve found a small amount of cash, another bag of crystals and herbs, a map of the city, and a subway card, along with ID and passport and a number of the flyers with Beata's image and information.

But taped under the friggie they found an envelope of cash with a peacock feather fixed diagonally across the seal.

"That's about ten thousand," Peabody estimated. "She didn't have to read palms to pay the rent."

"It's what she did. What kept her centered. Bag it, and let's seal this place up. We should get to the restaurant."

"She made it nice," Peabody repeated with another glance around. "I guess that's what travelers do. Make a home wherever they land, then pack it up and make the next one."

Beata hadn't packed it up, Eve thought, and wherever she was, it wasn't home.

Goulash did a bustling business on Saturday evening. Spices perfumed air that rang with voices and the clatter of silverware, the clink of glasses. The waitstaff wore red sashes at the waist of black uniforms while moving briskly from kitchen to table.

A rosy-cheeked woman of about forty offered Eve a welcoming smile. "Welcome to Goulash. Do you have a reservation?"

Eve palmed her badge. "We're not here for dinner."

"Beata! You've found her."

"No."

"Oh." The smile faded away. "I thought . . . I'm sorry, what can I do for you?"

"We're meeting Detective Lloyd on a police matter. We'll need somewhere to talk. And I'll need to speak with you and your staff."

"Of course." She looked around. "We're not going to have a table free for at least a half hour, but you can use the kitchen."

"That's fine. Your name?"

"Mirium Frido. This is my place, my husband's and mine. He's the chef. Is this about Beata? Beata Varga?"

"Indirectly."

"Give me one minute to put someone else on the door." Mirium hurried over to one of the waitresses. The girl glanced at Eve and Peabody, nodded.

Mirium signaled Eve forward, then led them through the dining room, past the bar, and through one of a pair of swinging doors into the chaos of the kitchen.

"Dinner rush. I'll set you up over here—our chef's table. Jan invites customers back sometimes—gives them a treat. I told Vee to send Detective Lloyd back when he gets here. He's been in several times about Beata, so everyone knows him. Can you tell me anything about her? Do you have more information?"

"I'll know more when I speak with the detective. She worked for you."

"Yes. A beautiful girl and a good worker. She was a pleasure." Mirium reached back to a shelf, picked up three setups, and arranged them on the table. "I know they think she just took off—Gypsy feet—but it doesn't make sense. She made amazing tips—the looks, the voice, the personality. And . . . well, she just wouldn't be that rude and careless, wouldn't have left without telling us. Or her family."

"Boyfriend?"

"No. Nothing serious and no one specific. She dated—she's young and gorgeous. But she was serious about her dancing. Went to auditions, took classes every day. She had an understudy spot in a small musical review. And she'd just landed a part in the chorus on a new musical spot off-Broadway. There wasn't enough time for a serious boyfriend. I'm sorry, please sit. How about some food?"

"We're good, thanks. You have flyers at the reservation station, I noticed."

"Yes. Her grandmother—well, great-grandmother—is here from Hungary. She had them made up and takes them around the city. She comes by here every day. Detective—"

"Lieutenant," Eve said automatically.

"Lieutenant, Beata worked here nearly a year. You get to know people who work for you, and I promise you, she wouldn't worry her family this way. I'm so afraid something's happened to her. I know Madam Szabo's determined to find her, but with every day that passes . . . "

"I'm sorry to tell you Gizi Szabo was killed this afternoon."

"No." Instantly Mirium's eyes filled. "Oh, no. What happened?"

"We're going to find out."

"She told my fortune," Mirium murmured. "Said I would have a child, a son. Jan and I haven't . . . That was two months ago. I found out yesterday I'm pregnant. I told her just today."

"She was in today."

"Yes, about eleven, I guess." Shaking her head, Mirium swiped at a tear while the kitchen bustle raged on around them. "She was so happy for me. She said she'd felt his search, my son's. An old soul, she said, who'd turned the wheel again. She talked like that," Mirium murmured. "I don't really believe that sort of thing, but when she looks at you . . . She's—she was—Romany, and a speaker for the dead."

So am I, Eve thought with a quick chill. I speak for the dead. "What time did she leave?"

"She was only here a few minutes. She said she was going home. She said she felt closer to Beata, felt something coming. Or someone. I don't know, she was—I want to say optimistic. She was going to rest and then do a new spell because she was breaking through, well, the veil. She said Beata was toward the setting sun, below the rays, um, locked beyond the red door. I have no idea what that meant," Mirium added. "Or if it meant anything, but she was *fierce* about it. She swore Beata was alive, but trapped. By a devil.

"I know how that sounds," she continued. "But—" She glanced over. "Here's Detective Lloyd. Sorry I went on like that."

"Don't be," Eve told her. "Every detail, every impression, is helpful."

"I just can't believe Madam's gone. She was such a presence, even for the short time I knew her. Excuse me. I need to tell Jan. Hello, Detective Lloyd, have a seat."

Lloyd was a square-faced, square-bodied man who transmitted *I'm a cop* from thirty paces. He gave Eve and Peabody a brisk nod, then sat at the little square table. Shook hands.

"It's too bad about the old lady. She had some juice, had some spine. She should've stayed back home."

She made home where she landed, Eve thought, remembering Peabody's take. "Tell me about Beata Varga."

He hitched up a hip, took a disc out of his pocket. "I went ahead and made a copy of the file for you."

"Appreciate it."

"She's a looker. Smart, from what I get, savvy, but still green when it comes to city. Used to wandering with her family—tribe, you'd say. Came here wanting to be a Broadway star, and the family wasn't happy about it."

"Is that so?"

"Wanted her home. Wanted her to stay pure, you could say. Get hitched, have babies, keep the line going, that sort of thing. But, the old woman—Szabo—overruled them. She wanted the girl to take her shot, find her destiny, like that. The girl got a job here and a place a couple blocks away. Started taking classes—dance classes, acting classes, stuff like that, at West Side School for the Arts. Went to the cattle calls regular. No boyfriend—or not one in particular. Dated a few guys. I got the names and statements, the data in the file there." He nodded toward the disc. "Nobody rang the bell."

He paused when Mirium came over with a tray holding three tall glasses. "I don't mean to interrupt. Just something cold to drink while you talk. If you need me for anything, I'll be out front."

"They're good people," Lloyd commented when she left them. "Her, her husband. They come up clean. Ran the whole staff when I caught the case. Got some bumps here and there, but nobody popped."

"What's the time line?"

When he didn't refer to his notes, Eve knew the case had him, and his teeth were still in it.

"Beata Varga went to her regular dance class, eight a.m. to ten. Hit a rehearsal for the show she just landed at Carmine Theater on Tenth at eleven. Reported here for work at one, all excited about the show. Worked a split shift, so she was off at three, hit her acting class from three thirty to five, back to work at five thirty, off at eleven. Walked down the block with a couple friends from work—names in the file—then split off to go home. That's the last anyone can verify seeing her. Eleven ten, then poof.

"Apartment's not big on security. No cams," he added. "No

log-in. The neighbors can't say whether she came in that night, but nobody saw her. A bag and some of her clothes and personal items are gone, and there was no money in the place. According to statements, she pulled in hefty tips and was saving. It looks like she got itchy feet, tossed what she wanted in a bag, and took off."

"That's not what you think," Eve said, watching his eyes.

"Nope. I think between here and home she ran into trouble. Somebody snatched her. I think she's been dead since that night. You know as well as I do, Lieutenant, we don't always find the bodies."

No, Eve thought. "If she's dead, then someone she knew killed her. Why else try to make it seem like she took off? Why pack clothes?"

"I lean that way, but I can't find anything." Frustration rippled around him. "It could be whoever did her used her ID for her address, had her key—she carried all that in her purse. Tried to cover it up. I'm still working it, when I can, as an MP, but my sense is it's more in your line."

He glanced around as he sipped his drink. "The old woman didn't buy it for cheap," he said. "Claimed she talked to the dead, and if the girl was dead, she'd know. I don't buy that for free, but . . . Now the old woman gets murdered? People get dead in the city," he added as he set his glass down. "But it's got a smell to it. I'd appreciate you giving me what you've got on it. Something or somebody might cross somewhere."

"You'll get it," Eve promised. Because something or somebody *would* cross.

Five

The ballet studio ranged over the fourth floor of an old building on the West Side. Under the glare of streetlights the pocked bricks were dull and grayed with time and pollution, but the glass in every window sparkled.

Out of Order signs hung on the chipped gray doors of both elevators. Students, staff, and visitors had expressed their opinions on the situation with varying degrees of humor or annoyance by tagging the doors with obscenities, anatomically impossible suggestions, and illustrations on how to attempt the suggestions. All in a variety of languages.

"Guess they've been out of order for a while," Peabody commented.

Eve just stared at one of the series of strange symbols and letters while her mind—something in there—translated it with a kind of dry humor.

"Fuck your mother," she murmured, and Peabody blinked.

"What? Why?"

"Not *your* mother."

"But you just said—"

Eve shook her head impatiently. "It's Russian. A classic Russian insult." She reached out, ran a fingertip over the lettering on the door. *"Yob tvoiu mat."*

Peabody studied the phrase Eve traced and thought it might as well be hieroglyphics. "How do you know that?"

"I must have seen it somewhere else." But that didn't explain how she knew—*knew*—the elevators had been down for weeks. Turning away, she started up the stairs.

Nor could she say why her heart began to beat faster as they climbed, passed the other studios and classrooms. Tap, jazz, children's ballet sessions. Or why, as she approached the fourth floor, the music drifting out hit some chord inside her.

She followed the music, stepped into the doorway.

The woman was whiplash thin in her black leotard and gauzy skirt. Her hair, wildly red, slicked back from a face that struck Eve as thirty years older than her body. Her skin was white as the moon, her lips red as her hair.

She called out in French to a group of dancers at a long bar who responded by sliding their feet from one position to another—pointed toes, flat feet, lifted leg, bended knees.

In a corner of the studio a man played a bright and steady beat on an old piano. He seemed to look at nothing at all with a half smile on his face, dark eyes dreamy in a sharp-featured face surrounded by dark hair with wide, dramatic white streaks.

As Eve and Peabody entered the room, one of the dancers, a man in his twenties, dark hair restrained in a curling tail, turned his head a fraction to stare, to scowl.

Interesting, she thought, a guy wearing a leotard and ballet shoes would make a couple of cops so quickly.

The woman stopped, planted her hands on her hips. "You want lessons, you sign up. Class has started."

Eve merely held up her badge.

The woman sighed hugely. "Alexi, take the class."

At the order, the scowling man tossed his head, sniffed, then strode out from the bar. The woman gestured them into the hallway.

"What could you want?" she demanded in a voice husky, impatient, and thick with her homeland. "I'm teaching."

"Natalya Barinova?"

"Yes, yes. I am Barinova. What do I want with police?"

"You know a Gizi Szabo?"

"Yes, yes," she said in the same dismissive tone. "She looks for Beata, who ran off to Las Vegas."

"You know Beata Varga went to Vegas?" Eve demanded.

"Where else? They think, these girls, they go make big money showing their tits and wearing big feathers on their heads. They don't want to work, to sweat, to suffer, to *learn*."

"Beata told you she was leaving?"

"No, she tells me nothing, that girl. But she doesn't come back. She's not the first, will not be the last. Her old grandmother comes—a good woman—looking for this flighty girl who has talent. Wasted now. Wasted."

The way she cut her hand through the air made her anger clear.

"I tell her this, tell Gizi, Beata has talent. Needs discipline, needs practice. Should not waste so much time with the tap and the jazz and the *modern* business. I tell Beata the same, but she only smiles. Then poof, off she runs."

"When did you last see Madam Szabo?"

"Ah . . . " Barinova frowned, waved a hand in the air. "A day ago, I think. Yes, on yesterday. She comes often. Sometimes we have tea. She was a dancer in her day, she tells me, and we talk. She's a good woman, and Beata shows no respect to her. She thinks harm has come to Beata, but I say how could this be? Beata is strong and smart—except she's stupid to run to Las Vegas. So, she asked you to come? Like the other police?"

"No. Madam Szabo was killed this afternoon."

"No." Barinova held out both hands as if to push the words away. "No. How does this happen?"

"She was stabbed in the alley outside her apartment building."

Barinova closed her eyes. "Such cruelty. I will pray she finds peace and her killer roasts in hell. Beata must bear some blame for this. Selfish girl."

"When did you last see Beata?"

"Ah." She cut a hand through the air again, but now there were tears in her eyes for the old woman and disgust for the young. "Weeks now, maybe months. She comes to class excited about a part in some musical. She works hard, this is true. I give her the pas de deux with Alexi in our autumn gala. My son," she added. "She dances well with him in practice, then she says she has this part—maybe she does, maybe she doesn't. But soon after, she doesn't come to class anymore. I have my brother Sasha to call her on the 'link, but she doesn't answer. We tell all this to the police when they come."

"Did Madam Szabo tell you she was concerned about anyone? That she had any leads on Beata?"

"She said the last she was here she believed Beata was close. She was Romany, you understand, and had a gift. Me, I have Romany in my blood, but from long ago. She used her gift and said Beata was close, but trapped. Below, behind a red door." Barinova shrugged. "She was very old, and gifted, yes, but sometimes hope and wishes outweigh truth. The girl ran off as girls do, and now a good woman is dead."

"It would be helpful if we could talk to your son and brother, maybe some of the students who took classes with Beata."

"Yes, yes, we will help. I will miss tea with Gizi and our talks." She turned back into the studio, moved to her son. She spoke quickly in Russian, gestured, then took his place as he strode out.

"You're interrupting my practice." Unlike his mother, he had no trace of an accent. What he had was attitude.

"Yeah, murder interrupts a lot of things."

"What murder?" His sneer twisted off his face. "Beata? She's dead?"

"I don't know, but her great-grandmother is."

"Madam Szabo?" His shock looked sincere enough, and so, Eve noted, did his relief. "Why would anybody kill an old woman?"

"People always seem to have a reason. In this case, maybe because she was getting close to finding out what happened to Beata."

"Beata left." He jerked a shoulder sharply. "She didn't have what it takes."

"To what?"

"To dance, to live life full."

Eve cocked her head. "Wouldn't sleep with you?"

He tipped back his head to look down his long nose. "I don't have a problem getting women into bed. If we'd danced together for the gala, we'd sleep together. One is like the other."

"I thought you did dance together."

"Practice."

"So it must've annoyed you that she wouldn't have sex with you."

"This woman, that woman." He smiled slowly. "One is like the other."

"Charming. When did you last see Madam Szabo?"

"Just yesterday. She'd visit class, and my mother, a lot. Talk to the other dancers here, and the other studios down on two and three where Beata took some classes. She'd have tea with my mother, sit with my uncle at the piano. She said she felt close to Beata here."

"And she mentioned something about Beata being close. Being below."

"She was a Gypsy—and took it seriously. I don't buy into that, but yeah, she said some stuff about it. Didn't make any sense, because if Beata was close, why did she stop coming to class? Why did she bail on the part she got, and screw the understudy position she had? Dancers dance. She took off, that's what she did, to dance somewhere else. Found a bigger brass ring to grab."

"Where were you today, Alexi? Say from noon to four?"

"Cops." He sniffed again. "I slept late in the apartment of Allie Madison. She and I will dance in the gala, and she and I sleep together. For now," he added. "We stayed in bed until about two, then met friends for a little brunch. Then we came here, to practice, then to take class. She's the blonde, the tall one with the tattoo of a lark on her left shoulder blade. I need to practice."

"Go ahead. Ask your uncle to come out."

Eve waited until he'd strode off again. "Did you run him?" she asked Peabody.

"Oh yeah. He's got a few drunk and disorderlies, a couple of minor illegals possessions, an assault—bar fight, which added destruction of private property, public nuisance, resisting. He's twenty-six, listed as principal dancer and instructor here at the school, and lives with his mother upstairs on six."

Got a temper, Eve thought as the piano player stepped out.

"Officer?"

"Lieutenant Dallas, Detective Peabody. And you're Sasha?"

"Sasha Korchov, yes. My nephew said you came because Madam Szabo was killed." His dreamy eyes were soft and sad, like this voice. Like the slow glide of a bow over violin strings. "I'm very sorry to know this."

"Were you here when she came in yesterday?"

"I didn't see her. Natalya was using the music disc—advanced students to work on dances for the gala. I am in the storeroom, I think, with the props when she was here. My sister tells me I missed her. We enjoyed talking music and dance. I saw her the day before, on the street, not far from here. I was going to the market. But she was across the street and didn't hear when I called out to her. We talked in Russian," he said with a ghost of a smile. "Her mother was Russian, like mine and my papa, so sometimes we talked in Russian. I will miss it, and her."

"What about Beata?"

"Beata." He sighed. "My sister, she thinks Beata ran off to Las Vegas, but no, I think something bad happened to her. I don't say so to Gizi, but . . . I think she knows I believe this. She could see inside if she looked, so I think sometimes she was sad to talk to me. I'm sorry for it."

"What did you think happened to Beata?"

"I think she loved her family, and to dance, and New York. I don't think she would leave all of that by choice. I think she's dead, and now so is Gizi. Now Gizi will find her, so they will, at least, have each other."

"Your nephew was interested in Beata—personally."

"He likes pretty girls," Sasha said cautiously. "What young man doesn't?"

"But she wasn't interested in him?"

"She was more interested in dance than in men. Pure of heart, and with music in her blood."

"Can you tell me where you were this afternoon?"

"I went to market after morning classes—I like to go most days. I came home to have my lunch and to play. I opened the windows so the music could go out. I came down to talk to my sister, and play for the two o'clock class. When that's done, we have tea, Natalya and me."

"Okay, thank you. Would you send Allie Madison out?"

"Will they send her body home?"

"I don't have that information."

"I hope she goes home," Sasha murmured, then wandered back inside.

"He immigrated here from Russia with his sister and her kid—Alexi was a couple months old—twenty-six years ago," Peabody added. "Sister's husband's listed as dead, right before the kid was born. Korchov was thirty-five and had been a big-deal ballet guy until he got messed up in a car wreck. They fixed him, but his career was shot. The sister was thirty, and had a pretty decent career herself. They opened the school. He has his own apartment on six. No criminal record. No marriages on record, two cohabs, both in Russia. The second one died in the same wreck that messed him up."

"Okay." Eve watched the willowy blonde glide out.

"You wanted to see me?" She had a breathy, baby doll voice that made Eve think it was Allie's good luck ballet didn't require vocals.

"Just verifying some information. Would you mind telling me where you were this afternoon?"

"Sure. Alex and I had brunch with some friends at Quazar's. Caviar and champagne—it was CeeCee's birthday—which probably wasn't a good idea right before practice. I'm still carrying those blinis." She smiled easily. "Doesn't bother Alex, I guess, because he jumped right in when we got here. Pushed me through that damn pas de deux until I thought about just sticking my fingers down my throat. But Barinova will skin you for purging, and she always knows. Anyway, I got through it. My Angel to his Devil."

"His what?"

"Devil." She lifted the water bottle she carried, took a long sip. "We're performing the final pas de deux from *Diabolique*. I'm dancing Angel. Alex is Devil. Let me tell you, it's a killer."

Eve looked past her to the studio doorway. "I just bet."

Six

"That's what I'd call a devil of a coincidence," Peabody commented when they stepped out on the street.

"Are you buying it?"

"Not even for the couple of loose credits in my pocket."

"I want you to check with the other people the blonde gave us, and the restaurant. We'll see if Alexi could've managed to slip away. See what the timing is from the restaurant to the alley, from the school to the alley."

"Beata turned him down, pissed him off. He kills her, buries the body." Peabody scanned the area. "God knows where, but that would fit in with the west of the alley, underground deal."

"She's not dead. She's trapped." Eve snapped it out furiously, shocking herself as much as Peabody.

"Okay . . . So you think—"

"It's what she thought. Szabo." Eve rubbed a hand between her breasts where her heart beat, hard and dull, a hammer against cloth. "I'm saying Szabo thought Beata was alive."

"Right. Behind a red door. Why do people have to be so cryptic?"

Think like a cop, Eve ordered herself. Facts, logic, instinct. "Szabo spends time at the school, with Alexi et al, sniffs it out, suspects, hints around. Maybe trying to get Alexi to make a move. He kills her." Eve rolled it around. "Awful damn tidy, but sometimes it just is."

"Well, the old lady told everybody Beata was still alive, so that doesn't ride the train very well."

"She poofs. She's got a job, her classes, landed a part. Sounds like everything's working out for her, but she poofs. Odds are she didn't poof voluntarily—that's Lloyd's take, and I agree."

"Three months is a long time," Peabody put in. "A long time to hold somebody who doesn't want to be held. And for what reason?"

"Szabo didn't want to believe the girl was dead, and who can blame her?" Eve added. "Not only her great-granddaughter, but she overrode the rest of the family so Beata could come to New York."

"Had to feel sick about it." Like Eve, Peabody scanned the street, the buildings, the traffic. "What did she say exactly? To you, I mean."

Eve didn't want to go back there, to kneeling in the street, the woman's hand clasped with hers. Blood to blood.

"She said Beata's name, she said she was trapped, couldn't get out. The below bit, the red door. She asked for help."

You are the warrior. I am the promise.

Fighting to stay steady, Eve shoved a hand through her hair. "She was dying."

But her eyes, Eve remembered, had been alert, alive.

"We comb through the alibis, check her other habitats." Do the work, Eve thought, take the steps. "I'm going to check in with Morris, contact the arresting officers about Alexi, get their take on him."

"Beata's disappearance and the old woman's murder—if they're not connected, it's another devil of a coincidence."

"We pursue the investigation as if they are. We figure out one, we've got the other."

"I could tag McNab, have him meet me, go by the theater where she was supposed to work. Lloyd covered it," Peabody added, "but we could try fresh eyes on it."

"Good thinking. Send me whatever you get."

She needed thinking time, Eve told herself as they split up. A stop at the morgue to confirm TOD—which was just stupid, since she'd been right there at TOD—to see if Morris or the lab had been able to get a handle on the type of blade used, if the sweepers had found any trace evidence.

Deal with the facts first, she thought as she got in her vehicle—then move on to theory. But she sat a moment, suddenly tired, suddenly angry. It felt as if something pushed inside her brain, trying to shove her thoughts into tangents.

Not enough downtime, she decided. No time to take some good, deep breaths between cases. So she took them now, just closing her eyes for a moment, ordering her mind and body to clear.

Alive. Trapped. Help.
Keep your promise!

The voice was so clear in her head she jerked up, had a hand on her weapon as she swiveled to check the seat beside her, behind her. Her heart pounded painfully against her ribs, in her throat, in her ears as she lowered her unsteady hand.

"Stop. Just stop," she ordered herself. "Do what you have to do, then get some sleep." She pulled away from the curb, but gave in to need and called home.

And her heart slowed, settled a little when Roarke's face flowed on-screen.

"Lieutenant, I was hoping I'd— What's wrong?"

"Nothing. Well, nothing except having some old Hungarian woman bleed out under my hands. Tired," she admitted. "I've got to head down to the morgue because there was a glitch with the TOD. I need to get it straightened out, then talk to a bunch of cops about a Russian ballet guy. Sorry," she added. "This one literally fell in my lap."

"I'll meet you at the morgue."

"Why?"

"Where else does a man meet his wife—when they're you and me?" She looked pale, he thought, her eyes too dark against her skin.

"Yeah, okay. I'll see you there."

When she broke transmission, Roarke stared at the blank screen of his 'link. Not even a token protest? More than tired, he thought.

His lieutenant was not herself.

*   *   *

She got lost. She would have deemed it impossible, but she couldn't find her way. The streets seemed too crowded, too confusing, and the blare of horns when she hesitated at a light had her jumping in her seat. Frustration turned to sweaty fear that ran a snaking line down the center of her back. Battling it back, she ordered the dash navigator to plot her route, then gave in and put her vehicle on auto.

Tired, she assured herself and closed her eyes. Just tired. But there was a lingering unease that she was ill—or worse.

Need a boost, she thought, nearly shuddering with relief as she arrived at the morgue. She'd grab a tube of Pepsi at Vending, down some caffeine. Maybe even choke down a PowerBar because, Jesus, she was starving.

What was wrong with the air in here? she wondered as she started down the white tunnel. The lights glaring off the tiles slapped into her eyes and made them ache. It was frigid, an icy blast after the heat of the summer night. Yet under her chilled skin her blood beat hot, like a fever raging.

She headed for Vending, digging into her pockets, her mind on food and caffeine. A woman sat on the floor beside the machines, her face in her hands, weeping.

"I'm scared. I'm scared," she repeated. "Nobody sees me now."

"What's the problem?" As Eve crouched down, the woman dropped her hands. Her face, livid with bruising, shone with shock and what might have been hope.

"You can see me?"

"Of course I can see you. You need medical attention. Take it easy. I'm going to get someone, then—"

"It's too late." Tears ran down the swollen face as the woman dipped her head again. "Look what he did to me."

Eve froze as she stared at the gaping wound on the back of the woman's head, at the dried blood matting the hair, soaking the blouse.

"Hold on. Just—" Eve reached out, and her hand passed through the woman's arm. "Jesus God."

"It was Rennie." Sniffling, she pushed the heels of her hands through the tears.

"What are you? What is this?"

"I don't know, but I have to tell *somebody*. It was Rennie," she repeated. "The bastard. He was mad at me 'cause I helped

Sara get away from him. He must've followed me from work, and when I was in the park, he was just there. And he yelled and he hit me. He kept hitting me, and I couldn't get away. Nobody came to help. Nobody saw, and he hit me and hit me, and I fell. And he picked up a rock and he killed me. It's not right. What am I going to do now? I'm scared to be here. I'm scared to be dead."

Eve couldn't swallow, could barely breathe. "This has to stop."

"Rennie killed me."

The woman—the hallucination—held out her hands. Tore them up, Eve thought in some cold part of her brain. Tore them up when she fell, when she tried to crawl away.

"He killed me, and now I won't ever get married or eat ice cream or buy new shoes and have drinks with Sara. Rennie Foster killed me with a rock in Riverside Park, and maybe he'll kill Sara next. What's going to happen?"

"I don't know."

"Aren't I supposed to go somewhere? I don't want to stay here. It's cold here. It's too cold and it's too bright. Can you help me? I'm Janna, Janna Dorchester, and I didn't do anything wrong. Is this hell?"

"No." But she wasn't entirely sure.

Maybe hell was cold and bright. Maybe hell was losing your mind.

"Eve." Roarke dropped down beside her, took her arms. "Christ, you're burning up. Come on now."

He started to lift her, but she resisted. "No. Wait." She sucked in a breath, shuddered it out. "You don't see her?"

He pressed a hand to her forehead. "I see you, sitting on the floor of the morgue looking like a ghost."

"At one," she murmured.

"I guess he can't see me because I'm dead and everything," Janna said. "Why do you?"

"I don't know. I need Morris," she told Roarke. "And God, I need something to drink."

"Don't leave me," Janna begged, dropping her head again so Eve could see the ugly wound that killed her. "Please don't leave me here alone."

"I'm just going to sit here. Bring Morris, will you? I just . . . need to sit here." Deal, she ordered herself. Deal with what's in front of you, then figure out the rest. "Could really use something cold to drink."

Roarke rose, cursing under his breath as he ordered a tube of Pepsi.

"He's gorgeous." Janna smiled a little even as she knuckled at tears. "Mega frosted. Is he your boyfriend?"

"We're married," Eve murmured.

"Seriously icy for you," Janna said as Roarke glanced down.

"So we are," he said. "And I'll be taking my wife to a doctor in short order. I'll get you Morris first, but then you're done here."

"He's got a really sexy voice, too." Janna sighed as Eve took the tube Roarke had opened, drank.

"Thanks. I'm going to sit right here," she said as much to Janna as Roarke, "while you get Morris."

And while she sat wondering if she had a brain tumor or had dropped into some strange, vivid dream, she put on the cop and interviewed the dead.

Minutes later, Morris hurried down the tunnel with Roarke.

"Dallas." He knelt, laid a hand on her brow as Roarke had. "You're feverish."

"Just tell me if you've gotten a body in—female, mixed race, midtwenties, ID'd as Janna Dorchester. Beating death in Riverside Park."

"Yes. She's only just come in. How did you—"

"Who caught the case?"

"Ah . . . Stuben's primary."

"I need to contact him. Can you get me his contact data?"

"Of course. But you don't look well."

"I'm feeling better, actually." Odd, she thought, how the cop approach steadied her, even when her interviewee was dead. "I think I'll feel better yet once I talk to Stuben. I'd appreciate it, Morris."

"Give me a minute."

"Eve." Roarke took her hand as Morris strode away. "What's going on here?"

"I'm not sure, and I need you to give me a really open mind. I mean wide-open. Yours is already more open than mine about, you know, weird stuff."

"What sort of weird stuff is my mind going to be wide-open about?"

"Okay." She looked into his eyes, so blue, so beautiful. Eyes she trusted with everything she had. "There's a dead woman sitting right beside me. Her name's Janna Dorchester, and some asshole named Rennie Foster bashed her head in with a rock in Riverside Park. She's worried her friend Sara might be next on his list. So I'm going to pass the information to the primary. I can read Russian."

"I'm sorry?"

"I can read Russian. I think I can speak it, too, and I'm pretty sure I can make Hungarian goulash. And maybe borscht, possibly pierogies. The old woman, the one who fell into my lap and happened to be a Gypsy speaker for the dead, did something to me. Or I have a brain tumor."

Staring into her eyes, Roarke cupped Eve's face in his hands. *"Kak vashi dela?"*

"U menya vsyo po pnezhne mu. Hey, you speak Russian?"

He sat back on his heels, rocked right down to the bone. "A handful of phrases, and certainly not as fluently as you, apparently. And despite your answer, I doubt you're fine."

They looked up as Morris came back. "I have what you need."

"Great." Eve took out her 'link, and staying where she was, contacted Detective Stuben. "Lieutenant Dallas," she said, "Homicide, out of Central. I've got some information on your vic, on Janna Dorchester." She looked at Janna as she spoke. "You're going to want to find Rennie Foster and get some protection to a Sara Jasper. Let me lay it out for you."

When she had, she answered his question on how she came by the information by claiming a confidential informant.

"Unless Stuben's an idiot—and he didn't strike me that way—that should do it." Eve got to her feet. "It's all I can do."

"I'm still dead, but I'm not as scared. It's not so cold anymore."

"I don't think you have to stay here."

"Maybe for a little while. It helped to talk to you. I still wish I wasn't dead, but . . . " She trailed off, shrugged.

"Good luck." Eve turned to Morris. "I don't know how to explain it. I need to see Gizi Szabo."

"Dallas, did you just have a conversation with the dead?"

"It sure felt that way. And I'd really appreciate it if you wouldn't spread it around. I need to work, I need to keep going, or I'm pretty sure I'm going to go crazy. So . . . " She started forward, glanced back, and saw Janna lift a hand in good-bye. "I need to confirm TOD on Szabo."

"I've run it three times, using various components. It's still thirteen hundred."

"It's not possible." She shoved through the doors of the autopsy suite. "I was *there*. Lopez was there, hours later. She fell off the curb, we administered first aid. She—"

"Eve," Roarke interrupted, "you just spoke with a woman killed more than two hours ago, and you're questioning the possible?"

"I know the difference between dead and alive." She stepped up to the body. "Why can't I see *her*? Why can't I talk to *her*? I look at her, and I feel . . . rage and frustration. And . . . obligation."

"I spoke with Chale," Morris told her. At the sink he ran cold water over a cloth, wrung it out. Then he came to her and smoothed it over her face himself to cool it.

"He said the same, but he also said that she took your hand, spoke to you, and there was a light—a blast of light and energy. And for a moment after it, you seemed to be blank. Just blank. He said something seemed to pass between you."

She took the cloth, mildly embarrassed he'd tended to her—that she'd let him. "You don't believe that kind of thing."

"The science says this woman died at one this afternoon—irrefutably—but there's more in the world than science."

Maybe, she thought—hard to argue about it right at the moment. But it had been routine and order that had gotten her through the experience with Janna. So she'd stay there as long as she could.

"Let's stick with science for the moment. What can you tell me about the weapon?"

"All right. A thin, double-edged blade. Seven and a quarter inches in length." He turned to a screen to bring up the image he'd reconstructed from the wounds, then turned back to the body. "You see here where the killer thrust it fully into her, the bruising from the bolster."

She leaned in, studying the gouges, the slices. "A dagger."

"Yes. He hit bone. The tip will be chipped." Morris showed her a tiny piece of steel, sealed in a tray. "I recovered this."

"Okay, that's good. He stabbed her in the back first—back

of the shoulder." She remembered the shocking, tearing pain. "Because he's a coward, and because he feared her. She didn't see his face—he wore a mask or makeup. A kind of costume, because he's theatrical. A devil," she murmured, "because it's a role he plays, or wants to. Because it's powerful, because it instills fear, because he wanted that image to be the last she saw."

"Why?" Morris asked.

"He has something she wanted, and she wouldn't have stopped until she got it back. Exposed him. Punished him. Deprived him."

"Now you'll get it back."

She turned to Roarke, nodded. "Yeah. I will. I need to go home. You could drive while I talk to some cops."

"Dallas," Morris said, "I'd like to talk about this at some point."

"Yeah. At some point." She hesitated, handed him back the cloth, then closed her hand over his for just a moment. "Thanks."

Cooler, steadier, she walked down the tunnel with Roarke.

"Is she there?"

Eve paused, looked down at the floor where she'd sat with Jenna. "No. I guess she's gone wherever she had to go. Jesus, Roarke."

He took her hand firmly. "Let's get to the bottom of this, because right now I don't know if you need a doctor or a bloody priest."

"A priest?"

"For an exorcism."

"That's not funny," she muttered.

"It's not, no."

Seven

Roarke gave her the time she needed while he drove. He said nothing, listening to her talk with a handful of cops about someone named Alexi Barin. Since her color was back, and her skin no longer felt as though it might burn off her bones, he checked the impulse to take her straight to a health center.

He considered his wife, among other things, cynical, stable, and often annoyingly rooted in reality and logic.

When she told him, straight-faced and clear-eyed, she'd had a conversation with the dead, he leaned toward believing her. Particularly adding in her unhesitating response to his simple *How are you?* in Russian.

She clicked off her 'link again, said, "Hmmm."

"How do you make Hungarian goulash?"

"What? I'm not making goulash."

"I didn't ask you to make it, but how you would."

"Oh, it's a test. Well, you'd cut up some onions and brown them in hot oil—just to golden brown, then you'd take this beef you'd cut in cubes and coated with flour, add that and some paprika to the oil and onions. Then—"

"That's enough."

"Why would you coat good meat with flour? I thought flour was for baking stuff."

"Which proves you know less about cooking than I do, which is next to nothing, and yet you can toss off a recipe for goulash."

"It's weird, and it's pretty fucking irritating. Which is why I'm going home instead of in to Central. I'm not going to find myself talking to some dead guy or whatever in front of other cops."

"You're still you," he murmured, foolishly relieved. "You're more embarrassed than frightened by the situation you appear to be in."

"I don't even believe this is happening, but I know it is. I'm not sure I wouldn't rather have a brain tumor."

She took a breath, then another. "I'm going back over it in my head. She was walking—staggering—bleeding all over the place. Science says she was dead, but Lopez saw her, too—and the medics when they got there. She talked to me. She looked at me."

She moved back to the scene. "But she'd walked that way for blocks—I followed the blood trail back. And no one helped her, no one called for help. I can't buy that, so, using the twisted logic of this whole deal, I have to conclude no one saw her."

"Continuing with that so-called twisted logic, she came to you. She had enough left in her to cross your path, to leave you a trail, to give you what you'd need to help her."

"You could theorize. And the first thing she said was the girl's name: Beata. That she was trapped, needed help. She told me her name, and when I asked who'd done this to her, she said the devil. And . . . "

"What?"

"She said I was the warrior. Her eyes were so dark, black eyes, so intense. She said I had to take her in, let her in. She asked me, begged me. Take me in, so I said sure. I just wanted to keep her calm and alive until the MTs got there."

"You agreed."

"I guess I did." Huffing out a breath, she dragged a hand through her hair. "I guess I did, then she grabbed my hand, and bam—blinding light and like this electrical shock. These voices. I saw her face—the girl—Beata. Next thing I know, Lopez is calling my name, the medics are there, and Szabo's dead. Cold and dead."

"Because, scientifically at least, she'd died hours earlier."

"It's fucked up," was Eve's opinion. "I felt shaky and off. I guess I haven't felt all the way steady since. I recognized things I shouldn't have and didn't recognize things I should. God, Roarke, I got lost driving to the morgue. I just couldn't remember the streets."

He thought of how she'd looked, face dead white, shiny with sweat. "I think we should call Louise, have her come take a look at you."

"I don't think a doctor's going to help, or a priest either. I can't believe I'm saying this, but I think it's like Janna. When we close the case, it'll be done."

She shifted to him. "She cut me a little with her nails, see?" She held up her hand, palm out. "Said all this stuff about blood to blood and heart to heart. I had her blood all over me by then. And she said it wouldn't be finished until the promise was kept. And the thing is, I promised to find Beata while I was trying to keep the old woman alive."

"You made a blood pact with a Romany."

"A Romany speaker for the dead, apparently. Not on purpose," she added with some heat.

"An accidental blood pact," he qualified.

"You'd have done the same damn thing." Peeved, she shifted away again. "And you're a civilian. I'm a cop. Protect and serve, goddamn it."

"Which rarely includes blood pacts with dead travelers."

"Are you trying to piss me off?"

"Got your color back," he said easily.

"Well, whoopee. Eyes on the prize. I have to find out who killed Gizi Szabo, and I have to find Beata."

"She's alive, Beata. You're certain."

"In my current condition, tossing out the logic that says otherwise? I think Szabo would have known if the girl was dead. And I think I'd know it now. Instead, I have this certainty, against all that logic, that she's alive, trapped by the same devil who killed her great-grandmother. He wants to keep the girl, and the old woman made sure people knew she was getting close to finding her. Maybe she did that to lure him out, maybe she did it because it kept her going. But she was a threat."

Her nerves throttled down a few more notches when Roarke drove through the gates, when she saw the house. Home. Hers.

"Beata's a liability now," Eve added. "And that may weigh heavier on him than his need to keep her. Szabo stirred things up, and now I've done the same. He may decide to kill her rather than risk discovery."

"This Alexi Barin?"

"He's heading the list. He knew her, wanted her, got shut down by her. He's got an ego the size of Utah. He knew where she lived, where she worked, very likely knew her basic routine. Added, they were rehearsing for this big dance—*Diabolique*, Angel and Devil, which is no fucking coincidence."

"I'd agree. That would make it easier yet to lure her. Extra practice, after hours."

"There you go. He's had violent run-ins, got a sheet, and the cops who busted him all say he's got a temper that lights him up—quick and fast. And that's why he's not in Interview right now."

"Because while Szabo was killed violently and perhaps on impulse, if Beata's still alive, being held against her will, that took some planning. And continues to take planning."

"Right now, it's a good thing you can think like a cop, because I don't know if my brain's firing on all circuits." She got out of the car. "I need to be home. I need to be back in control. And if you're up for it, I could use some help running everybody on my list who knows Beata, studied with her, worked with her. Her neighbors, her friends, people who saw her routinely. You want what you see—or have to see it to want it."

"You give me the names, I'll start your runs—on the condition that you rest. An hour," he said as she started to protest. "Nonnegotiable."

"I just need to clear my head. And I'm starving," she admitted. "I feel like I haven't eaten in days, like everything's burned off."

"Possibly a side effect of possession."

"That's not funny either." She stepped inside, gave Summerset a beady stare. *"Baszd meg,"* she suggested and watched his eyes widen.

Suspected she saw his lips twitch in what might have been a restrained smile.

"I see you're broadening your linguistics."

"That wasn't Russian," Roarke said as they headed up the stairs.

"I think it's Hungarian. It just came to me—and I figure he knows I just told him to fuck off."

"Rude, yet fascinating." He went with her to her office. "You, up." He pointed at the cat currently sprawled in Eve's sleep chair. "You, down," he ordered. "Give me your list, and I'll get those runs going." He brushed a hand over her hair, struggling against worry. "How about pizza?"

"I could eat a whole pie." She dropped into the chair. "Thank God my appetite's not running to that borscht, because I'd really rather have a brain tumor than beet soup." She dragged her notebook out of her pocket. "Most of the names are in here. I have to get more. Peabody and McNab were hitting the theaters where she worked or would have, and I need neighbors. But that's a big start."

"Food first." He walked into the kitchen.

Galahad didn't leap into her lap but sat eyeing her.

"I'm still me," she murmured. "I'm not her. I'm still me." When he bumped his head against her leg, her eyes stung. "I'm still me," she repeated.

Roarke came back with a plate on a tray. "I ordered up a whole one, but you start with that. And drink the soother. Don't argue," he warned. "I doubt you've looked in the mirror in the last few hours, but when I came in to the morgue, you looked like you belonged there. You'll eat, drink a soother, then we'll see."

With that, he turned to her desk, sat, and began inputting names into her computer. Eve ate like a horse.

"God, that's better. No shakes." She held out a hand, a steady one. "No queasiness, no jumps." Still she looked down at the cat. "He won't sit in my lap, even for pizza. He's not sure of me. I guess he senses something's off. That I'm off. How long do you think—" She couldn't say it.

"It's going to be fine." He rose to go to her. "We'll do whatever needs to be done, then we'll do whatever comes after that. You'll be fine."

"I have to live with the dead, Roarke, I don't want to chat with them. I see the advantage for a murder cop. Hey, sorry about the bad luck, but who killed you? Oh yeah, we'll go pick him up. Move on. I don't want to work that way. I don't want to live that way. I don't think I can."

"You won't have to." He took the tray, set it aside. "I swear to you, we'll find whatever needs finding."

She believed him. Maybe she had to, but she believed him.

"In the meantime . . . " She took his hand. "Can you be with me? I need to be *me*. I need you to touch me—*me*—and feel what I do when you're with me. Know that you feel me."

"There's no one but you." He slid onto the chair beside her. "Never anyone but you."

"Don't be gentle." She dragged his mouth to hers. "Want me."

She needed those seeking hands, that mouth hungry for hers. Needed to feel and taste and ache, needed to know that it was her mind, her body, her heart meshed with his.

Love, the dark and the light of it, was strength, and she took it from him.

He tugged her jacket down her shoulders, hit the release on her weapon harness as his mouth captured and conquered hers. And those hands, those wonderful hands lit fresh fires, a new fever that raged clean and bright in her blood. Her fingers fumbled for the chair controls so they tumbled back when it slid flat.

It wasn't comfort she wanted, he knew, but lust—the greed and speed. Perhaps he needed the same. So he pinned her arms over her head, used his free one to torment until she bucked beneath him, crying out as she came.

And there was more. Dewy flesh quivering under his hands, frantic pulses jumping at the nip of his teeth. The lust she wanted beat inside him as wildly as her heart.

His woman. Only his. Her flesh, her lips, her body. Strong again.

"Now. Yes. Now!" Her nails dug into his hips as she arched against him, opened to him.

Hot and wet, she closed around him, crying out again as he thrust hard and deep, as she bowed to take him. Holding there, holding for one heady moment as he looked in her eyes. As he saw only Eve.

Then the whirlwind, wicked and wild, spinning them both too high for air, too fast for fear.

And when the world settled back, all the colors and shapes and light, then came the comfort. She lay locked in his arms, breathing him in. Her body—*her* body—felt used and raw and wonderful.

Eyes closed, she ran a hand through his hair, down his

back. "No problem, considering you might have just indirectly banged a ninety-six-year-old woman?"

"If I did, she gave as good as she got."

She laughed, tangled her legs with his. "We'll still bang when we're ninety, right?"

"Count on it. I'll have developed a taste for old women by then, so this could be considered good practice."

"It's got to be sick to even be thinking this way, but it's probably like making jokes in the morgue. It's how you get through." She untangled, sat up. "What I'm going to do is grab a shower, then coffee, then go over your runs. I'm going to work this like it needs to be worked and keep this other thing off to the side. Because if I think about it too hard, I'm just going to wig out."

He sat up with her, took her shoulders. And what she saw in his eyes blocked the air from her lungs. "What? What?"

"You are who you are. I know you. You believe that?"

"Yeah, but—"

"You're Eve Dallas. You're the love of my life. My heart and soul. You're a cop, mind and bone. You're a woman of strength and resilience. Stubborn, hardheaded, occasionally mean as a badger, and more generous than you'll admit."

Fear edged back, an icy blade down the spine. "Why are you saying this?"

"Because I don't think you can put what's happened aside, not altogether. Take a breath."

"Why—"

"Take a breath." he said it sharply, adding a shake so she did so automatically. "Now another." He kept one hand on her shoulder as he shifted and touched the other to her ankle.

And the tattoo of a peacock feather.

Eight

She got her shower, got her coffee. She told herself she was calm—*would* be calm. Panic wouldn't help; raging might feel good, but in the end wouldn't help either.

"There are options," Roarke told her.

"Don't say the *E* word. No exorcisms. I'm not having some priest or witch doctor or voodoo guy dancing around me, banging on his magic coconuts."

"Magic . . . Is that a euphemism?"

"Maybe." It helped to see him smile—to think she might be able to. "But I'm not going there, Roarke."

"All right then. What about Mira?"

"You think she can shrink Szabo out of me?"

"Hypnosis might find some answers."

She shook her head. "I'm not being stubborn. Or maybe I am," she admitted when he cocked his eyebrows. "Right now I'd rather not bring anybody else into this. I just don't want to tell anybody I invited a dead woman to take up residence in my head, or wherever she is. Because that's what I did."

She shoved up, began to pace. "I said sure, come right in. Maybe if I'd been paying attention to what she was saying, what she meant, I'd have locked the door. Instead I'm all, yeah, yeah, whatever, because I'm trying to keep a woman science says was already dead from bleeding out. It doesn't make any sense, god-damn it. And because it doesn't, I have to set it to one side. I have to," she insisted. "I have to work the cases—cases—with my head, my gut. Fucking A *mine*. Which I damn well would've done anyway if she'd left me the hell alone."

"So you'll fight this with logic and instinct?" He decided they could both use a glass of wine.

"It's what I've got. It's what's mine. And if there's any logic to this other part, the part that makes no sense, when I find the killer, when I find Beata, it—she—goes away. If I don't believe that, I'm going to lock myself in a closet and start sucking my thumb."

He took her the wine, touched her cheek. "Then we'll find the killer and Beata. And for now, we'll keep the rest of it be-tween you and me. Twenty-four hours. We'll work it your way, and I'll find someone who can undo what was done. If this isn't resolved in twenty-four hours, we'll work it my way."

"That sounds like an ultimatum."

"It most certainly is. You can waste time arguing, or you can get to work. I'm not going to share my wife with anyone for more than a day."

"I'm not your possession either, pal."

He smiled again. "But you belong to me. We can fight about it." He shrugged, sipped his wine. "And you'll have wasted part of your twenty-four. Still, it might fire you up, so I'm open to it."

"Smug bastard."

"Maybe you'd like to swear at me in Russian or Hungarian."

"And you said *I* was mean. Twenty-four." She took a slug of wine, considered how she's push for more if she needed it. "Let's look at the runs."

Roarke ordered data on-screen, leaned a hip against the side of her desk. "Your prime suspect," he began. "You had most of this, but the second-level run added a bit, and I extrapolated from your notes. Allie Madison's apartment, where it's verified Alexi Barin began the day, is an easy ten-minute walk to the alley—considerably less if a healthy, athletic man took it at a jog, even a run. It's about the same from the restaurant where he had brunch. As is his own apartment," Roarke added, ordering the map he'd generated on-screen. "These locations are clus-tered, more or less, in the general area."

"So he could've slipped out, slipped away, put on a mask,

sliced Szabo up, and gotten back. Which would involve knowing she'd be in the alley at that convenient moment, and wearing something for the blood spatter. Because you don't hack somebody up the way she was hacked and walk away clean and fresh to take your alibi to brunch."

She paced in front of the screen. "He could have set a meet with her, pinning the timing. Told her he had some information on Beata. It's a lot of planning for an impulsive guy with a temper."

"Something set him off at the brunch if we go with your TOD, or prior if we stay with science," Roarke suggested. "He went to confront her, saw her in the alley—he'd have come from this direction, so he'd have passed the alley. He snaps, pulls the knife, goes in."

"Why is he disguised?"

"She could have seen his face, Eve. The condition she was in when you found her? It's not a stretch to believe she wasn't lucid."

"She didn't see it. She saw the devil." Eve paused a moment. "I know. It's what I saw. I had . . . a moment in the alley. I know what she saw."

"All right."

Because she'd expected an argument, even yearned for one, she rounded on him. "I don't know whether to be grateful or pissed off that you accept so easily."

"Not as easy as it might seem, just easier than you. So if you say you saw what she saw, I know you did. The occult, on some level, is involved—even that's logical."

"If you're a superstitious Irish guy."

"If you're currently able to curse in Hungarian and make goulash," he countered—and shut her up. "It could be your suspect has some power of his own."

"I'm not going there. Logic, facts, data. So while it's possible Alexi slipped out, did the murder, it's low on the logic and probability scale with the data we have at this time. Give me the guy Beata worked with. The one who walked out of the restaurant with her the night she was last seen."

"David Ingall, twenty-two, single. He's had two bumps. One for an airboard incident where he lost control and mowed down a group of pedestrians in Times Square, and another for manufacturing and using false ID—he was underage and got into a sex club before an undercover busted him. He dropped out of NYU and takes a couple of virtual courses a semester, lives in a one-bedroom apartment a few blocks from the restaurant with two roommates. He's worked at Goulash for three years."

"Doesn't sound particularly murderous."

"In addition, the file from your Detective Lloyd has a statement from one of the roommates confirming his arrival home—and the drunken night of computer gaming that followed, on the night Beata Varga went missing."

"Roommates make it harder for him to take Beata, hold her, unless they're complicit."

"The information on the roommates is as benign as this one."

"Switch to the theater," Eve decided. "Where she was understudying. What did Peabody get?"

She studied the data as it scrolled, listened to Roarke's summaries. And paced.

None of them popped for her. Holding a woman against her will for an extended length of time required privacy, soundproofing, supplies, and time.

Maybe she was wrong—maybe the old woman had been wrong—and the girl was dead. And the thought of that pierced her so deep, she shuddered.

"Eve—"

"No, it's nothing. Keep going. I need to set up a murder board. I should've done it already."

She pinned up her photos, let the information Roarke provided wind through while she arranged what she needed on the board.

"Work and the school," Eve said. "Her most usual and regular spots other than her apartment. We focus there. She went out on auditions, and that'll be another level if we bomb here. Work, school, her neighbors. Then the theater, then audition sites, shops, and so on.

"Let me see the map again."

She moved closer to the screen. "She takes this route basically every day. Home to morning class. Then from class to work if she was scheduled. Back to class, back to work or an audition. Evening class three nights a week, and work again four nights."

"A regular customer at the restaurant," Roarke suggested. "Someone she waited on routinely. Wanted her, took her."

She nodded. "Possible. Someone she knew is most probable. Someone who could lure her where he wanted her to go. Doesn't make the ripples a forced abduction would. Had to have a place. Underground. A basement? A cellar?"

"The underground itself," Roarke commented. "There are places under the streets no one would pay attention to a woman struggling, screaming, calling for help."

"Too many," Eve agreed. "But it'd be risky. Someone could take her from you. Private," she said again. "Can you get the blueprints for the building—the dance school?" When his answer was simply a long look, she rolled her eyes. "Go ahead, show off. Let me see the uncle's data. Sasha Korchov."

"I've got deeper data on Natalya Barinova as well."

"It's a man. Go with the man first."

Benign. That was the word Roarke had used to describe Beata's coworker and his roommates. It was a word that came to mind with Sasha. Dreamy eyes, she remembered—a little like Dennis Mira there—and indeed his ID photo showed the same, along with the soft smile.

But the images Roarke had dug up from before the accident that had cost him his career and his lover showed a dynamic, intense, passionate man. Leaping, spinning a long, leanly muscled body showcased in dramatic costumes. The mane of hair coal black, the eyes on fire.

"How do you lose that?" she murmured. "Lose that energy, that passion, that fierceness? It must be almost like death or losing someone to death. Something breaks, something more than a leg, an arm. Something gets crushed, more than a foot, more than ribs."

How do you get over the anger—that's what she'd asked Lopez about survivors, about families who lost someone to murder.

"You lost your badge once," Roarke reminded her. "What did it do to you?"

"Destroyed me. Temporarily. Cut me off from what I was. But I had you to help bring me back, and I got my badge back. He lost his woman, too. His woman," she repeated. "Another dancer. And look here, they danced the *Diabolique* ballet together. The Devil was his signature role. Son of a bitch. I should've seen it."

"The building has a basement," Roarke told her. "It runs the length and width of the building and holds a number of rooms, listed as storage and/or utility and maintenance on the plans."

"Who owns the building?"

"Funny you should ask. He owns it. He made quite a bit of money during his career and was awarded a large settlement after the accident."

"He's got no record anywhere. Unless it got covered up. No history of violence."

"Money can smooth the way."

"Yeah." She angled her head at Roarke. "It can. But you can usually find a few bumps in the media. Speculation, gossip. A man might not be charged and still be guilty."

"I'll see what I come across, and it's telling, I think, that he gave no interviews I can find, no public statements or appearances after the accident."

"He went underground," Eve murmured. "So to speak. Lost everything that mattered to him? That could be it. Had his sister, and she left her home and possibly the remains of her career to come here with him, bringing her infant son. Dreamy eyes," she recalled. "Medication? His medicals show extensive injuries from the accident, the kind a man's lucky to live through. Had to have a lot of pain."

More than physical, she decided, thinking of losing her badge again. Much more than physical pain.

"He sits in that studio now playing music for others to dance to. For this beautiful young woman who's about the same age, the same build and coloring as the woman he loved. She's going to dance that same role with his nephew.

"Would that piss him off, make him sad? They go to Vegas." She stopped as her gut twisted. "Natalya said they go to Las Vegas to be showgirls. Maybe Beata's not the first."

She strode to the auxiliary comp, started a search for missing persons, female of the same age group, coded in ballet.

"There's some speculation and juice regarding a young Sasha Korchov and his temper. Storming off stage at rehearsals, berating other dancers—neither of which is particularly unusual," Roarke added. "And more, here and there, about wild parties and breaking up hotel rooms and such. Before he met and danced with Arial Nurenski. She, it's speculated here, was balm to his troubled spirit and other romantic analogies. She changed him, calmed him, inspired him. They were to be married two weeks after the accident that killed her."

"Vanessa Warwich, age twenty-two, last seen leaving a café to go to rehearsal at the West Side School for the Arts. She was to dance the role of Angel in their autumn gala—just like Beata. That was two years ago. There are more." She looked over at Roarke. "I need to cross-reference, find a connection with the school or Barin, or the role."

"Send me your list. I'll take half."

She shot the data to his computer. "Roarke, if he's been taking these women, holding them, trapped in a basement? He is a devil."

They found eight.

Nine

It was no backyard barbecue, but it had nearly the same guest list. In the conference room at Cop Central, Eve laid out what she had.

"Nine women over twenty-three years," she began, "with a direct or indirect connection to the school, or a connection to the ballet, have gone missing. All were in their early to mid twenties, dark hair, slim build. All were dancers, and all vanished without a solid explanation."

She turned to the screen, to the images. "In some cases they'd made some noises about leaving the city; in most there were personal items missing from their apartments, as if they had done so."

"The nine includes this Beata Varga." Commander Whitney studied the board Eve had arranged with ID shots of the missing. "Who connects to your murder victim."

"She's the latest. Detective Lloyd can give you the background on that." She nodded at him.

Lloyd stood and walked to the board. "Last seen leaving the restaurant where she worked. Here." He used the laser pointer Eve handed him. "In the company of two coworkers. They separated here, with Beata continuing south in the direction of her apartment."

He went over the time lines, the other particulars, reviewed his interview statements. "Up to the point she went missing, she had regular contact with her family. Her work hours weren't regular, as her employers scheduled her around her classes and auditions and rehearsals, but when she was scheduled to work, she showed up, and statements from her employers, co-workers, customers corroborate she was responsible. Happy. Dedicated to forging her career. She'd just landed a part in an off-Broadway musical. She wasn't the type to just take off."

"Neither was Vanessa Warwich." Eve used her own pointer to highlight the photo. "Missing for twenty-six months, last seen leaving her apartment—here—to rehearse at the school. She'd enrolled only five weeks earlier, had a new boyfriend. Or Allegra Martin, age twenty-four, a principal dancer for the City Ballet who was starring in the role of Angel when she went missing four and a half years ago.

"Lucy Quinn, seven years missing," Eve continued, and worked down the line. "The pattern's clear, as is the victim type."

"You believe Sasha Korchov is replacing his lover with these women."

Eve nodded at Mira. "I know he is. He lost her, lost everything in one terrible moment. He left his home and is reduced to teaching others to dance, more to watching them—those young women—dance when his lover can't, while he plays for them."

"He plays the tune," Mira added. "They dance. If he's taken these women, it could be he needs them to dance for him— only him. He needs to keep them to himself, possibly to re-create the relationship he had with his fiancée, professionally and personally."

"Could they still be alive?" Peabody asked.

"I think there could only be one at a time," Mira told her. "One dancer, one lover, one partner if you will, or the illusion shatters. It would be more likely he's replacing the replacements over time than adding to the number."

"Beata's alive." Eve felt it in her bones. "But he's killed Szabo to protect himself. She made it known she believed Beata was alive and close by, trapped. Underground. A Romany, a dead talker, breathing down his neck."

She saw Baxter roll his eyes at that, stuck with logic. "He has some Romany blood. His sister and the old woman talked regularly—she's poking around, getting too close. He's afraid of her, superstitious. Enough so he disguises himself before he kills her. He doesn't want her to see his true face. And now he's had the cops at his door over it. How long can he keep Beata alive?"

"The pressure may push him to eliminate her," Mira agreed.

"I need a warrant. We need to search that basement, his apartment, the whole damn place."

"I can get one." APA Reo pushed to her feet. "The pattern and connections should be enough." She checked her wrist unit, winced at the time. "Waking up a judge or interrupting the Saturday night party isn't going to win me a popularity award."

As Reo left the room, Eve ordered the blueprints on-screen. "His apartment. We need to take him first, secure him so he doesn't have the chance to panic and take Beata out. We also secure the sister and nephew. They may be involved, may be protecting him. Feeney, I want to locate everyone in the building before we go in."

"We'll set it up. Get you heat source imagery."

"I need the exits secured," she continued. "And there are a lot of them: doors, windows, fire escapes, roof access. Elevators are down. If Korchov's in his apartment, we secure him. If he's not, we find him. We're also looking for the murder weapon. A dagger, seven and a quarter inches, likely a chipped tip. Renicki, Jacobson, you're on the apartment. Baxter, Trueheart, Peabody, we'll take the basement." She glanced at Roarke. "We'll take the civilian."

A locked door, she thought, would be easier to deal with if they had a thief—former—along.

"Feeney, McNab, Callendar, you run the electronics. I want locations, movements. Once the suspect, the sister, the nephew are secured, you'll move in."

She went over the rest of the assignments, detailing the operation stage by stage.

This is what she did, she told herself. This was the logic, the instinct, the training. And if there was something inside her urging her, all but begging her to hurry, she had to ignore it.

"I want all of you to watch your asses," she concluded. "This man is suspected of abducting and imprisoning at least nine women, very likely killing them when he was finished. He's suspected of slicing up a ninety-six-year-old woman in broad daylight. Just because he used to wear tights and ballet shoes doesn't mean he's not dangerous."

"Potentially very," Mira confirmed, "when cornered, when desperate. I'll ride with EDD," she added. "If any of his victims are alive, I may be able to help."

"Appreciate it." She looked at Morris. "And if they aren't."

He nodded. "Yes."

"Let's get moving. Load it up, ride it out. Father Lopez, if I could have a moment."

She gestured him to the side of the room. "I don't make a habit of calling a priest into an op, but—"

"I'm grateful you did in this case. I'll do whatever I can to help."

"You were there when Szabo died. You did the Last Rites thing. I figured if the old woman was Catholic, the girl probably is. Between you and Mira she'd be covered."

"It's kind of you."

She didn't know if it was—didn't know if it had been her impulse to call him in or if she'd been directed.

"How are you, Eve?"

"Hell if I know, and I don't have a lot of time to think about it right now."

"If you need me—"

"I'm hoping not to go there. No offense."

He smiled at her. "None taken."

"I'll need you to stay in the EDD van with Mira until we're clear."

"Understood, even if it's disappointing not to be able to get in on some of the action."

"This devil's my fight. Stick with Mira," she said before she started toward Roarke.

"I can't figure out how you connected the dots." Peabody stopped her. "The basement, all those missing women, the soft-spoken piano player. I feel like I missed a couple dozen steps."

"Things just started falling into place. Let's just say I followed Szabo. She was already closing in. Check with Reo. See if she's got the warrant."

She continued on to Roarke. "I need to ask you for something."

"Are you asking your husband or your civilian?"

"Looks like you're both. I need you to stay close to me. If I start to lose it—"

"You won't."

"If, I think you can help me stay grounded. She's in here." Eve touched a hand to her chest. "This is the guy who took Beata, the guy who killed her. She might want some payback. If it looks like I'd turn that way, stop me. You stop me."

"I have every confidence in Lieutenant Dallas, but if it makes you feel easier, I won't let you do anything you'll regret."

"Good. But be, you know, subtle about it."

He had to laugh. "You are absolutely you. All right then, while preventing you from taking a dead Gypsy's revenge, I'll do whatever I can to preserve your dignity. How's that?"

"It'll do."

She reviewed the blueprints again on the way to the building, checked in with her teams, focused on the work.

"We go in the front, pass the main stairs, to the right and straight to the basement access door. It's going to be locked. If the master doesn't work, we use the battering ram or"—she glanced at Roarke—"other means. If Feeney picks up images down there, we follow his lead. Otherwise, Peabody, Baxter, Trueheart, take this sector. Roarke and I this one. One of you sees a mouse riveting, everybody hears about it. We clear sector by sector. If a door's locked, take it down. Call for backup if you need it."

She toggled to the exterior view. "Locations of cams are highlighted. I don't see anybody watching them this time of night. But there are very likely cams down there not on the blueprints."

Think like him, she ordered herself. Not like a frantic old woman.

"He'd want to watch her, and want his area secured in and out. Can't have somebody stumbling across her, and can't let her find a way out. If Renicki and Jacobson lock him down, they can work him for more information—but we won't count on getting it. We'll bring in the others, and we'll go through every inch of that basement.

"Feeney," she said into her mic, "give me the word."

"Got nothing in the suspect's place. Got two in the other apartment. Everything else aboveground is clear. Got nothing for you in the basement, but there are voids down there, Dallas, either due to the thickness of walls, jammers, or sensor blocks."

"Tucks them up tight," she murmured. "Give me the location of the voids."

She keyed them in, felt the adrenaline begin to pump. "We hit those first. If he's not upstairs and didn't go for a goddamn walk, he's down there with her now. We're green. All teams, we're green. Move."

She jumped out of the back of the transport, weapon out. She prayed she hadn't missed a deeper level of security, prayed he wasn't monitoring the cameras as she used her master to access the main door.

Cops spread out to the exits, up the stairs, moving quick and quiet while she and her team rushed to the basement door.

"Master's ineffective."

"Give me a minute," Roarke told her. "Battering rams are crude, and they're noisy."

She stepped back to give him room, mentally checking off each exit as her men reported them secure.

When Roarke's clever tools and fingers unlocked the door, she signaled to Peabody. "High and left," she told her, "then straight down."

She went in low and right—and knew immediately her instincts had been on target.

Lights burned in the ceiling, dim but activated. The old metal stairs led down to a concrete floor, thick walls, narrow corridors.

She signaled Peabody to lead her team, then set off in the opposite direction with Roarke.

They passed through a cavernous room piled with old furniture, lamps, fabrics, down another dim corridor. She heard the clink and hum of the building mechanicals as they moved through a utility area where tools were neatly stored on free-standing shelves.

"This area needs to be maintained," she said quietly, sweeping with her weapon as Roarke did the same with the one he'd slipped out of his pocket. "Wherever he keeps them has to be soundproofed and fully secured."

"This sector's void's west. Down that way."

Eve started to turn, then went into a crouch, weapon up. Her muscles trembled as the ballerina blocked her way.

"I can't get out," the woman said and held out her hands. "We can't get out. Can you help me?"

"You have to wait."

"Eve?"

"It's Vanessa Warwich." Eve fought off shudders as her skin shivered from the sudden cold. "You have to wait a little longer."

"I couldn't dance anymore." She lifted her sparkling white skirt. "He cried when he killed me." She touched her fingers to the gaping slice across her throat. "But I couldn't dance anymore."

"Just wait." And gritting her teeth, Eve walked through the pleading woman. She reached out to try to balance herself when her head spun.

Roarke grabbed her, braced her. "Bloody hell. Stay here."

"I have to finish it. You know I have to finish it. I have to make it stop." She glanced back and into Vanessa Warwich's eyes but saw the others behind her. All the pretty girls in their sparkling skirts and toe shoes.

All those white throats gaping.

"She's waiting. Warwich waiting—trapped. And God, she's not alone. We have to move."

"Hold on to me if you have to."

He took the lead, brooked no argument. She steadied herself as she followed, cleared her throat as she listened to team updates.

Her op, she reminded herself. She was in command here. She had to be.

Natalya and Alexi were secured, Peabody had reached the first of her voids. An empty room. The search of Sasha's apartment was under way, but neither he nor the murder weapon had been found.

Roarke held up a hand, stopped her. "Sensors," he murmured. "They'll read us."

"Then we're getting close."

"They'll likely signal in his apartment but could very well alert him if he's down here. Give me a minute to jam them."

"You're handy."

"We do what we can." He took out what looked like an innocent PPC, keyed in various codes. "It's rudimentary," he told her. "Just a precaution to let him know if anyone's down this way."

"Or if his current ballerina managed to get out. Are we clear?"

"We are."

"Peabody, we hit sensors. Watch for them. We're moving."

Another turn, another twenty feet, and they spotted the door. "Secured door," she said into her mic. "Accessing now."

She rolled her shoulders as Roarke got to work. She was ready, she thought. She was herself.

When he nodded, they went through the door together, swept it.

She supposed it would be called a sitting room—windowless, but with a softly faded carpet, a sofa, a lamp. And a small monitoring station.

He could sit here and watch her before he went in, she thought, studying the blank monitor, then the second secured door, the one painted bright bloodred.

"The red door," she murmured. "Locked behind the red door."

Without a word Roarke went to the door, checked the security. She had to breathe deeply, slowly, fighting the voice inside her begging her to hurry, hurry, hurry.

"Got his lair," she said to Peabody. "Key in on me. Secondary door and inner security being bypassed. Feeney, I've got a monitoring station here. Send McNab in. We're clear," she said at Roarke's nod. "We're going in."

She looked at him, trusted him to keep her centered. She held up three fingers, closed to a fist, then held up one, two. On three they were through the door.

Ten

He'd set his prison with a stage with filmy white curtains on either side and lights to enhance the mood of the music that soared. Roses, their petals glowing silver in the light, scented the air. Eve spotted all this, and another door, in an instant, but her focus centered on the stage and the dancers.

Beata, her face pale with exhaustion, her eyes empty of hope, wore a white, filmy skirt, topped by a bodice glittering with gold like the ring that crowned her.

The same costume as all the others. All the pretty dancers.

Beata rose, fluid as water, *en pointe* and into an arabesque before turning into the arms of the devil.

He gripped her waist, lifted her high, while his eyes shone through the holes in his mask. His cape flowed from his shoulders as he dipped her head toward the floor.

Eve's weapon seemed to burn in her hand. She longed to fire it, craved it as her heart raged in her chest. And the words, the thoughts that roared through her head were in Romany.

Roarke touched a hand to the small of her back, just a bare brush of fingers. "Your move, Lieutenant," he murmured beneath the swell of music.

Her move, she thought, and took it when the dancers leaped apart.

"Nice jump," she called out, training her weapon on Sasha. "Now freeze, or I'll drop you off your twinkle toes."

She heard Beata's cry, swore she felt it rip through her soul, but kept her eyes on Sasha.

"You're interrupting the performance." He spoke with some heat—as a man would when bumped violently on the street by a stranger.

"Show's canceled."

"Don't be ridiculous." He dismissed her with a wave of the hand, then reached it out for his partner. Roarke had already moved in and put himself between them.

Sasha pulled the dagger from his belt. "I'll kill you for touching her."

"You can certainly try, and I admit I'd enjoy beating you to hell and back again, but I believe the lieutenant will indeed drop you if you take a step toward this girl."

"She's mine." He whirled back to Eve. "No one takes her from me. She is my Angel, and here she lives forever."

"I am Beata Varga." Beata yanked the crown from her head, heaved it. "I'm not your Angel, and you go to hell."

Sasha lunged for her, and even as Roarke braced to counter the attack, Eve kept her word. She dropped him, stunned and shuddering, to center stage.

As he fell, Beata covered her face with her hands and slid to the floor at the edge of those glittering lights. "I knew someone would come. I knew someone would come."

Eve moved forward, went to her knees, and wrapped her arms around Beata as Peabody's team rushed in.

Once again Roarke stepped between. "I think you might want to restrain your suspect before he recovers, and take him out. Give Beata a moment." He gave the dagger a light kick across the stage. "And there's your murder weapon."

"Yeah." If Peabody thought it strange to see her partner rocking the weeping girl, she said nothing of it. "We'll clear him out, and I'll tell Father Lopez and Dr. Mira to stand by."

"Crazy fucker." Baxter looked around the room as he locked restraints on Sasha. "All his world's a freaking stage. Trueheart tagged the MTs. For her," he added, and with Trueheart's help, hauled Sasha to his feet.

Eve let the police routine play out behind her—under control, she thought and concentrated on Beata. "Are you hurt? Did he hurt you?"

"Not really, not much. How long? How long have I been here? Sometimes he gave me something that made me sleep, and I lost track."

"You're all right now. That's what counts."

"He locked me in. In there." Though she continued to shake, she lifted her chin toward the inner door. "This horrible, beautiful room. He brought me flowers and chocolates, and all these beautiful clothes. He's out of his mind, out of his mind." She dropped her head back on Eve's shoulder.

"Did he touch you? Beata." She drew the girl back.

"No, no, no. Not that way. I thought he would rape me, kill me, but it wasn't what he wanted."

She continued to tremble under Eve's hands, but even as they streamed with tears, her eyes held fury.

"He said we would be together forever, and I would do what I was born to do: dance. Always dance. And night after night he would come and put on the costume. If I wouldn't wear mine, he'd give me the drug, and when I woke I'd be in it. So I put it on rather than have him touch me. And I danced, because if I refused or if I fought, he'd tie me and leave me in the dark."

"You did what you had to do," Eve told her. "You did exactly right."

"I called, but no one heard, and I tried to break the door, but I couldn't. I couldn't. I couldn't."

"Okay. It's okay."

"Every day I'd try to find a way out, but there wasn't one. I don't know where I am. How did you find me?"

"You're in the basement of the school where you took classes. We'll get into all the details later. We're going to get you out of here now."

"My family."

"You can contact them." Eve laid a hand on Beata's cheek. "Your family is always with you, wherever you are, wherever you go."

Beata closed a hand around Eve's wrist, let her head rest in Eve's hand. "That's what my grandmother would say to me whenever I was sad or scared."

I know, Eve thought, and helped Beata to her feet. "I want you to go with these officers now. They'll take you out."

"Aren't you coming with me?"

"I'll be there soon. There are things I have to do. Beata, did they know, were they part of this? Natalya, Alexi."

"No. He said it was only us, our secret—that they wanted him to be calm, to accept, to live without me. Her, Arial, the one whose name he called me. But that he never would. He wouldn't share me with them or the world. He wouldn't lose me this time. He told me often."

"Okay, go ahead now. Go outside. Go breathe the air."

Eve knew what it was to be locked up, to be trapped and helpless. And to want to breathe free.

Eve shut off her recorder, looked at Roarke. "It's not done. I hoped, when we found her . . . I have to find the others. I know where they are," she said before Roarke answered. "They're pressing on me. The dead. I know where they are, and I think—hope—I know what to do."

"Then we'll go find them."

She turned her recorder back on, reengaged her mic. "I need a unit down here with tools. We need to take down a wall. And I'll need Morris. I'm on the move. Key in on my location when I get there, and send a team down to process this goddamn prison.

"Let's go," she said to Roarke.

She didn't have to ask him to hold her hand, to keep her close as they walked those dim corridors, or to talk to her quietly, soothingly.

"He must've built that place years ago," she said. "And updated it, maintained it—down here in the bowels of the building. There were tools in that utility room we went through. A sledgehammer and—"

"I'll get something." She was pale again, he thought, feverish again. It had to end. "Are you all right alone?"

"I'm not exactly alone, but yeah."

While Roarke doubled back, she walked straight to the void, the empty room Peabody had reported, stared—her eyes burning dry—at the far wall. Old wood, old brick, so it looked patched and repaired and nondescript. But she felt the misery, the horror, and had to force herself not to attack it with her bare hands.

Morris came in behind her. "I passed Roarke. He told me to bring this."

She grabbed the pry bar out of his hands, began to drag at the boards, the spikes and nails.

"Dallas—"

"They're back there. Trapped in there."

"Who?"

"The others. All the others. They can't get out, can't get to the other side. They need to be seen, need to be shown." Her muscles trembled with the effort as boards splintered. "They need help."

"Step back," Roarke snapped as he strode in. "Eve, step back."

He slammed the sledgehammer he carried at the brick, exploding dust and shards. As he pounded again, again, she moved in, away from the arc of his swing to rip and pry.

The stench seeped in, one she knew too well. Death entered the room.

"I see her." Eve grabbed for the flashlight on her belt. "Her— them. Three, I think. Wrapped in plastic."

As she spoke, Roarke slammed the hammer again. Through the gap he created a skeletal hand reached out, palm up, as if in supplication.

"Careful now." Morris laid a hand on Eve's shoulder. "We need to go carefully now. This is for my team and forensics."

"Let me see your light." Roarke took it from Eve, shone it in the gap. "Christ Jesus. He's stacked them, like berths in a bloody train."

"And when bricks were too much trouble or he just ran out of them, he switched to boards. Can you see how many?" Eve asked him.

"Five, I think. I can't be sure."

"Hold off now. It's enough." She took out her communicator. "Peabody, we've got bodies. Eight, maybe more. I need a recovery team, the sweepers. Morris is calling his people in."

"Acknowledged. Jesus, Dallas, eight?"

"Maybe more. They're found now. And Peabody, send down the priest."

She clicked off, said nothing as Roarke picked up the bar and continued to carefully knock away loose bricks. Instead she reached in, laid a hand on the plastic covering the ruined shell of Vanessa Warwich.

You're found now, she thought. You're free now.

She stepped out of the room, just leaned against a wall as she struggled against waves of grief.

And the old woman stepped to her, spoke.

"You found our Beata."

"I'd have found her my own way. I'd have stopped this my own way."

"I think perhaps you would. But the child is so precious to me, how could I risk it? I was guided to you, or you to me, when I was between. Who can say?"

"I'd think you could at this point. Death ought to come with a few answers."

Now Gizi smiled. "Perhaps it will. You didn't kill him."

"It's not how I work."

"I would have," she said simply, "but your way will be enough. You are the warrior. I can leave the gift with you."

"No. Seriously."

"Then it goes with me. I had a good, long life, but he didn't have the right to end it. You'll see there is balance."

"He'll pay, for all of it." She hesitated, then asked what she had asked Lopez, asked herself. "Is it enough?"

"This time. For others?" Gizi lifted her shoulders, let them fall. "Who can say?"

"This time then. I have to finish. I have to finish my way."

"Yes. As do I. You've freed them. Now I'll guide them to the other side where there will be light and peace. Until we're called again. *Pa chiv tuka*, Eve Dallas."

"Ni eve tuka." Eve shook her head. "You're welcome," she corrected.

She saw the light again, not blinding now, but warm. She simply closed her eyes as the heat flowed through her, then out again. When she opened them, there was nothing but the dim corridor and the sound of approaching footsteps.

She pushed away from the wall, moved forward to direct cops and techs. To do her job. "They're in there," she said to Lopez. "Maybe you can do . . . what you do."

"Yes. The girl, Beata, she's waiting for you. She won't leave until she speaks to you."

"I'll go up."

"A very hard day," he said. "And yet . . . "

"Yeah." She reached over as Roarke came out, brushed mortar and brick dust off his shirt. "Let's go up."

"Tell me how you are."

"I'll show you." She stopped, yanked up her pants leg. Her clutch piece rode on her unmarked ankle. "No more tattoo. It's a lot less crowded in here." She tapped her head. "Say something in Russian."

"I only have a few phrases, but this one seems appropriate. *Ya liubliu tebia.*"

She grinned at him, felt a lightness she hadn't felt in hours. "I have no idea what you said. Thank God."

He grabbed her, held tight. Then he drew her face up, crushed his mouth with hers.

"On an op," she murmured but kissed him back before drawing away.

Linking hands, they continued down the corridor. "I said I love you—and it's true in every language."

"Nice. Let's just keep it all in English for a while. God, I'm starving again." She pressed her hand to her belly. "Anyway, thanks for the assist. In there and all around."

"No problem. But next time we have a barbecue, Lieutenant, we both stay the bloody hell home."

"That's a deal."

Upstairs she paused, walked over to where Natalya and Alexi sat on the steps, nodded at the cop standing by them. Natalya looked up, eyes flooded with tears.

"They said—we heard—there are bodies."

"Yes."

"My brother." Her voice broke as she pressed her face to her son's chest. "He was broken, but he took his medication. We went on—we both went on. What has he done? In the mercy of God, what has he done?"

"She didn't know." Alexi held her close while she sobbed. "We didn't know, I swear it. My uncle, he's such a quiet man. Such a quiet man. Beata? She's all right?"

"She'll be all right. We're going to have to take you and your mother down to Central. We need to talk."

He only nodded and stroked his mother's hair. "We didn't know."

"I believe you."

"A nightmare for them," Roarke commented as they stepped outside into the warm night.

"One that won't end anytime soon."

Gawkers pressed behind the barricades. Cops swarmed, lights flared, and the air was busy with voices and communicators. Reporters, alerted to the scene, shouted questions.

Eve ignored them all as Beata broke away from Mira and ran to her.

"They said Mamoka is dead. Sasha killed her—my great-grandmother."

"Yes. I'm very sorry."

The sound she made was deep, dark grief. "Mamoka. She came for me, to find me. And he killed her."

"He'll pay for that, for all of it." And this time, Eve reminded herself, it was enough. "She did find you, and that's what mattered most to her. She told me your name. She . . . showed me the way."

"She spoke to you?"

"She did. And I know she's okay, because you are. You can see her tomorrow. I'll arrange it. But now, you need to go to the health center, get checked out. You need to listen to Dr. Mira. We'll talk again."

"There were others." Her face stark, Beata stared at the old building with its glittering windows. "I heard—"

"We'll talk again," Eve said.

Beata pressed her fingers to her eyes, nodded, then dropped them. "I'm sorry. I never asked your name."

"I'm Dallas." Through and through, she thought, in and out and all the way. "Lieutenant Eve Dallas."

"Thank you, Lieutenant Dallas." Beata held out a hand. "For every day of the rest of my life."

"Make good use of them." Eve shook her hand, then sent her back to Mira.

Eve took a breath, then tuned in to the lights, the noise, the movement. Her world, she thought, and walked back to Roarke.

"Things to wrap up," she told him. "Reports to file, killers to question."

"You look pretty pleased about it."

"All in all, I am. But tomorrow? Why don't we stay home,

watch old vids and eat junk food, maybe drink a whole bunch of wine and have half-drunk sex?"

"A master plan. I'm in."

"Excellent. I have to go back down there. You could wait here or go on home."

"Lieutenant." He took her hand again. "I'm with you."

"Well, you're handy," she said, grinned again.

She walked back toward the building with him to do the job. She felt tired, violently hungry, and completely herself.

The Other Side of the Coin

Mary Blayney

For Paul, who I trust completely

One

"Admit it, Harry. You want to have an affair with that Melton woman." Bettina faced him and looked straight into his eyes, hoping to see the truth.

"No, my dear, I do *not* want to have an affair with her. Or with anyone else." He narrowed his eyes as if wondering what question she was really asking.

"You say that with such ennui, you would think I've asked it a dozen times before."

"I answer that way because it's an absurd question."

"Is it? You haven't been the same lately." He'd been distant, too considerate. Even in bed he'd been more careful than intense. "I find myself hoping that you are only thinking about an affair and not already having one."

"Bettina." Harry came to her, gathered her close, pressing a kiss to her cheek—not her lips. "There is only you."

Bettina laid her head on his chest. Their darling baby, Cameron, was almost six months old, but her passionate lover had not come back to her bed. Harry had been sweet and gentle, but that was not what she wanted from him. At least not every time they made love. Had her lying-in been too great a test of Harry's fidelity?

With a quick kiss on her mouth, Harry stepped back and

handed her a glass of champagne. "An excellent idea to have champagne waiting in your bedchamber." The Earl of Fellsborough tugged off his coat and did not seem to notice the sound of a seam ripping. He tossed it onto a chair.

As usual, she acted the valet, picking up Harry's coat and folding it with the care that the fine wool deserved.

He picked up his own glass of champagne and took a long drink. "As for Patricia Melton, did you notice that her dress was the same fabric as yours?"

"Oh no!" Bettina's cheeks burned at the thought, and she vowed to give her maid the dress the very next day.

Laughing, Harry continued, apparently unaware of his wife's dismay. "I doubt anyone remarked on it. Her décolletage had every man there watching her breasts. If the material slipped just one more inch, we all would have had an eyeful."

"You are an idiot, Harry." His countess grabbed the glass from his hand and put it on the table with enough force to draw his attention if her words did not.

"What? What did I say?" His humor disappeared. "I didn't *do* anything!"

His confusion was convincing and even more infuriating. "How can you be so unfeeling? You've as much as said that my gown was the inferior of the two and you called that woman by her first name. I did not even know what her given name was."

Bettina turned her back to him and was distracted by the glint of a coin on her night table.

"Do you want an argument?" he asked in an all too reasonable voice.

"Yes!" she yelled and picked up the coin. "What is this?" She held out her hand to show it to him.

"I would say it's a coin. Is that what you want to argue about?"

Rage roiled through her, aimed at him, at herself, at her life. "I just wish you could be in my shoes. Then you would not be so patronizing." Bettina threw the coin at him.

Harry caught it handily, his expression a mix of frustration and annoyance. "And I wish you would trust me." Then he dropped the coin as if it had burned his hand.

At the same moment Bettina's vision blurred. She had the feeling that her mind was being pulled from her body. She braced herself with a hand on the bedpost, but the world would not stop spinning.

She plunged into the vortex, feeling it forcefully separate her mind from the rest of her, taking from her control of limbs, mouth, eyes. There was no pain but confusion as terrifying as any sensation she had ever felt.

I'm dying. Her fear disappeared as her heart filled with regret, sorrow, loss. Oh, her poor son. Motherless or worse, with a mother like Patricia Melton. *Oh, Harry, I was only afraid you did not love me anymore.*

The sensation felt like it lasted forever and less than a minute, both at the same time. Finally the spinning slowed, and the room settled around her. Bettina did not feel dead, but something profound had happened.

She saw her body lying on the bed. Had she fallen there when she died? Was she in some kind of faint? Looking around, she did not see her husband. Where was he? "Harry! Harry!" she called.

She heard her words, not from where she lay on the bed, but from where she stood, as though her voice had come from someplace else.

"My God, Bettina, where are *you*?" Her body sat up on the bed. Were Harry's words coming from her mouth?

"Right here in front of you." She moved forward, awkwardly. Bettina looked down, and to her confusion and growing horror, it looked as though her mind were encased in Harry's body.

Bettina stopped and thought, *I will lift my hand.* Harry's hand rose, palm up, as she wished. She hurried to the bed and her actual body.

"Harry, what has happened? Are you hurt?"

"I feel damned strange dressed in your ball gown. These god-awful pins are sticking in my, I mean your, scalp."

"Yes, the pins work loose sometimes," she answered, as if explaining her body while someone else used it was normal. "Dear heaven, what has happened?" she asked again.

"My dear," her husband's distinctive drawl came from her lips, "I do believe your wish has come true."

Two

"My lord! My lord! You must come. The countess is dying!"
The maid burst into the earl's dressing room without even a
perfunctory knock.

"Freeba! Calm yourself." Bettina ripped the towel from
around her neck. The shave would have to wait. Before she
could stand, the valet grabbed the cloth, wiping the soap from
the earl's chin. Bettina, clad in trousers and shirt, still only in
stockings, dashed from the room in as much distress as Freeba.

Harry cannot be dying. She could not bear to live if he was
lost to her. Life without Harry would be empty, dull. The horror of it made her heart beat so hard and fast that she raised a
hand to her chest as if to keep it from bursting from her body.
The gesture reminded her that she had another reason to fear
losing him.

If he died in *her* body, she could well be trapped in *his* body
forever. Twelve hours ago she would have thought nothing
worse could happen than the two of them changing places. Now
she could see her imagination was not nearly vivid enough.

Bettina tore into the suite of rooms that had been hers for
the three years of their marriage. The curtains around the bed
were still drawn tight, and the bedchamber was in unusual disarray. Clothes tossed on the chair, shoes left under it, and a

stack of books opened, one atop another, on her writing desk. How like him, even in a woman's body, to not give a thought to his clothes.

"The countess would not allow me to do anything to help her prepare for bed last night, except unlace her stays." Freeba stepped in front of the earl to slow his progress. "I came in to bring her chocolate and found the room this way. She must be very ill, my lord. You know how careful she is with her clothes."

"Never mind, Freeba. It hardly matters right now." Bettina stepped around the maid and went straight to her bed, pushed aside the curtains. "What's wrong? What's happened?"

Harry was no more than a lump under the linen, but the groans as much as said, "I am in misery here."

"What is wrong? Explain!" Bettina demanded.

Freeba gasped at the unsympathetic tone of voice, and Bettina dismissed the maid from the room with a curt wave.

Alone with Harry, Bettina repeated the question, trying for a more sympathetic tone.

He spoke, though his face, which was actually her face, was buried in the pillow. Still, the words were quite intelligible. "I have the worst ache in my gut."

She understood in an instant. With a roll of eyes and a relief most profound, Bettina expanded on her husband's terse explanation. "Does it feel like some monster from hell is working its way through your stomach and below and the only relief will be when it explodes out of you? But before that can happen the pain fades, but only for a few moments."

"Yes." He sounded amazed at her insight.

"It happens every month, my lady," Bettina said with a sarcastic emphasis on the honorific. "Indeed, it will happen monthly right before your courses for the next twenty years."

"God help me."

"I endure it every four weeks," Bettina answered with a prosaic nonchalance. "Are you saying that I am able to tolerate pain better than you are?" If he had gone through childbirth as she had, he would not need prompting to answer.

"We have to find a way out of this, it's unbearable."

"The cramps will end."

"When?" he asked.

"Harry, they will end soon, and you will not die."

"What else should I expect? Tell me," he demanded as if facing a wasting disease. "Is this the worst of it?"

"The worst of your courses? Yes. Except for the bleeding. That usually lasts about four days for me."

"That had better be the worst part of my being in your body."

Exactly what was he going to do if there was worse to come? "This will pass, Harry," she said again. "But you will still have to look in the mirror every day. For me, *that* is the worst part of this switch. Every time I see your face where mine should be, I'm shocked all over again. And your body feels strange."

"Oh, that I understand completely. You have no idea how odd I feel." Harry paused. "Or maybe you do."

Bettina glanced back at Harry, his brain surrounded by her dark hair, green eyes, clear skin. She shut her eyes tight. If this went on much longer, she was going to have to find a way to rise above the upset it caused.

"I can't take the pain, Bettina," Harry said as another cramp struck. "Bring me some brandy. I'll drink it away."

"You can't do that."

"Why not?"

"Because I never do that, and we have to preserve the façade that life is normal for as long as we can."

"The façade being all there is." He struggled into a sitting position. "At least you have something beautiful to look at."

Oh, she thought, *that was rather sweet.*

"Did Freeba interrupt Roberts while he was shaving my face?"

Bettina nodded.

"How unfortunate. You know how disreputable I look with a day's growth of beard. Go back and allow him to finish."

"Believe me, Harry, the state of your beard is the least of our problems."

Another cramp seemed to convince him that she was right. "God help me, we have to find a way to undo this damned curse." He covered his face with the bed linen and groaned.

Bettina pulled the chair from in front of the secretary, amazed at how light it felt. With a firm grasp she tested her man's strength and easily lifted it, moving the chair to the side of the bed so she could face Harry.

She straddled the chair with her arms folded on the back of it. Just because she could. Trousers were as comfortable as they looked, even if she did feel self-conscious showing off the turn of her ankle and leg. Or rather Harry's ankle and leg.

"Harry," she said and waited until he pulled the linen down and she could see her face. She stared at it, trying to see him somewhere inside her. "The thing is, Harry, I don't think this is a curse."

"Semantics, Bettina. You made a wish, and God help us, it came true. Now we have to undo it." The last word was followed by a grunt of discomfort.

"I was not the only one who made a wish."

"Where is the coin?" Harry asked, apparently intending to ignore that fact.

"The one you threw at me after you made your wish?" Bettina insisted, but did not wait for an answer. "How should I know? Didn't we look everywhere last night? Today, when you are up and dressed, you must order the staff to search again. Roll up the rugs, move the furniture. It must be in this room somewhere."

Bettina stood up and pushed the window curtains open. Sun poured into the room, and she turned quickly, hoping to see the morning light glint off the coin. She circled the room, even looked under the bed. Nothing.

"It cannot have rolled out the door. The door was closed," Harry said, pushing the covers back but not rising from the bed. "Where did it come from? Maybe there is another one like it."

"Harry, do you truly think there are two coins that grant wishes?"

"It's the pain." His voice sounded suspiciously tear-filled.

Until he was comfortable she would not be able to reason with him. Harry was such a bear when he was ill.

The countess strode to the door, doing her best to imitate a man's stride. It was something she would have to practice. It felt forceful and aggressive, like she wanted to challenge someone to a shouting match.

Is that how men felt, or was it just that this sort of walk was not natural to a woman's sensibilities?

As she expected, Freeba was attending the door.

"Bring the warmed soother."

"I offered it to her, my lord, and have it at the ready, but the countess used a very crude word when I suggested it." Freeba paused but seemed to steel herself. "My lord, she is not herself.

This must be more than her courses. She would never call on you for feminine woes as common as that."

"I know, but she told me recently that her pains have been so much worse since Cameron was born."

"She told you that?"

"Yes, she told me." Bettina tried for the curt tone her husband used so well.

It worked. Freeba nodded and even bobbed a curtsy.

"Bring the soother. I will stay with the countess."

"You will?"

This time Bettina did not say a word, only looked at the maid with one raised brow. It was one of Harry's most annoying tricks, fraught with disdain and annoyance.

Without a comment, Freeba hurried away, and Bettina returned to the bedside.

"You do that rather well," Harry said with surprise. "Walk like a man, that is."

"I have four older brothers."

"Well, I have two sisters. What difference does that make?"

"As a child I followed them around as if they were gods and imitated them in everything."

"Really? I didn't know that, but that would explain why you are not at all missish, afraid of spiders and such." He paused a moment and then added, "And why you are so tolerant of practical jokes."

Bettina watched him grit his teeth, but he did not otherwise give in to the pain of the cramp.

"God, how I wish this was a joke or a bad dream I could wake up from. As it is, we *must* find a solution. And quickly."

Freeba scratched at the door and handed her the soother.

"Go until I send for you."

Freeba's expression implied insult, but she nodded very slightly and left.

"Here, Harry, take this and lay it across your belly and lower. I find it very helpful."

"What is it? It looks like a poor excuse for a pillow. One filled with very heavy feathers."

"It's a bag of soft wool filled with dried beans. You heat it inside a bed warmer and then lay it against what aches. Do you remember the time you wrenched your shoulder when you were thrown from your horse?"

Harry nodded, taking the bag from her hand. "Yes, I do. It worked wonders. Your mother invented it, did she not; and swears she could have made a fortune with it."

Harry settled against the pillows and sighed with relief. He closed his eyes and yawned.

"Do not fall asleep."

"I'm not!" he said, through another monster yawn.

Bettina began to pace the room, still unsettled at the thought of looking into her own face. "Let's take a moment to reconstruct what happened last night. We may find a clue to reclaiming our own bodies."

"Yes. All right," Harry agreed. "It may be more simple than we think."

Three

Bettina moved the chair and sat down again, doing her best to hide her anxiety. Harry thought this could be simple? Simple was the last word she would use. Insane. Impossible. Horrifying. The list of words only made her feel worse. What if this change was permanent? She would neither contemplate nor mention that possibility.

As usual, they sat in silence for a moment, for her part, trying to decide where it had begun. "We went to Ellsworth's musicale."

"Separately," he added with censure.

"You could have waited for me. I was not being frivolous. The first dress I put on had a tear in the hem."

She could see they were already poised on the downhill slide into their usual argument of who was at fault.

"I had to speak to Lord Osterman about my vote for his bill," Harry explained, "and I knew he would leave early. He only attends those events to do Parliament's business. His interest in music is nonexistent."

Bettina was not going to start an argument by calling her husband a liar, yet she was almost certain Lord Osterman was not the only reason her husband had been in such a hurry.

"We should have left the musicale when he did," Harry said.

"That first performance was abominable. You would think the young man would be over his nerves by now."

"He only missed one note."

"Come now, his play was as tentative as a boy with his first whore."

"Harry!"

"Oh, that's right, I'm you now, aren't I." Harry raised a hand to pat *her* hair and spoke in a voice too high to be hers. "He will be a wonderful musician. He only needs more practice. I will admit, my lord, that his play was tentative, like a babe afraid of his first steps."

Bettina sat back and folded her hands. Did he have any idea how hurtful it was for him to mock her so? She never spoke in such a shrill voice, and the boy *would* do better once he was accustomed to an audience.

"I'm sorry, dearest," Harry said quickly. "I can be a fool when things are not going as I would like." He reached for her hand but stopped. Bettina looked down at the hand that responded to her commands: dark hair about the wrist, a smattering of lighter hair around the knuckles ending in the blunt nails of Harry's very manly fingers. Harry looked away. Ah, so he, too, was having a hard time adjusting to the change of body.

"I am sorry," he said again. "I must remind myself that you are in my body, wearing my clothes, but you are still very much my Bettina. Even now I can tell I have hurt your feelings by the way you move back and become so formal as though I am preparing to strike you."

"Oh no—!" She began to reassure him, but he spoke over her protests.

"Yes, you know I would never take a hand to you. Never."

She did always move back. "That was something else I learned from my brothers. If I wanted them to stop teasing me, or otherwise being mean, I would pretend that what they said did not bother me at all. How odd that I do that even now." Bettina laughed. "I wish—"

"No!" Harry yelled. "Do not wish anything."

She bit her lips, pressing them together, and nodded. They were silent a moment. This time he touched her wrist, covered by shirt and coat.

"Continue with your memory of the evening. Where could

we have been given the coin? Someone must have slipped it to us."

"The butler when he handed us our hats and things? No, Harry, someone put it in this room while we were out. There is no sense in asking Freeba. She will insist she knows nothing if it might mean trouble for her."

"I will ask her anyway. Later, when I am dressing."

Bettina could tell he wanted to send for Freeba this minute but restrained himself. "You can try, but you will have to question her with my sensibilities and not with your inclination to browbeat her for the answer you want."

"I do not browbeat the servants."

"Yes, you do. Last week you left the footman in tears when you found him chatting with one of the serving girls while at his post. And just yesterday you practically gave a sermon on honesty when the youngest groom admitted he said he had checked the horses and was caught in the lie."

"Both of them are lucky to still have their positions, but we will discuss the subject another time, Bettina. Right now we are supposed to be talking about what happened last night so we are not faced with another night in each other's bed."

"Please do go on, Harry," she said with all the hauteur she could summon and forbore to mention that his mattress was much too soft for her liking.

"Very well," Harry said and thought for a moment. "We left Ellsworth's before supper, and when we arrived back home, you suggested that we have a glass of champagne here in your bedchamber, and I hoped that meant we would end up together in bed. Instead, you brought up an affair with Patricia Melton and were thinking the worst of me."

"Oh no, Harry, the worst would be if you went from her bed to mine."

He was silent for so long that she was afraid that is exactly what had happened.

"Patricia Melton lives to tempt and tease, Bettina." The edge in his voice made it clear this was a subject he had no desire to discuss.

"I was so angry with you last night." And still am, she thought. "I was about to tell you to leave my chamber when I was distracted by the coin."

"Why did you pick it up?"

"Because I didn't recognize it, and I wondered how it came to be on my night table." She could see it still, glinting as though demanding her attention. "Then we made those misguided wishes."

They stared at each other, her anger and his frustration replaced by the memory of the hideous moment of their transformation. The silence was long. Bettina had no idea what was going through Harry's mind, but for her part, she was praying, praying, praying that this would end soon.

"Bettina, we have to pray that this ends tonight and prepare for the fact it may not. But we cannot give up trying to find a solution."

"Of course not, but Harry, please, we have to teach each other how to go on. If this continues, we may well be sent to Bedlam. This morning, Roberts looked at me askance when I told him that he could choose my clothes." Bettina shrugged. "I had no idea what your calendar called for."

Harry nodded. "Yes, I see your point."

Bettina went on. "I'm sure Freeba thinks something is terribly wrong. We never spend this much time together in the morning. Cameron is most likely missing his mama, and Lord Osterman is wondering why you are not in Parliament." *And tonight we both know that Patricia Melton will wonder at your absence.*

"Do you not think that we should take a few days to teach each other what we need to know? Besides, you will not want to be in society this week."

He shuddered.

She waited while he thought about it.

"It seems that while we are in different bodies, our minds are very much our own." Harry waited for her nod before he went on. "Looking at myself when I look at you is not all that different from looking in a glass."

"Oh, yes, it is. I've noticed it as we've been talking. Look at the eyes, Harry." She moved from the chair to sit on the bed opposite him. "The color might be correct, but when I look into yours, I see you. You must surely see me."

They sat still a moment, staring intently at each other. He smiled, that rakish smile that was the first thing about him that fascinated her. It might be her lips, but it was his smile.

"Why don't we kiss," he said, moving closer.

"No!" Bettina jerked back. "It would be like kissing myself."

"Just a little kiss. I do not feel like any more than that. A kiss of comfort. Close your eyes. Let's see if it feels different."

Tentatively, Bettina moved toward him. She closed her eyes as she felt that first brush of lips. His lips were soft. So soft and full. Opening her eyes, she stared directly into him and forgot reality.

She opened herself to him. His tongue felt delicate as it swept into her mouth, then Bettina moved, taking over the kiss. She was in the bed beside Harry, fitting her mouth to his or his to hers.

It was so confusing, but then she forgot all about pronouns as sensation flooded her body.

Bettina had never felt this need before; anticipation raced through her, pushing all thought from her mind, arousing her so that all she wanted was to join together and find the pleasure that the kiss tortured her with.

She wanted more than the feel of his lips. She needed more than his tongue teasing her. Her body was barely within her control but not for much longer. She pulled her mouth from his. "I want you now, Harry."

Harry stiffened, pulled away. "All I wanted was a kiss, Bettina."

His words sobered her. "What's wrong?" she asked and then recalled him asking the same question with the same edge to his voice in their first days of marriage.

"I wanted only a kiss of comfort. Do you think I am trying to seduce you? Who would want to have sex feeling as I do?" His hand swept down to his lower abdomen. "Nor do I think that you would want to have sex while I am in this condition. All I wanted was a little soothing kiss."

He sounded like a . . . She paused. He sounded like a woman. He sounded like *her*.

Four

As Bettina paced the hall waiting for Harry to join her, she found herself actually praying. She had given up praying when her sister died in childbirth five years ago, despite hours on her knees in church, begging God to spare her.

Bettina's prayer today was proof that she had not abandoned her belief in God but rather that she had given up on the idea that prayers made a difference to His plans. But a man and a woman switching bodies had to have involved some kind of divine intervention, and she was not about to let Him forget what was going on in her corner of the world.

Now that they were facing their first public outing, she prayed. *Help us, Lord.* A simple prayer she repeated three times with her eyes closed, her hands folded, and all her concentration centered on those three words.

For her part, she felt well prepared for her role as the Earl of Fellsborough. She wished she was as sure of Harry's acting ability.

This moment was like so much of the last four days. A mix of anxiety and anticipation with a healthy dose of frustration to guarantee that neither of them grew overconfident.

The most significant moment, definitely not fun, had come

when nothing happened as midnight approached, twenty-four hours after their wish on the coin.

Bettina had cried. Harry had thumped her on the back, which had not been at all comforting, and told her, "Stop that whining. You make me look like a weakling."

"Harry, if I remember correctly, I wished you to be in my shoes. I did not think to say for how long. Cameron knows something is wrong, and he is only six months old!"

"We each hold him differently, that is all. Since neither of us holds anyone else, that will not give us away."

Harry was angry all the time. He had dismissed one of the footmen for no good reason and sent word to Cook that dinner was a disappointment. Finally Bettina had confronted him. "If you keep on like this, we will lose every servant in the house."

"They are all too sensitive," Harry insisted as they practiced dancing.

"Stop criticizing them!"

They separated, and Bettina had to concentrate to recall the man's steps for even the simplest of reels.

When they came together for a promenade down the imaginary line of couples, she went on, "By the way, I hired Kennet back. He is supporting his aging mother and cannot afford to be without a position. As for Cook, the housekeeper managed to convince her that 'The countess is still not herself.' She explained that Cameron's birth has left me short-tempered and indisposed. Thank you for that, Harry."

"Bettina, sarcasm is not attractive," he said with narrowed eyes. "I am doing the best I can. You have done me no favors. Your refusal to go to Parliament until 'you feel more sure of yourself' has raised concern for my health, not to mention making me appear less than reliable. I have a proposal of my own and no expectation of when I can present it or if I will have the support I need."

Aha, she thought, that is why Harry is so irritated by almost everything the servants say or do. Lack of control was the crux of his peevishness.

That was what unnerved him, Bettina thought. And, she admitted, it might well be what appealed to her. The chance to be in charge, rather like being king for a day, or maybe a week. If she knew how long it would last, it could prove a very interesting experience.

Like her, Harry refused to consider that this curse would last forever, but neither of them could think of a way to undo the wish, especially if they could not find the coin.

The coin was definitely not in her bedchamber. The servants had searched. It seemed to her that its disappearance was as magical as the magic it created.

Cameron's nurse had suggested that they stop searching for it. "If you stop tearing the house apart," Martha said, "I am sure it will turn up. At least that has always been my experience with lost things."

If she had not at that moment succeeded in quieting a wailing Cameron, Bettina was sure that Harry would have dismissed her for voicing an unsolicited opinion. Martha seemed to sense her error, though, and had kept her thoughts to herself ever since.

In the end they had abandoned the search for the coin, not because they thought that would make it turn up again, but because they had to prepare in case it did not.

She and Harry had begun to work at understanding how the other passed the day, up to and including the things that each should know about the other's friends and Harry's political colleagues, not all of whom would count as friends. When Harry balked she had insisted. "I need to know as much as I can if I am to go places without you."

His recounting of his cronies' various peccadilloes had taken all of an hour. Some were charming, like Lord Bright's promise to go to Almack's as often as his very shy sister did. And some were appalling, making Bettina sorry that she had insisted Harry tell her all that he thought she needed to know.

If Harry ever came downstairs, they were going to make their first test in public: a ride in the park. They had argued over whether to take a carriage or their horses. Harry had won. They would ride. They always rode on Rotten Row, he'd said, reminding her that they wanted to do nothing that would draw any particular attention.

If riding astride became too difficult for her, Harry insisted that they could dismount and lead their horses, pretending that they preferred to walk to more easily converse with friends.

"I rode astride with my brothers for years. Can I guess that you never rode sidesaddle with your sisters?"

"I would have looked stupid. But I'm sure I can manage."

As she watched Harry come down the stairs, she wondered if he could, indeed, manage. He was having a difficult enough time with the habit, the new one she had not worn yet. She bit her lip and did not complain.

The blue was gorgeous. Bright enough to make her look young again, but it did not demand attention the way Mrs. Melton's clothes did.

Bettina bowed to him, and he curtsied with studied grace. That was one lesson he had learned well. Then, for no reason at all, they both burst out laughing.

"I suspect that with the right air about us, it will be great fun to fool the ton." Harry smoothed his skirts and stopped in the middle of the gesture. "A lady is always confident and never gives any indication she is not dressed perfectly." He whispered the phrase to himself, but Bettina heard him.

"What have you been reading?" she asked. "I do not think there is a woman in the world who thinks she is dressed perfectly."

"I beg to differ. I've read several of the books you have on ways to command attention in society."

"Today, I have no desire to command anyone's attention. God forbid." Bettina drew on gloves and offered an arm to Harry. "The horses are out front. Remember what I told you about mounting, and for all that's good, do not refuse the mounting block. I never do."

Bettina waited patiently while Harry did his best to mount her mare. The horse cooperated, but Harry's ensemble did not. The groom held on to the reins as Harry hooked his leg over the pommel and adjusted the voluminous skirts so that they would drape properly.

It took all Bettina's control not to call out help, and she prayed that the groom was not aware of what an excellent rider the countess was reputed to be.

Once on the horse, she could see Harry could not find the stirrup, his foot lost in the fabric, so she stepped up and took his ankle, directing it properly.

Harry leaned down so that Bettina had a very clear view of her décolletage and breathed, "Thank you, my lord," in a surprisingly sexy voice.

Her body reacted with a feeling between her legs that could only be the beginning of something she had no desire to experience in public. Turning quickly, she mounted his horse with convincing ease.

It was Wednesday, and with Parliament not in session, the streets were more crowded than usual, all the better-looking equipages and riders headed for an afternoon on Rotten Row.

Harry's only mistake on the way to Hyde Park was when he took the lead as soon as they moved away from the gate of Fell House. Bettina cantered to his side and whispered, "The earl takes the lead." Harry winced at the obvious error and fell back.

The park was filled with familiar faces, just as she expected. There were several carriages, and knots of people gathered for a gossip here and there. With a bow and wave to several of them, Bettina led Harry to a spot where they could easily ride side by side.

"Will you stop waving that way? You will have people thinking I have turned into a nancy boy." Harry leaned toward her as he spoke, and Bettina nodded with a smile so that everyone would think the comment had been an amusing one.

"You must stop looking annoyed, Harry. I am supposed to be the love of your life. Act like it."

With a sniff, Harry gave his horse a nudge and rode off, making it obvious to every observer that they were not on the best of terms.

Come back here! Bettina wanted to shout. She might feel perfectly at ease seated astride, dressed as her husband dressed, but she did not feel at all comfortable pretending to be him among his cronies and, worse, his flirts.

When Harry's good friend, Lord Bright, called out, Bettina pretended she did not hear him, but a minute later she could not avoid Lord Osterman, who stopped his horse crossways in the path.

"Where the hell have you been all week, Fellsborough? I was counting on your vote, and now have had to put it off until you deign to return to Parliament."

"My apologies for the inconvenience. I was struck with some strange inflammation that left me too weak to even move from bed. It passed as quickly as it started." The excuse she and Harry had concocted sounded weaker when spoken than it had when they discussed it.

"More like you found a whore to your liking and spent the last three days with her."

"That would be more like you than me, Osterman." Bettina had no trouble recalling what Harry had told her about Lord Osterman. How he liked to find a prostitute and use her until the woman begged to give the money back if he would leave her alone.

Bettina wished now that she had not ignored Lord Bright. She would much rather tease him about his last visit to Almack's than have the image of a beast like Osterman in her head.

Her disgust stood her in good stead in this situation. It was not hard to look as revolted as she felt. In fact, she was having a hard time controlling her anger at his outrageous behavior.

"You only wish you had the kind of stamina I do," the man bragged. "I can fuck for hours without rest."

"And the pleasure is all yours." *You selfish pig.*

"The wife has no complaints."

Of course she doesn't, Bettina thought. *You probably avoid her bed as much as you can.*

"Not like your wife, Fellsborough. You don't seem to be in the countess's good graces. Have you been neglecting her? Perhaps I should offer to show her what a real man can do."

"She is a loyal and faithful wife, Osterman. There is nothing you could say or do that would tempt her." Bettina was pleased with her response. It's what Harry would have said; she was almost sure of it.

"Are you suggesting a wager? I could bed your wife and give her more satisfaction than you ever could, and put another child in her belly for you to call your own." Osterman licked his lips.

That the man could even make such a suggestion drove all rational thought from Bettina's head. She leaned forward and looked him straight in the eye. For a second her vision was actually clouded with red. "Mark my words, you lecherous fool. A whore is more of a lady than you are a gentleman."

Osterman's expression made Bettina realize that she might have gone too far. His face showed a mix of puzzlement and a matching anger, his skin a mottled red and white. "Watch what you say, Fellsborough, or I will call you out right now."

Bettina hoped her panic did not show. Harry was an expert shot, but she had never in her life handled a pistol.

"I need your vote, my lord." Osterman spoke with hatred coloring each word. "That is the only thing that is saving you.

Be advised you are on very tenuous ground." Osterman turned his horse with a jerk of his wrist and headed toward the park entrance without a farewell.

Bettina decided to allow him the last word, even though it left her feeling that she had lost the battle. Harry would never have allowed that.

Bettina looked around for her husband and found him conversing with the Duchess of Lowbray, laughing much too loudly at something she said.

The mare he rode was not comfortable, Bettina could see that, reflecting, she suspected, Harry's ill ease riding sidesaddle.

At least Harry's behavior was not threatening her life, as she had just threatened his. Bettina had had no idea how easily riled a man's body could become, even with a sensible female brain in command of the situation. No wonder they spent so much time boxing at Jackson's and racing horses.

She prayed again. *Please keep us safe and help us find our way back. Soon!*

Five

"Lord Fellsborough!"

Bettina looked around to see who was calling out, certain it was not the voice of God answering her prayer. God would never announce a name in so seductive a way, even if God was a woman, which was as likely as the idea that God was a man.

It was Patricia Melton, of course. This outing was turning into a living nightmare.

Mrs. Melton was driving her own carriage, a delicate-looking curricle picked in blue and silver. She was smart enough to wear a dark blue habit, *not* the same material as Bettina's this time. The lighter blue and silver of her conveyance framed her body as the habit and bonnet framed her blond hair and blue eyes.

With a smile that she had practiced in front of a glass, Bettina rode over to the woman with a little more haste than was seemly.

"Mrs. Melton." He bowed to her from his seat. Patricia Melton raised her fan so that all attention would be focused on her very sultry eyes. Probably because her teeth were so bad that she did not want anyone to see them. On the other hand, what one really wanted to feast the eyes on were her breasts. Bettina had never noticed how full-breasted the woman was.

She caught herself and decided that she was only noticing now because her male body was—um—fascinated. Yes, that was the word.

"You are here alone, my lord?" Patricia Melton asked.

"No, my wife rode ahead to speak with the Duchess of Lowbray, who is with us after visiting her first grandchild in Kent."

Mrs. Melton made a face, or at least her eyes crinkled unbecomingly. "I can see that you have better things to do than to hear about a newborn, even if he is going to inherit a dukedom."

"I do have a newborn of my own, you recall."

"Yes, I do. During your wife's lying-in we had that lovely interlude at the Graves' party. I was hoping we could reprise that experience." The woman leaned forward so that her breasts were on view for him alone.

Bettina had no idea what to say. Harry had sworn that Mrs. Melton meant nothing to him. Exactly what did an "interlude" mean? Before Bettina could think of a response more innocuous than, "I never want to see you again, you fat cow," they were interrupted by the groom who accompanied them. "My lord, the countess would like your help with her saddle."

"Isn't that what you're here for?" Bettina snapped and then waved her hand at him, appalled at how much like Harry she sounded. Besides, she wanted to know exactly what her husband had to say about the "interlude" Mrs. Melton referred to. "Excuse me, Patricia. My wife needs my attention."

"Oh, I am sure she does, my lord." Mrs. Melton spoke as though she were very familiar with just such an intimacy.

Bettina rode to Harry's side. He was on the edge of a grove of trees that gave them some privacy. Good, because this question would not wait. "What exactly does a woman mean when she reminds a man about an 'interlude' they shared?" She tried to sound as though it was idle curiosity that prompted the question.

"What are you talking about? Can you please check the saddle? It feels loose."

Bettina glanced at the perfectly snug fit of the saddle and ignored his question. "Tell me what happened between you and Patricia Melton at the Graves' party." The edge in her voice commandeered Harry's attention quite effectively.

"Graves' party? When was that?"

"While I was recovering from Cameron's birth."

"That was months ago. I don't remember."

She leaned forward, hoping to see the truth in his eyes. "You had sex with that woman and don't remember?"

"What?" Harry's horse sidled away, and Harry had to take a moment to settle her. "Bettina," Harry leaned even closer to her as he whispered her name, "I swear before God that from the moment we married, I've never had sex with anyone but you. Why can you not trust me?"

If she had an answer to that question, she might have told him. Instead she pressed her advantage. "Then what in the name of all that is good is an 'interlude'?"

"I'll tell you what it is. It's a figment of Patricia Melton's imagination. I danced with her or sat at supper with her or something equally innocuous. Nothing happened."

Maybe he was telling the truth. Then why did she doubt him? Because her enthusiastic, adventurous lover had not been in her bed since Cameron was born. He could not be any more satisfied than she was. She almost asked, when Lord Bright rode up to them.

"Truth to tell, I cannot decide if you are arguing or desperate to make love, but whichever it is, I suggest you save it for the bedroom. You are attracting all eyes."

"Thank you, Nick." Bettina did her best to appear jovial. "We were, indeed, teasing each other about, well, you are quite right. It is better saved for the bedroom."

Bright chatted with them for a moment more. Bettina was self-conscious at conversing while Harry watched, but when he did not interrupt, she decided she must be performing adequately.

Finally, Lord Bright turned to the countess. "You shine whenever I see you, my lady. I look forward to dinner at the Daltons' this evening. Shall we send this fool to his club"— he nodded at the earl—"and the two of us can play whatever game you wish?"

"I do enjoy chess," Harry said with a spark in his eye that was more anger than flirtation.

"Chess it will be." Bright laughed, swept off his hat, and bowed to them both. "Until this eveing!"

Bettina sent him off with a salute and almost groaned aloud at the reminder of the dinner performance facing them later.

"Fix this saddle," Harry said with a return to his usual commanding form.

"It's not loose, Harry. It's just that you are less than comfortable riding sidesaddle."

"Then we will go home. Now."

"No," Bettina insisted, even as she turned toward the gate. "We should stay so that no one thinks we were arguing or so anxious for sex that we are almost in each other's laps."

Harry gave her a withering look. "Must you question every single thing I say?"

"Yes, when I think you are wrong."

"We are both on the verge of a shouting row. If we lose our tempers here, lose control here, then we are going to have a more difficult time maintaining our pose. You are likely to start making those gestures with your hands, the ones that make it look like you want to strangle me. Or start crying."

"And you will try to leave or at the very least look away, as if what I say has no merit."

"I do not do that!"

"You just did. That very sentence rejects what I said. What's more, you rode off when we first arrived here when I suggested that you act like I, as the earl, am the love of your life." Tears filled her eyes.

With a look of panic, Harry moved as close to her as he could. "You are the love of my life, Bettina. Do *not* cry."

As if she could control that.

"Bettina, even you do not cry in public."

He was right. It was much too unseemly and would attract all the damned attention they were trying to avoid.

"Then let's go home, Harry. Not because I want to but because I have to tell you about the argument I had with Osterman. And what in the world did the duchess say that made you laugh that way? Not at all ladylike, Harry."

"She told me that having grandchildren was so much more fun than the children themselves."

"You laughed at that? I do not think she meant to be funny. Her three younger children have been nothing but an embarrassment to her."

"Lowbray's heir is a fine man. I knew him at school."

"Harry, I said her three younger children." Bettina stopped

her horse and, perforce, Harry slowed beside her. "The duchess's second son ran off with a married woman. Her daughter has chronic hiccoughs and cannot be in society, and her youngest daughter is so obese she cannot ride a horse. Believe me, there is nothing funny about having one child beyond the social pale and two daughters who will obviously never marry."

"You told me nothing about her," Harry said, with quiet vehemence. "How was I to know? Men do not gossip over such trifles."

"Stop acting so superior." Bettina nudged her horse, and they moved on, smiling and nodding to acquaintances but not stopping to talk. "I have had enough of this for now. When we are home I will tell you what Osterman said, and then I want to hold Cameron and pretend that everything is all right."

"Which means I will go visit our son, and you will retire to the earl's study and read the *Edinburgh Review* or the papers."

Bettina missed her baby and wanted to spend more time with him than the miserly ten minutes each morning. How could Harry stand to see so little of the boy? Unless he did not care for the child any more than as his heir.

The first night of this curse, alone in bed and afraid of sleep, Bettina had consoled herself with the idea that the purpose of this nonsense was to help her to understand Harry better. But the fact was that being in his body really did not give her any more understanding of how his mind worked than she had before.

What was the point of this then? She wondered if she would ever find out.

Six

They rode the rest of the way from the park to Fell House in silence, negotiating the heavy street traffic with care.

Once in the front hall, Bettina reminded her husband, "Before you go to see Cameron, come into the study. I would have a word with you, my dear." Harry followed Bettina into his study.

Bettina slapped her hand with her gloves as she considered what to say. Neither of them sat down. Bettina was too upset and Harry too much of a gentleman, despite his skirts, to sit down if she did not.

"Osterman is a rogue of the worst kind," Bettina began. Just saying the words renewed her anger.

"That is not news to me, nor should it be news to you. I told you about his habits."

"But he insulted me. Or do I mean he insulted you?"

"Which is it, Bettina?"

"He insulted the countess."

Harry's expression hardened. Even framed by curls, his expression was neither friendly nor understanding. "Tell me what happened."

Feeling as though she had been called before the magistrate and treated as if she were the criminal, Bettina recounted the conversation as best as she could recall it. As she came to her insult to Osterman and his half challenge, Bettina could see that Harry could no longer contain his alarm.

"My God! Be careful, or you will have one of us dead. Osterman was needling you. I never would have reacted that way, but you rose to the bait."

"A needle is not bait, Harry. It is in no way tempting. A needle hurts just as an insult to your wife should offend you."

"He did not insult the countess. At least that was not what he was trying to do. He was trying to find a way to pay you back for your insult of him. It was as much a dare as anything to proclaim the countess's virtue to a man like him."

"What should I have done?"

"Threatened him first, of course. Told him that you would meet him at Jackson's and prove who was more the man with your fists where everyone could see."

Bettina winced at the thought. She knew less about boxing than she did about guns. "Would we not be in the same situation?"

"No, neither one of you meant what you were saying. Not then. Not until your discussion became so heated that you spoke without thinking."

"And you think women play games with each other!" Bettina threw the gloves onto the chair and ran her hands over her face. "What do I do now?"

Harry rubbed his hands together as if itching for a fist-fight. "I think you should pretend nothing happened and if pressed"—he paused and shook his head in disgust—"if Osterman presses you, then you must apologize."

"Oh, Harry, no." She could see how much the idea distressed him. "I'm so sorry. If it came to a duel, surely Osterman would not kill me. It's against the law. Not to fight a duel, but to kill someone."

"I have no idea what Osterman will do when he's in a temper. We already know that his appetites often override his birth as a gentleman."

There was a scratch at the door. One of the footmen had a message. "I beg your pardon, my lady, but Nurse wants to know if you are coming to see Lord Cameron or if she should begin his bedtime ritual?"

"Tell her—" Bettina began, taking two steps to the door before Harry interrupted her.

"I can speak for myself, my lord." Harry's warning reminded her who was playing whom. "Tell Nurse that I will be there shortly to say good night to my son."

The footman left, and Harry shook his head. "See what happens when you are upset? Try to think, eat, breathe, and laugh the way I do." He headed for the door and paused. "Bettina, where did you find Martha Stepp?"

"She applied through the agency we always use." Bettina liked the girl, though she was younger than the usual nurse.

"Does she not act above her station?"

"Harry! Do not even consider dismissing her because she occasionally speaks out of turn. She is wonderful with Cameron. I worry sometimes that he is closer to her than he is to his mother."

"Yes, she is good with the boy, but she acts as if she knows more than we do."

Bettina could not help laughing. "She does know more about children, Harry. Almost anyone would."

They parted. Bettina watched Harry hurry off and felt a pang that it would be too much of a curiosity if the earl joined the countess. By this time of day he usually was at his club.

Tonight they had agreed to meet at nine o'clock to set out for their second test of the day. Dinner with some political cronies. Thank God, neither Patricia Melton nor Osterman would be among the guests. Now, there was a couple who deserved each other.

Bettina settled in Harry's favorite chair and looked through the *Edinburgh Review*, finding nothing that held her interest.

The papers yielded a few tidbits, and she thought she should make a point of checking them more often. Why hadn't any of her friends told her that Lady Quinton was increasing or that Faith Grimlin had retired to the country, supposedly because her mother was failing?

Faith and her husband had been very tense around each other for almost the whole Season. Perhaps tonight she could find out if they had formally separated.

Or Harry could. She would be in the dining room with the other gentlemen while the ladies retired to the salon. She would have to remind Harry to pay close attention to the conversation and not act as though he was thinking about something else, as he did so often with her.

For her part, Bettina had always wondered what the gentlemen talked about. As she sat in front of the fire, her eyes closed, but not really resting, Bettina tried to concentrate on the pleasure of finally learning the answer to that question and not on how nervous she felt whenever she was not in Harry's company, as if he could catch any mistake she made and help her rectify it.

Tonight would be a challenge. Lord Nicholas would be there. *Try to think of him as Nick,* she reminded herself. There would be twenty guests altogether, ten men who were as interested in politics as Harry was.

Bettina picked up the *Edinburgh Review* again. If she read one of the articles, then she would have something to talk about. She was positive Harry never lacked for conversation.

A scratch at the door distracted her from a fascinating piece on the life and times of the men of the Ninety-fifth Rifles. When she called out, "Enter," in what she thought was a perfect imitation of Harry's "why are you interrupting me" voice, Freeba stepped in.

Was Freeba wearing one of her old dresses? Most likely. Bettina only hoped that it had looked better on her before she passed it on to her maid.

"I beg your pardon, my lord, but the countess would like you to come settle a difference of opinion on fashion."

"What?" Bettina had never ever asked for the earl's help in such a trivial matter.

"I told you that all was not right with the countess. She is half dressed and will go no farther. She insists that she needs your help in this.."

What was Harry thinking? As Bettina remembered how many times she had used the half-dressed ploy as a way to seduce him, she almost laughed. Not likely, but that was the perfect way to convince Freeba that nothing was wrong with her mistress.

"Freeba, thank you." Bettina stood up, adjusting her trousers to accommodate the awakening of the body. "I will stop in and see what the countess needs. Why do you not leave us alone until an hour before she needs to dress?"

With a smile inviting her collusion, Harry waited.

"Oh, yes, my lord, I see." Freeba actually curtsied. "I will knock before I come back."

"Tell the footman to bring us some champagne."

"Yes, my lord." She bobbed another curtsy and hurried off.

In keeping with the pretense, Bettina went to the earl's suite and, with her valet's help, changed from riding clothes into comfortable trousers, a loose shirt, and Harry's favorite banyan overall.

Remembering to whistle the way Harry did, Bettina knocked on the connecting door and went into the countess's bedchamber.

"Tell me, do you whistle to announce your arrival or because you anticipate a treat?" She had always wondered, along with marveling that his tutor had allowed such common behavior to become a habit.

Harry looked up from where he sat near the fire, dressed in Bettina's favorite dressing gown. Why had she never noticed that the robe was threadbare, no good for anything more than the sickroom? Really, the moment their lives were back to normal, she was going to buy some new fabric.

"Oh, my banyan!" Harry stood up and slipped out of the dressing gown. "Trade with me. This thing of yours is not designed for warmth."

"That is not what a woman is aiming for when she wears one."

"If sex is why a woman wears this thing, why not just go naked? No confusion then." Harry laughed as soon as he had the banyan around him. "This is the closest I've come to feeling like myself since we wished on the coin."

Bettina took off the shirt and slipped into the old dressing gown. "How do you stand wearing a cravat? It's like a rope around the neck."

"How is it that you do not catch a chill on rainy days? I'm thinking that the dresses in fashion are designed for much warmer climates than England."

"In the winter I wear a wool petticoat and wool stockings. It's not so bad." She raised a shoulder to shrug and heard a rip. "Oh, that's much better. Now I can actually move my shoulders."

"You've ruined it!" Harry announced.

"I am just imitating you. You abuse your clothes constantly. Besides, this robe is not even good enough to give to Freeba." Bettina walked around the room, leaving the gown open. "Why did you send for me? You must know that Freeba is growing more suspicious by the minute."

"I needed to know where you keep the key to the jewel chest, and I could hardly ask Freeba."

Bettina nodded at the secretary. "In the topmost drawer." At that moment there was a tap at the door, and it opened before either one of them could give permission. Kennet, the footman who had already been dismissed once this week, came in, followed by Freeba.

Bettina could easily imagine how absurd they looked. Harry might look coy in the earl's banyan, but there was no doubt that she looked just plain stupid wearing a woman's robe over her trousers. Now there would be rumors that the earl had lost all interest in women.

As if to confirm her worst fears, the sight of the earl and the countess in each other's robes was more than Kennet could handle. He stopped short and dropped the tray he was carrying. Fortunately, the champagne was still corked, and the glasses merely rolled on the thick carpeting.

Freeba all but pushed him out the door and closed it behind her. "I'll send up another bottle, my lord."

"Do not bother." Harry spoke in a tone that announced the mood was quite spoiled. "Tell Kennet that if he gossips, he will be fired and blacklisted in every agency in town."

"Yes, my lady. Yes." She backed out of the room, bowing and curtsying at the same time.

Seven

Once again Bettina waited for Harry. It seemed that Kennet had kept his experience to himself, since none of the servants were looking at the earl as though he was bound for hell for wearing women's clothes.

When Harry finally came down the stairs, all Bettina could do was stare. He was wearing the Fellsborough diamonds, a string of twelve grand stones, each a treasure in their own right, one separated from the other by smaller diamonds. The glare fairly blinded those nearby. The necklace was too much for a quiet evening with friends. In fact, Bettina was hard-pressed to think of where she would wear it besides a coronation.

The dress, however, was perfect, though the style might emphasize the few pounds she had gained with Cameron. Was it time to find a new dressmaker?

When Harry reached her, they kissed each other on the cheek as they usually did, and he whispered, "These shoes already hurt."

She looked down. "They're new. Why are you wearing every single new item in my wardrobe? Though in this case I appreciate you wearing the shoes. They are not yet conformed to my feet. How generous of you to break them in for me."

Harry answered with a groan.

"But, darling," she said, raising her voice a little. "Don't you recall telling me the fastening on that necklace is weak? I've been meaning to take it to the jewelers for you. Why not step into the salon and have Freeba bring down the pearls instead. They will look magical with the pale pink of the gown. And she could bring the pearl combs, too."

"But I like the diamonds," Harry said, as one of the footman hurried upstairs to find Freeba, and Bettina all but dragged Harry into the salon. "I want to wear them more often."

Bettina closed the door before the footman could do it for them and faced her husband with her hands on her hips. "They are not the right jewels for this evening, Harry."

"That's it! I've had enough of this!" He reached back and unfastened the perfectly sound clasp and dropped the necklace on the near table. "How the hell am I supposed to know what jewelry is right for what occasion?"

Harry hit his forehead with his hand. "God! I cannot believe I asked that question. Before the damn wish I could have cared less. When this is over, I may well have to search for my manliness. It is being compromised more each moment."

As long as your search does not go beyond our bedroom. Bettina kept the thought to herself. If he had not considered it, she did not want to put such ideas into his head.

Instead she went back to the topic under discussion. "When you dress, listen to Freeba. She would never have let you wear the diamonds."

"Like you listened to Roberts? That waistcoat is ugly, and makes my skin look sallow."

"It does not! Roberts and I both agreed that it should be worn more often."

"Believe me when I tell you that Roberts is not the fashion expert Freeba is. Roberts keeps me organized and is a genius with the shaving blade and that is the only reason I keep him. He thinks Brummell is a fool with his ideal of dressing simply and prefers to hold the Regent as a model."

Oh dear, Roberts was wrong on both counts. Bettina wondered if there was time for her to change into another waistcoat.

Harry whirled around the room, pacing the floor as the earl did when he was annoyed. He paused in front of the full-length glass.

"Harry," Bettina began, looking at her dress in the glass. "Do you think that gown makes me look fat?"

"No more than that waistcoat makes me look sallow."

"For all that's good, that is no answer at all."

"Yes," he said with a withering smile. "I have learned the art of an answer that is not one in Parliament."

The reminder that tomorrow she would have to take his seat in the House of Lords made her feel sick.

Before she could say anything more, there was a knock and they were both surprised when Martha Stepp came in, carrying little Lord Cameron. "I do beg your pardon, my lord and my lady, but the babe sat up for the first time and, my lady, you told me today that you wanted me to show the earl any significant changes as soon as they happened."

"You did that?" Bettina looked at Harry, her eyes filling with tears. How sweet of him to know how much she would miss her time with Cameron.

"Well, yes, he is your son, too, *my lord*." Harry emphasized the last two words, and Bettina nodded.

Darling Cameron performed for them with infant enthusiasm. Moving from his stomach, to his side and up onto his adorable, cloth-clad derriere. As a finale, he slapped his hands on his fat knees and laughed at his success. By the time Freeba arrived with the pearls, they were all marveling at the child's genius.

"Thank you, Nurse," Harry said. "The earl and I will come tomorrow to see a repeat performance. This is not to be missed. Clearly the boy is more dexterous than the average child. He will be a marvel in the boxing ring."

"No son of mine is going to spend time boxing!" Bettina said with motherly outrage and then realized that she was not playing her role any more than Harry was. "I think his dexterity would be better developed fencing."

Martha Stepp curtsied and left the room, leaving Harry and Bettina in complete silence.

Bettina spoke first. "Do you think she suspects?"

"Suspects what? That I have left my manliness someplace?" He shook his head in disgust. "Without a doubt."

"I'm sorry, Harry, but you are as much at fault as I am. What mother would say that she wants her son to box? You might have said he would look wonderful on the dance floor."

"We have to find a way out of this, Bettina." Harry sat down in the nearest chair, looking dispirited and unhappy. "I am not sure we will stay sane much longer. The housekeeper was shocked when I approved the chef's menu without critique. Why do you pay the man so much to cook if you do not trust his menu choices?"

"Because the chef pays no attention to the cost of food. He thinks with the mind of an artist and is not practical at all. Someone has to rein him in."

"I see." He made a face that was all Harry's, brow furrowed and mouth turned down. If he kept doing that, her face would be wrinkled before she was thirty. "Good for you, then, to take such care of our money." Harry stared at the rug for a minute and then looked up again. "But what about the housekeeper's calendar? She wanted to know when the maids could beat the rugs and when the silver could be polished. I really don't care."

"The housekeeper asks because I keep the calendar and know when we will be using the rooms and have need of the silver."

"Isn't the calendar the majordomo's charge?"

"Usually, but I've found that the majordomo's weakness is keeping the calendar. He is excellent with the staff but has confused more dates than is acceptable. So I meet weekly with your secretary, and we compare calendars and consider invitations, which to accept and which to decline."

Harry stood and bowed to her, which looked very odd, considering he was wearing a pink silk gown and pearls.

"And I thought you spent all your time making calls and shopping. It seems to me that my countess has far greater responsibilities than I ever realized. I understand now that you are the reason this house runs so smoothly and our son is so content."

As Harry spoke, there was a small flash of light. Like the glint off a coin. They both recognized it at once and arrowed across the room to the spot where the light had come from. And there it was. The coin. The cursed coin that had changed their lives.

Eight

They both reached for the coin, but Harry was faster. "I wish that . . . ."

"Harry, wait!" For once the man listened to her. "Don't you think we have to word this carefully? You only have to look at us to know the coin has a very whimsical way of granting wishes."

"Hmmm" was all Harry said, a sign he was considering what she suggested. After a moment he put the coin on the table. "So what should we say?"

They debated the wording for a full five minutes, before agreeing that they would both hold the coin and make the same wish. "We wish that our world could be the way it was before our first wish."

Nothing happened. Harry released Bettina's hand, and they looked at the coin. It was a dull, tarnished bronze, communicating quite efficiently that it had no intention of granting *that* wish.

They spent another half hour trying similarly worded wishes with no success.

"Harry, if we do not leave for dinner now, we will be remarked on for being so late."

"Bettina! This coin controls our lives. It's more important than a political dinner."

"But we *have* the coin now. We can deal with it later. If our lives are to go on in this bizarre manner, then we had best go to dinner as is expected. We cannot behave in any way that will attract undue attention." How many times would she have to explain that to him?

"Why not? Missing a dinner is hardly a symptom of some depraved disease."

"No, but it will be one more proof that something is amiss with us, and the ton will watch us with more interest than either of us wants. I don't know about you, but I do not want Nick Bright asking too many questions, or, God forbid, Lord Osterman."

"Hmmm," he said again, seeming to mull over the options. "What do we do with this coin? It seems to be able to appear and disappear at will."

"That is worrisome. I agree with you on that." She waited to see what he would suggest.

"Let's put it with the jewels," Harry suggested. "At least it will be locked tight, and if it disappears we will know that no one has taken it."

Bettina nodded her head in agreement as that was what she would have suggested. Before Harry could begin a debate, Bettina rushed upstairs with the diamonds and the coin, putting them in the countess's jewel case. Freeba watched the earl come and go without comment.

It was a challenge to stop thinking about the coin, but when Harry reminded her that she was hardly an expert on politics, Bettina pushed worries about the coin to the back of her mind and faced the more immediate challenge of a dinner with men she knew only socially.

Harry gave her a detailed lecture on the issues before Parliament and who was on what side. "I feel strongly, as does Nick Bright, that Wellesley is the man for the task in Portugal. But he cannot succeed without support. Starting with funding, which is woefully inadequate. This is one of the rare times when I think Lord Osterman has the right of it. It's why I am willing to join him in promoting the legislation."

Harry went on and on, and Bettina listened, truly she did, and prayed that the words would come to her as needed.

They were greeted with effusive welcome at the Daltons' house, and even though they were the last to arrive, their hosts waited another good while before they were led in to dinner.

As the ranking gentleman present, the Earl of Fellsborough sat to the right of the hostess, and the countess would be next to Mr. Dalton.

Those seated around Bettina seemed affable, and one of the older gentlemen winked. "I never could resist the wife when she was dressed for a party. I can guess why you were late." The men and women around them laughed, and Bettina joined in, wishing for so simple an explanation of their predicament.

Would she and Harry ever make love again? The body her brain rested in assured her it would happen, but she could not imagine it. *Though I am curious. How does sex feel from Harry's point of view?*

"So what do you say, my lord?"

"Not much," the old man spoke for the earl. "He is still not thinking with his brain, are you?"

Bettina shrugged. Her husband wasn't the only one who had ways to avoid uncomfortable questions. Bettina looked down the table toward Harry and saw him raise a glass of wine and drain it in one gulp. The sommelier poured more immediately.

"No oysters for me," Bettina said when the footman paused at her side with a platter filled with the disgusting crustaceans.

"Harry, that's not like you," Nick Bright said as he slapped down his empty wineglass, which was instantly refilled. "Dalton's chef is a genius with oysters, and you love them."

Oh dear, Bettina thought, *Nick is right.* Harry loved oysters as much as she hated them. "But as Baron Helder has made clear, I don't need any oysters tonight," Bettina answered, and everyone laughed.

Nicely done, she thought to herself and looked toward the other end of the table where the sommelier was refilling Harry's wineglass yet again.

Slow down, she thought. *The countess never drinks that much or that fast.*

Bettina sipped the wine to see if it really was that special. A delicious red, but nothing that made her want to drink without stopping.

Deciding to take the bull by the horns, she asked one of the questions on the list Harry had given her on the ride over.

"Gentlemen, what are the prospects for Napoleon's legacy now that he is married to Maria Therese?"

And so the political discussion began. Everyone had an opinion on everything from Lord Byron's bizarre antics to James Madison's election as president on the other side of the Atlantic.

The meal passed in a haze of courses, wines, and conversation, and by the time Mrs. Dalton announced that the ladies were leaving, it was well past midnight.

The gentlemen stood as the ladies gathered their reticules and fans. They all laughed while Bettina cringed when the Countess of Fellsborough finished off the last of the wine before standing.

"Mrs. Dalton, you must give the countess the name of your vintner. I have never seen her enjoy the wine so much."

"I am among friends, am I not?" Harry responded with just the right coy note. "I cannot decide which wine was better. My compliments to the sommelier and our hosts."

Harry gave a graceful if overdone curtsy to both and was heard to whisper, "I wouldn't mind some brandy."

Bettina hoped that Mrs. Dalton did not have any in the salon.

The ladies were no sooner out of the room than the baron jumped up to relieve himself in the chamber pot behind the curtain. As soon as he sat down, another took his turn.

If Bettina had thought that the political discussions would continue, she was dead wrong. As the brandy was passed from man to man, the ribald stories grew more and more coarse. Finally Nick Bright did the favor of calling attention to the quiet Earl of Fellsborough.

"Eh, Harry, we know you are ever faithful to your lovely bride, but surely you have observed something worth sharing regarding Patricia Melton. God knows she wants your attention more than mine or even Dalton's, and everyone knows what a lover he is."

They all laughed, and Dalton raised a glass, not denying his rakish habits. "Tell us, Fellsborough, why do you not take advantage of Melton's charms?"

More than anything Bettina wanted to believe that Harry was faithful and that she could trust him in this. Was the answer to be had right here? "How do you know I have not been with her?"

"Because she would crow about it to everyone she met. Because it is all a game to Mrs. Melton. She wants to ruin every marriage in England." This from the baron who had proved his wisdom earlier. "If she is not happy, she wants no one to be happy." He smiled. "And her sexual appetite is prodigious." He winked again, and everyone laughed.

So Baron Helder knew from experience and handed her the truth. Harry had resisted her advances. Harry was faithful. She joined the others in laughter, and if a tear or two trickled out of her eyes, she could blame it on amusement.

"Patricia Melton should make friends with Lord Osterman," Bettina added as the laughter faded. "They are well suited."

The group was silent, and Bettina had the feeling she had said something untoward.

"I must needs remind you, my lord, that Osterman's name is not mentioned in this house."

Bettina stood and bowed her apology to the host. "I beg your pardon, Mr. Dalton. The wine confused me." For all that's good, Bettina thought, the earl and Osterman were supporting the same bill in Parliament. Did Dalton, with his powerful seat in Commons, favor the opposing view? How could anyone vote against financial support of the army?

Dalton went on. "He has forced his personal attentions where they are not wanted, and he is no longer welcome here."

Oh, so it was not political at all. "I understand." Bettina nodded, took a breath, and went on. "But I wonder how your personal concerns balance against the funding bill before Parliament."

The mention of the needs of the army introduced the subject of politics again, and before long they were in a deep discussion as to who could be counted on to support the government's desperate need for additional funding and who could be convinced.

The clock struck, and there was a discreet tap on the door. Dalton finished off his brandy in a gulp and stood with only a little bit of a wobble. "It's time to rejoin the ladies and see whom we can cajole into indiscretion. I seem to be having more than my usual luck with the countess tonight. Appears Fellsborough has her primed for more."

Bettina found it hard to control the wave of fury that overcame her at Dalton's salacious hint. Nick Bright saved her from further embarrassment when he whispered, "Calm down, brother. He's drunk, and we all know how he can be when he is in his cups. It means nothing."

Bettina nodded and went over to the chamber pot to relieve herself. This was one aspect of the masculine body that appealed to her. Yes, men had to shave every day, but the ease with which they could relieve themselves more than made up for the other.

Rather than wait their turn, two of the guests went out onto the terrace and used the back garden as their personal latrine, laughing at their range and duration just as her brothers used to do. It was disgusting, really. Did men never leave the boy behind?

As they made their way to the gold salon, Bettina decided that she enjoyed being with the ladies more than sharing brandy with the gentlemen. She missed the discussion of children and shopping and which of their friends was having trouble with servants.

For the most part, what she learned in the salon was a far more practical sharing of information than the lewd stories bandied about in the dining room.

Exactly what could a man do with the jokes he heard here but repeat them to other men? And politics. That was making a mountain out of an anthill. If Wellesley needed more money, then he must have it. The chance of Bonaparte succeeding in his lust for rule did not bear thinking about.

The gold salon had white walls and ceiling but all was embellished with gilded trim. It was the perfect setting for the ladies, all dressed to perfection. They were clustered in a group around one of their number, their colorful gowns shimmering around them. They looked like so many butterflies clustered around a very generous flower.

What was going on?

Nine

Bettina could smell tobacco smoke, which was odd, since the gentlemen had not smoked in the dining room. Baron Helder considered it a "disgusting habit," and the rest had bowed to his seniority.

Bettina had her answer when she discovered Harry in the middle of the circle of ladies demonstrating how to blow circles of smoke using a cigar.

The ladies were amused and intrigued, but Harry blushed when they realized the gentlemen had joined them.

"My lady, you smoke?" Mr. Dalton took the cigar from her and drew a puff before handing it back. "I had no idea."

"Something I learned from my brothers." Harry pronounced the words with studied precision, a sure sign he'd had too much to drink.

"Your wife sounds just like you do when you're drunk," Nick Bright whispered, and Bettina wondered how many others had noticed it.

"I taught her everything she knows," Bettina said, making for the center of the group, taking the cigar with one hand and the countess's arm with the other. "We will leave before you show them all the other things your brothers taught you."

"What they taught me is nothing compared to what I've learned from you, darling. Let's go home and practice."

The gathering laughed good-naturedly. Thank God this was a group of friends, or there would be endless gossip, though the teasing from friends might not be much kinder.

The carriage came quickly as they were the first to leave. Before they climbed aboard, Harry groaned and threw up into a pot that one of the Dalton grooms had the genius to have at hand. At least no one had come out to see them off, and they were spared that embarrassment.

Settled in the carriage, Bettina ordered the coachman to drive carefully and avoid bumps.

Harry shook his head. "I'm much better now." Rubbing his eyes, her husband settled across from Bettina, ignoring the way his skirts showed ankle and leg. "I have no idea how that happened. I did not drink more than I usually do, but it struck with all the force of a punch just as we left the dining room."

"Harry, my body is not nearly as sturdy as yours, and I never drink that much wine. At least when they bring up this evening, we can blame the idea of smoking a cigar on your intoxication. Where did you find one?"

"I tucked one in my . . . God, I mean, I tucked a cigar in *your* reticule, meaning to give it to you, as I always prefer my own blend. But I recalled that the baron does not like the smell of cigars, and, well, I decided that I would smoke it myself." He looked confused. "It reminds me of all that I am missing."

Bettina leaned across from her seat and patted Harry's hand. "We can spend some time with the coin this evening, and perhaps we will be able to restore your life before you ruin mine."

"Bettina, it was the most useless conversation. All the ladies talked about was Patricia Melton's modiste and if they should shun the woman or patronize her. Then Mrs. Dalton went on about her son's success at school and her daughter's preparation for the Season. Though I must admit I was intrigued by the news that Nick Bright's sister is about to become engaged to Lord Osterman's son."

"Oh, Harry! Please let that be no more than gossip. It would be an awful match if the boy is anything like his father. I wish I had been there to suggest she turn him down." Bettina made a mental note to mention it to Lord Nicholas when she saw him tomorrow before Parliament. "Besides, I thought Osterman's name was not to be spoken in Dalton's company."

"That was another thing I learned. That most wives never listen to a word their husbands say." He sat back, his expression glum. Bettina was not sure if it was because of his excessive drinking or the bits he had learned tonight.

By the time they reached their suite of rooms, the evening's misadventures were forgotten. Harry and Bettina were both focused on nothing but the coin.

The servants were hurriedly dismissed, and Bettina pulled the key to the jewel chest out of her pocket. *Please, please let the coin be where I left it.*

Bettina put the key in the lock and opened the chest. The coin winked amidst the glittering spill of diamonds, as if welcoming them home. Bettina picked it up, closed the lid, and handed the coin to Harry.

They stood there looking at it, Bettina's mind caught up in ways to have the coin do their bidding.

"Have you noticed how odd a coin it is? There is strange Eastern writing on one side, but the other looks as traditional as the King's English." Bettina took the coin from Harry and turned it over and over as she spoke.

"Yes, I noticed that, too. I expect it is from a shipment destined for India to be used in commerce there. But how it came to be endowed with magic, we will most likely never know."

"Perhaps some mage in India entrusted it to a servant to bring to someone here, and the coin was stolen. It could be that the coin is still trying to find the rightful owner."

The coin glimmered as Bettina finished her fanciful story, and they both stared at it.

"Please, please," Bettina begged the coin, "we will help you if you help us."

The coin did not respond, and Bettina felt a moment of fear as she worried that she was, indeed, beginning to go insane. Is this how dear King George felt? She persisted despite her fear. "Tell us what we have to do."

Just as Harry drew a breath—Bettina was sure he was going to rebuke her silliness—the coin grew brighter.

"You mean if we do some specific thing, then this will not be permanent?"

The coin twinkled again.

"What a relief!" Harry laughed as he spoke. "I will not be trapped in skirts forever."

"And I will be able to see Cameron whenever I wish."

"Now all we have to do is find out what the coin wants from us."

They sat very close to each other on the small settee near the fireplace with the coin on the table in front of them. Bettina loved the feel of Harry next to her and thought only of his breath on her neck and not the way his breasts pressed into her side.

"Think back, Bettina, what did we wish for?"

"I wished that you would know what it's like to be me," Bettina said and then went on in a rush. "Just this evening, before the coin reappeared, you told me that you saw how completely concerned I am with your happiness and how well the house is run." It made her smile. It was at least a step in the right direction. Her smile grew when the coin winked at them with a bright golden beam.

Now they needed only to remember what Harry wished for and all would be right with their world once again. Bettina knew better than to wish for a perfect life. What she had now was good enough.

Ten

"I wished you would trust me." Harry nodded. "Oddly enough, it is what I want above all things."

"Oh, Harry, of course I trust you." Had she not learned tonight that his fidelity was true and fast? She trusted him. It must not have been the right phrasing though, because the coin dulled. Bettina stared at it, willing cooperation. Nothing happened.

"And another thing I learned later tonight," Harry began. Bettina had the feeling he was trying to distract her from their mutual disappointment. He faced her, and Bettina looked into his eyes. "Do you, darling wife, have any idea how men look at you?"

"Look at me?"

"They want you. Every man who looks at you wants what I have. A loving, loyal wife."

"Nonsense. If they would practice a little love and loyalty themselves, every one of them would have the same from their wives. They want sex with me. They want my body and nothing more."

"Bettina! How can you be so cynical?"

"I spent the evening listening to your chums tell tasteless jokes and bet who would be Patricia Melton's next lover."

"What are the odds that it's the Regent?"

"Harry!" Bettina moved away from him a little. "I would not tell you if I knew." And she would never tell her husband that the male consensus was that the Earl of Fellsborough was Mrs. Melton's personal preference. "I *will* tell you this. I am forever cured of wanting to drink brandy and remain at table. I will go with the ladies happily."

They both looked at the coin, which seemed to have no opinion on the subject.

"I think we should go to bed. It's late and obvious that nothing is going to happen tonight."

Bettina nodded agreement and watched while Harry locked the coin in the jewel chest once again.

"Bettina, you left the key in the lock. It is not a wise habit to cultivate."

"Oh, Harry, we never left the room. Besides, I almost always remember to lock it and hide the key." Bettina shrugged off the criticism. She went to the connecting door and realized that Harry was following her.

"Let's sleep together in the big bed tonight," Harry suggested. "The way we did when we were first married."

"Oh, yes," Bettina said on a sigh. She closed the connecting door then stared at it for a moment, wondering if sleeping together in their current states was a wise idea. She didn't care. More than anything, she wanted the comfort of being close.

"Harry, I'll help you undress." *Like we did when we were first married and so in love.* Tears filled her eyes, and she fumbled with the buttons.

"Now you know why it took me so long to undo the buttons. A man's hands are not made for such delicate work."

He'd misunderstood her clumsiness, and Bettina did her best to hide the tears. When she reached the new shoes, she eased them off, lifted a foot, and began to massage the reddened toes.

"God help me," Harry sighed as he flopped back on the bed, dressed only in a chemise. "Don't ever stop doing that. It's almost worth wearing those torturous slippers to feel you work magic like that."

Bettina smiled and felt the male part of her respond. To what, she wasn't sure. To the feel of soft, warm skin. To the body spread on the bed in surrender. To the utter bliss in Harry's eyes. To the idea of giving with no expectations.

Bettina amended that. One expectation was now very much present. *Do not speak. Do not say a word. It will destroy the moment.*

Bettina undressed quickly and moved to lie on the bed crosswise but beside Harry, trailing a hand over the chemise, the fine, fine lawn chemise that was a favorite because it hinted at so much.

Harry lay still with eyes closed, and Bettina reached inside the scooped neck of the chemise and rested a hand on a full round breast.

She had touched her breasts dozens of times, but with Harry's hand it felt different. His hands were rougher, and her skin felt as fragile as a rose petal.

The most masculine part of the body she was in grew hard as a rock. Bettina moved her hand away, ended all contact, and lay back beside Harry, not touching, doing all she could to bring the lust under control.

"How do you do it?" she gasped.

Harry turned to look at her and sighed. "I think about something awful. The worst thing you can think of that does not have to do with sex."

"Sex is all I can think of. My whole body is begging for release."

"Then come to me." He leaned over her and smiled.

"No." Bettina tried to push herself deeper into the down mattress. "It feels as though I would be having sex with myself."

"Close your eyes and don't think. I find that amazingly easy to do at a time like this."

"I can't stop thinking. Besides, all I wanted was to know how you feel and now—I—do." She parsed out the last three words with effort.

With a speed that was totally unexpected, Harry moved over her and with one deft movement guided the erection into place inside the hot wet sheath of her body. Bettina closed her eyes and tried, really tried, to control the release, but it was impossible. The pleasure pulsed from her, concentrated in the core of her male body with an intensity unlike her female experience of sex. Not better, just very different.

"That was so fast," Harry said as Bettina rolled away from him and buried her head in her hands, embarrassed and relieved at the same time. "And it didn't hurt at all."

"Of course it doesn't hurt." She raised her head and leaned on her hand. "Have I ever said that it hurt?"

"No, but I thought after Cameron was born it would be different. Your body was used so brutally in the birth process I thought you would never welcome my advances again."

"Oh, Harry, is that the reason your lovemaking has become so tentative? Not because you are merely doing your duty?"

"Of course. I never make love to you out of duty. I want you more than I want water," Harry answered.

"Oh, Harry, I love you. Trust comes in so many different guises. I can see why the coin was not content with my simple statement. Harry, believe me, when it comes to our love life here together in bed, I trust you completely and can never have enough."

Bettina felt the male member leap to attention at thought of more sex. Harry noticed and laughed.

"Is it always like this? So easy?" Bettina asked.

"Almost always. Don't you remember the time we did not leave the bed for near twenty hours?"

"Oh, yes. I think that was the night, and day, Cameron was conceived. How do men ever learn control?"

"From a very young age and not without some embarrassing incidents."

"Harry," she began in a pensive voice. "Do you think that is why men hold their feelings so close? They have learned a physical control that women have no need for?"

"Possibly," Harry said with that vagueness that made it clear his mind was on something else. "In fact, Bettina, I can feel that the female body is much more circumspect. But I can tell that I want you as much as I do when I am fully myself."

It was an invitation Bettina could not, would not, did not want to ignore. She closed her eyes and proceeded to use her knowledge of her true body to show him that she felt exactly the same way.

Eleven

Harry was gone when Bettina awoke, and she could guess why. The body part she seemed to have no control over was ready again. Harry had never once asked for her to come to him in the morning, but she doubted this feeling was a unique occurrence.

Bettina lay back and waited for the arousal to pass, marveling at the differences between male and female bodies. What luck that they were so compatible in bed. She was even willing to acknowledge to herself that she had a more firm understanding of why some men were not faithful to their wives and why some women looked beyond the marriage bed for pleasure.

When Roberts came into the bedchamber with coffee, it was as good as a cold bath.

"Good day to you, my lord. You have three hours until you must leave for Parliament. The countess asked if you would let her know when you are ready for breakfast as she will join you to discuss your plans for the evening."

By the time Bettina reached the dining room, she was a bundle of nerves. Her performance at dinner last night had not been as brilliant as she would have liked, and today she would be faced with far more exacting tradition, traditions that she was not at all familiar with. To take the earl's seat in Parliament was like Harry taking a daughter to bow before the queen without a lifetime of preparation or personal experience to rely on.

Harry came into the room looking particularly lovely in a cotton frock washed a pale green with leaves embroidered around the square neck and hem. Bettina felt her manhood give a throb of approval. The constant interest in sex was beginning to annoy her. "Why have I never gone to observe Parliament before? I do not even know where you sit."

"It's my fault," Harry insisted. "I told you it was the most boring experience in the world. And I assure you it will be."

He started off by telling her where to sit, next to Lord Nicholas, and began to recount the other details of what was an everyday exercise for him. "This will be a new experience for me as well, my dear. I plan to be in the gallery observing today. If anything untoward develops, I will send a message asking for you to meet me. It is not precisely common, but no one will be shocked."

Harry went over a few more details, but they were not nearly as important as acting as though she belonged. Bettina was about to tell him to stop filling her head with useless detail when the nurse came in with Lord Cameron.

"I do beg your pardon, my lady. I know you are leaving and somewhat pressed for time and thought it would be easier if I came to you."

Bettina cringed. That was the sort of forward behavior that annoyed Harry. The woman should have just sent a footman to request the countess's presence.

"Very well. What is it?" Harry spoke curtly, but Martha Stepp did not notice.

"I do believe Lord Cameron is teething, and I wanted to know what your preferences are for keeping him comfortable."

Bettina watched as Harry stared at his boy and then ran a finger over his gums. Cameron stopped crying long enough to bite, and when Harry pulled his finger away, the babe began whimpering again.

"Is he feverish? Is he ill?" Harry used his browbeating voice.

"No, my lady."

"Then go back to the nursery, and I will come to you shortly. Do not presume so again."

"Yes, my lady." Martha Stepp turned away with the babe and left the room.

"Harry, if she gives her notice, then you are the one who is going to find a new nurse."

"What else could I do, Bettina? I have no idea what to do for a teething baby and need your advice."

Bettina forbore to explain he could have spoken in a more kindly tone. "Did you feel any teeth?"

"Yes, two, I think."

"Oh, the poor baby. All right. Be sure to tell Nurse not to use brandy or any liquor to soothe his gums. She should use cracked ice wrapped in muslin. And perhaps a smooth wooden toy for him to bite on."

"I understand," Harry said, nodding.

"Now I have to leave. I do not want to be too late." Though in her heart what she really wanted was to hurry after Martha and send her off so mother and son could comfort each other.

As Harry had predicted, Nick Bright came over the moment the earl passed through the doors. Though Bettina had arrived at almost the last minute, the room was not particularly crowded.

Lord Osterman held court at his usual table, or the one that Harry had described as his favorite. It reminded Bettina that she needed to talk to Nick about the inadvisability of marrying his sister into Osterman's family.

"What say you, Harry! You are here more than a minute before the bell rings. You will ruin the usher's timing." Bright handed him a cup of coffee. "How are you this morning? And, tell me, does Bettina have a headache, or is she her usual charming self?"

"She is feeling so well that she is coming to observe today. She said that dinner made her realize how woefully uninformed she is, and she is taking steps to correct it."

Nick raised his eyebrows. "Next she will be advising you on your vote."

"I will assume that is your idea of a joke." Why did men persist in thinking all wives meddled in business that was not theirs? "Bettina is very happy managing our house and family. As a matter of fact, she considers it time better spent than the endless hours here."

Nick nodded and, thankfully, left it at that.

"Nick, I am early because I wanted a word with you. My

wife told me that your sister is seriously considering an offer from Lord Osterman's son."

"The countess knows that? I was hoping it would not be gossiped about until it was done."

"You cannot let it happen. You are the head of the household, and you must not allow it."

"Indeed?"

Bettina heard the warning but went on anyway. "You know as well I do what an animal Osterman is. You cannot allow your sister to live in the same house with someone like him. And do you have any idea what his son is like? As far as I know, he has never been to Town."

"Harry, leave it alone. You do not know what is at stake, and I am not about to tell you when you gossip like a girl."

Bettina raised her voice a little. "Then think on this: is whatever compels you so important that you are willing to sacrifice your sweet sister's health and well-being?"

Nick Bright closed his eyes and shook his head. "It is not what I would wish for, but I am not the one in control here."

"But you are," Bettina insisted, close to shouting.

"Enough, my lord." Nick spoke with quiet vehemence, turning from the earl and walking away. Bettina looked around to see more than one group watching, including Osterman. Had she been that loud? Loud enough for the others, for Osterman, to hear? That was the last thing Harry needed.

Osterman stood up and began to walk to where Bettina was sitting, murder in his eyes. Bettina wanted to confront the man, wanted to tell him that nothing could keep the Earl of Fellsborough from defending the defenseless.

The bell rang, calling the lords to the chamber, just as Osterman came close. "Saved by the bell, Fellsborough. You are as meddlesome as a fishwife. What will it take to convince you to mind your own business?"

Lord Osterman did not wait for an answer but strode into the chamber, leaving Bettina wondering exactly what Harry would do in a situation like this. What kind of attention would it draw if the earl sent a message to his wife? Bettina knew she needed help.

Twelve

Nick had already taken his seat when Bettina joined him in the chamber. His ill humor had vanished, and Lord Nicholas made room on the bench for his friend.

Bettina looked up at the gallery and was surprised though not particularly upset to see that Harry was not yet in place.

There would be more traffic than usual, and Harry never left enough time, thinking that the world ran by his timepiece and always surprised when it did not. Hadn't Bright expressed surprise at the earl's early arrival just a few minutes ago?

It was an effort to pay attention during the prosing of at least ten members of Commons. Was it just that they liked to hear themselves talk, or did they hope to attract the notice of someone more important and move up in the political world that Harry had so luckily been born into?

It seemed a blessing of great magnitude to have the right to an earldom as Harry did. Yes, the family had earned it with a century or more of service to the crown, but the head of the family in the last two generations had only to maintain and add to the wealth.

It seemed to Bettina that Harry's brother, who was fighting in Portugal, was serving the king more directly and more purposefully than Harry was sitting here in Parliament.

She settled more comfortably when she noticed that Harry had finally arrived.

"What good timing on the countess's part, Harry. She has arrived to hear the best speaker of the day." Nick Bright nodded toward the other side of the floor where William Wilberforce stood.

The earl's good fortune was brought home to her even more strongly as she listened with unfeigned interest to the amazing Wilberforce, who had worked so long and tirelessly to end the slave trade.

Today he was speaking on the need to abolish slavery completely, and it was clear that support was awakening. She looked up at Harry, who nodded, smiling at the words ringing in the air and the enthusiasm on both sides of the chamber.

Then Lord Osterman stood up. "I cannot criticize Mr. Wilberforce's dedication to the issues he thinks are the most important. How could I when he has proved that perseverance will eventually wear down opposition?"

Oh, that was so annoying. As if the supporters of the slave trade had given up because Wilberforce nagged them to death. They had given up because they had been convinced of the error of their ways. Bettina was sure of that.

Osterman droned on, but when Bettina felt Nick's elbow in the ribs, she made herself listen again.

"I ask you," Osterman went on, "do you not think his concern is misplaced? Why waste our valuable time on concern for African slaves when we are in the midst of a war that should command all of our attention?"

There were some murmurs of interest, if not agreement.

"If we do not give all of our effort to the needs of the army, we may well find out what slavery is like under the French flag."

Bettina stood up, so incensed by Osterman's inflammatory rhetoric and the nods and grunts of agreement that she responded so without thinking about what Harry's stand would be. "Lord Osterman, your effort to strike fear in our hearts will fail. Englishmen are made of sterner stuff. We can defeat Napoleon and care for those in need. One does not exclude the other any more than a mother can only care for a sick child and neglect her other children."

No one moved to speak. No one moved at all. Bettina real-

ized that she must have done something awful and sat down
with a graceless thump.

A recess was called, and Bettina was not sure if it was a
blessing or a curse, since it left her words as the last heard.

Nick Bright shook his head. "Lord help you, Harry, what are
you thinking? You and Osterman are supporting the same bill
for monies for the army. You sound as though you are having
second thoughts. Stupidity like that will cost you votes."

It wasn't stupid, she wanted to shout, but at least had the
presence of mind to eat the words, to acknowledge her anger
had to be controlled.

Lord Osterman stopped by on his way out as well. "Fellsborough, have you gone mad? I will call you out if you persist."

Control seemed to be something that Osterman had not
learned at all. Faced with his bluster, Bettina felt more calm. "If
we duel, then there will be one less vote for the army funding."

Before Osterman could reply, a page came to them. "My
lord, the countess is asking to see you. She says it is an emergency."

With alacrity she was sure most men never felt, Bettina raced
out of the chamber and looked for Harry in the public hall. It
took a few minutes to find him as men milled about, talking in
clusters, some moving along as they conversed, most unaware
of the fact they were blocking progress. Finally she found him.
He was wearing an awful puce cloak, one she had pushed to the
back of her armoire months ago. It must be Freeba's half day
off. Bettina urged him to the side of the hall, where they could
have a little privacy.

"Oh, Harry, I'm so relieved you are here. Why were you so
late? Is Cameron all right? I did not think they would seat you
after the session had begun."

"No, no, all is well." He spoke as though she were overreact-
ing and it was his job to remain levelheaded. "Why will you
not trust me to put our son's welfare as high as you would?" He
looked away from her for a moment, and she was almost sure
his feelings were hurt by her lack of confidence in him. Harry
had never felt that way. Never.

"The thing is, my dear, it is both Freeba's and the nurse's
half day off, so I had to choose outerwear myself, and then I
stayed to make sure the second nurse knew what she was doing.

I left Cameron asleep with Nurse Stepp due back within the hour."

"Oh, Harry, I am sure you handled the upset perfectly. I am the one who is making a mess of things. I cannot think what we will do."

"Nonsense. It's never as bad as you think."

His confidence was such a comfort that tears filled her eyes.

"For God sake, Bettina, do not cry. That would be an even greater disaster." Harry looked around the space as if making sure no one was watching them. "I took care of Cameron exactly as you instructed, and now you must trust me that this will resolve itself. I can tell you exactly what to say."

Harry was about to go on, but Bettina interrupted him. "I'm afraid that I cannot handle the pose here. If I stand and speak whenever I am angry, I am sure to find more trouble for you."

"Trust me, Bettina. Together we can find a solution, and it will be forgotten in a day. Less than a day."

Bettina took both his hands as it struck her that this was what trust was. It was easy to trust when you heard proof as she had from Baron Helder at the Daltons' dinner. A situation like the one they were facing right now took trust from the heart.

"Yes, yes," Bettina said with a surge of trust and love so powerful that anything seemed possible. "The two of us together can do anything. Oh, Harry, I do trust you. I trust you completely."

At that moment the oddest thing happened. As they held hands, Bettina felt a shift, a massive shift of vigor between them. It was the same vortex she had felt once before, but this time she felt no fear at its onset, only elation. Yes, she trusted Harry completely, not only with her life but with her heart and her future.

When she was again aware of her surroundings, Harry was kneeling beside her, a crowd of anxious faces above him. But Harry was all she cared about. Harry in his own body, in his superfine green wool coat, with the cravat choking him just as it had choked her. Bettina decided that she must have fainted. Harry lifted her into his arms and carried her into the cloakroom nearby.

"Are you all right?" they asked each other in unison. Bettina threw her arms around his neck. They laughed and kissed and kissed and laughed with more relief than passion.

Any number of people may have witnessed the faint, but not a one of them could have guessed at the real reason for it. Assuring everyone she was well and felt fine, Bettina insisted that she would watch the rest of the session from the gallery, telling Harry that she did not care a whit if "it calls into question my sensibilities."

As Harry walked with her back toward the stairs to the gallery, Osterman came up to him.

When Bettina would have moved away, Harry held on to her arm. "My lord Osterman, my apologies if I embarrassed you. But you called it on yourself by making a statement guaranteed to alienate votes. We need the support of every man we can find, even men like Wilberforce."

Osterman made a series of blustering, unintelligible sounds and ended with, "Just stop sounding like a damned abolitionist. At least until we have this funding passed."

Harry turned to Bettina, kissed her fingers, and smiled, his eyes telling her, *You see how easy that was to fix?* She smiled back and went up the stairs to the gallery as happy as she had been in at least six months, possibly her whole life.

It was a long day and had been an even longer week, so it made perfect sense for Bettina and Harry to agree that they should retire early that evening.

As they walked upstairs to bed, Harry reminded her, "Now my dear, we must be very careful not to wish for anything again."

"Why would I?" she asked. "I have everything I could possibly want."

They kissed outside her bedroom, a deep, drugging kiss, a code Harry had long ago developed to tell her that he wanted to share his bed with her. With a smile she could not control, Bettina hurried into the bedroom and let Freeba help her undress. When only her chemise remained, Bettina bade Freeba good night, and the maid backed out of the room announcing that she would come "with my lady's chocolate in the morning."

Bettina hurried over to the secretary, took out the key, opened the jewel chest, and pulled out the ridiculously gorgeous Fellsborough diamonds. She tucked them near the bed warmer and took off her chemise. Draping the warmed diamonds over her naked body, she went to the door that connected her room to Harry's and tapped lightly.

Instead of answering, he opened the door himself. When he saw his wife before him naked but for the diamonds, Bettina could tell that he, or at least his body, was very pleased indeed.

As Harry gathered her up and carried her to his bed, Bettina whispered, "Regardless of what you learned at the Daltons' party, there are some wives who do listen to what their husbands say."

Epilogue

"It's so perfect outside, and now that he has his first teeth, it is the ideal day to take Cameron to see Miss Bright and her mother. Lord Nicholas assured me that they would both be receiving callers today."

Martha Stepp nodded and moved the blanket away from Lord Cameron's face so he could see the world around him.

"I beg your pardon, my lady, but have you had any further thoughts on what happened to the coin that you asked me about?"

"No, it's so odd. Yes, I foolishly left the key in the lock of the jewelry box the night before, so it's possible someone took it. But why take only the coin?" She had been very distracted about wearing the diamonds for Harry, so perhaps she had dislodged the coin when she pulled the diamonds out. "And you and Freeba were the only ones to come in that morning. Freeba was expected, and you came to show me that Cameron's teeth had broken through."

Bettina shook her head, trying to reconstruct the morning, for the fifth time in as many days, but she had been so happy and so happily tired that the first few hours of the day had passed in a haze. She thought she might be increasing again. Though it was impossible to know for certain yet.

"Not that I suspect you at all, Martha," she assured her favorite servant. "Whoever took the coin took nothing else. And really, that coin is worthless."

Bettina made a mental apology to the coin and the mage who had endowed it with magic. But who would believe her if she told the truth?

By the time they were settled in Lord Bright's sunny red and yellow salon, Bettina had let the coin slip to the back of her mind. She showed off her darling baby boy and then passed him to Nurse so she and the Brights could use the rest of the time to talk.

Bettina still hoped there was a way to save Miss Bright from marriage to the young, virtually unknown Osterman heir, but she realized that she would have to tread carefully. Today was the first step.

Miss Bright was very subdued and spent most of the first part of the visit staring out the window onto the street at the front of the house.

"Come over here, daughter," her mother commanded. "You spend so much time staring out that window you are going to take root there."

With a last wistful look out the window, Miss Bright joined Bettina and her mother in the center of the room. Martha Stepp, holding Lord Cameron, claimed the window that Miss Bright had just vacated.

As the three women chattered on about fashion, Bettina tried to find a way to introduce the subject of Miss Bright's engagement. In the end, Bettina said good-bye without having broached the subject, hoping she would have another chance. Any disappointment she felt was relieved by the thought that the marriage could hardly happen overnight. She would ask Harry. Together they could come up with a plan to save the girl.

Not one of the three ladies knew that only a few minutes after the Countess of Fellsborough completed her call, Miss Bright found a very strange coin on the sill of her favorite window, beckoning her with its golden glow.

Always a curious girl, she picked it up, studying it with interest, and wondered why she had such a strong urge to make a wish. She wrapped her fingers tight around the coin and thought. It would have to be just the right wish. Miss Bright knew exactly what that was.

The Dancing Ghost

Patricia Gaffney

For Bonnie Gaffney

From the Hartford Courant, June 10, 1895:
"Ghost Expert" Says Old House Is "Haunted"

A self-described "spirit investigator" has determined that a long-abandoned house on Portman Street is haunted by ghosts.

"After rigorous testing, using the most modern scientific instruments available, I find the evidence overwhelming," declared Henry Cleland, president of the World Society for Harmonial Inspi-Rationality. "In all my vast experience with the supernatural, never have I encountered a private residence more patently associated with elements from the spirit world."

Rumors have swirled around the decrepit mansion in West Hartford for decades. Skeptics laugh, but neighbors and passersby regularly report mysterious sights and sounds emanating from the house, including weeping, knocking, rapping, and the passing of disembodied shapes in the windows.

Last year, the Hartford Society for Enlightened Spiritualism decided to investigate the odd goings-on. According to Mrs. Horace T. Beckingham, the society's chairwoman, their investigations were inconclusive, and "as a result, we decided to engage an expert."

Enter Mr. Cleland, lately of Philadelphia, Baltimore, and New Haven, and author of the monograph "Examinations of the Metanormal with Scientific Proofs of the Odic Force."

"I spent several nights in the house," said Cleland, "performing experiments and gathering data."

"He had a lot of equipment, machines and gauges and devices, for detecting things out of the ordinary,"

Mrs. Beckingham confirmed. "In the end, it was the photographs that convinced us."

Cleland would not supply photographs to this newspaper. "They're proprietary," he explained. "Plus, I may write a book."

He and Mrs. Beckingham both claimed the photographs showed "numinous images" and "orbs of pure psychic energy."

For now, the society has no plans to continue the ghostly experiments, citing financial considerations. "We're a small organization with limited resources," Mrs. Beckingham explained. "Ghost experts don't come cheap."

Not everyone is convinced the Portman Street house is haunted.

"Ridiculous," said Arthur M. Mordecai, vice president of Hartford Mercantile Bank & Trust, holder of the house's mortgage. "Absurd. No such thing as ghosts." Hartford Mercantile has been trying to sell the mansion for many years. Will its new designation as a "haunted house" lessen its chances of sale even further?

"Of course not," scoffed Mordecai. "Unless everybody's gone completely insane."

14 Lexington Street
Paulton, Massachusetts

June 14, 1895

Mr. Henry Cleland
Post Office Box 127-B
Boston, Massachusetts

My dear Mr. Cleland,

Mrs. Horace T. Beckingham was kind enough to send me your new address. I had written to her after reading in the Courant of your extraordinary work in the matter of the haunted house in Hartford, Conn.

I am sure a gentleman of your exceptional background and talents is extremely busy, beset no doubt by appeals from a public eager for your unique skills and advice. Even so, I hope you will entertain one more humble request, and consider a commission not unlike the one you performed for the Hartford Society for Enlightened Spiritualism.

Many of us here in Paulton believe Willow House, my late grandparents' home, is inhabited by spirits from the beyond. A number of witnesses, yours truly among them, have observed many extremely convincing manifestations that cannot be explained otherwise. I have a personal interest in getting to the bottom of this mystery, and I believe you, Mr. Cleland, are the perfect, indeed the only, person who can help me.

I have taken the liberty of making a discreet inquiry of Mrs. Beckingham, who suggested (with similar discre-

tion) that your time and services might be secured for a certain remunerative consideration. Please see the attached, which details what I hope you will deem a suitable recompense.

I implore you to help me, Mr. Cleland. Time is of the essence. Your kind and expeditious reply will be most appreciated by

Your humble servant,
(Miss) Angiolina Darlington

June 16, 1895

Miss Angiolina Darlington
14 Lexington Street
Paulton, Mass.

Dear Miss Darlington,

Thank you for your kind letter. It is true that the particular services I am able to offer are much in demand, and only grow more numerous as time passes and human enlightenment expands. Ordinarily I would be unable to accommodate you on such short notice, but as it happens, I do find a small window of time has unexpectedly opened in my busy schedule.

As to recompense, my own needs are trivial—spartan—but my work is, as you say, so unique, so specialized, I am afraid I couldn't think of offering it at a discount. Please see the attached re: the matter of my fee.

Certain we can come to an agreement in this matter, and looking forward to a productive and mutually satisfactory spirit enterprise, I remain

Very truly yours,
Henry Cleland

14 Lexington Street
Paulton, Massachusetts

June 18, 1895

Mr. Henry Cleland
Post Office Box 127-B
Boston, Massachusetts

My dear Mr. Cleland,

Thank you so much for your prompt reply. Words cannot express how glad and grateful I am that you will be coming to Paulton, and not a minute too soon!

Alas, my personal circumstances are such that I am unable to offer you more than the amount mentioned in my last (see attached). But I have it on excellent authority (dear Mrs. Beckingham) that besides being brilliant in your unique field of endeavor, you are also a most kind, most generous person. I am praying that that generosity of spirit will impel you to help me, Mr. Cleland, for I desperately need your help!

Yours most sincerely,
Angiolina Darlington

Post Office Box 127-B
Boston, Mass.

June 20, 1895

Miss Angiolina Darlington
14 Lexington Street
Paulton, Mass.

Dear Miss Darlington,

You are, of course, not aware that I am obliged to move about with an enormous amount of special scientific equipment, all of a very delicate nature. As a consequence, travel expenses alone take up the vast bulk of the modest sum I request (see attached) for my services. And then there are the extra requirements for the transport of Astra, a vital part of any investigation I perform.

Since I will be a newcomer, I rely on you solely in the matter of accommodations whilst I am in Paulton. (And I hope I need hardly mention that financial responsibility in that regard will be yours, not mine. But I am a very simple man, never fear, so I assure you that burden will be light.)

Thanking you for your kind consideration, I remain,

Yours,
Henry Cleland

14 Lexington Street
Paulton, Massachusetts

June 22, 1895

Mr. Henry Cleland
Post Office Box l27-B
Boston, Massachusetts

Dear Mr. Cleland,

It is so unpleasant to speak of financial matters, is it not? Especially when the "product" one is discussing is a matter as abstract and precious as the Truth itself!

And how dearly I wish it were in my power to come to terms with you in the matter of your quite reasonable request. But, tragically, it is not. Once again, I can only rely on your good nature, generosity, and the unquenchable intellectual and philosophical curiosity I am absolutely assured you possess, dear Mr. Cleland.

One good thing—perhaps you don't own a map?— Paulton is just over half a day's train ride from Boston, thus very economical. You'll also be happy to know that, upon inquiry, I have learned that freight charges for passengers traveling on weekdays are extremely reasonable.

As to lodging, I'm sure you will find Mr. Smoak's Boardinghouse for Gentlemen on Lexington Street will not overtax your pocketbook, especially for a man of such spartan tastes. It will be convenient also, being ad-

jacent to my own rooms here in a similar establishment for ladies.

Looking forward with hope and eagerness to our meeting, I remain

Yours with great sincerity,
Angiolina Darlington

June 24, 1895

Miss Darlington:

Arrive 27 June, 1:28 p.m., on Boston train. Trust convey-ance from station to Smoak's won't put you out.

H. Cleland

One

Only Lexington Street and a hundred feet of lawn on either side of it separated Mr. Smoak's Boardinghouse for Gentlemen and Mrs. Mortimer's Boardinghouse for Ladies. One of the principal entertainments at each was observing the comings and goings of the occupants of the other, either from windows or their nearly identical front porches.

Angiolina Darlington usually had better things to do, but today she'd been watching from the window seat of her cramped, second-floor bed/sitting room for nearly an hour when, at about three in the afternoon, a horse-drawn van pulled up in front of Mr. Smoak's. The driver jumped down from one side, and a man in a checked coat and dark trousers jumped down from the other.

Mr. Cleland, she presumed. She put on her glasses to see him better. He looked nothing like the man she'd been expecting. Vague as that was. What did a "spirit investigator" look like? No telling, but she'd been thinking of someone at least middle-aged. This gentleman looked hardly older than she (twenty-eight, not that that was *young*), and in addition, at least from this distance, he appeared . . . normal. Perfectly sane, which struck her as an even more interesting feature than his above-average good looks. Oughtn't a man whose profession was "spirit investigator" to have a sort of *mad scientist* quality about him? At the very least he should look eccentric. He should look like—well, he should look like her grandfather.

Oh, and he had a dog. Medium size, brown and white, some sort of terrier. He released it from a wicker hamper, and it ran around Smoak's front yard in excited circles, relieving itself on the bushes.

Heavens, Mr. Cleland did have a lot of luggage. She'd assumed he was exaggerating, to drive up his price. Well, this was embarrassing. She muffled an aghast laugh as he and the driver hauled out bag after box after crate after carton in the hot June sun and lugged it all into the house. Which box contained "Astra"? she wondered. The biggest one, no doubt; "Astra" must be a giant spirit telescope or some such thing.

There, that was the last of his belongings. Mr. Cleland paid the driver in coins, not bills—that eased her conscience a bit. They tipped their hats to each other, he went inside, and the driver drove away.

She should go across the street and greet him. She'd thought of waiting for him to come to her, but now it seemed the least she could do—make the first move.

"Get up, Margaret," she told the cat in her lap—named after Margaret Knight, inventor of the flat-bottom paper bag–making machine.

At the wardrobe mirror, Angie decided she didn't like what she was wearing anymore. It was fine this morning, when she'd thought Mr. Cleland would be white-haired and strange, but now . . . Oh, it was hopeless anyway. Since she'd spilled motor oil on her best blouse trying to silence the squeak in her grandfather's automatic hat-tipping machine, she was down to three summer dresses and a handful of skirts and shirtwaists.

Good thing I'm not vain, she thought, leaning in toward the freckled mirror to adjust her hair, pinch more color in her cheeks. Her grandmother's onyx brooch made her look . . . like her grandmother. She took it off. Now she looked plain, "spartan," as Mr. Cleland would say. She put the brooch back on. Scowled at herself. "To hell with it," she said, and went out.

TWO

Miss Angiolina Darlington didn't look like the woman Henry Cleland had been expecting. Vague as that was, and not that he'd given it much thought: a paying customer was a paying customer. From the tone of her irritating letters, though, he'd thought she'd be older, and either big and boat-bosomed, like Mrs. Beckingham, or raisin-faced and stringy from pinching her precious pennies.

Instead she was younger than he, and tiny, not much over five feet. But with a carriage so erect, the flat-topped straw hat on top of her dark, upswept hair stayed in constant parallel with the ground. Neat, inexpensive dress of a hyacinth color; polished shoes creased across the tops and worn at the heels; small purse in one gloved hand, closed parasol in the other.

He took this all in from behind a porch pillar as she looked both ways, a gratuitous precaution on sleepy Lexington Street, and stepped out into the road. Astra, who had been sniffing at bees on a bush in the flower border, heard the light clip of her feet on the pavement and did something completely out of character: he went out to greet her. Henry, who would have liked a few more seconds of hidden appraisal, a little more time to size up his new patron, had no choice but to do the same.

The thought crossed his mind that she could be anybody, not Angiolina Darlington at all. Too late now, though; he'd already lifted his hat and stuck out his hand. He admired her wide-set eyes, dubious and alert, and her soft, politely pursed mouth. She said, "Mr. Cleland," and gave him the tips of her fingers, and he forgot his misgivings. Of course she was Angiolina Darlington. She could be no one else.

"A pleasure to meet you, ma'am. I was just coming across to make your—Down, Astra. *Down.* This isn't like him, he's taken quite a—"

"Astra?" Miss Darlington sank to her knees and laid purse and parasol on the grass. "His name is *Astra*?" Her laugh was a quick, bubbly outburst, unexpected and charming. Henry crouched down opposite, and they both petted the dog. He had to pull him away when Astra jumped on Miss Darlington's knees and tried to lick her chin.

"He's not usually like this," he said.

"He smells Margaret."

"No, he likes you. He's usually much more dignified. Margaret?"

"My cat." They stood up. "How was your trip, Mr. Cleland?"

"Uneventful, thanks."

"And your room?"

"Fine, fine."

"Not too . . . *spartan*?" Was that a twinkle in her eye? "I live there," she said, pointing behind her. White clapboard, two stories, wide porch, seedy yard. Same as his. They didn't bode well for his prospects, Miss Darlington's narrow circumstances. And yet in spite of that, he warmed to her. They had poverty in common.

"Shall we walk?" she invited, and they set off down Lexington Street, Astra forging ahead.

"I was hoping I might see the house today," Henry said, matching his pace to hers. After the train trip, it felt good to stretch his legs.

"It's not far, although in a completely different sort of neighborhood." Not as run-down as this one, he took that to mean. "But let's walk through town first. Paulton's growing—more of a city than a town now, as you'll see. Named, of course, after Paul Revere."

"Have you always lived here?" he asked.

"No, only since I was seventeen. Before that, I . . . visited from time to time."

"But now your grandparents have passed away?"

She nodded. "A little over a year ago now."

"I'm sorry. How did it happen? I only ask because it may be relevant."

"Influenza. One caught it, then the other. They died within days of each other."

"How terrible."

"Actually, I doubt they'd have wanted it any other way."

"And . . . " Always a delicate question. "You believe they're haunting the house now?"

The merry, surprised laugh bubbled up again. She cut it off quickly, putting on a sober face. "Oh, I think that's highly unlikely. Although they did love the house. I can imagine them not wanting to leave it."

"Who, then?"

She stopped. They were at an intersection, Lexington and Concord Avenue; downtown Paulton lay before them. "Shall I tell you now, or would you rather see the house first?"

Was it a trick question? Did she think he would know who haunted the house by looking at it? "It's up to you," he said judiciously.

"Let's wait, then. Tell me about yourself, Mr. Cleland. How did you get into your . . . line of work?"

"I think of it as a calling, a vocation. An ideal match between my interests and my talents."

"Ah. And how did you—"

"The *Paulton Republic*," he read in the curtained window of a four-story brick building they were passing. "Any good?"

"Excellent. It wins awards. And I'm not prejudiced, even if the owner is my good friend's husband."

Walker Hersh, Editor and Publisher, Henry read to himself, walking backward. The name didn't ring any bells. Good.

Strolling along the elm-lined streets, passing a white-steepled church about every other block, Henry confirmed the impression of Paulton he'd formed from the train: tidy, pleasant, typical New England village. A bit prettier than most, a little more prosperous. It even had a college; Miss Darlington pointed it out as they passed the archway to a small but handsome enclave of stone buildings. All in all, a fine place to spend a week or two in the fullness of spring. Particularly since he had, at the moment, no other plans.

"You were saying?" she reminded him. "How you came by your *calling*."

"Ah, yes. Well, actually, you might say it was passed down to me by blood. My great-grandfather, Baronet Spenser, was practically on speaking terms with the ghosts and spirits in his castle."

"His castle?"

"Just a small one, in Derbyshire."

"So you're a baronet, too?"

He waved his fingers in the air dismissively. "Oh, technically, but I think of America as my home. The family moved to Philadelphia when I was quite small. Where was I?"

"The castle in Derbyshire."

"Right. The gift skipped a couple of generations—my grandfather was busy shipbuilding, and my father, an amateur biologist, was too much of a natural skeptic to give credence to his own senses. But then it popped up in me."

"The gift?"

"The gift."

"How exactly did it pop up?"

"Intuition. Empathy. A mind open to the unexplained and the unexplainable."

"Aha."

"Also, I have a degree in engineering from the University of London, so I like to think my temperament embodied both essentials for the work I do: tolerance of the unknowable coupled with rigid adherence to the laws of science."

Hard to say what she made of all that. She had a way of pursing her lips that might mean she was thinking things over or might mean she was trying not to laugh.

Miss Darlington was anything but conventionally attractive, but he liked the way she looked. Neat and tidy. She'd be the smart one, the kind of girl you'd want on your side in a contest or debate. Or a game. A small, feminine package of humor and intelligence.

Just so she wasn't *too* intelligent.

"Your dog is awfully well behaved." The words were barely out of her mouth when Astra took the opportunity to lift his leg and pee on a lamppost. Instead of blushing or looking away,

Miss Darlington pressed down a smile. "A vital part of your investigations, you wrote. So he's a sort of . . . ghost dog?"

"Exactly. Enormously useful, has a kind of sixth sense about the supernatural. I got him in India."

"India."

"Bought him from a shaman in Calcutta."

"Really. I'm so ignorant—I thought shamanism was more of a *northern* Asian religion."

"Well, he wasn't *from* Calcutta. He just happened to be *in* Calcutta."

"Of course. And you were there . . . ?"

"Studying the occult. Researching."

She'd have pursued that, he could tell, but luckily they had arrived at their destination. "Here we are," she said with a small flourish. "This is Willow House."

Again, not quite what he'd been expecting. In fact, not at all. Quirky Victorian architecture made for the best haunted houses, and ideally they were in isolated locales, preferably near cemeteries. This one was on an elderly but fairly lively street, set back from it by a stone wall and a spread of mature willow trees in full bloom. He admired the stately, Adam-style front, three stories of white-painted brick divided by tall, linteled windows, four up, four down, and two graceful gables on top. "It's beautiful," he said truthfully.

Miss Darlington turned to him, her face transformed. "Yes. It is. That portico," she said, pointing above the front door to a small balcony surrounded by a waist-high balustrade. "That's where she dances."

"Who?"

"The ghost."

Of course.

"One of them," she clarified. "Let's go around to the back."

They went along a flagstone walk between yew hedges, past a swing hanging from the branch of another willow tree, past a stagnant lily pond. The hedges gave way, the vista opened, and they were in a rose garden.

"This was my grandmother's," Miss Darlington said with a note of shy pride. "I've been trying to tend it since she passed away, but . . . " She put her hands out and shrugged. "I'm not my grandmother."

"Gorgeous," Henry said, truthfully again. He couldn't

imagine how this could have been more beautiful, no matter who was tending it. Roses everywhere, in clumps, on trellises, climbing over low stone walls. Bees made a constant, industrious buzz, and the smell was intoxicating.

"We'll have to go inside through the basement—that's the only key I have." She went down a mossy cement stairway to a padlocked metal door, which she unlocked with a key she took from her purse. "Watch your head. Be careful, wait until I . . . " She moved away in the dimness, and presently a light came on. So the house was electrified. Henry saw that they were in a . . . he wasn't sure what. A plant, a workshop, some sort of laboratory.

"My grandfather did his work here. He was an inventor. William Darlington—you may have heard of him?"

"I may have," he temporized, eyeing a long center table laden with small machines and engines, jars, bottles, vises, tools, books, metal contraptions. She'd said her grandfather had been dead for months, but his workshop looked like he'd just gone upstairs for lunch. "What did he invent?"

"Well . . . here's a pocket ashtray. A gentleman clips it to his vest or coat pocket. You can even monogram it."

"A pocket ashtray. Say, that *would* be handy."

"And this is a compass you attach to your hat brim."

"Mm-*hm*."

"A bottle opener that fits on the heel of your shoe."

"Ingenious. And this?"

"Well . . . it was *going* to be a device to keep you awake. You wear this collar around your neck, and if you start to nod off, it activates an alarm."

"A-*ha*."

She looked at him levelly. "I know what you're thinking. But don't be fooled by the—the frivolity of these gadgets, Mr. Cleland. My grandfather's imagination could be a bit whimsical at times, but he was also a genius. And he never got credit for his greatest invention: the gramophone disk."

"Your grandfather invented the gramophone disk?"

"Everyone thinks it was Emile Berliner, but Grampa thought of it first. But then he forgot to send in his patent application, so he never got credit. And it was revolutionary—it made the old cylinder technology obsolete." She gave a quick headshake, as if she hadn't intended to go into all that. "Anyway. Let's go upstairs; I'll show you the house."

The inside of Willow House was no spookier than the outside. What it was, was peculiar.

"This used to be the library," said Miss Darlington, standing in the middle of the kitchen. "My grandfather thought the kitchen ought to be closer to the dining room, so he moved it."

Henry was perfecting the art of the noncommittal hum. "Very sensible. That, uh, thing up there . . . " He pointed to an overhead set of tracks or cables running along the ceiling.

"A moving tray. It goes to the dining room first, then down the hall to the front parlor. For transporting food and drink. Well, anything—books, the newspaper . . . "

"Hm."

She looked a little defensive. "My grandmother had terrible arthritis, so he was always thinking of ways to try to make life easier for her."

One of the ways in which he'd made life easier for her was to ruin the symmetry of the entry hall by installing a wire cage in front of the center staircase. It rose and descended via a hand-cranked rope-and-pulley gizmo attached to the wall.

"He called it the Elizavator," said Miss Darlington, "because—"

"Your grandmother was Elizabeth?"

"Precisely. Are you getting a *sense* of anything, Mr. Cleland? Any psychic vibrations or connections yet?"

He narrowed his eyes and allowed a dramatic pause. "There is something, yes. Definitely. Something. Too soon to speak of it, though."

What he was getting, in spite of the oddness of the house, in spite of not having a psychic bone in his body, was a feeling of warmth and comfort. Of home. It was in the graceful proportions of the rooms and in the retreats of nooks and alcoves and unexpected porches. It was even in the comfortable, unmatched furniture, some of it covered with sheets. But mostly, he decided, the feeling came from the light, a soft, pale-gold illumination that bathed every room, upstairs and down. This was a happy house.

"Skylights," Miss Darlington said when he remarked on the phenomenon. "Grampa hid them in unexpected places, behind cornices, valances. It was one of his hobbies—playing with light."

She showed him the well-stocked library, numerous parlors, a small music room—so small, an ancient grand piano took up most of the space. She ended the tour in the center hall on the second floor, before the double doors to the outside portico. "This is where she dances."

"Yes." He put his hand to his forehead. "I sensed it."

"Well, and also, I told you."

"Astra feels it, too."

Hearing his name, Astra leaned against Henry's knee and grinned at him. "Tell me about the ghost, Miss Darlington," Henry said with great seriousness. "Tell me everything. In your own words."

"Yes, I thought I'd use mine." She arranged her face so that it was as somber as his. Lowered her voice. Spoke slowly.

"It's always at night. When there's no moon. She wears white—they say she did in life, too: always dressed in shades of alabaster. Her long yellow hair is always down. Sometimes there's music. They say it's a Gypsy violin, and that would make sense. Her lover was a Gypsy."

"Who was she?"

"Lucinda Darlington. My great-great-great aunt, for whom this house was built. In 1801."

"Built by whom?"

"Eustace Darlington, her husband. For a wedding present. He was a wealthy merchant, much older, and she was young and beautiful and gay. Above all, she loved music and dancing— and he forbade both. He tried to make her a prisoner. In this house. But she fell in love—"

"With the Gypsy violinist."

"Yes. They had a mad, passionate affair, made plans to run away. A servant betrayed them—Eustace caught them. On a moonless night." She stepped to one of the portico doors and pushed it open. "They found her the next day—there. Dead and broken on the ground." Theatrical pause. "As for Eustace, he went mad and committed suicide. By drinking poison."

Henry let a suitable length of time go by. Miss Darlington looked quite splendid in profile, her features sharp-edged and tragic against the sky. "How many people have seen the ghost?" he asked in a stricken tone.

"Many. And not just Lucinda's—the Gypsy is buried somewhere on the grounds, and they say all three of them haunt the house."

"And do they? You lived here."

"Oh, that will be for you to decide, Mr. Cleland. But I'll tell you this." Her voice, which had gone low and sepulchral before, went more so now. Her eyes, a deep and gold-flecked gray, snared him in their gaze. "I have seen and heard things in this house that would curl your hair."

"Like what?"

She stared at him a little too long. The heavy, ominous look faltered. "Well . . . if I say, it might influence your impartiality. Wouldn't it be better to begin your investigations with a completely open mind?"

She was good. Either that or she believed everything she was saying.

"Up to a point," he started to answer, when he heard noises from downstairs—a door opening; voices. Miss Darlington began to pronounce a word he'd have sworn was going to be an extremely unladylike oath, but she cut it off before he could be sure. "Visitors?"

"My cousin," she said through her teeth. "Bringing buyers."

"Buyers?"

"I forgot to tell you. Willow House is for sale."

Three

Cousin Lucien's bulbous, corpulent features looked even more belligerent when he was annoyed, and he was annoyed now. Angie knew he turned a rude "What are you doing here?" or possibly even "What the *hell* are you doing here?" into a stiff "Angiolina, what a surprise," only because of the young, prosperous-looking couple he'd brought to look at the house. If she'd been alone, he wouldn't have bothered introducing her, but he couldn't very well ignore the presence of a strange man and a dog.

"Mr. and Mrs. Foster—Miss Darlington. My cousin," he added grudgingly.

"How do you do? And this is Mr. Cleland," Angie said with extra graciousness to make up for Lucien's lack. More hand-shakes and how-are-yous. "Oh, and this is Astra, Mr. Cleland's . . . um . . ."

"My ghost dog."

Mrs. Foster, who was blond, petite, and by Angie's estimation at least five months pregnant, covered her mouth with her hand. "Oh dear! Do you mean to say it's *true*?"

Lucien cut off a snarl with a cough. "Of course it's not true! Ha-ha! The man's joking."

"Not in the least," said Mr. Cleland. "I'll show you. Astra! Astra, do you *feel* something?"

At once the dog stopped sniffing at Mr. Foster's pants cuff and went still. His black eyes bulged; his nose lifted in the air. His peeled-back lips revealed a mouthful of stained teeth.

Mrs. Foster gasped and pressed back against her husband.

"Oh, for—" Lucien pinched his nose to rein in his temper. "Who are you? What are you doing here? Sir," he remembered to add; he wasn't a vice president of Paulton National Bank for nothing.

"Mr. Cleland," Angie answered for him, "is an investigator of the paranormal. He's a *ghost detective!*"

Mrs. Foster clutched at her rounded abdomen. "There, there," said Mr. Foster, patting her shoulder. "My wife is very sensitive."

"Come, let's look at the house," Lucien said, trying to move them away. "Never mind the elevator, an eyesore, I know, but it can easily be taken out. Unless you like it, in which case it's quite a handy—"

"Mr. Cleland uses *purely scientific* methods in his research," Angie said. "For which he is *world famous*. He's going to *study* Willow House."

"By God, he—"

"He is, Lucien—Mrs. Grimmett wants him to."

"Who?" said Mr. Cleland.

"Do you really believe the house is haunted?" Mrs. Foster asked him, rubbing her arms as if they were chilled. "We'd heard the rumors, of course, but Walter said it was all foolishness."

"It's too soon to say," Mr. Cleland said, stroking his clean-shaven chin. "When I've finished my experiments, I'll be able to hazard an opinion. In the meantime, however . . . "

"Yes?"

"In the meantime, relying on my many years of experience and a certain natural intuition, if I may, I would have to say . . . "

"Yes?"

"The environment, the *ambiance*, a certain something in the *aerosphere* of the house . . . Yes, I would definitely have to say there is . . . something."

Lucien snorted.

But that was enough for Mrs. Foster. "Terribly sorry—a

pleasure to meet you—come, Walter." Taking her husband's arm, she made a wide berth around Astra and flew out the door.

"Who's Mrs. Grimmett?"

Mr. Smoak's Boardinghouse for Gentlemen had a side porch as well as a front porch, the former screened from the street by rangy, never-pruned hydrangea bushes. The furnishings were sparse, just a few pieces of mildewed wicker, and flies and mosquitoes were a nuisance, but what it lacked in comfort the side porch made up for in privacy. *Respectable* privacy, since it was outdoors and thus, technically, a public place.

Angie pulled her skirts aside to give Mr. Cleland more room on the damp love seat cushion they were sharing. "She's the wife of Lucien's boss at the bank. A great believer in spiritualism. She's to Paulton what Mrs. What's-her-name—"

"Beckingham?"

"What Mrs. Beckingham is to Hartford, only more so. Mrs. Grimmett founded ISIPP."

"International Society for . . . "

"Institute for Scientific Investigation of Paranormal Phenomena."

"Oh, yes. Never heard of it."

"It's local." She stopped petting Astra and turned to face Mr. Cleland. "I'm sorry I didn't tell you the house is in foreclosure. I'm not sure why I didn't, except—well, really, does it matter?"

"Not to me, and it won't have any effect on my experiments. But I can see it matters a good deal to you. Maybe that's why you didn't tell me. Too painful."

He said that so matter-of-factly, she surprised herself by telling him the truth. "It is painful. I love Willow House, and I always have. It's home. And," she added more forcefully, "my grandparents *meant* for me to live there." Hadn't they said that to her practically on their deathbeds? "Don't let that money-grubbing saphead get it," Grampa had told her, meaning Lucien. And Gramma had said, "We don't want anyone living here but you, dear. That way it'll be as if we never left."

"What happened? Why didn't you inherit it?" Mr. Cleland asked.

"My grandfather . . . " She felt herself coloring. Why did everything she told Mr. Cleland about Grampa make him sound like such a nincompoop? "He used it as collateral for a loan, to buy equipment for experiments on a new invention. When that didn't work out, he couldn't pay the loan back. The bank foreclosed—or my cousin did, I should say, since he *is* the bank. Practically."

"Practically. Fortunately for you, Mr. Grimmett *is* the bank."

"Yes, exactly." How quickly Mr. Cleland got to the heart of things.

"Does your cousin want the house for himself?"

"Lucien? Oh no, he just wants the money." She jumped up to pace. "And I'm running out of time. I'm afraid he'll find a buyer before I can pay off the loan."

"Pay off the loan? But I thought . . . I assumed . . . "

"That I'm broke? I am. *But*. I have a *plan*." And she almost told Mr. Cleland what it was—until she remembered with whom she was dealing. He might not be what she'd been expecting, he might be a good deal smarter, nicer, and much, much more charming, but he was still a *ghost detective*. "Well, never mind that now," she said brusquely. "What is *your* plan, Mr. Cleland? What do you intend to do?"

"I'll stay at the house tonight. Move my equipment in, get things set up."

"Excellent. Lucien won't object—he can't."

"Mrs. Grimmett?"

"Mrs. Grimmett."

"Good. So. Leave it to me, Miss Darlington. Astra and I will perform our first experiments this very evening."

"*Dear* Astra." The dog had been pacing along with her. "What a good boy you are." She crouched down to ruffle his ears, which he seemed to like. "Your 'ghost dog,'" she said, laughing up at Mr. Cleland. "No 'investigator' should be without one."

Her confidential grin faded when not only did Mr. Cleland not smile back, he looked offended.

"Oh—I beg your pardon. I didn't mean to make light."

An awkward moment passed, but then he said, "Never mind," magnanimous again. "A hazard of my occupation."

Now she didn't know what to make of him. Was he fake or wasn't he?

"I have to go," she said, rising. "So do you, in fact—our respective suppers are served at precisely six o'clock, in case you didn't know." He walked her around to the front of the house. "May I . . . um . . . *count* on you?" she asked, keeping the question vague. She wasn't as certain of him as she had been.

"You may."

"Oh—good."

"I will open my mind and attempt to evaluate the atmosphere of the house fully and fairly, with the utmost objectivity."

"Of course, but it really would—*behoove* everyone concerned if you—everyone but my cousin, that is—if you, if your, if it did indeed turn out that there *were* . . ."

"I understand completely."

"Ah! Good."

"And I assure you I shall give the matter my complete, unprejudiced, unbiased attention."

Confound the man.

Four

The banker cousin must be selling the house furnished, thought Henry, readjusting the pillows against the headboard of Miss Darlington's four-poster feather bed. This room still had all her furniture, everything but her clothes and most personal belongings. Left behind was a watercolor portrait of her as a young girl—he assumed it was she; same all-seeing level gaze, same privately amused mouth—in what could only be her grandmother's rose garden. It hung on the wall at the foot of the bed, and he looked at it every time he got stuck for a word on the piece he was trying to write, under his Atticus Bent pseudonym, for *Leslie's Monthly.* Since he was almost as tired as he was distracted, he looked at the painting often.

Somewhere off in Paulton, one of the ubiquitous church bells tolled eleven. Henry stubbed out his half-smoked cigar— what good was a cigar without an accompanying shot of booze? None, and since he didn't drink anymore, he said to hell with it—and reached down to give Astra a good night pat. Everything was in place, all his ghost-detecting equipment, his cameras. He'd taken a few pictures of moonlight on window glass, and they might or might not look like orbs of spirit energy when he developed them, but tomorrow would be soon enough to get some good mists and shadow apparitions. He yawned, stretched, and blew out his reading lamp.

Nice bed. He imagined Miss Darlington in it. Something about her appealed to him in spite of the fact that she seemed to have his number. Or . . . maybe that was what did appeal to him, no *in spite of* about it. She was nobody's fool. And in his present circumstances, it was flattering to be seen through.

Also, she had nice ankles. Very small ears. Pretty skin. He fell asleep wondering how long her shiny, dark hair would be if she ever let it down.

The music didn't wake up Astra, the world's laziest terrier, and it only woke Henry gradually, gently, like a whisper in his ear. Piano music. Light as air, a quick, melodic tune. Gypsy music.

Well, well.

He'd gone to bed in his underwear, not expecting to have to get up, because he never had before, not once in his year-and-a-half-long career as a ghost detective. Where were his trousers? He fumbled with the switch on the wall, *click-click, click-click*. Nothing. No electricity.

Well, well, well.

"Don't you *hear* that?" he complained to Astra, who was finally yawning and stretching, scratching his ear. "You're not from Calcutta anymore, by the way, you're from someplace north. You're from . . . " Hell if he knew. Have to look it up in a damn atlas.

Luckily there was a nearly full moon; he didn't bother lighting the oil lamp. He could see fine. He could even check his . . . check his . . .

He stopped dead in front of the mirror over the bureau. His skin prickled with a cold that began in his bones and seeped into his blood—until his brain engaged and he started thinking, not just feeling. Scrawled on the mirror were the words:

Death stifles not the breath of true love

All right, she'd come into the room. How, though? Quietly, very quietly; Astra was a lazy cow, but he wasn't *deaf*. Then, too, it was her room, so she'd know how, which floorboards creaked, that sort of thing. Still, it was unnerving to think he *and* his dog had slept through such an intimate invasion.

He was halfway down the stairs when the music stopped. He sprinted the rest of the way, cursing himself for his slowness. No one in the shadowy foyer. No one in the dark hall. He raced to the music room door, bare feet skidding on the floor, Astra behind him.

Nothing. Unless she was—no, not inside the piano, and he felt like an idiot as soon as he looked. He tried the light switch—still off. Smart ghost; she must've done something to the circuit. Could she have gotten out of this room without him seeing her? Or was there a secret panel? Then he really felt like an idiot. "Secret panel"—the very words made him cringe. Of course she could have gotten out, and run down the hall to the kitchen, through the back door, out into the yard. She was probably halfway to Lexington Street by now.

But she wasn't. She was here. He didn't intuit it—he heard music again.

This time a violin. Very versatile ghost. More Gypsy music, in a tragic minor key. Henry crept out into the hall, listening, turning his head to discern the direction. "This is supposed to be your job," he muttered to Astra, who looked nothing but game and interested—not frightened, not threatened. Which was good. Henry had to admit that was reassuring.

He followed the music—"haunting" was really the only word for it—back the way he'd come, to the front of the house. It seemed for a moment, as he stood in the spacious hall, to come from everywhere. Then it stopped.

He thought at first it was his imagination that things were getting brighter, or maybe he thought the moon was coming out from behind a cloud. But no, this light slowly grew stronger from *above*, from upstairs, it came from . . .

He froze, one foot on the first stair tread. The dancing ghost swayed above him as if in thin air, and the light seemed to shine through her slender body. Certainly it shone through the thin white—*alabaster*—robe or billowy dress she wore, so that he could see . . . just about everything.

Afterward he would tell himself that that was what kept him motionless for so long, simply the pleasure of beholding a lovely naked lady, dancing. But the more complicated truth was that he could not have moved if he'd wanted to. For the length of time the apparition turned and bent and arched so gracefully, long blond hair rippling to her waist, her arms ethereal, like pale scarves floating in an unseen breeze, he honestly didn't know if she was real or not.

Only after the unearthly light dimmed and finally disappeared was he able to move. And by then it was too late. He and Astra—whom he'd completely forgotten about; what was *his* excuse for doing nothing?—rushed up the steps to find the hall . . . empty.

But the portico doors were open.

And there was a scent in the air, a subtle perfume of . . . roses.

He searched every room in the house, including the basement. Also the elevator, although he had no idea what he was looking for there. He didn't expect to find anything, and he didn't. Last, he checked his equipment, although he had less than no faith that his thermometers, barometers, wind socks, compasses, and chimes could actually detect anything. If only he'd had some notice, some warning—if only he'd taken a *picture* of the dancer with one of his cameras. Then he'd know.

Then he'd know? What rubbish. He knew now! Angiolina Darlington had outfoxed him, that was all. He wasn't used to that. He was the spook*er*, not the spook*ee*.

In bed, he talked himself back into a state of calm. *Look how rational I am,* he thought. *About to drift off to sleep in a haunted house. If I believed in ghosts, I'd be up all night.*

He made the mistake of opening his eyes and letting his drowsy gaze drift to the mirror over the bureau.

The message had changed.

> Who loves
> Believes the Impossible.

Very literary ghost. Either that or he'd just been visited by Elizabeth Barrett Browning.

Five

Then Angie went too far.

But she was having such fun, and everything was going so *well*. Besides, after she'd gone to all the trouble of bringing Margaret and the leftover halibut, it would be a shame not to use them.

She got the music room ready in no time, making hardly a sound—easy when one was barefooted. And when one's "ghost dog" antagonist was either deaf or the dimmest terrier on earth. She took a final look around. Window ajar so Margaret could escape, check. Fish bits scattered on and between piano keys, check. Door closed, check.

"It's up to you now, sweetheart," she told the cat as she released her from her pillowcase prison. "Hope you're hungry. Make a *lot* of noise, Margaret; otherwise they'll both just sleep through it." Instead of waking in fear and confusion to the eerie, tuneless sound of piano music in the dead of night. And finding nothing but—

"Oh, I almost forgot." *Pssssst*, a spray of rose cologne: the dancing ghost's signature scent. Also, it would mask the smell of halibut.

—And finding nothing but an empty, moonlit room, redolent with the mysterious odor of roses. And then, just when Mr.

Cleland decided he was imagining things, what would he hear? Chilling strains of the Gypsy violin again, coming from . . . he knew not where. And by the time he figured out where, it would be gone. And so would Angie.

All in all, an excellent night's work.

Setting Margaret gently on the piano bench, she gave her a kiss, retrieved the pillowcase, perfume atomizer, and fishy-smelling paper wrapper, went to the mantel, tilted the portrait of her parents over it (dressed as Beatrice and Benedick for a burlesque production of *Much Ado About Nothing*), and disappeared into the black maw of the fireplace.

Luckily she knew these stairs, wasn't likely to stumble in the pitch black en route to the second floor. When she reached the tiny landing, though, she trod carefully, not anxious to knock over any of the props she'd hastily stashed here after her dance performance, the shuttered lantern with the gauzy lens, the footstool, her yellow wig. And her violin, which she found now by feel, propped against the cool brick wall where she'd left it.

She hadn't planned this third trick as carefully as the other two. *I'll play it by ear,* she'd thought. And now it was time to do just that, with a piece by a Belgian violinist she'd learned, sort of, from a gramophone record. But should she start playing it now, here, just down the hall (but behind a floor-to-ceiling mirror in a gilt frame) from Mr. Cleland and his dog? Or should she wait for—

Never mind. Margaret took the decision out of her hands by bounding up onto a bottom octave just then—a tremendous leap, it sounded like, reverberating with a nice atonal *bang*. Angie waited, holding her breath. More piano notes, higher— Margaret was making her way up the scale—and then the sound of feet and paws nearby. Muttering. A rustle of movement, of rushing. *Well, wait, not so fast,* Angie worried; *give her a chance to finish eating.* Pounding feet on the stairs now. Oh dear. And now—why hadn't she foreseen this?—a din of horrendous barking and hissing, screeching, howling, the crashing of objects and the yelling of oaths.

A distraction, that was the ticket. But suddenly she couldn't remember how the Gypsy piece started! *Play anything,* she thought, and struck up a mazurka she knew well—she taught it to her music students. Sort of Gypsyish. She slowed it down, gave it a mournful edge. The cursing downstairs stopped, but not the animal ruckus. She kept playing, straining to hear what was happening between long, sad violin strokes.

Bow poised, she felt the hair rise on the back of her neck. A muted scrabbling was coming through the false wall—the mirror's back. He was out there. She was found.

Run!

No, don't! Stay still, don't make a sound. He'd never figure it out, that pineapple finial at the bottom corner blended into the mirror's gilt edge too well, he wouldn't turn it, he'd never . . .

The mirror tilted. Pale light streamed in. Angie set her violin down and ran.

Down instead of up—a mistake. She might have lost him in the attic, but the mayhem waiting for her in the music room doomed her escape. Anyway, how could she leave Margaret halfway up the wall, clinging wildly to the window drapes, spitting and terrified? "Astra!" she yelled, grabbing for his stubby, ecstatic tail, missing.

And then the worst. A horrible, horrible thumping in the wall above the mantel, all the more horrible for how long it went on. Mr. Cleland crashed into the fireplace and lay dead.

Six

"I'll pay you more. Not *much* more, but then, you don't have to *do* much. Just say nothing."

Henry made a show of being unable to raise his head to the glass of water Miss Darlington was holding to his lips. It worked; she moved even closer to him on the sofa and slid her cool fingers to the back of his neck. "You don't *have* any money," he pointed out, taking a small, pitiful sip. His head throbbed, but Miss Darlington's ministrations were making up for it.

"No, but I *will* have as soon as my grandfather's lawsuit is settled. Any day now, I expect a *windfall*."

"The gramophone disk?"

"No, his new bicycle pedal. Someone else took credit for it, so now it's in court. If we win, the A. A. Pope Company will market his recessed-cleat, dual-sided, spring-actuated, clipless pedal, and I'll be rich. Well." She made a deprecatory moue. "Not rich. But, by God, I'll have enough money to buy this house back from the bank!" She set his head back on the sofa cushion with a bit too much force; he winced. He sensed a sore subject.

They were in the small parlor off the dining room, where she'd moved him, with some difficulty, so that they, or rather she, couldn't be seen from the street when she switched the electricity back on. Now she rose from the sofa and started pacing. A habit, he'd noticed.

"The lawyer says a decision is coming down soon, so all I have to do is stall—make sure nobody buys the house in the meantime. Which means all *you* have to do is keep quiet. You just continue your 'experiments,' during the course of which you determine that Willow House is definitely haunted."

"There's no need to make those little quote marks in the air," he said testily. "What makes you think I'm not a genuine, legitimate spirit investigator?"

She stopped pacing and looked at him. A minute passed. Somebody's lips twitched first, or it might have been a tie. Their hoots of laughter were definitely a tie. A good sound, in which Henry heard not only hilarity but immense relief on both sides. Thank God, the jig was up. He threw his feet to the floor and sat up, holding his head, groaning and laughing at the same time.

She came to him and put a hand on his shoulder. "Are you sure you're all right? Nothing feels broken?"

"A bruise or two," he said manfully, "nothing serious." He felt as if he'd been beaten with planks. How many steps had he fallen down? "So tell me, Miss Darlington. Why are there hidden staircases and secret sliding panels in your otherwise beautiful home?"

"It's not a secret—you'd probably have found out anyway. Eustace Darlington's brother inherited the house after Eustace's suicide, or whatever it was—"

"You mean he didn't drink poison after murdering his wife?"

"Well, he *might* have. He died not long after she did, and they say he was complaining of stomach pains."

"What about the musical Gypsy lover?"

"I'm not sure how that story started. She fell in love with *some*body, but I've also heard it was her music teacher. Who was Jewish. Anyway—after they died, Eustace's brother got the house, and when he died, he left it to his son, who was a strict abolitionist, very religious. He's the one who built the secret stairs—they go from the first floor to the attic. So escaping slaves could hide here."

"The Underground Railroad!"

"It's a fairly well-known fact in Paulton, but I was hoping you'd be gone before you heard about it." She sat down again beside him. "So tell me, Mr. Cleland," she said, mimicking him. "Were you scared?" Her twinkling eyes invited him to be honest.

"Don't be ridiculous."

"Oh, come on. Not even a little bit?"

"Of course not." The writing on the mirror might have given him a slight start, but he wasn't going to admit that to *her*. "I take it you don't believe in ghosts at all?"

"Certainly not. And neither do you."

"So you're quite positive Willow House isn't haunted?"

"Don't be silly. Not that I haven't heard things—yes, I have, but they certainly weren't *ghosts*."

"What kind of things?" he asked, interested.

She regarded him for a moment, but instead of answering, she waved her hand and said, "Nothing, never mind."

He'd have pressed, but they were interrupted just then by the sound of yipping, whining, and toenail scrabbling: Astra trying to get to the cat, still closed up behind the music room door.

"Astra!" Henry hollered, and after a moment the dog trotted into the parlor. "Come over here and behave yourself." Instead, Astra made a beeline for Miss Darlington, to whom he seemed to have taken a shine.

"Naughty ghost dog," she chided, playing with the two front paws he put on her knees. "Shame on you for terrifying poor Margaret."

"He really is a ghost dog, you know. You don't believe it?" he said when she rolled her eyes. "Astra! Astra, do you *feel* something?"

Astra lifted his head and sniffed the air, bulging his eyes and snarling his lips.

Henry thought Miss Darlington might slide off the couch, she laughed so hard. Delight filled him. For some reason, he blushed.

"So he's not from Calcutta?"

"A little west of there. Baltimore, to be exact. I inherited him from a friend."

The clock struck one. They had an argument about whether he would walk back with her to Mrs. Mortimer's ("You're not going anywhere—you've just fallen down a flight of stairs!" "You are *not* walking home alone in the middle of the night." "I do it all the time!"), which he won when they remembered there was no reason for him to stay here tonight anyway. He could walk home with her, then slip into Smoak's from the back.

They passed no one on the quiet, empty streets—as she'd predicted. "We have a lot to discuss, a lot to arrange," she said, resettling Margaret in her pillowcase. "The first thing is to get a story published in the newspaper about Paulton's new ghost detective. I'll take care of that; you just wait for a call from Walker Hersh."

"Of the *Republic*," Henry recalled.

"After that, I'm quite sure you'll be getting an invitation from Mrs. Grimmett. She's *dying* to meet you."

The moon had set. Nothing stirred on pitch-dark Lexington Street, not even a cricket. But when they arrived at Mrs. Mortimer's, they huddled together under the branches of a white dogwood to say good night. Just in case.

"Shall we meet tomorrow, Mr. Cleland?" she asked softly. "I have a music lesson in the morning, but we could have lunch—"

"Please. If we're going to be partners, don't you think you should call me Henry?"

"Henry, then. And I suppose you should call me Angie."

"A pleasure." He smiled.

She frowned. "We still haven't discussed the *nature* of our new partnership. I said I would pay you more, but we never settled on a fee."

"Partners don't charge each other fees. They're *partners*."

"Oh. Well." She sounded surprised, almost incredulous. "Well. That's . . . Thank you."

"Don't mention it. What instrument are you studying? Could it be the *Gypsy violin*?"

He was growing addicted to that delighted burst of a laugh. "No, I *teach* the violin," she said. "And the piano. I did it at Willow House as well, to supplement my grandfather's . . . irregular income, but now I do it to keep body and soul together."

"He left you nothing?"

"The house and his debts. They've canceled each other out."

Her wistfulness made him want to cheer her up. "I forgot to tell you: the dancing ghost is an absolute triumph. Quite a brilliant illusion."

She shifted Margaret in order to clap her hands—gently, so they made no sound. "I know! Isn't it? I've only done it twice before, but people are *completely convinced*."

"What, ah, what garment is that the ghost is wearing?" he couldn't resist asking.

"Oh, just my nightgown."

"Your *summer* nightgown, I assume."

"What do you mean?"

"The, um . . . " Why was he getting into this? "The, um, transparent nature of it."

"Trans—" She stood very straight. "Surely not. Do you mean it's—you can—"

"See through it."

"No, that's impossible. Dear heaven." The whites of her eyes went very big. "You're teasing me."

He shook his head.

"But no one's *ever* said that, never even *hinted*—and they *would*, you know they would, if you could—if you could—"

"Oh yes, they would. So it must've been just tonight," he said quickly. "Perhaps the lighting was different."

She seized on that. "The light! When I've danced on the balcony, I've always shined the lantern from the side, but tonight, in the hall, I had to do it from below, and I stood on a footstool. Did it look like I was in midair?"

"Amazingly."

"That's it, then. The light." She buried her face in the pillowcase. "You're not teasing?" came out a cottony mumble. "You really could—see—"

"No, not really, hardly anything. Don't know why I mentioned it. The barest glimpse, a mere suggestion, certainly nothing—*lewd*, just the reverse, in fact, quite natural and delightful—"

A soft, rising scream in the back of her throat finally shut him up. She backed away, clutching the cat to her chest, pivoted, and ran.

"Oh, well done. Good job." Henry rapped his knuckles against his skull. "Blockhead." But crossing the lawn to Smoak's back door, he looked up at the sky and laughed. What a day this had been. It didn't say much for the quality of his life lately, but he couldn't remember when he'd had so much fun.

Seven

"" "I know what I saw," said Cleland, "but I never rely on my senses alone. That's what my extremely sensitive gauges and sensors are for; the tricks of my trade, as it were." '

"Hm," Angie said, looking up from the front page of this morning's *Paulton Republic*. "Not sure you should've put it quite like *that*."

"Come at 'em head-on, that's my motto. Say it before they can." Mr. Cleland—Henry, rather—swung at an insect with the fly bat she'd just given him for a present. "Got him! Say, this is ingenious. This screen thing on the end, it doesn't displace much air, so the fly doesn't know it's coming."

"That's the idea." She went back to the newspaper. " 'Besides witnessing a dancing ghost, Cleland claims to have heard violin music "coming from everywhere and nowhere." In addition, mysterious writing appeared on the mirror in the bedchamber in which he was sleeping.' Oh, that's good; everybody loves *mysterious writing*. What did it say?"

"As if you didn't know."

"Me?" She laughed. "Even *I* can't be in two places at once. ' "Taken by surprise, I was unable to photograph the ghost at the moment of her appearance. However, often a spirit's ectoplasmic shadow can be captured after a materialization, and I submit that this photograph represents just that: the vestigial imprint of a spirit manifestation on the atmosphere."' Ha-ha!"

They chortled together. When Henry leaned in to see the photograph better, she could smell the bay rum on his freshly shaved cheek. "Came out pretty well, don't you think?" he said.

"Considering it's crumpled tissue paper on a string, I think it came out beautifully." More chortling. "How long have you been a photographer?"

"Not long," he said vaguely—but he was vague on almost anything that had to do with his immediate past. She, on the other hand, found herself telling him all sorts of things about herself she normally wouldn't tell someone, especially a man, on a mere three days' acquaintance. But Henry was so easy to talk to. And unshockable, at least so far. He seemed more of a friend than he possibly could be—so much so that she'd begun telling herself to be careful.

"Here's the only part I don't like." She pointed to a paragraph in the article. "'In addition to changes in temperature, wind direction, and barometric pressure in the vicinity of the ghost's materialization, Cleland claims there was also a bad smell. "It permeated the house. Indescribable. I can only call it the odor of Death."'"

"What's wrong with it?"

"You said my house stinks."

"Ah, but think of the deterrent effect. Who wants to buy a house that smells like death?"

"That's true."

"I like that he capitalized Death," Henry said. "You know, this is a very good article, all things considered."

"I told you it would be."

"Compared to a few other things I've had written about me, it's a puff piece."

"A puff piece?"

"Journalism term, I believe. I liked Hersh—he seems like a good fellow."

"He is."

"And I didn't get the impression he's a fool."

"No." She understood the question Henry was implicitly asking. "I admit, he's also a friend. He knows what this means to me. Otherwise . . . you're right, he might not have treated the author of 'Examinations of the Metanormal with Scientific Proofs of the Odic Force' quite so gently."

She folded the paper and set it aside. "So. I call phase one a smashing success, don't you? And phase two has already been set in motion, because today I received—"

"Angiolina."

"Yes?"

"Angiolina," he repeated, slowly, drawing out the ridiculous number of vowels. It didn't sound silly when he said it. "An unusual name."

"One of my mother's fancies. She admired Angiolina Cordier, the French opera singer."

"How interesting."

That was how he charmed her, by looking directly into her eyes and saying, *How interesting,* as if he'd never said anything truer in his life. "Oh," she said lightly, "you don't know the half."

"Tell me."

"Should I?"

He had such an innocent face for a charlatan. And smiling made him even handsomer when it compelled that dimple on the side of his mouth. "Why not?"

"Oh, well," she said—backtracking, now that she was going to tell him—"it's not *that* interesting. She was a singer, my mother, as well as a dancer and an actress. And my father owned and managed"—she took a deep breath—"Wild Johnny Darlington's Traveling Musical Theatre Extravaganza."

Henry was speechless.

She laughed at his thrilled, amused, fascinated face—just what she'd wanted. No judgment, no veiled horror. Those she was used to.

"He fought in the Union cavalry during the war, and afterward I guess Paulton wasn't exciting enough to come home to, so he joined a Wild West show and rode horses and shot guns and things. After a time, he formed his own theatrical company. He and my mother met when he hired her to play Eva in a musical version of *Uncle Tom's Cabin.*"

Henry shook his head in awe. "Where were you born?"

"Where? In Wood River, Illinois. Wild Johnny's had an engagement in St. Louis, but they never quite made it because I came a day early." She smiled, thinking of all the times she'd heard her mother or her father tell the story, much embellished, of her untimely arrival. Even at birth, she'd been an inconvenience.

"So you grew up in a theatrical troupe?"

"Partly. Half the time I traveled with the company; the other half I stayed here with my grandparents."

"Two different worlds."

"Completely different." His instant understanding prompted her to elaborate. "My parents never really planned to have a child. I'm not saying they weren't fond of me, but in some ways they were children themselves, and I—well, I spoiled the wonderful party they'd been having."

"So they sent you away."

"But I was always longing to come home. My grandparents had their quirks, yes, but Willow House was a *monument* to peace and stability compared to—"

"A traveling musical theatre extravaganza."

"Exactly. They used to try to put me in productions—once I had to play Little Nell! But I was no actress, as everyone soon realized, plus I was plain instead of beautiful, so that was the end of that. Thank God."

"Oh, I don't know," Henry said, eyeing her interestedly. "I can see you in both worlds."

He must be remembering the dancing ghost. About whom the less said the better. "Oh, no," she said quickly. "This is what I'm suited for, this is what I want—my little town, my independence, my music students. And my house," she added, punching her fist into her hand. "I want my *home* back."

"You'll get it. When we're through, no one will want to come near your smelly old house. Your cousin will offer it to you for a dollar."

She laughed. "Then I'll have to rehabilitate it. Can you exorcise ghosts as well as detect them?"

"You forget, I'm the president of the World Society for Harmonial Inspi-Rationality. I can do anything."

"I almost believe you."

He made a face, pretending to be hurt by *almost*. "You were about to tell me about phase two," he reminded her.

"Oh, yes." She found her pocketbook and took Lucien's folded note from it. "We've been invited to my cousin's house for dinner!"

"You don't say. I could've sworn he didn't like me."

"I'm sure he detests you—he's not that fond of me either—but this is really a dinner to pacify Mrs. Grimmett. She's the key to everything, Henry, even more than an article in the *Republic*. If we can convince *her* Willow House is haunted, we'll be home free."

"Literally. So she's that powerful?"

"She's the gatekeeper to Paulton society—and don't you dare say 'such as it is.' "

"Never."

"She only deigns to notice me because she's also the president of the Paulton Garden Club, where my grandmother was worshipped as a goddess."

"When is this dinner?"

"Saturday night. So I was wondering, do you, um, have a . . . "

"A good suit?" he guessed.

She put her hand on his sleeve. "I'm sorry to ask, but it's bound to be formal. Edwardia never misses a chance to show off her jewelry." Now, that was a catty thing to say. What was it about Henry that made her want to skip past reticence, a lifetime of it, and tell the truth?

"*Edwardia?*"

She loved the way he pronounced that name, too. "My cousin's wife. She's . . . well, you'll see."

"You're frightening me. And yes, I can probably muster up some duds that won't embarrass you."

"It's not *me*—"

"I know." He smiled with his whole face. "I know it's not you," he said, and she was caught up in the warmth of that smile, those guileless eyes that seemed to say, *I like you. I admire you.*

She pulled herself together. "Ordinarily I'd ride my bicycle, but since this is formal, Lucien will send his buggy for me. But I don't think we should go together, do you? We don't want to look like a *team*."

"No, indeed. Although we are."

If he'd reached out just then, she'd have taken his hand. That's how lost to discretion she was. "Good, it's settled," she said briskly and got up. "Seven o'clock, Saturday evening."

He stood, too. "But perhaps we should meet before then. Lunch tomorrow?"

"Oh—do you think we should?"

"For planning purposes."

"Ye-es, I suppose. We want to be on—"

"The same page," they finished together. "Shall we say noon at Grogan's again?" Henry asked.

Walking back to Mrs. Mortimer's, the thought crossed Angie's mind that having lunch in public twice in three days might send a message that they were a team even more than sharing a ride to Lucien's would. But, oh well; business was business; first things first. The important thing was, she'd be seeing him again tomorrow instead of the next day. For planning purposes.

Eight

The home of Lucien and Edwardia Darlington was big, pretentious, and *hot*. So hot, the Darlingtons and their guests were having their before-dinner sherries outside in the "folly." The perfect name, thought Henry, for this domed, concrete thing supported by Doric columns and overlooking a nondescript field—pasture, really—on the outskirts of Paulton. He was sweating under his stiff white collar and necktie. He grabbed another glass of seltzer water from the tray of a passing maid and thought wistfully of the "oscillating fan" in the living room at Willow House. Angie had built it with a sewing machine motor and a wooden paddle. A little noisy, but otherwise quite a miraculous creation. She should patent it.

He liked watching her as she leaned against a column and chatted with her friends the Hershes, Walker and Norah. Fresh as a crocus she looked in a white linen dress—a subtle tribute to the dancing ghost? He could imagine that tickling her sense of humor. She laughed at something Walker said, and Henry smiled in sympathy, wishing he were with them, over there instead of over here. With Mrs. Grimmett.

"*So* exciting to think we have our *very own haunted house* right here in Paulton," she was saying in her flutey bray, her face animated but not always visible because of the shifting angle of an ostrich plume attached to the bosom of her gown. She had iron-gray hair coiled in loops around her ears, like small animal appendages. "My own house has a cold spot, a definite cold spot, Mr. Cleland, right under the bay window in the library, and of course Chester says it's a draft, but I remind him that the builder is *dead*, isn't he, a Mr. Clyde Stottlewort of Boston, and I don't see why it's not possible that he's come *back* to one of his creations, if not to haunt it, then perhaps merely for a *visit*. Have you ever heard of such a phenomenon?"

That called for an actual answer, not a "Well said!" or "Very astute," with which he'd been deflecting Mrs. Grimmett for the last few minutes. What a dismal insight: that he knew her type so well, he could respond to most of what she said in his sleep.

"Indeed I have," he said, leaning in confidentially. "Most people don't notice, but these *aural areas*," a term he invented on the spot, "are more common than you might imagine. And yet, only the very, very sensitive can discern them."

"So true," she simpered, "so very true. I know you'll want to come to my house and experience the phenomenon yourself."

He was saved from a commitment to visit Mrs. Grimmett's cold spot by the arrival of the Darlington children, Lucien Jr. and Little Eddie, come to say good night. Angie had told him she would "rather die" than be their nursemaid or nanny or governess or anything else whatsoever—all posts she'd been offered by Cousin Lucien after her grandparents passed away. A tepidly handsome offer, he'd thought, depending on how you looked at it. Angie looked at it with horror. "Wait until you meet them," she'd said.

Well, no one could claim they were *attractive* children, since the family resemblance had unfortunately gone cross-gender; the little girl looked like her thickset father and the little boy like his bloodless wisp of a mother. Otherwise, they seemed all right.

But then, after the joky introductions and condescending baby talk were out of the way and no one but Henry was looking at them, Lucien Jr. poked Little Eddie in the eye with his toy soldier, and Little Eddie retaliated by shoving Lucien Jr. down the two steps from the folly to the gravel path. Shrieking, wrestling, and hair-pulling ensued, leaving the combatants bloody, dusty, and vowing revenge.

Over the heads of the intervening parents, nanny, and servants, Angie caught Henry's eye. *You see?* her expression asked. He made a terrified face and nodded back. *I see.*

"May I?" Walker Hersh asked, waving the lit end of a cigarette at him.

"Be my guest." Henry held still while Walker flicked ash into the collapsible brass receptacle clipped to his lapel—Angie's grandfather's "traveling pocket ashtray," patent pending. Henry was wearing it to please her, but it turned out to be a lot more useful than he'd thought.

Walker was about forty, according to Angie, but he looked older. He had narrow, slumping shoulders, tired eyes, and an air of amiable distraction that hid, Henry suspected, a shrewd and canny mind. "Norah and I used to want a big family," he said in a wistful voice, watching the Darlington children being led away, still caterwauling.

Henry smiled. "It's a good idea in theory."

"I've got four brothers and two sisters. You?"

"Just a brother. Three years younger." A straight answer, and it felt good. How long since he'd told the truth about himself to anyone? Under other circumstances, he could imagine Walker Hersh and himself becoming friends.

"I see you're a smoking but not a drinking man," Walker said, lighting his cigarette for him.

"True," Henry said. "Nowadays."

"But not always?"

"Not always."

"Well, good for you while it lasts. Drink's a ruinous thing," Walker said, slugging down the rest of the sherry in his glass. "Runs like a river through my profession."

"Does it?" Henry said innocently.

"Oh, yes. Something about newspapering just seems to bring on a powerful thirst." He kept his tone humorous and impersonal, but Henry thought he saw something in the other man's eyes. A spark of knowledge. A hunch.

Relax, he told himself. Hersh was no fool: why wouldn't he have doubts about a strange man in town whose alleged profession was investigating ghosts? Henry was getting complacent, that was the problem. That, and Paulton had too many seductive attractions. Like Angiolina Darlington. The solution was easy—be more careful. Especially around agreeable, sensible, clever Walker Hersh.

*   *   *

Mrs. Grimmett dominated conversation at the dinner table, holding forth on a lot of subjects, including her view of xeno-glossis (trance speaking in tongues). Henry valued any chance he got to speak to Norah Hersh, the lady on his other side, an attractive brunette as neat and tidy as her husband was disheveled. They said polite things to each other about the unseasonably early heat, how he was finding life in Paulton, if he'd dined at the Gryphon House yet. Then Mrs. Hersh leaned in and said in a low voice, "I count Angie as one of my closest friends."

He replied that he knew that, and started to say something about how lucky both ladies were in their friendships. She interrupted him.

"Angie doesn't have very many friends. That may surprise you, but think about it. She had the most unconventional upbringing imaginable, and some in this town regard it as nothing less than scandalous." She lowered her voice another degree. "Certain people, I think you can surmise who, treat her as if she's not quite respectable—they hold her at a distance."

"I can imagine that," he said slowly.

"On the other hand, people with not as much . . . social status to uphold find her the delight she is—and yet they, too, keep her at arm's length, because they think she's not one of them. Do you see what I mean?"

"I'm not sure."

"Most people are kind, but each . . . class, if you will, believes she belongs to the other. So she's betwixt and between. And, therefore, often neglected. You think she's self-sufficient, that she revels in her independence—and she is, she does, but that doesn't mean she's not lonely. Why else would she want to hold on to Willow House so badly?"

Henry was silent, his mind churning.

"I'm telling you these things for two reasons, Mr. Cleland. One, because despite all the evidence to the contrary, you don't seem like a dishonest person."

He put his fork down and stared at her.

"Two, consider it a warning. If you do anything to hurt my friend, I'll pay you back. I don't know how, but I promise you won't get away scot-free."

He could think of absolutely no response. He felt angry, guilty, misjudged, enlightened. Across the table, Angie was saying something to gloomy-faced Chester Grimmett that actually made him laugh. She glanced over at Henry and smiled with her eyes, friendly, sweet, conspiratorial. *How are we doing?*

A rush of affection seized him, a palpable twist in his chest. He wanted to excuse himself, go somewhere and think—but Mrs. Grimmett was soliciting his views on what the Bible had to say about ghosts. Unbelievably, he was up to speed on that, and could cite 1 Samuel 28 and Job 4:15 for her.

For Cousin Lucien, who had been making subtly skeptical faces and scoffing noises whenever Henry said a word, that was the last straw. "Sir!" he burst out. "Do you really claim justification for this—this *nonsense* in the Scriptures? I know many people who would find that offensive."

"The Scriptures say what they say," Mrs. Grimmett pronounced, as if that settled it.

If Lucien had been paying more attention to her tone, it would have. "Indeed they do," he retorted, "but Satan is wily. He has it in his power to easily fool the senses of the weak and the credulous."

A thunderous silence fell.

Lucien quailed, realizing his error too late. A purple vein in his forehead began to throb.

But there was no explosion. Mrs. Grimmett merely pruned her lips at him and made a suggestion.

"Fortunately, there's no need to argue this matter in the abstract. We have an actual edifice, a *structure* that appears to be the habitat of spirits from the Other Side."

"We have a haunted house," Angie simplified.

"Hypothetically haunted," Henry said mildly. "More research is required." With Angie as the true believer, he could afford to be the objective one, the scientist.

"Have you ever attended a séance?" Mrs. Grimmett asked him.

"Oh, yes, many times."

"Have you ever conducted one yourself?"

"Yes, indeed. Many times."

"Excellent." She rubbed her jeweled hands together. "Then I propose we have a séance at Willow House, as soon as possible, to lay this matter to rest. I've heard that the optimum number of attendees at a séance should be divisible by three—is that true, Mr. Cleland?"

"Why, yes. Ideally." His casual gaze locked with Angie's for a split second. She was trying to look interested instead of jubilant—so was he. What luck! According to their plan, whoever got the most natural, least contrived-seeming opportunity to bring up the idea of a séance was the one who should broach it first. And now Mrs. Grimmett had done it for them!

"Then I think it should be all of us, plus one. And you, of *course*, Mr. Cleland, by virtue of your experience, must be our medium."

Lucien looked apoplectic. But when Mrs. Grimmett asked if anyone had any objections, he stayed mum. What choice did he have? Henry almost felt sorry for him.

"What a wonderful idea, Mrs. Grimmett," Angie said, all surprise and admiration. "At last, the mystery of Willow House will be solved."

"*May* be solved," said Henry, once again the rational one. "Séances, even when everything goes perfectly, often disappoint. The spirits are fickle and don't always come at our bidding."

"Who should be our ninth member?" wondered Walker Hersh, who had the look of a kind man sitting among children, trying not to let it slip that there was no Santa Claus.

Everyone thought.

"Mrs. Mortimer?" Angie ventured. "You don't know her, Mrs. Grimmett, but I've been living in her home, and I count her as a friend. But more to the point, she's extremely *sensitive*."

"Sensitive how?" Lucien asked irritably.

"In the psychic sense. She has a way of—of knowing things in advance. It's quite extraordinary. Not like a fortune-teller, but just . . . "

"A special sensitivity to the metaphysical?" Mrs. Grimmett guessed. "She sounds *perfect*. But what do you think, Mr. Cleland?"

"Hm." Henry pulled on an imaginary beard. "The only absolute requirements for séance participants are mental stability and an open mind. Beyond that, you want as many diverse temperaments as possible, positive and negative, male and female, so forth and so on, in order to form a battery, as it were, on the principles of electricity, or galvanism, so that the magnetic spheres emanating from the circle may empower the spirits."

So it was decided. Angie's landlady, who read tea leaves for a hobby, would be their ninth.

Nine

"You were wonderful."

"No, *you* were wonderful."

"*You* were."

"Definitely you."

Angie sighed, sinking back against the stiff horsehair cushion of her cousin's closed buggy. "All right, we were both wonderful. Also splendid and brilliant and crafty and clever. Especially *you*." A passing streetlamp lit Henry's face long enough for her to see his smile—a lovely thing, and she was falling into the habit of trying to provoke it. "I'm beginning to understand," she said, "the appeal of your profession."

"That's because it's not *your* profession," he said, and in the darkness she could tell he wasn't smiling at all.

A silent moment passed. She said, "Then why—"

"Your cousin doesn't have much use for me, does he? He looks at me with a lot of loathing."

Henry sidetracked certain subjects so regularly, she was getting used to it. "My grandfather used to call him the white sheep of the family, and he didn't mean it as a compliment. I think Lucien probably does loathe you, because you're everything he isn't."

Henry turned his whole body to face her. "That's absurd." His incredulity was real, and it made her like him even more.

"Oh, Henry. Nobody likes Lucien. Everybody likes you."

"That can't possibly be true."

"It is true. He's homely and plain, you're—not. He's stiff and uncomfortable, not just with other people but with himself, and you . . . you're the sort of man people want to be around, because you seem so at ease with yourself."

"I do?"

She laughed. "Don't you know it?"

"No. I suppose that might've been true once, but . . . " He shifted to face forward again. As the buggy turned a corner, she was vividly aware of the part of her thigh that pressed against his. He, she was sure, didn't even notice.

"What changed?" she asked when he didn't continue.

"Life. Circumstances." He shook his head. "Anyway, thank you for the compliment."

"It wasn't a comp —"

"Do you think we can be ready for the séance by Thursday? I can tell Mrs. Grimmett something about the moon if we need more time—it needs to be full, it needs to be new."

"No, because the longer we wait, the longer it gives Lucien to find a buyer for the house. I'm afraid to delay."

"Then we'll just have to work quickly."

"Yes. Even if we don't know what we're doing. *I* don't. One thing I don't understand, Henry. If everyone's holding hands around a table, how can we play any tricks? Our hands will be tied—literally!"

"Don't worry. It can be done."

"Oh, I forgot to tell you—I can make smoke."

"You what?"

"It looks like fog or haze. Very ghostly. Nothing to it, you just mix glycerine and distilled water in a ratio of about thirty to seventy."

The buggy had stopped in front of Mrs. Mortimer's. Henry didn't move, though, so Angie didn't either. "You are," he said, and stopped. "You are the most . . . " She thought it would be another of their jokes—*You were great; No,* you *were great*—but his voice changed. "Angiolina Darlington, you are . . . the most amazing woman I've ever met." His eyes, glowing with warmth, seemed to see nothing but her. He leaned nearer.

He was going to kiss her. She was going to let him. Their faces were so close, she could feel the soft exhale of his breath on her skin. *Hell with it.* The dim thought floated past, and every scruple, every misgiving she'd ever had about him—and she'd had many—drifted away. They didn't matter. Nothing did but this.

The long, delicious moment stretched. *I'm going to die,* she thought clearly. She lifted her hand to touch him—just as he pulled away. "Late," he mumbled, and opened the buggy door.

With her own light out and the curtain open, Angie could see, across Lexington Street, the rectangle of gold that was Henry's window. Once he even walked past it, a dark, fleet silhouette, but that was a quarter of an hour ago; since then, no sighting. But his light was still on. She imagined him in bed, reading.

A flash of movement in the yard made her press her nose to the glass and peer harder. Oh—Astra. He'd recently fallen in love with the dog next door, a spaniel named Lulu with long, curly ears and saucer-sized eyes. Henry said he was hardly ever home anymore.

Margaret, curled up at the bottom of the bed, never fell in love. Never came into her estrous cycle, was the technical term. She'd been born that way. Neutral.

Angie used to feel a kinship with the cat in that way. Not literally, of course; metaphorically. Passion was something that afflicted other people, she'd thought, not her. She *knew* all about it, though. You could say she'd spent her childhood watching other people behaving passionately. What a *mess* it was. Chaos, absolute chaos—her parents' marriage was a perfect example in miniature, and a traveling theatrical troupe was a perfect example in . . . whatever the opposite of miniature was. Maxiature.

Her grandparents' marriage—that was her ideal. They'd completely adored each other, but their love had been steady and deep and calm. Fight? Never, not a cross word. They'd lived a rich, satisfied life, like two devoted fish on the bottom of the ocean. Shouting was the sound that had characterized her parents' marriage; her grandparents'—laughter.

That's what she wanted—if anything. Really, she was fine the way she was. But if she ever *did* have a chance for a partner, a life companion, God forbid it should be anyone like Henry Cleland. That would be like—like marrying her father.

Another huckster, another showman, just in a different field. *Please*, God forbid.

She might be an aging spinster, but she wasn't completely inexperienced, no indeed. She'd had a suitor once, a serious one, too—Abel Odenton, of Spears, Rank, & Odenton Insurance Agency; they had an office on the square and one in Springfield as well, so he was an "up-and-comer," or so he had often assured her. Maybe she should've married Abel. If anyone. Or someone like him: steady, even, safe. (*Safe*—an underappreciated quality, practically ridiculed in romantic novels, where the hero was always the risky, exciting one. How childish.) Abel, unfortunately, had had a disqualifying flaw she'd managed to rise above until the first (and last) time he'd kissed her: fishy-smelling breath. (Why? Why? Did he eat tuna every day? It had been like kissing Margaret.)

Henry . . . would be lovely to kiss. She even liked the smell of him. The way his hair fell. His strong, straight shoulders. His wrists. His sideburns. She could go on.

Obviously he didn't feel the same, although she would prefer to attribute other motives to him: he was too much of a gentleman to kiss her—he never mixed business with pleasure—he didn't feel he'd known her long enough. But she couldn't have it both ways. If he was the confidence artist she'd hoped for when she'd hired him, then he was unlikely to have gentlemanly scruples about something as frivolous and unimportant as kissing old maid Angie Darlington.

He simply didn't fancy her.

What a cruel irony. She got in bed, and when the cat crawled up to snuggle, she asked her, "How do people *ever* get together?" Margaret yawned, reminding her again—twice in one night—of Abel Odenton. "Why couldn't I have loved *him*? Why can't Henry love *me*?"

Pointless questions, the kind not to ask yourself right before trying to fall asleep. Anyway, this was no time to be distracted by a hopeless crush she'd be over as soon as Henry was gone. *Focus,* she told herself. *You've got a house to haunt.*

Mrs. Mortimer had already gone to bed when she'd gotten home tonight, but tomorrow, first thing, Angie would pop the question her landlady had probably wanted to hear all her life but never realized it: "Would you like to go to a séance?"

Ten

Henry liked Paulton. That was curious in itself—he was a big-city man, or so he'd always thought—but even more curious was that Paulton seemed to like him.

"Say, you're that ghost feller, aren't you?" Mr. Burt, the barber, asked him on Monday afternoon when he stopped by for a haircut. Three customers put down their newspapers to take a gander at him. He girded himself for skepticism, even derision—he was used to both—but all he got was curiosity and some good-natured joshing. By the time Mr. Burt slapped tonic on his cheeks and whipped the towel off his shoulders, everybody in the shop agreed it would be "a fine thing" if Paulton had its very own genuine, expert-certified haunted house.

It wasn't just at the barber's either. Everywhere he went, people were nice to him. After two visits to the Acorn, Home Cooking Fit for a King, he had a regular table and a waitress who called him by his name. On the street, men tipped their hats and women came close to smiling. His fellow boarders at Smoak's were friendly to a man, and Smoak himself never complained about his odd hours, or even about Astra. At first Henry thought all this politeness was because he was Miss Darlington's protégé, and the town was tolerating him out of respect for her. Eventually, though, he decided it was just that good manners were part of the Paulton civic character.

"How many people work for you, Walker?"

"Seven or eight, depending. More if you count my news-boys."

They were in the printing room, where a man was setting slugs at a Linotype machine and another man was jamming wedges into a printing press. The noise, that rackety-clackety click of metal striking metal, flung Henry back into the past like a slingshot. The smells of ink and hot lead almost made him dizzy, they were so familiar, and he'd missed them so much. He hadn't known how much.

"That makes you kind of a one-man band," he said as they walked back upstairs to the main office—what, on a bigger paper, he'd have called the city room.

"I guess it does. I'm the news editor, the managing editor, and the chief editorial writer."

"And the publisher," Henry reminded him.

"And sometimes the rewrite man and the copy editor. I'm the photographer when my regular man's too drunk." He flung himself into the chair behind his big desk, as if listing all his jobs had exhausted him. Reaching into a bottom drawer, he pulled out a bottle. "Care for a— Oh, sorry. Forgot, you're not a drinking man."

"No, but you go ahead."

"Not me." He put the bottle back. "Just being polite. Got a paper to get out tonight, and my lead reporter's down with the flu, or so he claims. I think he's down with the barmaid at Wayne's Tavern, but I could be wrong."

A rummy-looking old-timer at a distant desk looked up from his typewriter and chuckled. Another wave of nostalgia washed over Henry. Were all city rooms the same? All over the world?

"Circulation's up because we've got a Springfield edition now, plus Paulton's spreading out, getting bigger." Walker stuck his fingers in his thinning hair and pressed down on his skull. "Not enough hours in the day anymore."

Henry made sympathetic noises. An overworked managing editor was nothing new, but Walker looked done in. "You love it, though," Henry said to console him. "As tough as it is, you wouldn't be doing anything else."

Walker reached into another drawer, pulled out a couple of cigars, handed one over, lit them both with a safety match. They smoked for a while.

"Actually, I would."

Henry thought he'd heard wrong. "Would what?"

"Rather be doing something else. I inherited all this"—he swept the high-ceilinged, skylighted room with his arm—"from my old man. He started it, built it up from nothing. I just made it bigger."

"What would you rather be doing?" Henry asked, still in disbelief.

Walker sent him some kind of a look—measuring? shy?—and blew a smoke ring. "Something quieter. A journal, maybe."

"A magazine? Like . . . "

"Like . . . *The Century*, but with a focus on New England. Sort of a common man's *Atlantic Monthly*." He said that with a self-deprecating laugh.

"So, literary and political . . . "

"Topical, thoughtful. Progressive. Not stuffy. Some art, some pictures, but all grounded in good writing. It's just an idea," he said, waving his cigar in the air like an eraser, "one of my daydreams. Hits hardest around deadline time. Or when my wife tells me I'm never home and my son's growing up fatherless."

They talked a while longer—Walker did; Henry mostly listened—until Walker said he could do this all day, but he had to get back to work. Henry thanked him for the tour. They shook hands and said they should have dinner sometime.

Henry walked home wondering two things: why Walker had confided in him about his "daydream," and why any man would want to do anything else besides run a newspaper.

He slept over at Willow House that night. To perform more ghost experiments, he told anyone who was interested, but the real reason was to reconnoiter—explore the house's possibilities in preparation for the séance.

Lying in bed, he wrote down a few thoughts to run by Angie tomorrow—they were to meet in the afternoon and go over their plans. He missed her; he hadn't seen her since Saturday night.

Sunday she had church and whatnot—she was a Unitarian—
and today she had too many piano lessons to get away.

He'd caught sight of her once, though, yesterday on her way
to church, dressed in a plain gray skirt with a high-collared
blouse and a little black jacket. Prim-looking, if you didn't
know her. If you'd never seen the dancing ghost. She'd stuck
a clutch of yellow daisies in her hatband, and for some reason
that had made him laugh. He'd watched her from his window,
angling and craning till she was out of sight, thinking her out-
fit summed her up: perfectly proper but with flair. If she only
knew it. But then again, maybe that was part of her appeal:
the fact that she honestly thought she was plain. Somebody, or
maybe everybody, had put it into her head that she was an old
maid, so that was how she saw herself. Perhaps that made her
sweeter-natured, who knew, but still. A woman ought to know
herself better. Not to presume, but maybe he could help her out
in that area. No, no thanks necessary; it would be his pleasure.

He yawned, blew out his reading lamp. Miscellaneous
creaks and cracks he hadn't particularly noticed before sounded
louder in the sudden dark. MWS&G, he reminded himself—
the four main causes of all house-hauntings. Mice, wind, settling, and gullibility. But what accounted for that faint bubbling
noise that came from time to time and sounded like nothing so
much as laughter? Indulgent, delighted laughter, not the evil,
mustache-twirling kind. Well, it had to be something; unless
Angie was playing another trick on him, it couldn't really *be*
laughter. He probably just needed to add a P to his list of haunt
causes: plumbing.

The quarter moon would be mostly gone by Thursday,
luckily—the darker a séance room, the better—but tonight it
was sufficient to pick out the outlines of objects in the room.
The frame around the painting of a young Angie, for instance.
He didn't need to see the details; the picture was as clear in his
mind as if the light were still on. A sweet one to fall asleep to.

Wait. "What the hell?" He sat up, squinting at the mirror
over the bureau. No, that was impossible—surely he'd have noticed it if it had been there before. He threw back the covers and
got up to read.

'Til I loved
I never lived—Enough.

He knew the poem; even if he hadn't, the distinctive dash and that capital E would've given Miss Emily Dickinson away.

Not a very chilling message this time; you'd think the dead, dancing Lucinda would have more baleful sentiments about true love to convey. But why, why had Angie scrawled those lines, those *particular* lines, on his mirror?

The possibilities kept him awake for hours.

Astra barked an ecstatic greeting when Angie came down the basement steps—Henry had left the outside door open for her. He abandoned the saw where it was, halfway through a plank, and went to greet her, smiling, not even thinking about hiding his gladness. "You're late," he said. He took both her hands, a purely spontaneous gesture—it felt as if he hadn't seen her in days. "I haven't seen you in days."

"I know." She beamed back, color dotting her cheeks, while Astra ran around her in circles. "I almost called you on the telephone last night, but we wouldn't have had any privacy." Both Smoak's and Mrs. Mortimer's telephones were in their respective communal living rooms. "Oh, it's so nice and cool down here," she said as she dabbed at moisture on her upper lip with her hankie. She must have come on her bicycle. She bent over to kiss Astra on the nose—nothing else would stop his frantic welcome. "What are you making?"

Henry led her over to his basement worktable. "The séance table has to be round, so I'm making these sort of half-moon extensions out of some wood I found in the shed. What do you think?"

"Hmm . . . " She unpinned her hat and threw it on another table.

"Don't forget, I'm a ghost detective, not a carpenter."

"We'll put a tablecloth over it," she said kindly. "What room are we having the séance in?"

"Well, that's our first decision. Is the music room too small? Course, we'd have to move the piano."

"The music room? Why?"

"So we can use the secret stairs. Unless you think—"

"No, we can't—everyone knows about the secret stairs."

"I was afraid of that."

"Uh-oh. Does that ruin everything?"

"By no means. Plenty of ways to skin a cat."

"Henry, have you really done this 'many times'?"

He made a broad gesture with both arms. "What is 'many'? Isn't everything relative to everything else? In the grand scheme of things—"

"Henry."

"Hm?"

"Have you ever *been* to a séance?"

"Angie." He put his hand on his heart. "You wound me." There, he'd made her laugh, his favorite pastime. "Right, then, we'll use the dining room. Big room, big table, *and* it has two more valuable amenities."

"What?"

"A wainscoting, behind which it will be child's play to construct a sliding panel. Through the wall behind that alcove in the drawing room, which we can seal off with a bookcase."

She looked thrilled. "And the other amenity?"

"Your grandfather's ceiling trolley system."

"I thought of that! What will we do with it?"

"I don't know yet, but we'll think of something. By the way, can you make the elevator go up and down without being anywhere near it?"

"I've been thinking of that, too!"

They grinned at each other for a while.

"I need to hammer a few nails in the dining room floor. Is that all right?" he asked.

"Sure. Why?" '

"The floorboards squeak. There must be absolute silence when you're moving around the room."

"Will I be moving around the room?"

"I hope you're going to be dancing."

"Oh, Henry. This is going to be such *fun*."

He went back to sawing while Angie put on an apron that was too big for her, probably her grandfather's, and said she was going upstairs to oil the cable. "I've got an idea for the elevator, too. It might not work, but—"

"If it doesn't, it doesn't. We are nothing if not resourceful."

"And ingenious," she called back from the stairs.

"Versatile and adaptable."

"Clever and adept!"

Half an hour later, she returned, carrying a small wooden

box. "Look what I found in the attic." She opened the lid, and inside, a tiny porcelain man held a violin and a tiny porcelain woman danced with her arms over her head. A music box. "It was mine when I was little, a present from my grandparents."

"Does it work?"

"No, but I think I can fix it. It plays something from *La Traviata*. Which is 1850s, but I don't think anyone will recognize it."

"What do you mean?"

"Well, I was thinking we could say it was Lucinda's—it certainly *looks* old enough. And we could play it during the séance, say it's to help call up her spirit, but the real reason would be—"

"To cover up any noises we make. Brilliant!"

She laughed with delight. "I couldn't sleep last night, trying to think of a way to turn the gramophone on by itself. I thought of wiring it to a clock, or rigging it to some kind of dripping water mechanism, but nothing worked, and then I thought of this."

"Such a clever girl. How did you get so smart?"

She laughed again and started rummaging in a corner shelf.

"Seriously. Did your grandfather teach you?"

She turned around, holding a black metal cylinder. "He taught me to love playing with things, you know, physical objects, figuring out why they work this way instead of that way. And my grandmother taught me how to read."

"Not your parents?"

She studied him for a second. "I'll tell you something, but you can't repeat it to another soul."

"Not a word."

"I've never been to school."

"No!" He was surprised but not shocked.

"No time for it in Wild Johnny Darlington's Traveling Musical Theatre Extravaganza. So when I'd come home, my grandmother, who was a great reader, would take me in hand."

"And her favorite poets were Emily Dickinson and Elizabeth Barrett Browning."

"Yes!"

"Emily Brontë, too," he added, remembering this morning's message: "Whatever our souls are made of, his and mine are the same." If he'd had a pen handy, he'd have written back, "I *am* Heathcliff." She'd have laughed at that.

"How did you *know*?" she asked, all wonder and amazement.

"A wild guess." He grinned and wriggled his eyebrows, inviting her to confess.

"Oh, you saw the books in the library," she said, fiddling with the metal cylinder until it emitted a thin ray of light.

Henry lost his train of thought. "What in the world is that?"

"This? Oh, something I made. I sent in a patent application for it a long time ago. I called it a 'portable electric hand torch,' which in retrospect may not have been snappy enough. Titles can make a big difference—my grandfather taught me that."

"Let me see it."

"You slide this tab, and it presses against the band and switches on the light. It won't stay on very long; the battery's too weak. I'm working on a smaller, lighter one that would take a number six."

Henry flashed the light around the floor, the wall.

"I can imagine many uses," Angie said, "but one of the main ones would be finding things in a dark closet. Think of all the fires that have started with somebody holding a candle or a—"

"I can imagine an even better use. At a séance, after you've contacted the spirits and now they're trying to contact you. With a strange, unsettling beam of light."

Angie drew in her breath. "Of course."

"Rapping is old hat."

"Rapping's passé."

"But blinking—"

"*Blinking*. It's so much more—twentieth century!"

They whooped with laughter. "Oops." Henry almost knocked over a seamstress's dress form beside the worktable. "Beg your pardon," he told it, sending Angie off again. "What's this, a robe?" He lifted the edge of a soft, wooly garment covering the dress form.

"Actually, my grandmother invented that. She had an idea that people would buy something you could wear inside in cold weather. Not a blanket, not a robe, but sort of a combination of both. The sleeves leave your hands free."

"But you'd look so silly."

"That's what we told her. She was going to call it 'The Comfy.'"

They laughed some more.

"I have a question." Angie leaned back against the worktable and folded her arms. "Is everybody going to be holding hands at this séance? Because if so, I don't see how we're going to be able to do anything."

"Ah, but we will."

"Yes, but how? A false hand? Even if we stuffed a glove with cotton or something, it would never really *feel* like a hand, would it?"

She ought to look like a sexless child in that too-big apron, but she didn't. She looked adorable. He perched on the table beside her. Their hips bumped. "First of all," he said, taking her hand. The slim, smooth feel of it excited him; so did her low intake of breath when he nudged back the lace of her sleeve, exposing her wrist. "Such a clever hand," he murmured, then cleared his throat, trying to clear his head. "In order to call up a spirit from the other side, you need power, so at a séance you must act *in concert* as much as possible—act as one. To that end, the most propitious and effective contact between sitters is not hand in hand."

"It's not?"

"No. It's hand on wrist. Like so." He surrounded her small wrist with his hand, pressing gently, feeling the fragile bones. "This way, each can feel the other's pulse. The group's heart beats as one. The collective magnetism is liberated, and the force becomes . . . irresistible."

He bent toward her. "And then, if the medium momentarily breaks the circle"—he let go of her wrist—"because he needs his handkerchief, for example, or he must write something down, any excuse will do—to reunite the circle, he simply shifts a little, grasping his right-hand neighbor's wrist again"—he took Angie's wrist back—"while the neighbor on his left, thinking he—or she—is taking the medium's left wrist again, actually takes . . . his right."

Angie's face, so close, was a study in awe.

"And now the medium has a free hand with which to do . . . anything he likes."

And what he wanted to do was touch the side of Angie's face with his fingers, caress her soft skin, gently tilt her mouth to his and kiss her. But he held perfectly still. If either of them was breathing, they made no sound.

Then something wonderful happened. Angie slid her hand from Henry's grasp and laid it on his shoulder. Slowly, her eyes downcast, she moved her head toward his. Their lips met. So lightly. As if—almost—by accident. The moment held, stretched, until the flutter of her eyelashes undid him. He pulled her close with both arms and kissed her.

When he let her go, something—an excess of belated gentlemanliness, perhaps, although that seemed unlikely—prompted him to say, "I'm sorry."

"You . . . are?"

Too late to say, *No, that was a lie*, and instead he compounded the error by adding, "I shouldn't have done that."

She colored, looking away, and he remembered that she'd started it. "I'm the one who's sorry," she said.

"Well, what I meant—"

"No, you're right, seduction wasn't part of our bargain." She stepped away. "But don't worry, you'll still get—"

"Angie!" he said in alarm.

"You'll still get paid without adding *that* to your duties."

"Stop it, you know that's not—"

He froze: so did she. Footsteps sounded directly above them. *Who?* he mouthed.

My cousin, she mouthed back.

They couldn't be found down here, manufacturing séance props. Angie hid her portable electric hand torch in a dark shelf corner, and Henry shoved the music box under the workbench. The half-sawn boards were all right, nothing wrong with making the séance table round. But the dressmaker's form might make a good ghost, so he pushed it behind a cabinet and threw a burlap bag over it.

"Hurry," Angie urged. "Go."

He went ahead of her up the outside stairs while she switched off the light and locked the door, then raced up the steps after him. Astra, who had been dozing under a dogwood, jumped up to greet them, expecting a game.

"Now what?" said Henry.

She'd left a canvas bag on the grass. She found a pair of pruning shears in it and pushed them into his hands. "Now prune something. But not really! Just pretend."

"Thanks for your vote of confidence."

She didn't smile. He'd ruined everything.

She took a pair of garden gloves from the bag, knelt down, and started to weed under a rosebush. "Quick, before he comes out. You're pruning. You're helping me."

"Fine." He made a few snips in the air near a rose trellis. "But as soon as he leaves, you and I are going to have a talk."

Lucien's affection for Henry hadn't increased any since last they'd met. His doughy, vacuous face soured when he saw him pretend-clipping roses. "You," was his cordial greeting. "What are you doing here?"

"Lucien," Angie said, rising, brushing pretend grass from her knees. "Lovely to see you. To what do we owe the honor?"

He didn't even glance at her. "Why are you here? This property belongs to the Paulton National Bank. You're trespassing— you both are."

A futile stratagem, of course, and he knew it. When Angie said, "As you know, Lucien, Mrs. Grimmett very much wants Mr. Cleland to investigate the house—" he cut her off with a stifled oath and a slash of his hand. Frustration made his cheeks turn darker than their normal puce. Just the sight of Henry seemed to set him off.

"Investigate! You, sir, are a scoundrel. If you're thinking of profiting from my cousin's gullibility, think again. I'm on to your deceptions. My advice to you is to leave town before you're exposed for the conscienceless trickster you are." *Conscienceless trickster* was hard to say; it made a dot of spittle form at the corner of his lips.

It was quite an insult, too. Henry weighed the pros and cons of calling him out. Was dueling legal in Massachusetts? On the whole, it didn't seem worth it. If he'd been angrier, maybe, but it was hard to muster up enough indignation to take a shot at Lucien when half of what he said was true.

Angie was the furious one. Henry could imagine *her* smacking him across the cheek with her garden glove. "What have you come here for?" she demanded. "If it's just to insult Mr. Cleland, you can leave right now!"

"I'll leave when I'm good and ready." He smiled a smug

smile and reached into his coat pocket. "For you," he said with a little bow, and handed her an envelope.

She eyed it suspiciously. "It's been opened."

"It was never sealed," he corrected. "Mr. Wimrode works for the bank."

"Who's Mr. Wimrode?" asked Henry.

"He's my lawyer. *My* lawyer," she repeated to Lucien, whose smile only widened. "Why would he share *my* business with *you*?"

"Don't be silly, my dear. We're all just acting in your best interests."

If she was angry before, that made her livid. She almost tore the envelope in half to open it. A two-page missive, Henry saw by craning his neck, cover letter and short document. Angie's face paled. "Oh," she said and sat down on the garden bench.

"I'm sorry if the news disappoints you," Lucien lied, "but I can't say it surprises me. I never thought Uncle William's lawsuit ever had any merit."

Henry stepped in front of odious Lucien, as if he could shield Angie from him. "The bicycle pedal?" he asked softly.

She looked up at him, miserable-eyed. "He forgot to pay the maintenance fee on the patent application. It expired."

Having done his worst, Lucien took his leave. More false sympathy for Angie first, though, and then another warning for Henry. "If you really plan to go through with this absurd séance business, you'll be sorry. None of your cheap tricks will work here."

Thick-witted, unimaginative, acquisitive, capitalist blockhead. Henry let him have the last word and sat down next to Angie when he was gone.

"Everything's going to be fine."

"No, it's not." She put her head back and closed her eyes. She wasn't crying, but she looked as if she'd been mugged. "Even if the séance works and nobody wants to buy Willow House, there's no windfall now, no money coming. I have to face reality," she said, looking him in the eye. "I've lost my home."

He took her hands. "We'll think of something. We'll stall *longer*, and something will happen. You can't give up now."

"Does it seem like giving up to you? I've been fighting this fight for so long. I'm tired, Henry. I'm beaten."

"No, you're not." He shook his head, not letting her look away. "You've been fighting on your *own* too long, but now you've got me. And I'm not going to *let* them beat you."

The gold flecks in her eyes swam in a sudden river of tears. "Why?" she whispered, trying to wipe her cheek on her shoulder—he wouldn't let go of her hands. "Why would you want to help me?"

"Don't you know?" He wished she did, so he wouldn't have to say it. He wasn't any good at saying it. "This brings us back to where we were before knucklehead came."

She laughed wetly. He put his arm around her, and she let him, even rested her cheek on his shoulder. "When I said I was sorry for kissing you, I was, of course, lying."

"You don't have to say this. I know I'm—"

"Be quiet. Where I went wrong was, I mistook you for a different sort of girl. A conventional girl, if you can believe that. The sort of girl who would mind, or at least pretend to mind, if a man she liked a little bit tried to kiss her."

Angie lowered her head.

He touched his lips to her forehead. "What about it? Do you like me just a little?"

She heaved a sigh. "Oh, Henry. What a silly question. But I need someone . . . "

He was tired of chatting. He pulled her close and kissed her, a long, deep kiss, the sweetest he'd ever given or received. With his eyes shut tight, everything merged, the warm breeze, the perfume of roses, Angie's soft, unpracticed lips. "You need someone . . . "

"Completely . . . "

"Completely . . . ?"

Her eyes cleared for a second. "Different. From you. You are *exactly* the kind of man I don't want. Need, rather. I do . . . I do want . . . "

They could argue or they could kiss. They kissed again, and again, but then he had to say, "You don't know me. I *am* the kind of man you need; I just don't look it."

When she smiled, her kisses tasted even sweeter. "Oh, you look it."

"What if I were?"

"Were what?" She caressed his cheek with her fingertips, dreamy-eyed again.

"Someone you could—be with. Stay with. What if I were that kind of man?"

"But you're not, Baronet Spenser."

"But if I were."

"Oh, then." She took his hand and held it to her lips for a long time. "Then I would be quite the lucky girl, wouldn't I?" The faintest trace of sadness in her voice said she didn't believe it, though.

He surrounded her face with his hands and came so close, their noses touched. "Let's get this séance behind us and start over. Start all over—I'll leave town and come back. And everything I say will be the truth."

"Oh, my. Wouldn't that be something?"

Again, though, he could tell she didn't believe it. He'd just have to show her.

Eleven

Angie felt a raindrop on her wrist and quickened her pace. She was almost home, just two more blocks to Mrs. Mortimer's. Would a rainstorm be good for the séance tonight? Thunder would certainly enhance the dramatic atmosphere, but flashes of lightning might reveal too much. Such as the fact that a certain "ectoplasmic manifestation" was a ball of netting suspended from the ceiling trolley with wires. And many other ingenious phenomena, not the least of which was the fact that the dancing ghost would really be Angie in her nightgown, spookily illuminated by a portable electric hand torch.

Everything was ready. She'd just left Henry at Willow House tacking a black metal plate onto the toe of his shoe, the better to make rapping sounds under the table. Well . . . actually, she'd left him holding her in his arms and kissing her. Something they'd done quite a good deal of in the last two days. Quite a good deal. She was still in a daze from their good-bye embrace.

Never in her life, despite all she'd seen and heard in her profoundly irregular childhood, never in her least inhibited *dreams* had she imagined how enjoyable the . . . the pleasures of the flesh could be. Henry had made the *most* improper suggestion this afternoon, straight-out, no flowery figures of speech to dress up the blunt meaning. And instead of feeling insulted, she'd melted. Almost melted—she'd come to her dizzy senses at the last second and told him she wasn't quite *that* unconventional a girl. But that she wished she were.

They'd laughed—they did a good deal of that, too—but with a mutual edge of frustration this time. The situation couldn't go on. What kind of girl *was* she? What kind of girl was he turning her into? Shocking, but also thrilling, to think she might soon find out.

In front of Mr. Smoak's house, she was about to cross the street to Mrs. Mortimer's when Smoak himself darted out the front door and accosted her. "Miss Darlington!"

"Mr. Smoak! What's wrong?"

"Someone's broken into Mr. Cleland's room—he's been robbed!"

"Robbed!"

"I think so! Should I call the police? The lock on the door is broken, everything's tossed about—it must be a robbery!"

"Goodness. Yes, I suppose you'd better call them, then."

A little old lady of a man, Mr. Smoak rubbed his hands together, pink face crinkled with alarm. "This is terrible. Nothing like it has ever happened before. I run a respectable house!"

"Of course you do. Maybe it's nothing—an accident, a misunderstanding."

Mr. Smoak didn't look reassured.

Curiosity is a powerful motivator. Wasn't it what had inspired her grandfather to invent things? When Mr. Smoak trotted back into his house to call the police, Angie went around the side and up the back stairs. To investigate.

In truth, she'd always wanted to see Henry's room. Not like this, though. From the look of it, someone had used a crowbar to break the lock on the door, and inside everything was topsy-turvy, drawers open, bedsheets askew, his clothes thrown about willy-nilly. Papers everywhere. A burglary? But then why not steal his most, really his *only* valuable possession—his typewriter? There it was, a Caligraph New Special No. 3, sitting on the pine desk under the window. It still had a piece of paper in the platen. She went closer to read:

Should the Nation Own the Railways?

By Dexter C. Broome
(for Atlantic M'ly*?)*

and then a paragraph and a half about whether we should nationalize the rail system.

Who in the world was Dexter C. Broome?

She found more essays and articles scattered on the floor, all typed by the Caligraph: "The Irrigation Problem in the Southwest," by Seymour Bixby; "Great Plains Heroine," by Helen A. Buchanan; "An Afternoon at the General Store," by Billy Ray Bobbick. Even a poem, "Evening Falls Over the Hiawatha" by Miss E. L. H. And magazines and journals scattered about— *North American Review, Harper's Weekly, The Critic.*

Was Henry a writer? And if so, why did he use other people's names?

Not much else to see in the chaos. He used Dr. Caswell's Tooth Powder. His comb was missing several teeth. His only spare pair of shoes had recently been resoled. If he had any photographs of loved ones, they weren't visible, and she was not the kind of girl to snoop. Or so she told herself as she backed out of the room and tiptoed down the back stairs, not anxious to encounter Mr. Smoak again. Or the police.

She'd wanted to see Henry's room in hopes of unraveling the mystery of him, but all she'd done was tie it tighter.

"I'm not saying I don't understand the *attraction*," Norah Hersh murmured behind the cup of tea she held to her lips. "*Appreciate* it, even. Heavens. Look at him."

Angie was already looking at him. Maybe it was the way Henry had combed his hair tonight, straight back from his high, handsome forehead, that made him look not only magnificent (in her completely unbiased opinion) but also somehow Mephistophelian. She assumed the effect was deliberate, and that he knew what he was doing. Mrs. Grimmett certainly appreciated it—she was practically drooling on him. But then, so was placid, moon-faced Mrs. Mortimer. They had him cornered over by the fireplace, where Mrs. Grimmett was trying to impress him with her knowledge of the five different types of ghosts (apparitions, shadows, mists, orbs, and poltergeists).

Angie eyed the very slight bulge in his waistcoat pocket—no one else would notice it, she was sure. Inside was a glove, saturated with a mix of turpentine and pulverized luminous paint. When put on in the dark and then illuminated by a shuttered lantern, it looked like a disembodied hand.

They might or might not use it, though. The turpentine smell was still pretty strong. "We'll play it by ear"—they'd said that to each other so often, it was their mantra.

"I'm only saying—"

"I know what you're saying," Angie interrupted her friend. "That I should be careful. And that's good advice, but unfortunately it's come a little too late."

"Oh, dear. I was afraid of that."

"But you mustn't worry about me, Norah. Heavens, I'm older than *you* are."

"By six months. The point is, I'm older than you in *other* ways."

"The ways of *love*?" Angie raised and lowered her eyebrows the way Henry did.

"*Shh.*"

"Oh, who cares." She laughed, but then she lowered her voice so the threesome on the sofa—Edwardia Darlington, Chester Grimmett, and Norah's husband, Walker—couldn't hear. "I'll concede that you might have more . . . *hands-on* experience in that particular field." Norah had to giggle at that. "But I'm more sophisticated than you in other ways."

"You're an infant, my dear."

"No, I'm quite worldly."

"A child."

"Well, anyway—your advice has come too late. I've fallen in love with him."

Norah put her hands over her ears. "Oh, this is terrible."

"No, it's not. Why?"

"Because where can it lead? He's . . . "

"A ghost detective? He's not."

"What is he, then?"

"I don't know," she had to admit, "but it doesn't matter. After tonight we're starting over."

Across the room, Mrs. Grimmett looked at the watch pinned to her bosom and said something impatient-sounding to Henry.

"Norah, listen," Angie said quickly, "if you should notice anything odd or—*funny* tonight, if anything should catch your eye that seems . . . "

"Just say it. If I catch you faking some spirit manifestation, will I kindly keep my mouth shut?"

Angie blushed. "Just—you don't have to *lie*. I'd never ask that, and I don't want you involved in any way—"

"Don't be ridiculous. There are many things about this whole business I disapprove of heartily, but I would never, ever betray you."

Angie seized her friend's hand and squeezed it in gratitude.

Mrs. Grimmett looked at her watch again. "Where is Mr. Darlington?" she asked the room at large. "It's ten minutes past nine."

They had been assembled since 8:30, the séance to begin promptly at nine. Everyone was here except Lucien.

"I'm sure he'll be here any minute," Edwardia said timidly.

"Did he tell you he was going to be late?" the great lady asked.

"No, only that I should come by myself, as he'd be leaving from the bank. I should think he's just working late," Edwardia turned to say to Mr. Grimmett and was rewarded with an approving nod.

"I *suppose* we could start without him," Henry said, with admirably convincing reluctance, Angie thought. No one was looking at her, so she winked at him. His cheeks reddened faintly—her reward.

"But then we wouldn't have a number divisible by three," Mrs. Grimmett noted. "Do you think that would affect our powers?"

Henry frowned and *hmm*-ed thoughtfully. "In this case, I don't really think so, given the goodwill, the collective intelligence, the *intensity* of our group as it enters the harmonious and social spirit of fraternal intercourse and endeavors to promote the most powerful magnetic mode for which . . . "

Curses! A perfunctory knock, the squeal of the front door opening. Lucien appeared in the living room archway.

"Good evening. Sorry to be late, but something's come to my attention that I think you will all find quite interesting."

* * *

Angie had no idea what Lucien's interesting news might be, but as soon as he spoke, a terrible sinking feeling came over her. A premonition. She clutched the top of the wing chair, just for something to hold on to, her only thought a hopeless *Oh, no.* Henry—she wanted to go to him, but he looked white and frozen with the same dread paralyzing her. Lucien began to speak. She heard "drunkard," "knave," "philanderer," "habitual liar," but the words sounded like dialogue in a play, descriptions of the villain in a cheap melodrama. Not real.

Mrs. Grimmett's strident voice was like a slap in the face. "Mr. Darlington, please! You're a guest here, sir. How dare you impugn Mr. Cleland's character in this way? Unless you have proof, these insults are intolerable."

"I do have proof, madam. Indeed, I do." Lucien took folded papers from an inside pocket, and Angie's sinking sensation threatened to swallow her. "I have a report. From an agent, my good lady, a reputable person I employed to look into Mr. Cleland's, or should I say Mr.—"

"An 'agent'?" Mrs. Grimmett cut in, patrician lips curled in distaste. "A *detective*, do you mean? To investigate Mr. Cleland?"

But Lucien wasn't intimidated by her anymore. "Mr. *Wilde*, madam—his name isn't even Cleland! He's Henry Wilde, also known as Harry Wilde, also known as Wild Harry Wilde!"

Oh God, thought Angie. *Another wild man.*

"And he's not a ghost detective, he's a newspaper reporter. Or he used to be—he worked for the *Baltimore Sun* until a year and a half ago, when they fired him for stealing another man's work!"

Angie sat down hard.

"Born in Yonkers, father a railway conductor, mother deceased, one sibling, so on, so on . . . " Lucien turned a page of his report. "First job, copy boy for the *Brooklyn Daily Eagle*, then a junior reporter for the *New York Journal*, followed by two years at the *Boston Globe*—that's where he acquired his nickname. Hired at the *Sun* in 1891 as assistant city editor; worked there for three years, where it's well known he was often drunk, disrespectful of authority, and of a low moral caliber. In fact, numerous people swore he carried on a sordid 'love' affair with the fiancée—the *fiancée*—of a fellow journalist."

Gasps all around.

"And then, the coup de grâce. In '94, an investigation revealed that he plagiarized significant portions of a national news story on the Pullman strike, whereupon he was summarily dismissed!'"

Into the deafening silence Henry said, "I was framed."

Lucien continued as if he hadn't spoken. "Not long after that, Harry Wilde turned into Henry Cleland. For the last year and a half, he's made his dubious living as a confidence artist, preying on the hopes of innocent people and bilking money out of the credulous and unwary."

Mrs. Grimmett drew herself up. "Mr. Cle—" She faltered. "Mr. Cleland? You deny these claims, I'm sure?"

Angie wanted him to shout, swear, stamp his feet, excoriate Lucien—challenge him to a duel! But he did none of those things. He swallowed several times. He looked glassy-eyed, as if he'd been concussed but was inexplicably still standing. "Not all. I wish I could deny them all. I can't."

"No, he can't," Lucien gloated, "because they're true. The man's no better than a thief. He took advantage of all of us—I *assume*," he added nastily. "I can't speak for my cousin."

Henry seemed to wake up. "Angie knew *nothing* of this. I won't let you insinuate otherwise."

"How gallant," Lucien said with a sneer. "The fact that you lied to her as callously as you lied to the rest of us doesn't improve your case, though, does it?"

"It was you, Lucien," Angie realized, "you and your *agent*—you broke into Henry's room, didn't you? That's—illegal!" It was all she could think of to defend him.

"My man may have gotten a little too eager, but I never authorized him to do any such thing. Anyway, nothing was stolen, was it?"

Henry shook his head slowly.

"I can't believe this. It's outrageous." Mrs. Grimmett had sucked in so much air, she looked like a pigeon. "If what you say is true, Mr. Darlington, then we've *all* been duped."

"Has he taken money from you?" Lucien asked her hopefully.

"Certainly not."

"What about you?" He turned to Angie. "How much did *you* give him?"

"That's personal. And irrelevant," she thought to add, like a lawyer.

Mrs. Grimmett whirled on Henry. "Well? What have you to say for yourself? We're waiting." She was furious, but she was hurt, too, or at least embarrassed. She kept blinking, as if tears might form if she didn't. Angie knew exactly how she felt.

She'd never seen Henry like this before. He looked ill. He reminded her of someone . . . who was it? Oh, she remembered. One of the plays in her father's road show repertoire had been *The Tragic End of John Brown*. Henry looked like the John Brown character just before they hanged him.

"There's nothing I can say," he said, and on the first words his voice cracked. "Except that I'm sorry. Yes, I took advantage of you, and you didn't deserve it."

He turned from Mrs. Grimmett and faced Angie, who felt Norah's hand tighten on her shoulder as if to say, *Brace yourself.* "There are things in my past I'm not proud of. It's not an excuse, but I was young, just eighteen when I got into the newspaper business, and it's . . ." He reached out a pleading hand to Walker. "You know this, you can vouch for me here. It's a rough job, even rougher on a big paper, lots of drinking, and stupid dares, men behaving like boys—or like soldiers in wartime, because everything's so fast and intense, it's like—"

"Spare us your self-serving blather," Lucien butted in. "Is your name Henry Cleland? Is it? If not, are you or are you not a liar?"

Henry kept looking at Angie, no one else. "My name is Henry Wilde. Cleland's my middle name. But I never plagiarized anything. That was a put-up job, I swear."

"That's it?" Lucien asked, as if amazed. "That's your defense? You admit all the rest? You're a drunk, a philanderer, you seduced another man's fiancée?"

"Yes. I mean, no. I didn't 'seduce' her."

Angie stared at her hands in her lap.

"I got fired because this guy, this *injured party*, filed a story under my name that he swiped from another paper. For revenge. A frame, he even planted fake notes in my desk. But believe me, Angie, Walker—I swear, I never plagiarized. I *could* never."

Walker said nothing, and his face was unreadable. Angie remembered the articles and essays she'd seen scattered about Henry's room, all written by people with other names. Stolen?

She would never tell—they could torture her before she would tell anyone about those papers—but the evidence seemed damning. And he looked so ashamed. He looked destroyed. She wasn't sure whose disappointment in him hurt him more, hers or Walker's.

"I've heard enough. Come, Chester," Mrs. Grimmett ordered, and her husband dutifully rose from the sofa.

Mrs. Mortimer got up uncertainly. She'd fallen under Henry's spell, too; "Such a *charmer*," she would say whenever she saw him. She looked as if a beloved pet had snapped at her.

"Shame on you," Chester Grimmett said in a low voice to Henry—but Angie heard it because every one of her senses was focused on him. "You've insulted my wife. If I can think of a law you've broken, I'll prosecute you for it." And he followed Mrs. Grimmett out of the room.

Lucien and Edwardia left next.

When Angie stood up, Henry came toward her quickly, one hand up as if to stop her from leaving. She hadn't been going to. She didn't think. She really had no idea what she was going to do.

"We'll be out in the hall," Norah told her in a low, urgent tone. "Are you all right?"

Angie nodded.

Norah took her husband's arm. Walker's face was still a blank, but Norah's said if looks could kill, Henry would be stretched out on the floor, stone dead.

When they were gone, a new awful silence filled the room, and she wondered who would have the courage to speak first. Henry looked . . . so very guilty. At length, with a ghastly attempt at a smile, he said, "Where's a secret sliding panel when you need one?"

Another exquisitely painful pause. She couldn't help contrasting it with all the easy times, the banter and laughter, everything so natural between them. Good-bye to all that. "You don't owe me any explanations," she said eventually. "We both knew how this would end."

"What do you mean? I didn't. Angie, I'm sorry, I honestly thought I could save the house for you. That *we* could."

She hadn't meant that ending, but she was relieved that he'd misunderstood—now they wouldn't have to speak of it at all.

"It doesn't matter. Apparently I'm not meant to live here, that's all. It's not a tragedy."

He made a move toward her; she retreated.

He yanked on his tie, a habit when he was frustrated. "Christ, I've ruined everything."

"It really doesn't matter."

"Stop saying that. I *know* you're angry."

"Why would I be?" Although now that he'd said the word, she could feel the emotion. As if he'd opened a gate and gestured her through it. "I hired you because I thought you were a crook. Nothing's new, except now there's proof. Don't, Henry," she said when he reached out again. "I mean *Harry*. Mr. *Wilde*." She shut her eyes for a second. "Is anything you said to me true? Any of it?"

"No."

She turned to leave.

"But that's because I ran out of time! I was going to tell you my real name, my past, how I got into this stupid business—"

"I don't even care about that. I knew you were lying about almost everything. But Henry—*plagiarism*. Stealing someone's *words*. That's—the worst thing."

"Yes. And I knew you'd know it, too—that it's the worst thing. But I didn't do it."

She tried to laugh. "Why would I believe that?"

"Because it's true."

"That *one thing* is true?"

"Yes."

"How convenient."

"Could I explain? Will you listen to me?"

"No," she decided quickly. "I've listened to you enough. I'm afraid all you know how to do is tell lies."

"Well—hang on a second." He shifted his stance, moving from defense to offense. "Aren't you being a little selective all of a sudden?"

"What is that supposed to mean?"

"It means you were fine when I was telling lies *for* you; that didn't bother you a bit. And what about all the lies you told *me*?"

She opened her mouth, but then couldn't think of anything to say. "Very well. You're right, I'm a hypocrite. Does that make you feel better?"

"No."

"Henry, I can't do this anymore."

"Wait."

"I wish you luck. I bear you no ill will," she said with difficulty, and turned away.

"Angie, wait, don't leave. You must know—I'm in love with you."

Well, that was the final straw. Tears stung behind her eyes like vinegar; if she didn't go now, she would humiliate herself. "No, you're not. You just want me to not stop loving you."

He looked stunned. "You—you—"

"But it's too late. I already have."

"Angie!"

"Good-bye, Henry."

In the hall, Norah took one look at her face and said, "You're coming home with us."

Twelve

Henry woke up in his chair with a stiff neck and the bright sun in his eyes. Groaning, stiff-legged, he got up and walked to the bed, where he'd thrown his clothes last night, fumbled in his trousers until he found his watch, and cursed. How could it be ten thirty? Then he remembered: he hadn't fallen asleep till dawn. That was when he'd given up on a light ever coming on in Angie's room, or her shadow ever passing behind the drawn shade. Either she wasn't there or she preferred darkness. He couldn't decide which was worse.

He got dressed mechanically, without interest. Stared at himself in the mirror while he shaved and thought, *You look hungover.* Interesting. Who knew you could teetotal all night and still wake up resembling the corpse of a bloodhound.

Speaking of hounds, where was Astra? There, he saw through the window, curled up in the sun on the landing of the outside steps. His usual spot. Since he'd fallen in love, he'd taken to staying out all night, sleeping all day.

Henry's luck stayed bad when he encountered Smoak in the lounge, tidying up with a feather duster. At least the landlord didn't know anything yet, either that or he'd acquired tact overnight; all he said was, "You're up mighty late," and "Afraid you've missed breakfast by a mile," to which Henry responded with grunts. And Smoak wouldn't leave. Now he was running a damn carpet sweeper over the rug. Nothing for it: Henry would have to telephone Angie with an audience.

"She's not here," Mrs. Mortimer informed him, chilly-voiced.

"She's not?"

"Nope. She didn't come home last night."

That explained it. In the pause that followed, he heard all the disappointment, disgust, and condemnation with which he'd punished himself last night. But then Mrs. Mortimer said, "I expect you'll find her over at the Hershes'."

His emotions were raw; he couldn't speak for a second. "You're a very kind woman."

"Just a silly one," she said and hung up.

Norah Hersh was neither kind nor silly. "Yes, she's here. No, she won't come to the phone. Because she doesn't want to talk to you. No, I won't give her a message. Write her a letter, why don't you, and then go away."

He'd run out of choices. He took her advice.

Dear Angie,

I worked at the Sun *with a man named Finster. It's true he was engaged to the lady your cousin spoke of. I won't talk about her, but I promise that what passed between us was as much of a "love affair" as the one Astra's conducting with Lulu. But I take all the blame for it. Not my proudest moment, and it seems we reap what we sow. That's all. You won't care, but I had to tell you that anyway.*

Finster found out. We were up for the same job, assistant managing editor. While I was out on a story, he called in an op-ed under my byline, and they ran it the next day. Somebody cried foul, said it was almost the same as an editorial in the Cincinnati Post *a couple of weeks earlier, which it was. I recognized it myself. Great copy. Finster had laid his plans well, and his future father-in-law was the associate publisher. The rap stuck. I got sacked.*

Newspapering draws a lot of scoundrels, wastrels, drunks, and degenerates, and we tolerate them. We consider them color. What we don't put up with is copiers, at least not the egregious kind, and never at the high end of the profession or on the good papers. They're scum.

They get pitched out on the dunghill, and ever after their names are used as curses. If you love what you do, and I did, it's the end of you.

One friend stuck by me, name of Paddy, an old rummy who took pictures for the Globe. But his liver rotted out and he died, leaving me an inheritance: all his cameras and a dog with one trick.

Here's the funny part. Paddy had a not very lucrative sideline, cooking up photos of ghosts in haunted houses. You wouldn't think there'd be much call for that, but fakers have to get their pictures from somewhere, and in a lot of the Northeast, Paddy was their man. Then I was their man.

Only I took it further than Paddy did and became one of the fakers. More money in that if you do it right, although never what you'd call a gold mine. For a while I enjoyed what Lucien called "bilking the credulous and unwary." I was in a bad way, and it felt like getting in a punch of my own for a change.

What I liked best, though, was changing my name. I can't make you understand this, so I'll just say it. Taking my reputation from me was the same as killing me. I didn't do what they said, but it felt like I had. Hard to explain, but I felt as ashamed as if I'd done it. If booze is poison, I should've died, because God knows I gave it my best. But I couldn't even pull that off, so I did the next best thing. I disappeared.

Sorry, this must be tedious for you. I'll skip to the middle. By the time I met you, I'd given up drinking and started writing again, started sending pieces out under pseudonyms. To make a few extra bucks, sure, but also because it turns out I couldn't stop. So Lucien was right again—I am a newspaperman, not a ghost detective.

A lot of scurvy, defrocked journalists end up at the cheap papers, the kind with more pictures than words, or else they become press agents. I thought I was too good for that, but, wrong again. I'm tired of sinking. You probably don't want the burden of knowing it's because of you that I saw what I was turning into. So I'll spare you, and lie, and say it was my better nature finally surfacing. One thing is true: the thought of leaving you and going

back to my old life is like ice water in the face. I can't
do it. So I'll try for any job now, and I'll write anything,
tripe probably, under my own name.

That's it. I wish we could've gotten your house back. I
came to love it, too—I never told you that. I see you there.
I want it for you. These cameras are worth something,
the typewriter's almost new. They won't be enough, but
even a little money could be a new start. Since no one's
more resourceful than you, I don't count out the possibility. Especially if the dancing ghost returns to Willow
House some moonless night . . .

I'll never forget you. I'm sorry you can't believe the
main thing, the truest thing I said last night. That you
cared for me for a little while is the memory I'm holding
closest. My highest honor. The gift I don't deserve but
will keep with me the rest of my life. Be happy.

                                              Harry Wilde

Thirteen

Angie jumped off her bicycle in a billow of petticoats and exposed stocking—luckily nobody was around to see—and leaned the machine against a tree in front of Mr. Smoak's house. They should invent something to hold it up once you landed, a swiveling metal bar or rod you could kick into place, up or down. A kickstand, you could call it.

She knocked on Smoak's door with one hand while trying to smooth her wild hair with the other. How she must look. A fright, but she'd left Norah's in a hurry and raced all the way. Her hope was that Henry would be too glad to see her to notice her shortcomings.

Mr. Smoak, wearing an apron and holding an uncooked pie, opened the door. His sweet baby face crumpled when he saw her. "Oh dear, you've just missed him. He's gone."

"Gone?"

"Left an hour ago for the train station. He walked."

"He walked?"

"You won't catch him now, I'm afraid. He was taking the two forty-seven."

She sagged against the doorframe. "I see."

"Come inside."

"No. No, thanks—"

"He left you something. Please, come inside."

So in she went, weak-legged and empty-headed, and followed Mr. Smoak up to Henry's room.

"He threw a lot of stuff away, all them machines and thingamabobs for detecting, you know, ghosts. Gave me his barometer, but the rest he said is for you."

Oh, Henry. His cameras and all the tripods, lenses, plates. His typewriter! "Did he leave anything else? A note," she specified when Mr. Smoak looked blank.

"Oh. No, sorry, no note. Just paid his rent, whistled up his dog, and left."

"And . . . no forwarding address?"

"No, ma'am."

She must have looked alarmingly bereft, because all of a sudden Smoak remembered he had a pie to put in the oven and excused himself. He meant to be kind, but she had no desire to sit alone in Henry's room and think or pine or cry or whatever Mr. Smoak imagined an abandoned lady might do. She closed the door on Henry's heartbreaking legacy and went down the outside steps to the yard.

What to do? She couldn't think. To have come this close and missed him—she rapped her knuckles on her forehead in frustration, skewing her hat. *Idiot! You think you're so smart, and look what you've done.*

She had to find him, that was all. He'd go to Boston first—that's where the two forty-seven went—but then he might go anywhere, anywhere in the whole wide world, so she'd have to act fast. An ad in the newspaper? *Henry Cleland Wilde, please come back. A. D. was wrong about everything.*

Walker would help her. He had all those journalist connections. If anybody could track Henry down, he . . . he . . .

What was that *thing* that just streaked by? A blur of brown and white dashed through the hedges between Smoak's and the neighbor's yard. A cat, she'd thought at first, but no. No, now that she considered, it had looked more like a dog. Yes. It looked like . . .

"Astra!" A man's weary, irritated, out-of-breath voice. Henry's.

Everything tingled. Weird, because simultaneously, everything went numb. She could easily have let her knees give out and collapsed in the grass, prostrate from gladness. *A miracle*. Here came Henry, loping down Lexington Street with a bulging gladstone bag in one hand, empty dog collar in the other.

"Henry!" she called, and "Henry!" again, before he could burst through the hedge and disappear. She never wanted him to disappear again.

He heard her and skidded to a halt, twisting around slowly, pink, perspiring face registering hope and surprise. "Angie?" Oh, the way he said it, just her name. He thought she was a miracle, too! She picked up her skirts and ran to him. Cannoned into him—almost knocked him over. Talking would take too long; she wanted to *kiss* his amazement and disbelief away. He was the first to remember they were standing in full view of the world; they clasped hands and ran to the side porch, *their* side porch, and then it was time for words.

"I'm so sorry I doubted you! I never will again. Can you forgive me?"

"You read my letter?"

"You wrote me a letter? Oh, Henry."

"You couldn't have—I just mailed it."

"I'm so glad you wrote me! But, no, Walker told me."

"Told you what?"

"About that horrible man, Finster."

"What does Walker know about Finster?"

"Everything! Walker's been investigating you! Not with a detective, like Lucien, but by calling up and sending cables to his newspaper friends. He said he knew you were in the business almost right away."

"He did? How?"

"I don't know. Oh—he said what cinched it was when you said 'bulldog edition' while he was showing you around the *Republic*."

"Wow." She loved his bewilderment, his continued incomprehension. She felt like a god, a deus ex machina saving the day. Giving Henry back the thing he wanted most (after her): his reputation.

"Did you know he's been fired?" she asked rhetorically.

"Who?"

"Finster! No, you didn't know, because nobody could find you!"

"Finster got fired?"

"Yes, and you got exonerated, sort of, but nobody could tell you, because Harry Wilde had vanished!"

Henry fell back against a porch pillar. "Wait, Angie. Hold on. I'm not—"

"And it wasn't in the papers, unlike when *you* got fired, because Finster's future father-in-law wanted to keep it quiet to protect his daughter. Your, um, your . . . "

"Angie, you have to know—"

She flipped her hand. "I do know." She didn't know how, but she did. Finster's unfaithful fiancée, Henry's former . . . indiscretion, was not a person she needed to worry about, now or ever. "Walker says even though there was never a formal exoneration, *everybody* knows you didn't do what Finster said."

"Everybody knows?" Henry's eyes, just for a second . . . no, those couldn't be tears. But he swallowed twice, and he couldn't seem to speak.

"Everybody." She took his hands. "Do I have to call you Harry now? I don't mind. It's rather dashing, actually. Harry—can you forgive me?"

"Oh, Angie. For what?"

"For thinking the worst of you. I'm ashamed, Henry. I should've *known*."

"Well, I don't see how. I had a lot of sins to overlook." He stopped kissing her fingers and turned serious. "There's still one that's not forgivable."

"Impossible."

"I mean it. Because of me, you've lost Willow House."

"Are you going to marry me?"

His jaw fell, but she gave him credit for a fast recovery. "If you'll have me," he said, with all the devotion and enthusiasm she could hope for.

"I will have you. And then, for all I care, we can live in a tree house."

"Sweetheart." He kissed her so tenderly, she thought *she* might weep. "I couldn't agree more. Because wherever you are—"

"I know. Wherever *you* are—"

They finished the sentence together, a trick they would continue for years. "Is home."

Epilogue

"Nice hat."

Angie jumped. "I didn't hear you come in." She snatched off the flashlight she'd tied to the top of her head with a pair of garters. "I was trying an experiment."

"Very fetching." Henry crossed to the bed and kissed her. He smelled good, like newsprint and tobacco and excitement.

"You're early," she said against his lips. "Not even midnight yet. Did you put it to bed?" She liked using newspaper jargon. She was dying to say "bulldog edition," but so far the *Paulton Republic* hadn't done one.

Henry turned on the tasseled lamp and sat beside her. "Can't quite see it in church, though," he said, examining her flashlight-suspender contraption.

"I was seeing if it's any good for reading in bed."

"And?"

"Well, you'd have to shorten the cylinder, which would also make it lighter. But it struck me that the really important application will be for miners."

"Miners! Of course, instead of candles. How brilliant you are. Have I mentioned that lately?"

"Yes, but it bears repeating."

"And how clever I was for marrying a genius?"

"*I'm* the one who married a genius. You're the best managing editor the *Paulton Republic*'s ever had, and circulation's up to prove it. And that's just *one* of your innumerable sterling qualities."

"*Innumerable Sterling Qualities*—good title for my biography." He got up to get ready for bed.

"Your *auto*biography."

She tried to read a few more paragraphs from an essay on Mark Twain in *The Bay State Reader*, Walker Hersh's new journal. It was an interesting piece, but how much more interesting to watch her husband undress. He had such handsome shoulders. And what a nice, straight back. And, my, those long, strong legs, clad now only in drawers. All hers.

"What's this?" he said, leaning closer to the mirror over the bureau to read the writing on it—pretending he was just seeing it. His little joke. He also liked to pretend *she* wrote the messages on the mirror. Tonight's said:

Combination Rocking Chair/Butter Churn?

They alternated, the messages, between suggestions for inventions and love notes. She liked both, but the love notes were her favorite. Yesterday's had said, "Reader, I married him." Of course she'd recognized the line from *Jane Eyre*, her grandmother's favorite book. It wasn't Henry's, though, so how had he known of it? Oh, her husband was a man of many parts.

"Darling," he said, turning from the mirror, his eyes shining with tenderness. "What a beautiful sentiment. Elizabeth Barrett Browning?"

She blinked at him stupidly. "The rocking chair/butter churn?"

"The what?" He blinked stupidly back. Who knew how long that might've gone on, but just then Astra bounded into the room, followed by Eveready, the new puppy—named after the company that had bought Angie's portable electric hand torch. "Flashlight," they were calling it, and she had to admit that had a nice ring. ("Willow Light," she'd wanted to call it, in honor of the house it had helped to buy, but Eveready hadn't seen the marketing potential in that.)

"Was my dog door a good idea?" she wondered out loud,

far from the first time, while dodging sloppy kisses from both animals. They couldn't seem to absorb the lesson that the bed was not a legitimate part of their territory.

Henry tossed them both onto the floor (but so gently, no wonder they weren't getting it) and climbed in beside her. "Sure it was, especially after the patent comes through. How are you liking the *Reader*?"

"It's grand. Norah says they've already passed the first subscription quota. And Walker's so happy now—she says he's a different man."

"It's a fine journal. He should be happy. He's thinking of selling it, you know."

"The *Reader*? Walker wants—"

"No, the *Republic*."

"Oh." This was news. "But that's wonderful! Henry—we could buy it!"

"Hang on there, moneybags."

"Think of it: you'd have your very own newspaper!"

"It would be . . . "

"A dream come true!"

"Ye-es, but—"

"No buts. Let's buy it!"

"Sweetheart," he said, laughing, rolling over on top of her, sliding his hands under her shoulders and nuzzling her neck. "You scare me."

"I do?"

"No, not you. Our life."

She pulled away to see his face. "I *love* our life."

"Me, too."

"Then—"

"But we have everything. Willow House, your work, my work—"

"Don't forget each other."

"The best part. But you see what I mean? We already have everything, so how could we want more? It almost seems greedy. Like tempting fate."

"Since when do you believe in fate? You sound like Mrs. Grimmett. That reminds me. I got a note from her today, asking if I'd like to join the garden club."

They made amazed faces. "The power of the nouveau riche," Henry said.

"More likely the power of your irresistible charm attack. She couldn't take it anymore; she folded like a . . . "

"Like a gutless poker player."

"Like an accordion."

"Like a well-read love letter." Henry was so much better at words than she was. "Thank you, darling," he said, "but I think it was the ad rates I gave her husband's bank. So? Are you going to join the garden club?"

"Should I? What if we become pillars of the community?" She gave a mock shudder.

"What if we do?"

"Wouldn't it be funny? The ex-ghost detective and Wild Johnny Darlington's girl, leading the way in Paulton high society."

"Now *that's* supernatural. What was I saying? Before Mrs. Grimmett—"

"Something about tempting fate."

"Sweetheart, it's just that my cup runneth over already—"

"Oh, all right, we won't buy the *Republic*. Yet. But isn't it nice to know that we could if we wanted to?"

"Yes, Mrs. Vanderbilt."

"Not as nice as this, though." She squirmed under him, wanting to feel all of Henry on all of her. "This is very high up on our list of blessings."

"Possibly the top." He undid the buttons on her nightgown so he could kiss her between her breasts.

"I do love you, Henry," she said, while she could still think. (She'd tried calling him Harry, but it didn't stick. Except at certain *special* times.) "I wish I could tell you how much. Oh, I wish I knew the *words*."

He had the hem of her gown up around her thighs. "You did tell me," he murmured between intimate kisses. "You wrote it on the mirror."

"No, you did, you wrote 'rocking ch—' "

"Shh."

"You wrote . . . mmm . . . " She forgot what she was going to say. "Oh, Harry . . . "

Later, after the moon rose and the world was at its stillest, Angie pushed back the covers and padded down to the kitchen for a drink of water. She loved her house in all hours, but most of all in the thick of night, when its deep, benign silence wrapped her up like a comforter. Of course, sometimes there were noises. Creaks and cracks, nothing to be afraid of. Tonight that far-off, quicksilver sound that might be laughter played with her as she ran back up the stairs, holding up her gown in one hand, water glass in the other. It followed her back to her grandparents' bedroom—hers and Henry's now. It didn't scare her; it made her smile. *My house is so happy, it laughs.*

She stopped shy of the bed. Bluish moonlight slanting through the window picked out writing on the mirror. Quite a lot of writing. She *knew* it read, "rocking chair/butter churn?" but she went closer anyway, just to . . . to . . .

"Oh, Henry," she whispered, stricken with love. "Look what you did."

> I love thee with the breath,
> Smiles, tears, of all my life!—and, if God choose,
> I shall but love thee better after death.

Her heart turned over. All her life she'd wanted the sort of love her grandparents had, complete, passionate, fulfilling. *Eternal* love. And now it was hers.

In bed, she laid her head on Henry's chest and carefully arranged his sleeping arm around her. *Lucky, lucky me,* she thought, and drifted into a dream that began with the sweet, tickled sound of laughter.

Afterword

Alas, Emile Berliner, not Angie's grandfather, invented the gramophone disk.

I don't know who invented the self-tipping hat or the rocking chair/butter churn, but both have legitimate patents. Same with the pocket ashtray, the hat brim compass, the shoe-heel bottle opener, and the collar alarm.

Philip H. Diehl invented the first ceiling fan, and patented it in 1887.

The fly bat was invented by Frank H. Rose, but it didn't really take off until Dr. Samuel J. Crumbine renamed it the "flyswatter."

As for the flashlight, David Missell invented an early one around 1895, and sold it to the company that would later become Eveready.

Oh, if only Angie's grandmother had invented the Comfy! It would have predated the Snuggie by about a hundred years, and the Darlingtons would've been millionaires. Fortunately—this isn't in the story, but only because I ran out of room—while nursing the twins, Angie was playing with a piece of wire and accidentally invented the paperclip. Some people think it was William Middlebrook of Waterbury, Connecticut, but no, it was

Angie. That's how the Wildes got their wealth, eclipsing that of the Grimmetts by a mile. Henry and Angie's proudest moment came in 1917, though, when the *Paulton Republic* won the first Pulizer Prize for journalistic excellence. Not long after that, the town was renamed Wildeton.

Almost Heaven

Ruth Ryan Langan

To my beautiful daughter-in-law,
Patty Langan,
for planting the seed that grew
into this heavenly tale.
And to Tom, my heaven on earth.

Prologue

"Attention, everyone." Ted Crenshaw waited until the waiter signaled that every glass in the room had been filled with champagne. Copper Creek, one of the most prestigious private country clubs in northern California, was the perfect setting for this joyous celebration of the engagement of his only daughter, Christina, to handsome Mark Deering.

Drawing his wife Vanessa to her feet to stand beside him, the silver-haired man exuded wealth and success, and on this particular evening, great happiness.

He held aloft a fluted glass of Dom Pérignon. "To our daughter, Christina."

The young woman who was the object of his affection was seated at the other end of the oblong table and was positively glowing.

"And to Mark, who will soon be joining our family."

Mark Deering, charming owner of a successful Internet software company, had long headed the list of California's most eligible bachelors. No one was surprised that he had finally lost his heart to a woman like Christina Crenshaw. She was her parents' pride and joy. A brilliant student while at Harvard, with an MBA from Wharton, she had taken over an executive position at her father's company, one of the most solid advertising agencies on the West Coast. Under her leadership the company managed to land Lyon Entertainment, an account they'd been coveting for years. The future of Crenshaw Advertising looked even brighter with Christina leading the way.

Ted looked down into his wife's shining eyes before adding, "My only wish is that Mark and Christina will come to know the happiness her mother and I have enjoyed for the last thirty years."

While the others cheered and drank their champagne, Ted took only a sip before setting aside his glass to draw his wife close. "I don't need champagne tonight, babe. Nothing could make me happier than seeing those two together."

Vanessa brushed her lips over her husband's cheek. "I know what you mean. Look at them, Ted. They're so perfect together, aren't they?"

"You bet." He caught his wife's hand as the piano player started the last set of the night. "Come on. I want to dance with my best girl."

Watching them glide and dip in perfect rhythm, cheeks touching, eyes closed, Noelle Morgan, one of Christina's best friends since childhood, leaned across her escort. "I'm always amazed at your parents, Chris. Nobody their age should act like that." Her tone lowered with sarcasm. "My dad isn't even that goofy over his latest child bride."

"I don't know." Christina glanced across the room where her friend's father was whispering in the ear of the gorgeous redhead who had recently become his fifth wife. "They look pretty cozy to me."

"Give them time." Noelle's lips turned into a pout. "My dad's wives have a shelf life of approximately five years. Once they turn thirty, they realize they've outgrown him."

Christina was still laughing when her parents ambled over. She was on her feet at once, eager to hug them both. Ted and Vanessa drew their daughter into the circle of their arms.

"Happy?" Ted whispered against her cheek.

"You know I am, Dad."

"Then your mother and I are, too." He clapped an arm around Mark's shoulders, drawing him into the circle as well. "We need to get home now. Mrs. Mellon never falls asleep until she knows we're in for the night."

Christina smiled at the mention of the woman who had been

the Crenshaw housekeeper for the past twenty-five years. Both Mrs. Mellon and Bonnie Waverly—caregiver-tutor to her little brother, Tyler—had suites of rooms in the Crenshaw home. Blond, blue-eyed Tyler was called their bonus baby by her parents. Their late-in-life son had the face of an angel, but by the time he was three, they all realized something wasn't quite right. Now six years old, after having been examined by some of the finest specialists in the country, the family had been told that Tyler was a puzzle. He could be a high-functioning autistic, though he didn't fit the mold. He might also prove to be a nonverbal genius or just a very late bloomer. They were all patiently making their way through the maze that had become Tyler's personal challenge. Christina and her parents were actively involved in every aspect of the little boy's life. Though Tyler remained unresponsive to most of the things that went on around him, his family was convinced that they would eventually hit upon the key to help him live a normal, productive life.

Ted had a sudden thought. "Just because the party's starting to break up, it needn't end. If you and Mark would like to come back to our place, we can keep the celebration going a little longer. I'm sure Mrs. Mellon and Bonnie would enjoy the chance to offer their congratulations."

Christina nodded. "Oh, I'd like that. Maybe we could even wake Tyler and let him join us." She turned to Mark. "What do you say?"

He gave a pained expression. "Sorry. I asked a few of our friends to stick around." He turned to Christina's parents. "I hope you don't mind if we do it another night."

"Not at all." Ted kissed his daughter and then, in a moment of pure joy, drew Mark close for a bear hug. "Just take good care of my girl."

"You know I will." Mark leaned down to kiss his future mother-in-law's cheek before taking Christina's hand in his.

When her parents reached the door, they turned and blew a kiss, and Christina did the same.

As soon as they stepped outside, Mark led Christina toward the bar, where a number of their friends had gathered.

When a round of drinks was served, Mark reached into his pocket. The waiter shook his head. "Sorry, Mr. Deering. Mr. Crenshaw insisted that the entire evening was on his tab. Even the tip."

Mark glanced around with a grin. "Looks like my money's no good tonight." He lifted a glass. "Here's to Ted and Vanessa. My soon-to-be family really knows how to throw a party."

The valet escorted Vanessa to the car under the shelter of an umbrella. As he held the door, he glanced across to her husband, settling himself behind the wheel. "Be careful of these rain-slick roads, Mr. C."

"Don't you worry, Casey." Ted fastened his seat belt. "I've been driving this route for thirty-odd years. I have a lot of respect for what rain can do to hairpin curves. We'll see you tomorrow for Sunday brunch."

Ted put the car into gear and started down the curving ribbon of driveway.

Minutes later they were cruising along the highway that boasted some of the most expensive real estate in California. Multimillion-dollar mansions clung precariously to the sides of hills, looking as though they might at any moment lose their grip and slide into the jagged canyons of rock and pine far below.

Though she'd made this trip hundreds of times, Vanessa never tired of the amazing view. She sat back with a sigh of pure contentment. "That was such a grand party, Ted."

"Nothing but the best for our girl." He glanced over. "I wish they could have come back with us."

Vanessa nodded. "I know Tyler would have loved to share in the celebration for his big sister."

Ted pressed his foot on the brake pedal as they started around the first curve. Instead of slowing down, the car actually seemed to be accelerating. Surprised, he pressed harder. The car careened around the curve, swerving dangerously close to the edge of the road.

Vanessa grasped the door handle. "Darling, slow down."

"I'm trying to. The brakes must be damp. I've never had the car behave like this before."

Keeping both hands on the wheel, he managed to bring the car back to the proper lane, but no amount of pressure on the brake pedal could slow the forward thrust. By the time they'd rounded another curve, the car was speeding like a missile down the rain-slicked highway.

"Ted." Vanessa's finger was trembling as she pointed. "Headlights."

"I know, babe. I know." It took all Ted's strength to keep his car from swerving into the path of the oncoming vehicle.

As the headlights moved past, Ted fought to maneuver around the hairpin turn, but by now the car was traveling at such a rate of speed, it was impossible to handle. With a sickening jolt the car broke through the guardrail and plunged like a child's toy over the embankment.

Vanessa's screams mingled with the sound of breaking glass and twisted metal as the car continued down the steep side of the hill until it came to an abrupt halt against a tree. The sheer force of the impact sliced the vehicle nearly in two, sending shards of glass and metal shrapnel raining everywhere.

After the deafening sound of the crash, an eerie silence settled over the land, broken only by the steady patter of the rain.

One

"Ted? Oh, Ted, darling, where are you?" Despite the horrible events of the past minutes, Vanessa's voice sounded as strong as ever.

"Here, babe." Ted, too, showed no sign of the trauma he'd just endured, his voice low and deep and filled with gratitude that his wife was able to call to him.

"Oh, thank heaven. For a minute I thought . . . " Vanessa glanced down at the scene of twisted wreckage, then caught sight of the mangled, bloody body lying on the passenger side, still held firmly in place by her seat belt.

The front and side airbags had inflated before having been shredded by tree limbs, looking like giant balloons with the air gone out of them, swaying gently in the breeze that blew through the shattered windows.

Vanessa pointed. "That woman looks like me."

"And that guy looks an awful lot like me." Ted indicated the lump of bloody flesh trapped behind the twisted steering wheel. The driver's section of the car gave a sickening lurch before sliding farther downhill until it came to rest several hundred yards beyond the rest of the wreckage.

"Oh, darling. I don't understand. What's going on here?"

Vanessa reached for her husband's hand, needing the comfort of his touch to assure that she wasn't hallucinating.

He drew her close, wrapping his arms around her, before glancing over her head to where the two bodies still lay. Against her temple he whispered, "I can't be certain, but I believe we're dead."

"Don't be silly. We can't be." She pushed a little away to look up into his familiar, beloved face. "If we were dead, would we be able to speak and think and feel? I can feel your arms, Ted." She tightened her grasp. "Can you feel mine?"

"I can." He gave her one of his rogue smiles. "And you feel really good, babe."

"So do you." She couldn't hold back the little sigh. "So. What do you make of this?"

"There's no denying that our bodies are there in that wreckage."

"If that's so, why aren't we . . . gone?"

"I don't know. I guess it means we're still us, only . . . different." He took in a deep breath, struggling with dozens of conflicting emotions. But the one that seemed stronger than all the others was an overwhelming sense of peace. Of knowledge. Of acceptance that everything was as it should be. "It means, I think, that we're now in the spirit world."

"And this is it? This is all there is to dying? Just . . . stepping outside ourselves?"

He shrugged. "I don't know. I guess I thought there'd be rays of white light. And angels. Or guides of some sort, to show us what was expected and how to behave in this new place."

"You rang?" The woman's voice came from directly beside them, though it took them a moment to see her.

When they did, Ted gave an excited shout. "Gram!"

"Hello, Teddy. My, haven't you grown up to be a fine, handsome fellow. I was allowed to see you occasionally, so I'm not at all surprised. You see, I was one of your angels during your lifetime."

He kissed her cheek, marveling that she hadn't aged since he'd last seen her more than forty years earlier. In fact, she was as lovely as the portrait of her as a young debutante that hung in his office. "I thought I saw you once, when I was dreaming."

"You were troubled. It was during that time when the doctors were running all those tests on little Tyler, and I wanted to comfort you."

"I remember waking up and feeling at peace with everything. Thank you."

"You're welcome." She dropped an arm around his shoulder. "I was gone before you and Vanessa married, so we've never been formally introduced."

"Gram, this is my wife, Vanessa. Darling, this is my father's mother, Sarah Graham Crenshaw."

"How nice to finally meet you." After hugging her, Vanessa held out her left hand. "I've been wearing your ring on my finger since the day I married Ted. I feel as if I've known you all my life, Gram." Vanessa smiled. "I hope you don't mind if I call you that? It's what Ted always called you when he spoke of you. And always, I might add, with great affection."

"The feeling is mutual." Sarah Crenshaw dropped a hand on the younger woman's shoulder. "I was always so pleased that you wanted to wear my ring. My Thaddeus gave me that ring the day we wed, and it never left my finger until the day I passed into this other world." Her tone warmed as she turned to her grandson. "Welcome to the other side. I've come to escort you and your lovely wife to your eternal reward."

"Wait." Vanessa looked back at the twisted wreckage; the bloodied, mangled bodies. "Ted, darling, think of the pain this will cause Christina. This should be the happiest time of her life. Instead, she'll be grief-stricken over her loss, as well as overwhelmed by all the details. And then there's the care of little Tyler." She turned to Ted's grandmother. "Is there any way we can stay around and ease our daughter through this horrible time?"

Sarah smiled. "As a matter of fact, yours is not an unfamiliar request, Vanessa. Often, when someone dies unexpectedly, there's a great deal of worry about the well-being of the loved ones who are left behind. If requested, a grace period can be granted between the former life and the hereafter. Otherwise, there would be many souls who wouldn't be able to properly enjoy their eternal reward. And, as you'll soon see, it's meant to be enjoyed."

Vanessa exchanged a look with her husband before turning to Sarah. "We can wait? Here on earth?"

"Of course."

"Oh, thank you, Gram." One wet tear rolled down Vanessa's cheek. "I'm sure we won't need more than a couple of days. Just enough time to get Christina and Tyler through the funeral. Thank heaven that little Tyler has his big sister to get him through this."

"And thank heaven," Ted added softly, "they both have a strong, loving man like Mark to lean on."

"Yes. Mark." The older woman's words became clipped. "I must warn you. There are certain rules by which you must now abide. Though you can see and hear, you can no longer be seen or heard by those on the other side. Furthermore, you cannot physically intervene with the free will of those still living."

Vanessa's brows lifted. "Intervene? Why in the world would we want to do that?"

"You are apt to see things that may displease you or annoy you or upset you."

Ted winked at his wife before turning to Sarah. "That might be true in some families, Gram, but not in ours. You've had a chance to see Christina. You know what an amazing young woman she's become. And little Tyler. There's an innocence in him that can't be denied."

Sarah sighed. "Be that as it may, I must warn you that however much you may try to persuade earthly creatures to get involved in solving the problems that you see from this side, you may use only peaceful means. No matter what you see or hear, no matter what you learn about those still living, you cannot resort to violence."

"Violence?" Ted grinned. "Gram, why would we even consider such a thing?"

"Just so you understand the rules." His grandmother touched a hand to his arm. "You may want to ask for more than a few days before you join me."

"I'm sure a levelheaded girl like Christina will be able to pull it together in a matter of days." Ted looked over, but his grandmother's image had begun to fade to a pale, shimmering light until even that gradually disappeared, and she was gone as quickly as she had appeared.

Drawing his wife into his arms, Ted brushed a kiss to her cheek. "Silly rules, if you ask me. We can watch but can't touch. We can interfere but can't intrude on free will. I'm not sure I like being . . . one of them."

"Not that it matters what we like, Ted." Vanessa sighed. "At least we can take comfort in the fact that our family will be taken care of now that we're gone."

"You bet." Ted lifted his head. "I hear sirens. Brace yourself, babe. I think someone has spotted the wreckage. Once they learn the identities of the victims, Christina is in for a shock. It's not going to be easy to stand by and watch her grieve."

"Thank you, Mrs. Mellon." Christina accepted a cup of strong, hot tea from the housekeeper, whose eyes were as red-rimmed as her own.

"You should get some rest, Miss Christina."

"I will. Soon." Christina, drained by grief, glanced at her little brother, who was standing by the big windows, watching as the last of the mourners' cars headed down the long, curving driveway.

The old woman turned to Mark, who hadn't left his fiancée's side since they had first heard about the fatal accident. "She's had a long day, Mr. Deering. If she won't sleep, at least coax her to get off her feet for a little while."

"Right." Mark steered Christina to an overstuffed chair and settled himself on the ottoman before lifting her feet to his lap. Without a word he removed her shoes and began massaging her feet.

Setting her cup of tea on a table beside her chair, Chris let her head fall back, forcing herself to relax. With her eyes closed, she said, "It was a beautiful service, wasn't it? Reverend Henderson gave such a lovely eulogy. Did you know that he presided at my parents' wedding?"

"He told me."

"And the articles in the *Dispatch*, in the *Times*, and even in our local *Gazette*. All of them said such kind, loving things about my parents."

"And why not? They gave generously of their time and money to so many charities."

Christina made a mental note to send additional checks to the food bank and the women's shelter that had become her mother's favorite causes. She would embrace them as hers now.

Mrs. Mellon bustled into the room and set a tray of tea sandwiches on the coffee table. "I noticed that you were too busy with the guests to think about food, Miss Christina, but now that you're alone, you really should try to eat something."

Chris caught the older woman's hand as she straightened. "And who's going to see that you eat or rest, Mrs. Mellon?"

The housekeeper wiped at a sudden tear. "You're so like her, you know. Your mother was always looking out for everybody but herself."

Without warning, this stoic woman, who had directed a staff of servers through the long day of the viewing in the formal parlor and the luncheon that had followed the funeral, now burst into tears. Horrified, she tried to turn away, but Christina was on her feet at once and drawing the older woman into her arms.

"I can't believe they're gone." Mrs. Mellon's words were muffled against Christina's shoulder.

"I know." Chris smoothed the woman's hair, absorbing a quick shaft of pain. "It doesn't seem possible."

"I didn't want to cry. Especially in front of you. You've been so strong."

"Me? I've shed buckets of tears. It's all right to cry, Mrs. Mellon. You miss them. We all do."

"How will we go on without them?"

"I don't know." Chris reached into her pocket and withdrew a lace-edged handkerchief. "You've been such a comfort to me, Mrs. Mellon. And to Tyler. We couldn't have gotten through this without you."

"I did what I could." The woman blew her nose and stepped away. "I need to stay busy."

"I know. I feel the same way. I don't want to stop and let myself think about what I've lost." Christina glanced over at her little brother, still standing silently by the window. "What we've all lost."

The housekeeper sniffed, dabbed at her eyes, and turned away. "The catering people have probably finished up in the kitchen by now. They'll be wanting a check."

Christina nodded. "I left it on the desk in the library."

"Don't bother yourself. I'll see to it."

When the older woman was gone, Mark dropped an arm around Christina's shoulders. "I agree with Mrs. Mellon. The best way to deal with grief is to stay busy. If you don't mind a suggestion, darling, I think you should get back to your routine as soon as possible."

"I suppose." Distracted, Chris picked up her tea. Sipped.

"That's my girl." Mark crossed to the fireplace and rested an arm on the mantel. "The sooner you return to your apartment in the city and tend to your father's business, the better you'll feel. And when you feel like crying, I'll be there with a strong shoulder. I promise."

"Thanks, Mark." Chris gave a long, deep sigh. "You're right, of course. Routine would be good for me. For all of us."

"Good." He started across the room. "Since you agree, I'll get the car."

When he was gone, Christina set aside her tea and studied her little brother. He hadn't moved from the window. What was he looking at? she wondered.

"What do you see, Tyler?" She crossed to him and dropped to her knees, so that they were eye to eye.

His tutor, Bonnie, stepped into the room and crossed to them but remained silent, watching and listening.

Outside, Christina could see Mark's vintage Corvette just rounding a corner, coming into view. For the funeral, he'd left it in the family garage, choosing to ride with her in the limousine. Now, with the top down and his pale hair tousled by the breeze, cell phone to his ear, he looked younger, more at ease than he had in days.

Thank heaven for Mark. He'd been her rock. Her pillar of strength.

Tyler, she realized, wasn't watching Mark. He was looking beyond him, as though waiting for something. Or someone.

Of course.

When the truth dawned, Chris felt as though she'd taken a knife to her heart.

She turned to Bonnie Waverly, who looked as sad and forlorn as the little boy.

Tears filled Christina's eyes as she gathered her little brother close and buried her face in his hair. "Oh, Tyler. They're not coming back."

Though he stiffened slightly, he made no sound.

His silence made her tears flow all the harder. "I know who you're watching for, baby. But you won't see them." She wondered that her poor heart didn't simply break from the pain that washed over her in waves as she forced herself to speak the horrifying words aloud. "Mom and Dad are gone for good, Tyler. And we're never going to see them again."

Mark strode into the room to find Christina still holding her little brother in her arms, sobbing gently against his hair.

She lifted her tear-stained face. "I'm sorry, Mark. I won't be going back to the city with you tonight."

He stepped closer, barely keeping his impatience in check. "Look, I've already been here more days than I'd expected. I really need to get back."

"I know. I understand. You have a business to run. But you'll have to go without me. Tyler needs me here."

"He has Bonnie and Mrs. Mellon."

"Yes, he does. And he has me."

"You're forgetting. I'm not the only one with a business to run. You're now in charge of your father's company. How long do you think it can flourish without a strong, steady hand at the helm?"

"We have good executives, Mark. They're loyal to me, just as they were to my father. They'll cover for me until I'm ready to return."

"And how long do you intend to hide out here?"

Was that what she was doing? Hiding from the truth? Hiding from the horrible loss of the two most important people in her life?

Though the words stung, she chose to ignore them. "I don't know. I only know that I need to be here with Tyler as much as he needs me here."

She looked up as the housekeeper paused in the doorway, holding an overnight bag. "I won't be needing that after all, Mrs. Mellon. I've decided I'm not ready to leave yet."

For the first time in days, the housekeeper's eyes lit with a smile. "I'm glad you're staying. Tyler needs you. And so do I."

The older woman glanced at Bonnie, who nodded her agreement. "She's right. We need you here a while longer."

"It's settled then."

Christina kept her little brother's hand firmly in hers as she got to her feet and started across the room. "Good-bye, Mark." She brushed a kiss over his cheek. "I'll call you tomorrow, when I've had time to think."

"You know I don't like being apart for even one night." He closed his hands over her upper arms and gave her a long, slow kiss. Then he stepped back and managed a smile for Tyler, and another for the two women who were watching, before turning away.

As he started out of the room he called, "But I suppose another night won't make much difference."

Christina watched as he strode away. When the door closed behind him, she thought about his words. He was right, she supposed. What difference could one night possibly make? Wouldn't she be just as sad and just as lost tomorrow as she was tonight? Still, one look at her little brother's haunted eyes and she knew she'd made the right decision. For now, for this night, she would do what she could to bring him comfort.

She'd deal with tomorrow's pain tomorrow.

TWO

"We'd like to stay here a few more days, Gram." Ted Crenshaw kissed his grandmother's cheek. "Vanessa and I aren't ready for eternal happiness yet. I guess we weren't prepared for so much chaos in our children's lives."

"Grief-stricken, are they?" The old woman looked from her grandson to his wife.

"Deeply." Ted drew an arm around his wife's shoulders. "It doesn't help that Tyler has no way to communicate his feelings. But Christina is doing all she can to reach him. What worries us is the way she's dithering. One day ready to pick up the pieces of her life, the next wanting to do nothing more than walk the gardens with her little brother. It isn't like her to be so indecisive."

"She's suffered a life-altering blow, Ted. It takes time for mortals to sort things out."

"If she waits too long, we're both afraid she's going to drive Mark away." Vanessa caught the older woman's hand. "Would it be possible for us to take a few more days here? Just until Christina gets her bearings?"

Sarah Graham Crenshaw smiled gently. "I've been authorized to tell you to take as long as you wish."

Her image seemed to glow like the sun before fading completely.

"Miss Christina." Mrs. Mellon paused in the doorway of the library.

Chris looked up from her father's desk, where she was busy recording checks in a ledger. "Yes?"

"I just saw Mr. Deering's car pulling up the drive."

Before Chris could stow the ledger, Mark strode along the hallway and paused behind the housekeeper. She stepped aside, and his tall figure seemed to fill the doorway.

His tone was incredulous. "Now what's this about hiding out here in your parents' place indefinitely?"

"Mark." Chris rounded the desk and flung her arms around his neck. "You didn't have to drive all this way. I thought I'd made myself clear on the phone."

"Clear as mud. You're giving up your apartment in the city? You actually think you can run your father's complex company from an office here in your family home? Come on, darling. Get a grip. That doesn't make any sense, and you know it."

"It makes perfect sense to me." She caught his hand and led him toward the leather sofa across the room. "Sit here and let me tell you what I've been thinking."

Mrs. Mellon cleared her throat. "Would you like me to make some tea, Miss Christina?"

Chris turned. "Yes, please. That would be nice." She glanced at Mark. "Have you had lunch?"

He nodded. "On my way up here. But I could use a vodka and tonic."

The housekeeper crossed the room to the wet bar and began fixing the drink. When he took a seat on the sofa, she handed him a crystal tumbler before hurrying from the room.

While Mark sipped his drink, Chris paced in front of him. "Every night, when Bonnie and I tuck Tyler into bed, we see him looking past us toward the doorway. We've talked it over, and we both feel that he hasn't grasped the fact that Mom and Dad are gone for good. He thinks they're off on a trip. He still expects to see them coming in to kiss him good night."

"That's natural enough. He's just a kid. He'll get used to it, in time."

Chris sighed. A long, deep sound that rose from the depths of her soul. "I know, Mark. But you can't imagine the pain I feel when I see my little brother watching for someone who's never going to come into his room again."

"Look." He set aside his drink and caught her hands in his, drawing her down to sit beside him. "I know Tyler isn't like other kids his age. I realize that he requires a lot of extra care. But he has an expensive tutor and caregiver in Bonnie, and he also has Mrs. Mellon. They were good enough for him when your folks were alive. Now that they're gone, you're acting as though you have to hover around him every minute of the day, just to get him through his grief. But in fact, you're not even certain he is grieving. For all you know, he's off in some fantasy world, waiting for fairy dust to land on his shoulder."

"Don't, Mark. Don't make light of this." She placed a hand on his chest and pushed a little away. "I may not know exactly what's going through my little brother's mind, but I can see that he's suffering, and I want to help."

"You're suffering, too." He lowered his voice. "And I want to help you."

"Then try to understand that I need time to work through all this."

"Take all the time you need, darling. But in the meantime, I suggest we move up the date of our wedding, so that I can properly take care of you and Tyler the way only a husband can."

"That's sweet." She paused while Mrs. Mellon walked across the room to place a silver tray on a side table.

"Shall I pour, Miss Christina?"

Chris shook her head. "Thanks, Mrs. Mellon. I'll do it."

She crossed to the table and filled a cup, taking time to squeeze a wedge of lemon into her tea.

When they were alone, she turned to Mark. "In fact, I've been thinking of postponing the wedding for a while." At his sound of disgust she added quickly, "It simply isn't possible for me to make wedding plans while my life is in such turmoil."

"Just like that?" He tossed back the rest of his drink and got to his feet. "Without consulting me, you've decided to cancel all our plans?"

"It's only for a while, Mark. Just until things settle down in my life. How can I possibly think about designer gowns, caterers, wedding lists, celebrations, at a time like this?"

He walked to her and smoothed a hand over her hair. His tone lowered to a whisper. "I'm not some insensitive clod. I know how devastated you are at the loss of your parents. Why don't you think about this instead? Forget about the extravagant wedding your parents had planned for you. Instead, we'll have a simple morning ceremony before Judge McShane. He's an old friend of your family. I'm sure he'd be happy to choose a time in the next few weeks when he could fit us in. Then we'll wait to celebrate the happy event with family and friends at a more appropriate time, after you and Tyler have had time to get past your grief."

"You'd do that for me? Forgo the fancy ceremony and the celebration we'd planned?"

"You know I would. All I want is your happiness, darling."

Tears sprang to her eyes. She pressed her hands over her face, muffling her voice. "Let me think about it, Mark."

"Of course." He gathered her close. Against her temple he muttered, "All I want is your happiness. I want to help you. And I can't think of a better way than by being a permanent part of your life. Promise me you'll give my idea some serious thought."

She drew in a deep, shuddering breath. "I will. Thank you for understanding and for being so patient. Can you stay for supper?"

"Sorry. I've already had to shuffle several appointments today. I'll be playing catch-up the rest of the week." He kissed her before turning away. In the doorway he paused. "I'll call you later today. I hope by then you'll have had a chance to speak with the judge and you can give me your answer."

She nodded and blew him a kiss.

As his car started down the drive, she turned to find Tyler sidling up beside her to stare out the window. With a smile Christina dropped an arm around his shoulders and waved until Mark was out of sight.

"Tyler is lucky to have such a loving sister." Ted watched with satisfaction as Christina led her little brother outside to the garden, where they stood together in the dappled sunshine.

"You're right. But I wonder if we haven't placed too much of a burden on her young shoulders."

"What do you mean, babe? Look at her. She's doing all the right things, putting her own happiness on hold while watching out for Tyler."

"That's just my point. If she isn't careful, Ted, she's going to lose Mark. You can sense his frustration." Vanessa pointed to a distant vision of Mark taking the hairpin curves of the highway at a dangerous speed.

"You heard him. He understands Christina's need to look out for Tyler. In fact, I like his suggestion that they have a small, private wedding now, and wait until later, when Christina is more settled, to celebrate with family and friends."

"Maybe." Vanessa crossed her arms over her chest and began tapping her foot, a sure sign that the wheels were turning in her brain. "I sensed a real tension in him. Didn't you?"

Ted's eyes narrowed. "Now that you mention it, I did."

"Christina has been so caught up in her grief and in Tyler's confusion that she may be completely unaware that Mark is grieving, too. After all, we were the only family he had. He often said that he loved us so much he actually thought of us more as parents than future in-laws." Vanessa caught her husband's hand. "Let's drop by his place in the city and see if we can't offer him some comfort."

As they passed through the walls of their familiar home, Ted grinned at his wife. "You know, there's something to be said for this kind of travel."

Her smile was as bright as the sunlight. "It beats the freeway."

"I'm not taking any calls, Joanna." Mark never even paused at the desk of his assistant before closeting himself in his office. Once there he stared morosely at the stack of papers on his desk before picking up the phone.

"Henderson? Mark Deering here. I know. I know. You're going to have to wait a while longer for that check. But it'll be there before the deadline. You have my word on it."

He paused, listened, then said dryly, "How about if I add a ten percent late fee? Will that satisfy you?"

Again he listened before saying, "All right. We'll do an electronic deposit. As soon as I have the funds available, you'll hear from my banker. The end of the month at the very latest."

As soon as the call ended, he dialed again, saying almost the same thing to someone named Julian. While he promised full payment of his debt, Mark looked up as a knock sounded on the private entrance to his office. Cutting short the call, he set down the receiver and hurried across the room.

"Mr. Smith?" The man speaking wore a grease-stained mechanic's uniform with a faded yellow company logo on the pocket. Dark hair hung to his shoulders.

"Come in." Mark closed the door and crossed to his desk. Unlocking the drawer, he removed an envelope and handed it to the stranger.

The man counted the money quickly before pocketing it.

Mark followed the man to the closed door. "You did a good job."

"Told you I would. I was the head mechanic in the joint."

"I can see why. As I told you earlier, I want no further contact between us. Understood?"

"Don't worry. For this much money, I'd cut out my own tongue." The man patted his pocket. "You ever want me to do you another favor, you know how to reach me."

"Yeah. I'll keep it in mind. I may have something for you in a couple of months. In the meantime, no contact. We've never met." Mark held the door while the man stepped outside, then closed and carefully locked it before returning to his desk.

Hearing the phone ring, he pushed the intercom and snarled, "I told you, Joanna. No calls."

"I thought you'd want to take this one, Mark. It's Christina."

With an audible sigh of impatience he composed himself before picking up the phone. "Hello, darling."

He listened and frowned. "How long will he be in Venice?" His hand closed into a fist. "That long? What does his schedule look like when he returns?" A moment later he broke into a wide smile. "He'll be back the first of next month? Perfect. Why don't you go ahead and book the date with his secretary now?" He paused before saying, "Now, now. I know you have some doubts about this, but it's the best thing for all of us. And you won't have the complication of fretting over all those details. We'll have a simple ceremony in his chambers, and we can even bring along Tyler and Mrs. Mellon and Bonnie, if you'd like. I don't want you to worry about a thing. Just remember that I love you, Christina. That's all that matters now."

He disconnected, rifled through his papers, and dialed again.

"Morgan? Mark Deering here. I'm calling about that little debt I owe you. You can expect a check the early part of next month." He paused, then sat back, smiling. "Not this time, old buddy. I know you've heard it before, but this time you can take it to the bank. I've just learned that I'm about to come into some serious money."

Ted and Vanessa stared at each other with matching looks of stunned disbelief. How was it possible that this handsome, charming man, whom they loved like a son, had another side to his personality? A dark, frightening side.

"Ted, did you hear what he just said? He's talking about the wedding and Christina's inheritance. He intends to use Christina to clear his own debts."

"I heard."

At his desk, Mark felt a sudden draft. Papers began rippling across his desk, almost as though human fingers were rifling through them, invisible eyes scanning their contents.

Ted flipped through the papers, pointing to the figures on each page as he mentally began tallying the total. "From the little I've seen so far, Mark is up to his eyebrows in debt. So much so, that unless I miss my guess, he's fighting to keep his precious company from going under."

Sweating, Mark glanced at the open window. With a muttered oath he pushed away from his desk to cross the room and close it before fiddling with the air-conditioning thermostat on the wall. When he returned to his desk, the papers lay perfectly still. Satisfied, he removed his suit jacket and returned his attention to the pile of bills atop his desk, going over each one and circling the totals.

"And that awful man." Vanessa indicated the closed door. "What was that about?"

"It was about our deaths." Ted's voice held the cold note of fury. "Now I realize why the car behaved so badly on those wet curves. It was no accident that the brakes wouldn't work. They'd been tampered with. By that . . . prison mechanic."

"We were murdered?" Vanessa stared at him with a look of

horror and revulsion. And then an even worse truth dawned. "Oh, Ted. Think about it. It stands to reason that if Mark was willing to kill us to get to Christina's money . . . "

Ted finished for her. ". . . he'd be more than willing to kill again, as soon as he controls her estate."

Three

"Oh, Ted." Vanessa's eyes were round with fear. "This is like some horrible nightmare. We have to stop Christina from marrying Mark."

"Exactly. But how? You heard Gram. I can't just reach out and throttle him within an inch of his life." Ted slammed a fist into his open palm. "Though I'd love to." He paused a moment, considering. "We can't use physical force. We can't interfere with a mortal's free will. Where does that leave us?"

"I don't know." Vanessa was pacing, her fingernail tapping a nervous tattoo on her crossed arm. "From Mark's phone conversation with Christina, we only have a month to figure this out. That is, if we're allowed to stay here that long." Tears filled her eyes. "Darling, we can't leave. We can't let this monster win."

"I know, babe." Ted drew his wife close. "Now, don't despair. We'll think of something."

Vanessa pushed away as a sudden thought intruded. "I have it. We need to find a mortal who'll interfere for us."

Ted arched a brow. "I recognize that look, babe. What've you got in mind?"

"What better way to stop a marriage than by having the bride-to-be fall hard for another man?"

"A bit late for that, don't you think? Christina has been dating Mark exclusively for more than a year. If you'll recall, they paired up just about the time she hooked the Lyon Entertainment account, putting our company on the map." He paused, eyes narrowing. "Come to think of it, that's probably why Mark became so interested. It was right after *California Business Weekly* wrote that flattering article about Christina."

"Proclaiming her the fastest rising star on the advertising planet," his wife put in dryly. "Now that we know what kind of snake he really is, it's beginning to add up." She gave a sigh of disgust. "Why didn't we see all this before it was too late?"

"Because he's an expert at dazzling people with his charm. That's what made his company so popular in the first place." Ted caught his wife's hand. "Come on. I can't stand to be in the same space with that maggot another minute."

As they passed through the walls of Mark's office, Vanessa's voice sounded soft and whispery. "Where are we going?"

"I don't have a clue." Ted added in an angry aside, "Maybe we can find that 'other man' you were hoping for. Preferably in a boxing ring. Or maybe at a rifle range."

"Ready for a lunch break?" Christina stepped into the playroom, where Bonnie was trying to entice Tyler to add a wooden block to the tower she had constructed.

Bonnie was considered one of the most qualified teachers in the state of California, having spent more than twenty-five years working with special children. After just six months with Tyler, she had formed a bond of trust with the boy. Though he had yet to speak, he had begun to interact with her, occasionally joining in the activities she initiated, and once or twice stopping to listen to certain words as she read aloud to him from a book. Small steps to some, but to the Crenshaw family, each simple act of normalcy was a milestone.

Bonnie shoved a hand through the wild tangle of salt-and-pepper corkscrew curls that refused to be tamed. "Lunch sounds good to me. How about you, Tyler?"

The boy was holding a wooden square, turning it around and around in his hand, as though enjoying the feel of the smooth, polished texture.

"I think he's hungry. I know I am." Bonnie got slowly to her feet and tugged on the colorful cotton shirt covering her ample bosom.

Christina was always amazed that this woman could spend hours on the floor, playing with toy trucks and tractors, stacking wooden blocks, or just kneeling eye to eye with Tyler while patiently telling him something, without ever knowing whether or not he heard a single word. To most people it would seem a thankless job. To Bonnie, with her boundless enthusiasm, each quirk of the boy's eyebrow, each pause in his constant pacing meant a breakthrough of sorts.

Christina led the way to the kitchen, where Mrs. Mellon was just adding a fat bowl of flowers to a glass-topped table set in a little window alcove. Since returning to her parents' home, Christina had asked the housekeeper to serve all their meals in the kitchen. The dining room felt far too formal. Besides, it still caused her pain to think about the joyous meals she'd shared with her mother and father in that special place.

Special. Everything about this house was special to her. The lush flower gardens that had been lovingly tended by her mother. The master bedroom upstairs, now closed off, where she and her mother had sat together for endless hours, planning her wedding. But of all the spaces in this house, the one most dear to her was her dad's office, which still bore the scent of his occasional cigars. This was where she'd gone to him with plans to attend Wharton. And where she'd confided that, more than anything, she wanted to follow in his footsteps and make her mark in the advertising world.

Theirs had been a special bond that few fathers and daughters were fortunate enough to share. Though Ted Crenshaw had urged his daughter to follow her own dreams, he'd been fiercely proud when she'd joined his advertising agency. And when she landed the Lyon Entertainment account, garnering national attention not only for herself but for the agency as well, he'd been over the moon.

She felt tears prickle and had to blink hard. At least she'd had the satisfaction of making her dad proud before he'd been swept out of her life without warning.

In the years to come she'd surely find some comfort in that. For now, her heart lay like a stone, and she wondered if she would ever again feel even the smallest measure of happiness.

* * *

"Why are we here, darling?" Vanessa studied the drab metal desks littered with file folders and half-filled paper cups of luke-warm coffee.

"I want to see if the investigators have made any progress on our"—Ted's nostrils flared in anger—"accident."

He studied the faces of the men and women at work behind the desks. "Fascinating. I've never had a reason to be in the state police crime lab before."

He peered over the shoulder of a man whose sleeves were rolled above his elbows, reading from scribbles on a notepad and entering them on a computer.

"This one isn't ours." Ted drifted to another desk. "Not ours." He paused in the midst of two young men commiserating over their long hours and lack of overtime pay. "Let's hope they're not working on our case."

One of the men glanced at the open file on the desk in front of him. "What've we decided about the crash up in the hills that claimed the millionaire and his wife?"

"Wickham wants every test in the book before we write up our report."

"Wickham." The second investigator spat the name with a snarl of disgust. "Easy for him. Now that he's being forced to retire, he's looking to go out in a blaze of glory. Nothing he'd like better than to uncover some sort of evil conspiracy so he can grab some headlines."

"So what do we do?" the first detective asked.

The second bent to initial the document. "Simple. This was open-and-shut. Rain-slicked highway. Plenty of cham-pagne flowing. Old geezer took the turns too fast and lost control."

"Geezer?" Ted's hands fisted at his sides as he turned to his wife. "Did you hear that idiot? He called me a geezer."

"What's more, darling, he's decided that you were drinking and couldn't handle the curves."

"Did they test for blood-alcohol level? Did they even think to take a look at the car's brakes?"

"You heard him, darling. Case closed. And we're not al-lowed to interfere."

Ted and Vanessa watched with matching looks of distress

as the young detectives strolled away, still complaining about the hours they'd been forced to work lately and the lack of pay.

Vanessa turned in time to see her husband positioning a fan in front of the open file. While she watched, he plugged it in, causing the blades to begin turning furiously, whipping up the papers on the desk.

He picked up their file and carried it to the next desk, bearing the name Henry Wickham. Ted dropped the document on the desktop, then kept a hand on it as other papers fluttered about on the breeze.

Minutes later a paunchy, gray-haired man in rumpled suit, tie askew, walked to the desk and sat, sipping a fresh cup of coffee from the vending machine. Idly picking up the file, he began to read, before muttering furiously, "Young fools. Thought they'd rubber-stamp this, did they? Not if I have anything to say about it."

Ted turned to his wife with a look of triumph. "Now maybe we'll get the investigation we deserve."

"Wickham?"

"You heard those young smart alecks. This guy's probably seen enough in his day to know that no case should be closed until all the tests are conducted and the results are in. If, as they said, he wants one big important case before he retires, he's our man. I'm betting he'll put our car through a battery of tests. And though the guys in the field will grumble about the extra work, old Henry has enough seniority to get what he wants."

"Oh, Ted." Vanessa's smile bloomed. "That was brilliant."

"Thanks, babe." He dropped an arm around her waist and led her through the walls of the building and out into the fresh air. "Now that our investigation is in good hands, we can concentrate on a way to keep Christina and Tyler safe from that murdering scum, Mark."

"Chris?" Noelle Morgan's voice drifted over the phone. "I ran into Mark yesterday, and he said you've given up your apartment to live in your parents' house."

"Yes. I want to stay close to Tyler while he gets through this."

"What about your business? Mark told me that you haven't been in your office once since the accident."

"I'm perfectly capable of conducting business from here, Noelle."

"I suppose that's true. But what about Mark?"

"What about him?"

"He's grieving, too, Chris. You know how he felt about your parents. He told me that you seem vague and distant, unable to concern yourself with anything but your little brother. It may be noble. It's certainly understandable. But honey, Mark's a man. If you're not around to comfort him, there are plenty of women out there who would die to have Mark Deering in their beds."

"Mark isn't like that, Noelle. If he were, I'd sense it. Now, I really have to go. Thanks for calling. I know you're only concerned with my happiness."

"I am. I wish I could ease your grief, Chris. But I think the sooner you marry Mark, the sooner you'll start to move on."

Hovering, Ted and Vanessa turned to one another with matching looks of dismay.

"You see?" Vanessa began to pace. "Even her friends are pushing her into his arms. We need to act quickly, Ted, or Christina and Tyler could very well be facing the same fate that we did."

"I know, babe. I know." He caught her hand and led her through the walls to the garden.

"Where are we going, Ted?"

He shrugged. "I don't really know. But I always enjoyed being out here." At a sudden thought he said, "Gram? Are you around?"

"Hello, Teddy." His grandmother appeared directly in front of him. "What can I do for you?"

"You know what's going on?"

The older woman nodded. "I know that Mark Deering arranged for you to suffer a fatal crash. And now you know, too."

"We do. Shocking," Vanessa added. "We're still reeling from it. But now our concern is to keep Christina and Tyler safe from him. Since we can't physically stop him from his evil scheme, I'm thinking that our children need a champion."

Ted put a hand on his wife's shoulder. "You know Vanessa. Ever the romantic. She's thinking that if we can find a good man . . ."

"A good, decent, honorable man who is big, strong, handsome, and single," his wife added.

Ted chuckled. "See what I mean?"

"You know I'm right." Vanessa smiled. "Having an honest man around might be the temptation Christina needs to take a step back and get a good look at the man she's engaged to marry."

Ted's grandmother sighed. "That's a tall order, especially since we're on a time limit here. But I'll see what I can do."

She shimmered and glowed before disappearing from their sight.

Four

". . . and all the animals in the kingdom, after roaring a welcome to their new king, lived happily ever after."

Christina closed the book and set it aside, all the while smiling at the sight of Tyler, sleeping peacefully in his bed. She tucked up the covers and brushed a lock of fine hair from his forehead, allowing her hand to linger on the warmth of his skin.

He'd fought to stay awake. This was one of his favorite books, and he loved the happy ending. She knew because his eyes always lost their vacant stare when she read those beloved words.

"Good night, Tyler." She felt her heart swell with love as she bent to press a kiss to his cheek. "Stay safe."

She swallowed the lump that always rose to her throat whenever she whispered the same words her mother had always said to him at bedtime.

"Oh, Mom. Dad. How I miss you."

When she walked from the room, Ted and Vanessa remained, watching their little boy as he slept.

They looked over as a young woman appeared.

"What are you doing here?" Ted reached out a hand as though to shield his son from danger. "Are you lost?"

"I . . . I guess I am." The young woman seemed surprised

by the unfamiliar surroundings. "I'd planned on seeing my husband. I must have been even more distracted than I realized."

"Distracted?" Seeing the sad, haunted look in her eyes, Vanessa attempted to soothe. But when she touched a hand to the woman's arm, she was startled to see it pass completely through, as though in a mist. "Why, you're . . . one of us."

The young woman's head came up sharply. "You're spirits, too?"

At their nods of agreement, she seemed relieved. "Then I'm meant to be here, though I have no idea why. But if there's one thing I've learned since entering the spirit world, it's that I ought not to question the why of things. For, you see, there are reasons for everything. Even, it seems, for death. Still, in my case, I have no answers. Why should I"—she touched a hand to her middle—"and my unborn baby have to die, leaving a husband to grieve so deeply he has turned his back on everything that once mattered to him?"

"It sounds as though you need to unburden yourself." Ted patted the edge of his son's mattress, and he and Vanessa sat on either side of the sleeping boy, their hands resting lightly on his hands atop the blanket.

In sleep, Tyler smiled. Seeing it, the two shared a tender look before turning their attention to their visitor.

The young woman perched on the edge of the bed. "My name is Lily Ridgeway. My husband Jake and I were so happy when we learned that we were having a baby, even though the doctors had warned me that I carry a dangerous gene that could claim my life and that of any child I might conceive." She looked away. "Perhaps I was foolish, but I believed myself invincible. And though Jake worried, I think I'd halfway convinced him as well. Then one night, before I could even call out to him for help, I was gone. Of course he blames himself, though it was never his fault, and there was nothing he could have done. But I'm so worried about him. His grief is wide and deep. He has given up a successful business, one that made him millions of dollars and gave him such joy, and has given away most of his money to a foundation he started that is researching the terrible illness that took my life and that of our unborn child."

"But that's so noble." Vanessa reached out to catch Lily's hand, careful to touch her lightly enough to keep from passing through. "Surely you understand that making piles of money won't bring your Jake as much pleasure as finding a possible cure for your illness."

"Of course. I'm pleased that he's using his fortune for a just cause. That isn't what worries me. But he's become so reclusive. He takes only an occasional job as a carpenter and cabinet-maker, and then only when he thinks the work will satisfy him. He's turned his back on his friends. There are weeks at a time when he speaks to no one. It isn't right. It isn't healthy to be so grief-stricken that he turns away from all the good things that could build happy memories. I want him to find some joy in his life before it's too late. It breaks my heart to see him so sad and lonely."

Vanessa's eyes narrowed with sudden concentration. "Is your Jake handsome?"

Lily's smile lit up the room. "Very handsome. I was so proud to be his wife."

"And brave?"

"Now Vanessa . . . " Ted tried to silence her, but she got to her feet and stood facing Lily across the bed. "Tell me. Is Jake brave?"

"I know that he would have died for me if he could. He's the bravest man I know."

"Oh, Ted." Vanessa clapped her hands together. "He's the one."

"You don't know . . . "

She shook her head. "Oh, but I do. Don't you see? Jake Ridgeway is the perfect guardian for Christina and Tyler."

"Guardian?" Lily looked from Vanessa to Ted. "What is this about?"

As quickly as possible they told her what they'd learned since entering the spirit world.

She listened in silence before giving a slow nod. "It sounds as though your daughter and son are in grave danger. This man who caused your death will stop at nothing to have their fortune."

"Exactly." For a moment Vanessa looked as though she might break down and cry.

Lily's voice grew stronger. "As I said, I knew I was meant to be here in your space, though I didn't know why. Now I do." She took a deep breath. "If Jake can save your loved ones from peril, and if your daughter can bring joy back into Jake's life, I'll do whatever I can to bring them together."

Vanessa hesitated. "It won't cause you pain to see your husband . . . love someone else?"

Lily smiled then. "Love has a very different meaning in the spirit world. Here, love is completely unselfish. We want only the best for all those who matter most to us. And if your Christina can bring the joy and laughter back to my Jake's life, I will ask no more." She paused. "Do you have a plan to bring them together?"

Ted glanced at Vanessa. "Jake Ridgeway may have been a successful businessman, but our families moved in different circles. And it would seem that despite his wealth, he now spends all his time in woodworking, while Christina is in advertising. I just don't know how we'll get them to meet."

"We'll find a way." Vanessa was smiling now. "After all, darling, it's meant to be."

"So you say."

"I know it." She touched a hand to her heart. "I can feel it here."

"So can I." Lily stood and circled the bed, embracing first Vanessa, then Ted. "Just meeting the two of you, I feel a renewed sense of hope. I believe that you are more than capable of resolving this without me. But if there is anything I can do to help, please let me know. I have already extended my stay here, but I will never be able to enjoy my new world until I'm satisfied that Jake has found a measure of peace and happiness in his. It means more to me than anything else in heaven or on earth."

When she turned away, some of the pain in her eyes had faded, to be replaced with a look of bright anticipation.

As quickly as she had appeared, she was gone in a shimmer of light.

"What's wrong, Miss Christina?" The housekeeper paused in the doorway to see Christina standing at the window, staring into space while chewing on her lower lip.

"I'm having quite an argument with myself, Mrs. Mellon."

"What about?"

Christina gave an embarrassed little laugh. "I was searching through a pile of file folders that I'd stashed in the corner, and it occurred to me that Dad's office just isn't adequate for all the work I'm trying to do here. But I'm reluctant to give up and go back to the city. It would mean leaving Tyler, and neither of us is ready for that."

The housekeeper pointed to the doorway leading to a lovely sitting room beyond the office. "It was always your mother's intention to convert that into her own office, to oversee all her charitable work while remaining close to your father. It seems to me it would be a simple matter for some workmen to remove that wall and double your office space so you could continue working right here instead of going into the city."

Christina crossed her arms and began tapping a finger nervously, reminding Mrs. Mellon of the very thing Vanessa always did when she was thinking. "I'm not sure I'm ready to make any changes to Dad's office."

"It's your office now, Miss Christina. And if you don't mind my saying, not only would the remodeling project give you the space you need, but it would give you the chance to put your own personal style on this office as well."

"I wouldn't know who to call to start making such changes."

Mrs. Mellon lifted a hand to her mouth as a thought came to her. "That reminds me of something. Susan, the Wallingfords' housekeeper, mentioned an excellent carpenter and cabinet-maker they'd hired to do some custom work in their library. He's a bit reclusive as I recall, but Mr. Wallingford couldn't stop singing the man's praises. If you'd like, I could call her and ask for his name, along with references."

Christina nodded. "I suppose it wouldn't hurt to ask. If and when I decide to move ahead, at least I'll have the name of someone highly recommended."

The housekeeper turned away. "I'll call her right now."

When she was gone, Christina looked around the office. She loved this room, loved knowing her father had spent so much time here. Still, as she walked through the doorway from the office to her mother's sitting room, she could see the possibilities. Combining the two rooms made perfect sense. She began mentally measuring the walls for more cabinets, tucking a larger desk by the big bay window, seeing in her mind's eye a fire on the hearth when the cool winds blew in off the ocean, and imagining herself being able to sip tea and work late into the night after tucking Tyler in.

Her musings were interrupted by the ringing of the phone.

"Hello." Her smile fled as she listened to Mark chiding her for forgetting their luncheon date. "Oh, Mark, I'm so sorry. Something . . . came up here, and I got sidetracked. Can we reschedule it for tomorrow?"

"Now I've become someone you have to pencil in on your calendar?"

She listened in silence, then soothed his ruffled feathers before replacing the receiver. Mark was angry, but then, Mark always seemed angry lately. And he was right when he accused her of neglecting him.

She really needed to begin moving forward, not only in their relationship but in her business life as well.

She came to a decision. She would begin the remodeling project as soon as possible. After all, if Brian Wallingford, one of the toughest board members of her father's country club, was happy with the work done by this carpenter, what did she have to lose?

Feeling confident in her decision, she strode out of the office and made her way to the gardens, where she'd seen Tyler strolling under the watchful eye of Bonnie.

Jake Ridgeway took a moment to admire the lush gardens as he parked his truck in the circular driveway. When he stepped out, he took another long minute to study the house he was about to enter. Though he no longer designed houses, the love of architecture was in his blood. He'd earned a great deal of money designing some of the best-known mansions in northern California. Now he used his skill designing custom cabinets in those same mansions. But only if the job appealed to him.

He climbed the wide stone steps and rang the bell. Minutes later, a plump woman ushered him inside and led the way to a suite of rooms on the main level.

"Miss Christina, the young man I told you about is here."

If he was surprised by the woman's youthful figure as she pushed away from her desk and hurried forward to shake his hand, he was even more surprised by the firm handshake and the brisk, businesslike attitude.

"Mr. Ridgeway. You come highly recommended. My neighbor, Brian Wallingford, has nothing but praise for the work you did in his library."

"Thanks." He broke contact and turned to study the thick wall of plastic sheeting used to keep the dust of the newly remodeled addition to a minimum in her office space. "That's quite an addition. What did you have in mind in there?"

Christina led him across the room and lifted a flap of the plastic to permit entry into the now-empty space. "I'm thinking of a desk here, in front of the window. That will give me more light while I work. Then a wall of custom cabinets on this side, with perhaps a marble countertop and open shelves above."

He could see it clearly. "Nice fireplace. You'd want the marble to match that surround?"

"I hadn't thought of that, but yes, I think that would be lovely." She continued to move around the room. "Maybe you could add some bookshelves on either side of the fireplace?"

He nodded. "Not a problem. Anything else?"

She crossed her arms, tapping a finger on her arm. "I love the look of old wood. Something rich and dark that matches my current office. I don't want it to look as though it's been added, but rather like something that was always here."

"I could bring some samples."

"Fine."

He waited. When she offered nothing more he pulled out a pad. "I'll take some measurements. Make a few drawings."

"Then I'll leave you to it." She turned and made her way back to her office and her father's desk, leaving him silhouetted beyond the plastic sheeting.

Within minutes she was lost in her work.

While Mark rolled up his sleeves to measure and make notations on his pad, Ted and Vanessa hovered.

"You see, Ted? He's just what we hoped for. Look at those muscles."

"I see them. But it's obvious that Christina didn't."

"Not yet. But she will. And that handsome poet's face. She can't ignore a face like that for long. Just look at those dark, soulful eyes. What woman could resist them?"

Ted chuckled. "It's a good thing he can't see you drooling, babe."

She joined in the laughter. "As long as we're choosing a champion, why not one who's easy on the eyes?"

Ted glanced at his daughter, fielding a call at her desk while her fingers sped across a keyboard. Like Jake, she was completely lost in her work. "He could look like a Greek god and be as noble as any mythological hero, but if he and Christina don't connect, it won't matter at all."

His wife followed his gaze and sighed. "That's why we're here, darling. If they don't connect on their own, we'll just have to nudge them along."

"Remember the rules. We're not allowed to meddle."

"No, darling. We're not allowed to interfere with their free will. Gram didn't say anything about nudging them in the right direction."

Ted chuckled again. "If I've learned anything after a lifetime with you, babe, it's this: I should never argue when you're about to play matchmaker."

"This is much more than playing, darling. This time, it's a matter of life and death."

Five

Jake opened a box and took out one of the hand-carved medallions he'd been perfecting in his workroom at home. He'd been pleasantly surprised by the beautiful old wood that Christina Crenshaw had chosen for her custom cabinets. Most of his clients wanted something more contemporary. The old wood suited this house. This room. And since he rarely slept more than a few hours at a time, he'd welcomed the chance to lose himself in work and avoid the dreams that often plagued him in the night.

He loved the feel of aged wood in his hands. It wasn't just the grain and texture, but the history. It pleased him to think about the tree it had once been and the men who had helped to cut it, plane it, sand it. This particular wood had come from a supplier he knew and trusted, who had assured him that it had once been a wall of an ancient abbey.

Holding up the medallion, he was pleased to note that it perfectly mirrored the medallions carved into the marble fireplace surround. He'd drawn one to scale and had used that as a template for the others. He had a feeling that his client would welcome this special touch on her cabinets.

His client.

He was particularly pleased that she left him alone with

his work and never tried to engage him in conversation. Even though they were essentially working in the same room, the plastic sheeting gave each of them a sense of privacy. That's what he liked most about this job. He didn't have to interact with other people. They left him alone to create something with his own two hands, with wood and tools, without ever having to talk to people except in passing. And the work kept him from thinking about what he'd lost and would never be able to regain in this lifetime. It was too painful, too heart-wrenching. There were times when he felt like an open, bloody wound that would never heal.

Jake was so absorbed in his work he wasn't even aware at first of the little boy who had sidled up beside him. It wasn't until the boy reached for a medallion and began turning it over and over in his hands that Jake noticed the movement. Seeing the way the boy was studying the wood, Jake smiled.

"You like it?"

The boy took no notice of him.

Instead of being annoyed by his brush-off, Jake was enormously pleased. It would seem that this was another family member who knew how to allow a man his privacy.

Jake turned away, like the boy, lost in his own thoughts.

"Any other questions?" Christina sat at her desk and gazed into the camera on her computer monitor, studying the faces of the men and women in her advertising agency who'd been part of the computer-generated conference call.

"I think we've covered everything." Amy Morrow, her executive assistant, smiled at the oversized flat-screen monitor mounted on the wall of the agency's conference room.

"It's plain to me that you have all given this latest campaign a great deal of thought, and it shows. When I decided to spend more time here, my chief concern was that you might think I was letting you and the company down." Christina cleared her throat and swallowed the lump that was threatening. "Dad always bragged that he had the best team in the advertising business. He was right. You've all been amazing."

Bright smiles broke out on all the faces as the camera panned the group.

"Thank you. All of you. I'll be in touch tomorrow. Same

time." As Christina exited the program, she sat back and swiveled her chair to stare out the window.

When she'd composed herself, she pushed away from her desk and got to her feet.

As she crossed the room, she couldn't resist pausing at the flap in the plastic sheeting. Curious to see how the work was progressing, she stepped inside.

The first thing she saw was Tyler, wielding a hammer, pounding nails crookedly into a piece of wood.

Catching sight of her in the doorway, Jake paused in his work. "Your son?"

She shook her head. "My little brother."

Jake didn't know why her response pleased him. "Doesn't talk. But he seemed interested in what I was doing, so I thought I'd let him try his hand at it."

"Thank you. That's kind of you. Tyler rarely shows an interest in anything outside his own mind."

"I'd know a thing or two about that." With a smile Jake returned to his work.

Christina stood quietly watching Tyler for several minutes. When she realized that neither he nor the carpenter even noticed her there, she turned on her heel and went in search of Bonnie.

"I hope you don't mind that I left Tyler there with your handyman for a couple of minutes." Bonnie looked up from the journal in which she kept meticulous notes about Tyler's improvements, no matter how minor. "I wanted to record this while it was fresh in my mind." She set aside the pen and clasped her hands in her lap. "We were passing by when he just stopped dead in his tracks. Then, before I knew what was happening, he walked over, picked up a piece of wood, and became fascinated by the shape and texture of it. He's done that before, of course. But then, instead of remaining fixated on the wood, he actually discarded it and picked up a hammer, imitating the man. I believe this is the most animated I've ever seen Tyler."

"Oh, Bonnie." Christina crossed the room and grabbed the woman's hands. "I wonder what it was that attracted him?"

"Maybe the carpenter reminds him of someone. Maybe it's because the man never talks, and that suits Tyler so perfectly. Or it may be something as simple as the tools he uses or the smell of wood. Whatever the attraction, there's a light in Tyler's eyes that I've rarely glimpsed. And if your carpenter doesn't mind, I'd like to encourage Tyler to spend as much time in there as he's willing to spend, under my watchful eye, of course."

Christina nodded, too overcome to speak.

On her way to the kitchen, she circled back to her office for another look. Tyler was exactly where she'd left him, happily hammering nails into a piece of wood. When Bonnie entered and took a seat across the room, Tyler took no notice of her.

Jake Ridgeway was across the room, standing on a stepladder, screwing a strip of wood to the wall. For a moment Christina merely watched, her attention caught by the corded muscles of his arms as he worked. Her gaze moved to the plaid shirt stretched tightly across those wide shoulders, then moved lower to his narrow waist and muscled legs encased in faded denims. When he reached for something in the tool belt at his waist, she quickly looked away. What in the world was she thinking? Until now she'd been so caught up in her own work and in the overwhelming task of this remodel, she hadn't even noticed the man doing the work.

But he was so easy on the eye.

She chanced one more look. At that very moment he glanced over, and she felt the pull of that dark, haunted gaze.

Jake paused in his work. "Did you want something?"

She felt the heat stain her cheeks. "Nothing. Just . . . checking out how the work was progressing. Would you care for some lunch?"

He pointed toward a cooler in the corner. "I brought my own."

"All right." She watched as he returned to his work.

Tyler hadn't even acknowledged her presence. Bonnie was busy recording in her journal.

Feeling slightly foolish, Christina turned away.

Mrs. Mellon paused in the doorway of the office. "I've brought you some tea."

Christina looked up from her computer. "Thank you." She pressed a hand to the back of her neck and stretched cramped muscles.

"You're working too hard." The housekeeper set a silver tray on a sideboard and filled a steaming cup.

"It helps to be busy. And everyone at the office has thrown themselves into this latest ad campaign."

"Of course they have. They all love you. But it's all right to let them do some of the work without you, Miss Christina."

Chris smiled. "Yes, ma'am."

Mrs. Mellon glanced at the figures silhouetted behind the plastic sheet. "In the past week Bonnie and I have been delighted at the way the lad has taken to Mr. Ridgeway."

"Mr. Ridgeway? Oh, Jake. Yes. Isn't it amazing?"

"Indeed." She lowered her voice. "Would you mind if I invited him to stay for supper tonight?"

Before Christina could respond, she said softly, "It was Bonnie's idea. She thinks he might be able to engage Tyler in conversation."

"I don't know." Christina began tapping a finger on her arm.

"And if nothing else, we might learn a bit about the man and determine just what it is that attracts the lad to him."

Christina gave that some thought before nodding. "All right. I suppose it wouldn't hurt. Would you like me to invite him?"

The housekeeper brightened. "It would certainly mean more coming from you."

Christina picked up her tea and sipped. "I'll take care of it."

A short time later she stepped into the work area and watched for several minutes as Jake held a level to a strip of wood and made some markings on the wall.

When he turned and saw her, he paused. "Sorry. I didn't hear you come in. Do you need something?"

From his position on the floor, Tyler looked up, glancing from Christina to Jake. The mere fact that he seemed to be following their conversation had Christina's heart rate climbing. He almost never paid any attention to the words being spoken by the people around him.

She saw Bonnie, seated silently in the corner of the room, smiling broadly.

"I came to invite you to dinner."

Jake seemed about to refuse but he caught sight of Tyler, staring at him with such eagerness, and he found himself nodding against his will. "I guess I could."

"I'll tell Mrs. Mellon. Dinner will be at six. I'll come and fetch you if you lose track of time."

Jake watched her walk away before returning to his work.

While he measured and marked and prepared to set the cabinets in place, he found himself wondering what had just happened.

He couldn't imagine making small talk over a meal with strangers for an hour or more. The thought of smiling, nodding, answering questions about life in general, or worse, about himself, had him mentally cursing his momentary lapse.

If he chased after her right now, he could excuse himself before he was committed to this. An appointment he'd forgotten. Or even an emergency that had just come up. There must be something he could say to get himself off the hook.

He looked at the boy, who had picked up one of the wooden medallions and was turning it over and over in his hands. For one brief instant they made eye contact, and the boy's lips curved into a half smile.

Jake felt a quick tug on his heart. Damn. The kid had him. Those sad eyes. That sweet smile.

He was trapped. He would just have to get through this.

"So, Mr. Ridgeway . . . "

"Jake."

The housekeeper smiled. "So, Jake, how did you happen to become a carpenter and cabinetmaker?"

The woman was as transparent as the glass that overlooked the gardens. She was bound and determined to engage him in conversation. Thinking about glass had him noticing the way the sunlight streaming in turned the ends of Christina's hair to gold, surrounding her like a halo. He found himself itching to reach out and touch a strand, to see if it was as silky as it looked.

She could have been a model for one of those California beach commercials. All flawless tawny skin and a lush body that she tried to camouflage in a simple knee-skimming dress of pale yellow silk. She could wear an old paper bag, and she'd still look gorgeous.

What the hell was the matter with him? It was barely a year since he'd lost Lily and their child, and he was thinking about things he had no right to.

He closed his hand into a fist in his lap, grateful that they were eating in the kitchen. In his faded jeans and work shirt he'd have been completely out of place in the formal dining

room he could see just beyond the doorway. If he found it odd
that the lady of the house was eating in the kitchen with her
staff, he didn't bother to dwell on it. She seemed as comfortable here as she did in that big office. And from the looks of it,
she didn't consider them staff at all, but more like family. These
two older women, he noted, were very protective of Christina
Crenshaw and her little brother.

"It was a natural progression from architect to builder to carpenter. They're all related fields, and I've always loved working
with wood. I enjoy making something with my own hands."

"I should think it would be very satisfying." Bonnie sat beside Tyler and noted the way he kept watching the man.

When Jake drank his milk, Tyler did the same. When Jake
ate a forkful of mashed potatoes, the boy did the same.

There was definitely a fascination here, a connection, no
matter how fragile.

Bonnie glanced over Tyler's head. "Do you live alone, Jake?"

He blinked and, across the table, Christina caught a glimpse
of sudden pain. For some unexplained reason, she wished she
could erase Bonnie's question.

"Yes."

"I used to, also, until I was fortunate enough to be employed
here." If Bonnie felt his discomfort, she covered it quickly. "I
can barely recall my life before moving into this lovely place.
From the first day, it has never felt like a job as much as a
homecoming."

Jake had felt it, too. Each time he set foot inside this house,
there was a very strong feeling of family, though he couldn't
explain it.

He took a bite of Mrs. Mellon's fabulous meat loaf, enjoying
the way it almost melted in his mouth. "Tyler, you're one lucky
boy to have such food every day of your life. I believe, Mrs.
Mellon, this is the best meat loaf I've ever tasted."

The boy's eyes widened, and he took a bite of meat loaf,
causing Bonnie to watch with approval. Tyler rarely ate meat
unless he was prodded. Another of his idiosyncrasies.

Mrs. Mellon blushed. "I hope you'll be just as pleased with
the dessert."

"As long as it's chocolate, I'll love it."

His words had her smiling brightly. "Home-baked brownies
with ice cream and fudge sauce."

He returned her smile. "Be still, my heart."

Across the table, Christina marveled at the way he'd managed to put them all at ease, despite Bonnie's careless question. She found herself wondering what had caused him such pain. Whatever the reason, Jake Ridgeway, it would seem, had an innate kindness that had him putting aside his own discomfort for the sake of others.

As the housekeeper began clearing the table and passing around the desserts, the mood lightened even more. By the time they'd finished eating and were sipping coffee, they were laughing comfortably together, as Bonnie regaled them with stories of her first job as a camp counselor, fresh from graduate school.

"I had a boy in my group who was absolutely terrified of anything in the lake that might touch his skin." She glanced around the table. "As you can imagine, there are thousands of things floating in a Wisconsin lake. Bugs, fish, algae to mention just a few. And every time something brushed against him, he would let out a screech that had the entire camp scrambling out of the water, thinking they were being attacked by monsters. By the end of the week, we were all exhausted."

Christina leaned closer. "Did he ever lose his fear?"

"No. He lost his voice. And for the next two days, until he got it back, peace reigned in the camp."

That had them all laughing out loud.

At that precise moment, Mark stuck his head around the corner. "Sounds like you're having a party in here." He stopped in midstride when he caught sight of Jake seated at the table.

Christina smoothly handled the introductions. "Mark, this is Jake Ridgeway, who's making the beautiful cabinets in my expanded office. Jake, this is Mark Deering."

"Christina's fiancé." Mark dropped a proprietary arm around her shoulders and drew her close. "Ridgeway." He gave Jake a long look as he shook his hand before turning to Christina, pointedly ignoring the others at the table. "I thought, since I was running late, you'd be ready to go."

"Go?"

Seeing the confusion in her eyes, his tone sharpened. "The club. I invited some of our friends."

She was already shaking her head. "Mark, you know how I feel about going back there. I'm not ready."

"It's been weeks. Sooner or later you have to get back on that horse and ride." He took both her hands in his. "Look, sweetheart. I know it brings up memories you'd rather forget. But the sooner you face it, the sooner you can move past all this. Now, go upstairs and get into something elegant, and we'll dance the night away."

"Mark, I said I'm not ready." Seeing the others watching and listening, she struggled to find her smile. Instead, her lips trembled.

Taking pity on her, Jake got to his feet, hoping to deflect the attention from her. "Mrs. Mellon, that was an excellent dinner. Thank you." He smiled at Bonnie. "I enjoyed your camp stories. You ought to write a book."

"Maybe someday." She returned his smile.

He placed a hand on the boy's shoulder. "Night, Tyler. See you tomorrow."

When there was no response, he turned to Christina. "Thanks again for the dinner invitation. I had a great time."

It was true, he realized. Though he hadn't expected to enjoy himself, the time had flown by.

Christina started after him, eager to escape the room. "I'll show you out."

"There's no need."

He glanced over his shoulder to see Mark following Christina from the room.

As he started down the hall, he heard Mark's voice, low, angry. "What the hell is he doing eating dinner like one of the family?"

"Don't be rude, Mark. I invited him."

"And you were having so much fun with that . . . carpenter, you forgot all about our date."

"I told you I wasn't interested in going to Dad's club."

"It's your club now, Chris. Ours, in fact. And maybe it's time to think about what I want. Or don't I matter anymore?"

"Don't, Mark." There was a weariness to her tone as Jake opened the front door and let himself out.

As he made his way to his truck, he glanced at the expensive convertible parked behind it. It seemed the perfect vehicle for a man like Mark Deering to show off his woman.

His woman.

The thought of it left a bad taste in Jake's mouth. There was something unpleasant about Mark Deering, something shallow and phony. It was hard to picture a man like that with Christina. In the short time he'd worked here, he'd formed an image of a kind, compassionate, hardworking woman who was deeply involved in her little brother's care. She deserved better than Deering.

Not his business, he reminded himself.

He climbed into his truck and drove away. But he couldn't resist a glance in the rearview mirror. Bonnie had been right. Though he couldn't explain it, just stepping inside the Crenshaw house each day was like coming home.

Leaving it had him feeling as empty as death.

Six

Henry Wickham blessed the inventor of the GPS as he took the twists and turns of the highway at a slow, careful pace. As he drove, he tried to imagine what it would feel like to discover, while maneuvering this rain-slicked stretch of pavement, that the brakes weren't working and the car was hurtling out of control.

No matter how cool the head or calm the demeanor, Ted Crenshaw must have been horrified to realize that he was unable to save his life and that of his beloved wife.

As he rounded the curving driveway, Henry Wickham slowed to a stop and sat a moment admiring the sprawling stone house set amid lush gardens. It was, quite simply, every man's dream house.

He climbed the steps and rang the doorbell. Moments later the door was opened by the housekeeper.

He handed her his card. "Detective Henry Wickham to see Miss Christina Crenshaw."

Mrs. Mellon read the card before stepping aside. "Please come in, Detective." She led him along the hallway and indicated a sitting room. "If you'll wait in here, I'll fetch Miss Christina."

"Thank you."

Minutes later, Christina entered, followed by Mark, who had been trying to persuade Christina to go to the city with him for the day. She seemed almost relieved to have a reason to refuse.

She offered a handshake. "Detective, I'm Christina Crenshaw. This is my fiancé, Mark Deering."

"Miss Crenshaw. Mr. Deering."

Chris stared pointedly at Mark. "Mr. Deering was just leaving."

He nodded at the detective, then kissed Chris's cheek before sauntering from the room.

When they were alone, Christina said, "What is this about, Detective?"

"It's the policy of our department to conduct several tests on all vehicles involved in fatal accidents." He handed over a manila envelope. "I've brought you a copy of the test results."

"Thank you. That's very kind of you, Detective. Such a long drive just to deliver these. Wouldn't you have preferred to mail them?"

"Perhaps, if the results had been different."

"Different?" She arched a brow.

He indicated a chair. "Perhaps we could sit?"

"Of course." She settled herself into a chair by the window, oddly touched by his courtly gesture of standing until she was seated before he perched on the edge of the nearby sofa.

She waited a beat before asking, "What did the tests reveal?"

"That the brakes on your father's car had been tampered with."

For long moments she was speechless. Finally finding her voice, she said in a barely audible breath, "Are you saying this was a deliberate act?"

"Without a doubt."

She blanched and sucked in a sudden breath. "But . . . that can't be."

"I'm afraid it is. And now I must ask. Did your parents have any known enemies?"

"No. Of course not." She fought tears. "Everyone loved my parents."

"Most children believe that." He chose his words carefully. "Your father was a very successful businessman. Could he have angered someone? Perhaps won an important account that someone else was counting on winning?"

She shook her head. "Dad was successful, but not at the expense of others. He would never cheat or scam a competitor. He was good and honest and decent. And my mother was actively involved in several charities, not because she was some bored, wealthy matron but because she honestly cared about people. Nobody could possibly want to harm my parents."

"It appears that someone did. I'm afraid I must ask you this, Miss Crenshaw. Who benefited from their deaths?"

She simply stared at him. Then, as his question became clear, her eyes widened. "Are you asking who inherited their estate?"

When he nodded, she said simply, "My little brother and I are their only heirs."

"There's nobody else?"

"Nobody."

Henry Wickham pointed to his card in her hand. "Keep that handy. If you think of anyone else who might have benefited from the death of your parents, or who may have had a grudge to settle, I'd like to hear from you at once." He paused. "You should realize that anyone willing to go to such lengths once, will do so again. You and your little brother could be targeted for the same fate. If I were you, I'd stay close to home and stay close to your brother."

"I'm sorry, Detective." He saw the tears that sprang to her eyes. "You must be wrong. Nobody could be that cruel. Not to people as good and kind as my parents. And certainly not to a little boy who suffers the way Tyler does." She looked away. "He's a special child, locked in his own world. But though he doesn't communicate, I can sense his grief. He . . . " She struggled to speak over the tears that clogged her throat. "He means everything to me. Tyler is my whole life."

"Then keep him close." Wickham got to his feet. "Call me day or night. I've written my private number on that card." When she started to get up, he shook his head. "I'll find my way out, Miss Crenshaw."

As he walked to his car, he realized that he was relieved by her reaction. He'd come here thinking that he could be meeting some rich kid who'd wanted to do in her parents in order to fatten the pot. It was seen too often in his line of work. Not even an Oscar-winning actress could have faked grief as real, as deep, as Christina Crenshaw's. She'd been not only stunned by the revelation that the brakes had been tampered with but had been completely unable to imagine anyone doing harm to her parents.

So, if it wasn't the daughter, who was it? He sighed as he turned the ignition and started away from the lovely mansion in the hills. The truth would come out eventually. He just hoped it was sooner rather than later. His retirement was coming up at the end of the month, and he hated the thought of any unsolved cases he'd have to leave behind.

Furthermore, that young woman had touched a chord in him. He'd been prepared to meet a spoiled, pampered socialite. Instead, he'd met a lovely young woman who was dealing with a great deal of grief.

"Ted, what are we going to do now? The work on Christina's office is finished way ahead of time." Vanessa watched her husband pace back and forth in their daughter's empty office. "We're about to lose our champion."

"We have to find a way to keep him here. We need to get those two young people alone somewhere, so they can connect."

"You mean talk?"

He winked. "I mean connect. As in turn up the heat, babe."

"Why Ted. You romantic. What do you have in mind?"

"You know that upstairs room that we use for storage?"

She nodded. "I used to talk about turning it into a sitting room for Christina, until she took an apartment in the city."

"Right. Well, now that she's back home, it's time to reconsider the remodeling job. I think, with the right amount of persuasion, she'll think it's all her own idea."

"And how do you plan to persuade her?"

He dropped a glossy remodeling magazine onto Christina's desk, then flipped through the pages until he came to the one he was seeking. "Maybe this will give her a nudge."

As the workmen put the last of the new cabinets in place under Jake's careful direction, Christina stood back, admiring the look of them. The dull patina of old wood gave just the right touch of elegance to the room.

Jake turned.

Seeing her there, he walked over. "The marble countertops will be installed tomorrow, as well as the bookshelves on either side of the fireplace. Then I'll be out of your hair."

"Maybe not." She showed him the magazine she'd found on her desk, depicting a suite of rooms very similar to her own upstairs. "Now that I'm living in my family home, I'd like to put the space to better use. Would you mind taking a look at my suite to see if you could do something like this?"

He studied the pictures before nodding. "Let's take a look."

As they started up the stairs, Ted grabbed his wife's hand, and they floated along behind.

"Why are we following them?"

"You'll see." Ted was smiling broadly.

"My rooms are over here." Christina led the way through her bedroom to the sitting room beyond. It was a large open space with a balcony overlooking the gardens.

She indicated the pale lemon-washed walls. "After seeing what was done in this brochure, I like the idea of adding shelves and cabinets. What do you think?"

Jake studied the room with an architect's eye to size and scale. "I agree. Besides giving you more storage, it will add depth and dimension to a flat space. What sort of wood do you have in mind?"

"Nothing as ornate as the wood you used in my office. Something with cleaner lines, I think. Something bright."

"Yes. Contemporary. With some built-in lights, and possibly some glass panels here and there for variety. I'll do a few drawings tonight and see if any of them meet with your approval." As he turned toward the door, the curtains billowed inward on a gust of wind, slamming the door between the bedroom and sitting room.

Startled, Christina grabbed his arm. "Oh." She let go at once and gave a nervous laugh. "Sorry."

"It's all right."

As he reached for the handle, Christina stood very still, feeling an awareness that was as startling as the slamming of the door. In that simple touch she'd been acutely aware of the ripple of muscle beneath her fingertips and had experienced a quick sexual tug. In truth, her fingertips were still tingling from the touch of Jake Ridgeway.

"That's odd." He glanced over his shoulder. "The knob isn't turning."

"It sticks sometimes." Without thinking, she placed her hand over his. At once she became aware of her mistake. The heat was back, stronger and hotter than before.

She removed her hand as though burned, but not before seeing a hungry look in his eyes that had the breath backing up in her throat.

He attempted to turn the knob again, and again was met with resistance.

He gave her a devilish grin. "You sure there aren't ghosts in this place?"

She managed a laugh. "Not that I know of. What'll we do?"

He looked around. "We could phone someone to come upstairs and lend a hand."

She shook her head. "The phone's in the other room. And my cell phone is on my desk downstairs."

He patted his shirt pocket. "Mine's down there as well, on top of my toolbox." He reached into his tool belt and removed a hammer.

"What are you doing?"

"Breaking us out of here." He began tapping the pins inside the hinges until both slid out of place.

Lifting the door from the hinges, he set it aside and made a sweeping motion with his hand. "After you."

Watching them make their exit, Vanessa chuckled at the scowl on her husband's face. "It was a good idea, darling. And certainly not your fault that our hero knows how to use a carpenter's tools."

"That's all right." Ted's brow was furrowed in thought. "At least that little experiment proved one thing. For one quick moment there, Christina became aware of Jake Ridgeway."

"And how would you know that? Are you a mind reader now?"

"A father. And I could see her heart in her eyes. It's a start. Now to find a way to force those two together until they really connect."

Christina was having trouble concentrating. Despite a successful teleconference with her staff and the acquisition of a new and very influential client, she couldn't seem to keep her mind on business. Instead, she had a burning desire to walk across the room every few minutes to check on the progress of the bookshelves.

This was her third time in less than two hours, and this time they were complete.

"Oh, Jake." She clasped her hands together as she admired the way they looked in the afternoon sunlight. "They're perfect."

"I'm glad you like them."

She glanced at Tyler, who was proudly wearing a smaller version of Jake's tool belt. "Oh, Tyler. Look at you."

The little boy actually smiled.

She turned to Jake. "Where did he get that?"

"I made it. I figured, if he was going to be my helper, the little guy deserved his own tools."

"That's so sweet." Without thinking, she opened her arms and hugged him.

At that moment, Mark stepped into the room. His eyes narrowed on the couple as Christina abruptly stepped away.

"Mark. I wasn't expecting you."

"Obviously." He forced a thin smile to his lips and made an attempt at a lame joke. "If that's how you thank all your workmen, where do I sign up?"

Jake walked to the doorway. "If you don't need me for anything else, I'll be upstairs taking some measurements."

When he was gone, Mark turned to her with a puzzled frown. "Upstairs?"

"I've decided to have some work done in my sitting room."

Mark surprised her with a wide smile. "I guess that means that the carpenter's going to be hanging around for a while." Ignoring Tyler, he put a hand to her elbow. "I asked Mrs. Mellon to bring our lunch to the library."

"Why?"

He shrugged. "With all the people underfoot, it's the only place I can have some private time with my fiancée."

"You know I like to have lunch with Tyler."

"Yeah." His smile faded. "I'd think you could miss just one afternoon in order to spend it with me." When they reached the library, he led her inside and closed the door.

While she walked to the window, he crossed the room and opened a chilled bottle of champagne, filling two glasses.

When he handed her one, she merely stared at him. "Are we celebrating something?"

"I hope so. I spoke with an old friend of mine, Judge Mc-Clelland, and he's agreed to clear his calendar to witness our marriage tomorrow afternoon."

"Tomorrow." Her hand shook, causing some of the liquid to spill over the rim of the glass.

"This isn't the reaction I was hoping for. I thought you'd be thrilled. I expected to hear you say, 'Oh, Mark, darling, what a happy surprise.' "

"It's certainly a surprise. But I'm not ready, Mark."

"You were ready a month ago."

"That was before . . . "

"Chris, you know this is what your parents would have wanted. You and Tyler need me. I need the two of you. Let's help each other. Let me into your life."

Spilling more champagne, she set the glass aside to mop at the front of her dress with a handkerchief.

Just as Mrs. Mellon knocked and entered, Christina gave a firm shake of her head. "I'm sorry, Mark. I know you mean well. But I'm not ready to marry you tomorrow. Or the day after. Right now I can't say when, or even if I ever will be."

Before he could say a word, she bolted from the room, leaving Mark and Mrs. Mellon to stare after her wearing matching looks of astonishment.

Mark was in a black rage as he drove back to the city. He'd come here determined to persuade Christina to go with him to city hall tomorrow and exchange vows. He'd even primed their friends to be ready for a post-wedding party at the club.

She hadn't just put him off, she'd indicated that she might never be ready to tie the knot.

By the time he reached his office, he was struggling to put aside a feeling of panic. He needed an infusion of cash soon, or his troubles would become public knowledge. If that happened, all his carefully laid plans would unravel.

He needed Christina's money, and he needed it now. There had to be a way to force her hand.

In his fury, he focused on the kid. Tyler was the key. That sick, needy little brat was the reason she'd moved back home.

The reason why she insisted on being there day and night, playing the role of little mother, curtailing her social life. Eating dinner in the kitchen with the help. Laughing with that low-life carpenter. Hugging him.

In his office Mark began to pace. As he paced, a plan began to take shape.

He was in such a dark mood, he was muttering aloud under his breath. "Maybe the carpenter is a blessing in disguise. If the kid were to disappear, the authorities would need to focus on someone suspicious. Who better than an itinerant laborer? And with the kid missing, Christina would have no one to turn to except me. While she quietly falls apart, I'll be more than happy to take charge. Of everything."

He gave a chilling laugh while he dug through his wallet, located a slip of paper, and dialed a number.

At the sound of a slurred, sleepy voice he said, "I told you I might have need of your services again. I'll be calling you in a couple of days to come pick up a . . . package and dispose of it where it can't be traced. Think you can handle it?" He listened, before saying, "Good. Wait for my call."

He was smiling as he leaned back in his chair and steepled his fingers. "Now it's only a matter of days."

Hovering beside Mark's desk, Vanessa looked at Ted. "Oh, darling. We have to find a way to stop this monster before he can carry out his hideous plan."

Ted's hands were curled into fists at his sides. It was obvious that he wanted, more than anything, to give Mark Deering the thrashing of his life. But when he tried to pummel him, his hands passed directly through Mark's flesh.

Frustrated, Ted caught Vanessa's hand, and together they flew through the walls of Mark's office. "Come on, babe. Time's wasting. We need to step up our effort to get Christina and Jake Ridgeway together."

"What if we can't?"

"We have no choice left. There's no time to develop a plan B."

Seven

Ted and Vanessa floated between Christina, working alone in her new office, and Jake, taking measurements upstairs.

"Oh, Ted, what have we done?" Vanessa watched as Jake made notations on a sheet of paper. "They're never going to get together at this rate. And Christina and Tyler are in grave danger. I can't bear this feeling of helplessness."

While they watched, Jake set aside his measuring tape and descended the stairs.

Ted and Vanessa exchanged hopeful glances.

As Jake started past Christina's office, he paused. Seeing her on the phone, he motioned that he wanted to talk to her before continuing out the door and to the driveway, where his truck was parked.

Christina replaced the receiver and hurried out of her office to follow Jake. "You wanted to talk to me?"

"Just to give you some drawings to look over before I leave."

Hovering beside them, Vanessa sighed. "They're wasting time. I don't care about the sitting room shelves. They need to connect, Ted. But how?"

"Look, babe, they're both dealing with guilt. She's still engaged to Mark and, knowing our daughter, is too honorable to cheat on him. Jake is still grieving the loss of a wife and unborn baby, and probably suffering the same guilt for having feelings for another woman. But they're human. They're alive. They've got so much love to give. Now we just need to point them in the right direction."

"What will it take?"

"Some kind of spark. It's a guy and girl thing. We connected, didn't we?"

"Did we ever." She sighed. "Do you remember that long walk in the rain?"

He grinned. "How could I forget it?" He snapped his fingers. "That's it."

"What?"

"A walk in the rain. Maybe that will get their juices flowing."

Vanessa scanned the sky. "There's not a cloud in sight."

He scowled, then brightened. "I'll call on Gram. Maybe she has some pull upstairs."

In a shimmer of light the old woman appeared beside them. "I heard what you said. Are you certain you want rain, Teddy?"

"Gram." Ted hugged his grandmother just as a fierce black cloud gathered overhead. He looked up. "Are you some kind of genius?"

"Like you, I'm just an incurable romantic."

Without warning, the cloud opened up, and a drenching rain began to fall.

"Oh." Because the open garage was closer than the front door, Christina raced through the rain to the garage, with Jake running along behind her.

The two were laughing as they shook rain from their hair. Jake's plaid shirt was plastered to his chest. Christina's silk dress clung to every line and curve of her body.

Embarrassed to be caught staring, each turned away.

Seeing it, Ted shouted, "We need more, Gram."

Just then there was a tremendous burst of thunder that shook the very foundation of the garage.

With a cry, Christina flung herself against Jake.

His arms encircled her, and he drew her close. With his

mouth to her ear he whispered, "Wow. That was quite a boomer. But it's okay. We're safe in here."

Despite the delicious shivers that raced down her spine at his whispered words, she did feel safe. Safe in the circle of his arms. It wasn't just his deep voice, calmly reassuring her. Or his strong arms, offering her shelter. It was this man. This quiet, competent man who stirred her in a way that no other man ever had.

She lifted her face. "I'm not usually afraid of storms. Sorry."

"Don't be." He stared down into her eyes. "It gave me an excuse to hold you." His arms tightened. "And I've been wanting to hold you for a very long time."

Her pulse started racing like an out-of-control train. "You have?"

He nodded. "Yeah. And not just hold you."

She saw his gaze lower to her mouth and could feel the heat of his kiss even before his lips brushed hers. "I've been wanting to do this for such a long time."

Her heart seemed to stop as his mouth moved over hers, tasting, touching, until she could feel her toes curling. In fact, she could feel him in every part of her body. A body that was now tingling with awareness.

There was such hunger in his kiss.

She answered with a hunger of her own, wrapping her arms around his neck and pressing herself so close to him she could feel the wild pounding of his heartbeat inside her own chest. The barely contained passion in him fueled her own, causing her to sigh and give herself up completely to the pleasure.

He changed the angle and took the kiss deeper, while his strong, clever hands moved along her spine, igniting a fire that raged like an inferno through her veins. When his fingers moved upward to encounter the swell of her breasts, his thumbs teased and stroked until she was straining against him.

"Jake." The word came out in a rush of heat.

He framed her face with his big hands and stared with naked hunger into her eyes. "Say that again."

"What?"

"My name."

She sighed. "Jake. Jake."

Inflamed, his fingers tangled in her hair, and he drove her

back against the wall, all the while kissing her until they were both breathless.

Outside, thunder roared and lightning streaked across the sky, while wind and rain battered the roof. The two people inside the garage were too lost in the excitement of their newly discovered passion to take any notice of the storm.

Jake lifted his head and filled his starving lungs with air. "Do you know how much I love hearing you say my name?" He lowered his face and pressed small butterfly kisses on the side of her mouth, her cheek, the tip of her nose. "Or how long I've wanted to say yours? Not Miss Crenshaw, but Christina. Beautiful, perfect Christina."

The way he spoke her name, almost like a prayer, made her feel like weeping.

"While I was working in your office, I used to close my eyes and listen to the sound of your voice while you talked with clients."

She glanced at him shyly. "And I used to walk over and pretend to look at the cabinets just so I could look at you."

They stared at each other in awe, like two people who had just discovered a rare and wonderful treasure.

It was Christina who pulled away first. Taking a step back, she moistened her lips with her tongue, avoiding Jake's eyes. "I have no right to have these . . . feelings for you. I'm engaged."

"Do you love him?"

She stared at the floor. "I thought I did. But lately . . . " She looked up. Met his direct gaze. "I guess I've known for some time that it's over. I just didn't want to probe my feelings too deeply. But honestly, Jake, I never expected to feel like this about you. About anyone. I've never felt this way before."

He closed his eyes a moment, letting her words wash over him, savoring the knowledge, before dragging her close. Against her temple he whispered, "Before we take this to the next level, I need to tell you about myself. I . . . was married. My wife and unborn baby . . . "

Vanessa caught her husband's hand. "This has become much more intimate that I'd expected. I think Christina and Jake deserve some privacy, Ted darling."

"Right." He drew her close and brushed a kiss over her mouth. "They're on the right track now. I have no doubt they'll connect in every way, thanks to Gram's absolutely brilliant thunderstorm. It worked so much better than a walk in the rain."

He and Vanessa looked around, but all they could see of his beloved grandmother was a haze of light lifting into the sky.

They hurried away, leaving Jake and their daughter to their much-deserved privacy.

It was more than an hour before Jake and Christina emerged from the garage, having shared their life stories before giving in to the passion that had caught them both by surprise. By the time they walked back to Jake's truck, they were holding hands and staring at one another as only intimate lovers can.

The sudden storm had fled as quickly as it had appeared, leaving the gardens awash in glistening sunlight.

Christina felt the softest of touches against her cheek, like the press of her mother's fingertips. She glanced around. Instead of the expected breeze, the leaves on the trees were completely still.

She stopped in her tracks as she caught a whiff of her mother's favorite perfume.

"What is it, Christina?"

At the sound of her name on Jake's lips, she smiled. "Nothing, I guess. Just a memory."

"A happy one, from the look in your eyes."

"It is. It always will be. A sweet, beautiful memory."

Beside her, Vanessa and Ted wiped tears from their eyes.

Though Jake was reluctant to leave, he opened the truck door. Before he could slip into the driver's seat, Christina drew his head down for a slow, lingering kiss.

Against his mouth she whispered, "I intend to call Mark as soon as I go inside. He deserves to know the truth."

"I hope you won't have regrets."

"I won't, Jake. I feel at peace with my decision. I feel . . . suddenly free."

"And I feel more alive than I ever believed possible." He settled himself behind the wheel and turned the key in the ignition. "I'll call you later tonight."

"You'd better." She blew him a kiss through the open window. "Better yet, why don't you come back and have dinner with us? Tyler will be as happy to see you as I will."

"I'd like that." He smiled. "I'll see you around six."

As he drove away, Christina turned toward the front door.

There was a spring to her step that hadn't been there in such a long time. And her heart was so light, she wondered that she didn't simply float through the air.

"Oh, Miss Christina." Mrs. Mellon's face bore a pinched, agitated look. "I've been searching all over for you."

"What's wrong?" Chris wondered how anyone could be worried on such an amazing day.

"It's Tyler. Bonnie is upstairs right now, going room by room. So far, we haven't found him."

"Can't find him?" Christina struggled to digest the news. "How long since you last saw him?"

"I'm not sure. Bonnie and I were with him at lunchtime. Then she read to him before his nap. That would have been around two o'clock. She retired to her own room, and when she came back around three thirty, his bed was empty. Even his blanket is missing."

"Have you phoned the police?"

"I was waiting until I found you, hoping the lad was with you."

With a feeling of absolute panic, Christina dialed nine-one-one.

After speaking privately with each of the three women who lived in the house and interviewing neighbors who might have spotted any strangers in the area, a police detective asked for the names of anyone who had been a frequent visitor to the Crenshaw residence.

Mrs. Mellon gave him the names and addresses of both Mark and Jake, while Christina and Bonnie continued searching every inch of the house and grounds.

Mrs. Mellon, trailed by a police officer, found Christina sitting on a garden bench, sobbing.

Taking her by the hand, the housekeeper gently led her toward the house. "Come inside, Miss Christina."

"I can't bear to go in there, knowing Tyler isn't with me."

"The police will find him. You must hold on to that thought. This kind officer has come to ask you a few more questions."

Once inside, Christina sat quietly in a chair in the kitchen, sipping a cup of strong tea, while a police detective sat across the table from her.

"You are engaged to a Mr. Mark Deering?"

Chris nodded wearily.

"We went first to his home. He was extremely friendly and helpful, and very concerned about the missing boy, saying he was like his very own little brother. He invited us in and suggested that we might want to check out a carpenter who has been working here."

"Jake Ridgeway."

The detective read from his notes. "That's right. Mr. Deering said he'd seen the carpenter palming some of the silver and crystal that you have lying about on some of the tabletops. We're wondering if he might have thought the boy would be worth a ransom."

"Jake?" Christina struggled to focus. She blinked. "Jake Ridgeway is a good and decent man. He would never do such a thing."

"How long have you known this carpenter, Miss Crenshaw?"

"A few weeks. But I . . . "

"And what do you know about him?"

"He's been despondent over the loss of his wife and unborn child. In fact, he has started a foundation to search for a cure for the rare illness that caused their deaths."

"Would you say he is depressed?"

"He may have been, but . . . " She huffed out a breath when she saw the detective writing furiously in his notebook. "Jake would never harm my brother."

"Mr. Deering suggested that you may have developed a . . . romantic attachment to the carpenter. Is this true?"

Christina saw Bonnie Waverly and Mrs. Mellon staring at her with open astonishment.

She blushed and avoided their eyes. "It's true. But Jake would never . . . "

The detective got to his feet. "I'm sorry, Miss Crenshaw. This happens more often than you can imagine. Faking a romance with a wealthy woman is the easiest way for a criminal to ply his trade."

"Oh, Ted. Our poor darling. Her heart is breaking."

"I know. But there's no time to comfort her now." Ted caught his wife's hand. "I know we can't interfere, but we have to find a way to redirect the police investigation. And quickly."

"Where do we start?"

They flew across the countryside and dropped into Henry Wickham's office, where his desk, as usual, was littered with reports.

Wickham was bent over, plugging in a fan. That gave them the perfect opportunity they needed.

"Here, babe. Go through these." Ted shoved a pile of documents toward Vanessa, while he took another pile for himself.

"What are we looking for?"

"I don't know. Anything that can get him to make some sense of this mess."

Fingers flying, papers ruffling, they read page after page of legal documents until Vanessa gave a cry. "Ted. Look." She shoved a paper toward him.

He read it, then placed it on top of the pile and set them right in front of old Wickham as he took his seat at his desk.

"Huh. I remember this." Henry glanced at one of the cold cases that had never been closed. An elderly woman had lost control of her car and was killed. The tests hadn't yielded enough information to make an arrest, even though at the time he'd suspected her much-younger lover of being more in love with her software company than with her.

As he began to set aside the document, he caught sight of the name of that young lover: Mark Deering.

He glanced at his watch and then snatched up the documents and hurried out of his office. Instead of phoning Christina Crenshaw with the news, he would go to her house.

If what he suspected was true, she and her brother were in grave danger.

Henry Wickham pulled up in front of the graceful mansion, grateful that the long drive had given him time to think about what he would say to the young woman who lived there. He would gently but firmly suggest that Miss Crenshaw hire an armed guard until the murder of her parents was solved.

Instead of the charming young lady he'd first met, Christina entered the room looking distraught and teary-eyed.

"Miss Crenshaw, has something happened?"

"It's my little brother. He's missing . . . "

They both looked up as Mrs. Mellon stepped aside to admit Jake Ridgeway, with a murderous expression in his eyes.

"Jake." Christina fell into his arms. "The police told me that they suspect you of taking Tyler."

"They've made it very clear that I'm their only suspect, thanks to Deering." Jake led her toward a chaise and knelt in front of her, taking both her hands in his. "How are you holding up?"

"Not very well. Oh, Jake. I'm so afraid."

Henry Wickham spoke up. "You said thanks to Deering. What did you mean by that?"

For the first time, Jake noticed the rumpled detective across the room. "Christina's fiancé suggested that I'm some kind of itinerant laborer looking for a chance to make a fast buck. He has the police wasting all their time investigating my background instead of searching for Tyler."

"Which is precisely what he'd hoped for."

At Wickham's words, both Christina and Jake stared at him in silence.

Watching and listening, Ted and Vanessa embraced.

"Finally we have everyone on the same page, babe. Now, if only they can rescue Tyler before he can be harmed, arrest that monster Mark, and put him away before he can hurt anyone else."

"Oh, Ted. I pray it's so."

"From your lips, babe . . . "

"But we know from experience that we don't always get our happy ending."

"Shhh. If we can see Tyler safely back home and Mark Deering locked up, we won't ask for anything more."

Ted kissed his wife soundly before turning back to listen as Henry Wickham phoned the police detective who was handling the case.

Eight

Mark Deering was feeling supremely confident. With the police focusing all their attention on the carpenter, he'd bought enough time to carry out his plan without interference. The kid would never be found. Christina would turn to him in desperation. He'd be more than happy to comfort her. And take charge of her and her bank account.

He made his way to his car parked in the garage and drove to his office, pulling around to his private entrance. Once there, he picked up a blanket-covered burden from the backseat and carried it inside, dumping it unceremoniously in a corner. There was a faint moan, the only sound the kid could make with his hands, feet, and mouth taped. Mark intended to add more tape in a minute, after he made a call.

He sat at his desk and dialed a number, then waited for the familiar voice.

Mark sounded almost euphoric when he finally spoke into the phone. "Time to get over here and pick up the package."

With a smile, he replaced the receiver.

He was still smiling when the hammer caught him on the side of his head, causing him to let out a cry of pain and rage.

Stunned, he watched in horror as the boy lifted the hammer a second time, hitting him with such force, he slumped forward, his bloody head dropping to the desktop. Through a shower of stars he watched helplessly as the boy ran out the door and disappeared down the steps.

It took several minutes before he was able to clear his head enough to stumble after Tyler.

Henry Wickham couldn't keep the gloom from his voice. "Detective Maloney said the police found Mr. Deering's residence empty. They then went to his place of business and found an ex-convict there, who claimed to be awaiting a package. They're holding him for questioning. They also found traces of blood on the desk and chair and on the floor around the desk. It will be sent to a lab for testing."

"Oh, no. My little brother . . . ?" Christina had her hands clamped tightly together, as though holding on by a thread.

"He wasn't there. Nor was Mark Deering. But the crime unit did find a blanket in the corner of the office that bore blond hairs that may or may not have come from the boy's head. There were also several torn strips of tape that could have been used to bind and gag him."

"Oh, Tyler." Tears spilled over, running down Christina's cheeks. "That monster."

"And they found one more thing in the blanket. A pair of small shears, which the boy may have used to cut those strips of tape and free himself."

Jake nodded. "They were part of the tools I put in that tool belt I made for him."

Christina lay a hand on Jake's arm. "Bonnie said he refused to take it off, even for his nap."

Henry Wickham arched a brow. "If he was snatched while sleeping, the kidnapper wouldn't have had time to remove it. That belt, and the tools in it, may have just given the boy a fighting chance."

"But the blood? Is it Tyler's?" Christina asked the question she most feared. "Do you think he's still alive?"

"We can't be certain, Miss Crenshaw. Detective Maloney thinks the ex-con was there to pick up the boy and dispose of him elsewhere. But with both the boy and Deering missing, nothing is certain. The question is, if Deering changed his plans, why didn't he alert the ex-con?" He paused, wondering how much to tell them. "Detective Maloney thinks Tyler managed to run away, and Deering was forced to give chase. That would explain why the two of them are missing."

"Where could Tyler run to?" Christina struggled with a rising sense of desperation. "It's getting dark. He's never been away from home alone. And he can't ask for help."

Jake drew an arm around her shoulders. "Tyler may not be able to speak, but he isn't helpless. He proved that by messing up Deering's plans." He glanced toward Henry Wickham. "What are the police doing?"

"The photo Miss Crenshaw provided is being broadcast on all the networks. Folks are being informed that the boy doesn't speak, but anyone who sees him should alert the authorities."

Too agitated to sit, Christina stood and began to pace. "I want to help search for him."

"That's always a family's first instinct. But the best thing you can do is remain here and wait for a call."

Seeing the tears in the eyes of the two older women, Christina gathered them close. "He's a brave, clever little boy. If there's any way to get word to us, he'll find it."

She prayed these weren't just hollow, empty words. Her little brother had to stay safe. Had to. Or what little joy she had left in the world would be forever shattered.

"Oh, Ted, darling. Where can he be?" Drifting across the city, clinging to her husband's hand, Vanessa scanned the streets below.

They'd begun their search at Mark Deering's office. From there they'd crisscrossed the city for any sign of their son or of Mark.

"I wish I knew how Tyler's mind worked. There was a time when I believed him incapable of thought. Now, watching him imitate Jake Ridgeway, I've begun to alter my thinking. He may not speak, but he's bright and clever. And best of all, brave. Brave enough to fight back and escape."

"We don't know that."

"It's the only thing that makes sense. If he hadn't run away, he'd already be in the clutches of that ex-convict. The same one who arranged our deadly accident."

"But he's only a little boy. And Mark is a cold-blooded murderer."

Ted drew his wife close. "I know, babe." He pointed downward. "What was that?"

She peered through the gathering darkness. "I don't see anything."

"Neither do I. But I thought I spotted movement." He drew her down with him to street level. "Look."

She followed his direction and saw Tyler hiding in the shadow of an empty building, peering around cautiously. "Oh, darling."

She rushed to the boy and wrapped her arms around him.

For just a moment Tyler shivered, as a feeling of warmth spread through him. Then, blinking furiously, he continued looking around.

"He can't feel me." Vanessa was openly weeping. "Ted, he doesn't even know I'm here."

"It's all right, babe. We know he's safe, at least for now. And that has to be enough."

"It isn't enough." She stomped her foot, but it made no sound. "I want to comfort him. I want my son to know he isn't alone." Tears of frustration ran down her cheeks. "And all I can do is watch and wait for some killer who has no conscience."

"Okay. Time to end the pity party." He knew he was being tough, but it had to be done. "Let's see if we can find out where Mark is and figure out how to distract him until the police can find Tyler."

"You want to leave Tyler alone?"

He thought a moment before saying, "No. You stay with him. I'll just fly around a bit and see if I can spot our resident creep."

Vanessa wrapped her arms around Tyler and watched as Ted disappeared into the night. She didn't care what Gram had told them; if Mark Deering came anywhere near her son, she would find a way to thwart him if it meant moving heaven and earth to do it.

Jake pulled Henry Wickham aside. "What put you onto Mark Deering?"

"He was a suspect in an earlier case that has never been re-solved. A wealthy widow who, shortly after marrying Deering, died in a suspicious automobile accident. We could never prove it wasn't an accident, so the case is still pending."

"You might want to see where that ex-con was when that accident occurred."

Wickham nodded. "I've already asked my office to run a check on him."

Jake lowered his voice. "What are Tyler's odds?"

The detective avoided Jake's eyes. "He's a gutsy kid. But he's just a kid. I'd hate to think what his chances are against a pro with no conscience. Especially one with so much to lose. If you ask me, Deering will do whatever he can to get to the kid before the police do."

"Thanks for the honesty." Jake turned away. "If Christina asks about me, tell her I had to file a report with your office."

The rumpled detective put a hand on his arm. "You inter-fere, you're apt to get yourself killed."

"Maybe. But if there's a chance to even the odds in Tyler's favor, I've got to try."

Ted dropped down beside Vanessa, who was still clinging to Tyler. The little boy hadn't made a move since her arrival, and that suited her just fine. She was content to just stand there, breathing him in.

"We've got to get him to run." Ted's voice held a note of desperation.

"Why, Ted?"

"Deering is headed this way. With murder in his eyes. From the look of him, Tyler gave him a pretty good whack with some-thing heavy. His head's bloody. His eye's swollen. I know one thing. He won't give Tyler a second shot at him."

"Oh, Ted." Vanessa grabbed Tyler's hand and tried to pull him, but her fingers passed through air. "How can we get him to move?"

Ted was looking around, hoping to think of something. Just then he spotted Jake's truck heading in the direction of Mark's office.

He floated through a block of tall buildings and dropped down into the street ahead of Jake's vehicle. Desperate to get his attention, he caught sight of a stray dog digging through an overturned garbage can. Ted reached inside and found some discarded fast-food burgers. Tossing them into the street, he watched with satisfaction as the dog raced toward them.

Jake was so deep in thought he almost didn't see the dog in time. Standing on his brakes, he managed to bring his truck to a halt inches from the hungry animal. A car trailing Jake wasn't so fortunate. He slammed into the truck, causing shards of glass and pieces of metal to litter the street. With a litany of swear words, the driver slammed out of his car.

The dog snatched up the meat and took off running.

Hearing the crash, Tyler peered around the corner of the building. Spying Jake in the headlights, he started running toward him.

Jake couldn't believe his eyes. He opened his arms and scooped up the little boy, hugging him to his heart.

"I've been looking for you. Your poor sister is waiting at home, worried sick about you."

The boy buried his face in Jake's neck.

"Thanks for making this easy." A voice behind them had all the blood freezing in Jake's veins.

Mark gave a chilling laugh. In his hand was a small, silver pistol. "Now I get to kill two birds with one stone." He turned to the driver of the car. "If you value your life, you'll get back in that wreck and drive."

The man, seeing Mark's gun, scrambled into his car and drove away, tires screeching.

Vanessa grabbed hold of his door and clung before climbing in beside him. As he swerved around a corner she reached into his pocket and held out his cell phone. Seeing it, he stood on the brakes, brought his car to halt, and dialed nine-one-one.

Very deliberately, Jake set Tyler down and muttered under his breath, "When I make a move, you run as fast as you can between those buildings."

He straightened and took up a position in front of the boy, shielding him with his own body.

"Trying to be a hero, are you?" Mark gave an evil smile. "It won't work. You've meddled for the last time, carpenter."

As he took aim, Vanessa returned to Ted's side and the two

hovered beside Jake and Tyler, desperate to stop the carnage but unable to come up with anything more.

Just then, police cars appeared from both directions, filling the street with lights and sirens. Half a dozen officers leapt from their cars and took aim with automatic rifles at the man holding the gun.

A bullhorn announced, "Police. Toss aside your weapon at once."

Mark hesitated, but seeing the number of armed men, was forced to comply. In the blink of an eye the scene was swarming with men shouting orders, with Mark facedown in the middle of the street.

Jake and Tyler were whisked off to a police car.

As they headed away from the scene, the little boy wrapped his arms around Jake's neck and burrowed against his chest. Riding along, Ted and Vanessa were alternately laughing and weeping with relief.

"Oh, Ted. You did it. Luring that dog right in the path of Jake's truck was brilliant."

"Sheer desperation, babe. But it wouldn't have been enough if you hadn't forced that other driver to do the right thing and phone the police. We saved our boy, and that's all that matters."

"No, Ted darling. This is what matters." Vanessa pointed to Christina, Mrs. Mellon, and Bonnie, all standing on the porch as the police car pulled up the driveway, and all of them weeping copious tears of joy.

It was one of those perfect California days, the sun shining brightly in a clear, cloudless sky.

Guests sat on chairs arrayed with white satin skirts and bows that had been arranged in a semicircle around a platform dressed with urns of white hydrangeas and trailing ivy.

Ted and Vanessa watched their daughter as she made her way along the white carpet. Her gown was a long sweep of ivory silk. The veil was the same one that had been worn at her mother's wedding.

Christina paused to hug Mrs. Mellon, who was weeping softly, and Bonnie, who handed her a lace-edged handkerchief for luck, before she ascended the platform where Jake and Tyler, in matching tuxedos, stood proudly waiting.

While the judge spoke the words that united them, Vanessa turned to her husband, tears of joy sparkling on her lashes. "We chose well, didn't we, Ted darling?"

"That we did, babe. See how much he loves our children?"

"Jake Ridgeway turned out to be the perfect champion."

Seeing a shimmering light, they turned to welcome Lily as she drifted toward them. The young woman embraced them, then looked at Jake as he spoke his vows.

Her eyes were shining when she turned to Ted and Vanessa. "Look how happy he is."

"Thanks to your generosity."

"And yours. Perfect love. That's what we strive for on earth and finally achieve in this place."

As the three were smiling their approval, a fourth light joined them.

"Are you ready now?"

Ted pressed a kiss to his grandmother's cheek. "I guess there's no point in asking if we can hang around for the party."

The old woman merely smiled. As she lifted her arms, they began to shimmer and glow.

"Wait. One last good-bye."

Ted and Vanessa hovered on either side of their daughter, kissing her cheek.

Christina lifted a hand to her cheek and felt the whisper of a breeze. As before, she caught a whiff of her mother's perfume, and a thought came to her as clearly as if it had been spoken aloud.

She smiled at the man facing her. Her hero. And the great love of her life.

"Jake." She pressed her lips to his. "I was wishing that my parents were here to share this day with us, and suddenly the knowledge came to me that, without any doubt, they are here, looking down on us right this minute and smiling. And I know, too, that they love you every bit as much as Tyler and I do."

"Love."

They both turned to the little boy who had spoken. It seemed only fitting that his first word should be the most important word in the universe.

"Yes, love, Tyler." Jake knelt down so that his eyes were steady on the little boy's. "I love you and your beautiful sister."

The boy's smile gave him the look of an angel.

With Tyler walking between them, holding tightly to their hands, the bride and groom mingled with those who had come to celebrate this happy occasion.

While the guests watched, twin beams seemed to shine like a benediction from high above, casting the bride in a halo of light. Some said it was merely a typical bride's joy on her wedding day. Others thought it was a reflection of the sun off her shimmering gown.

Tyler looked up. The smile on his face was one of pure happiness as he lifted his hand to wave to his parents until they were out of sight.

They weren't really gone, he knew. They had just gone to a place he couldn't follow. But they had left behind two people who would love him and keep him safe.

And wasn't that what made heaven on earth?

Never Too Late to Love

Mary Kay McComas

For Shirleen Peplinski Bold, an old friend found anew

One

"Mr. Brown, that doesn't make sense." M. J. Biderman flipped a folder closed on her desk and leaned back in her soft leather chair. She swept a swag of soft brown hair from her face and blinked her hazel eyes twice, slowly, to help her concentrate. "I gave you the keys to the house and a list of furniture items I want removed and put into storage. Then I want the house torn down and the lot evacuated for the sale of the property. What seems to be the problem?"

"For one thing, the key doesn't work. I can't get into the house." The contractor's voice was already straining for patience.

"Break a window."

"That's the other thing; I tried. Several times. Several different windows. They crack but don't break."

"That's ridiculous."

"That's what I said. The house is so old and brittle I would have thought a stiff wind could blow it over. But apparently it's not ready to come down yet."

"It's not what?"

"I know how it sounds, ma'am, but it happens sometimes. These old places take on a life of their own. Not often, I admit, but my dad told me about one over in Harrisburg when I was a kid. They finally gutted the place and let the woods around it swallow it up. Fifty years later they went back in, and time had rotted away everything but the old stone chimneys."

"I don't have fifty years, Mr. Brown, or a woods in the middle of town to swallow it up. I do, however, have a gentleman interested in buying the lot for a Smoothie Hut franchise, but only if it becomes a *vacant* lot. Which is why I've hired you."

"Well, you're going to have to do more than just hire me, ma'am, because the house doesn't want to come down just yet."

"Please stop saying that."

"I rammed my backhoe into its southeast corner this morning. There was a rumbling noise and dust flew everywhere. When it cleared, the house was the same. I didn't even crack the foundation. It ain't coming down."

"Mr. Brown, will you hold for just a moment, please?"

Tears of frustration pressed against the back of her eyes before the line was muted. She blinked slowly at the ceiling until the stinging subsided, and she curled her fingers into fists. *This* was her mother's fault. If just once her mother had listened to her when she advised her to sell Hedbo House and buy into an easy-turnover residence in a retirement community, it wouldn't be happening. Her mother *never* listened.

And now she never would.

She didn't have the time or energy for this. She needed every second, every ounce, to make partner at Wilson and Bows, and the audit and analysis of Longwire Industries was the deal breaker. She could feel it in her bones. All eyes would be on her for the next few weeks, and she couldn't miss a step.

She took a deep breath and splayed her hands out flat on the desktop, trying to relax. The only house she ever heard of that refused to fall down was in a nursery rhyme about pigs, and even then, she thought the wolf gave up too soon. There were laws of physics that applied to this situation, so there had to be an answer somewhere.

She adjusted her headset and reconnected with Mr. Brown. "Maybe I'd better drive out there Friday after work and see for myself. Can you meet me at the house about six?"

The drive from Alexandria, Virginia, just outside Washington, D.C., to Loudon County and the barely there, drive-through

town of Johnnie's Bend was easy enough. Despite the fact that
she'd spent time there as a child and her mother had lived the
last ten years of her life there, her trips out had become fewer
and fewer in recent years as her life became increasingly con-
sumed with her job and the responsibilities thereof. But she
could see immediately that Johnnie's Bend was changing . . .
growing.

At last.

And no one, including her, was going to miss Hedbo
House—a ramshackle, three-story, brick colossus built in the
late eighteen hundreds by Horatio Hedbo, who invented and
manufactured a modern press that put holes in buttons and left
his fortune and home to his only son, Hobart Hedbo, when he
died in 1930. Hobart, something of a womanizer, married late
in life and had three daughters—Imogene, Odelia, and Adeline.

Imogene married and had a son, Rufus, who died of pneumonia at a young age. Odelia never married. Adeline married
four times, producing only one descendant: M.J., who was as
convinced as any completely unsuperstitious person could be
that it was living in the very old and truly dreary Hedbo House
that had killed them all.

But it wasn't going to get her. She'd planned to raze the
house even before the lucrative offer from Smoothie Hut, Inc.,
arrived at the family lawyer's office almost a year after her
mother's funeral.

However—and wasn't there always a however somewhere—
certain family heirlooms needed to be removed and looked
after: given to distant relatives and donated to specific museums
or charities to be auctioned off according to her mother's will.
With so little time in her schedule, she'd given the list to her
contractor, Mr. Brown, who owned a deconstruction company
out of Leesburg. He planned to salvage the doors, hardware,
wood paneling . . . everything he could, actually, and recycle
the rest. Profits to her would come in the forms of sale of the
salvage, a tax-deductible donation of the refuse, and selling the
land rights to Smoothie Hut, Inc.

"Okay. Give me the key, and I'll try it this time." The stan-
dard key in the dead bolt worked fine. It was the long, nondescript skeleton key that fit into the ancient lock under the
doorknob that he was struggling with. She pulled her gaze
from the second of two large picture windows on the front of

the house that were cracked, shattered in fact, yet inexplicably intact. "Old locks get rusty, Mr. Brown. It's as simple as that. This house will come down, no matter what you think it's trying to tell us."

"Yes, ma'am, and I'll be right here waitin' on it." He stepped back with his hands low on his hips. His fifty-year-old beer belly looked taut under the green T-shirt he wore with an unbuttoned blue-plaid cotton shirt. He was shorter than her five-foot-nine frame and looked every bit as much a demolition man as she did a financial analyst. Well, she at least hoped the distinction was that clear. No offense to Mr. Brown, but she'd worked very hard to get where she was, and she liked to think that people could tell merely by looking at her that she was diligent and good at what she did.

"I hope you'll be doing more than just waiting. Contrary to what you think, this house has no magical powers, and it's not going to simply fall down on its own when it feels like it." She slipped the strap of her purse up high on her shoulder, put the key in the lock, and gave it a hard twist. There was no give inside, so she rattled the knob a little and twisted more gently the second time.

Mr. Brown was watching intently with a patient but smug expression on his face, and it was making her edgy. She realigned her body and the strap of her purse so he couldn't see, then shook the knob twice, good and hard, before twisting the key—this time in the opposite direction.

Truly. She didn't have the time or the energy for this. A scream of frustration started to build in her throat.

"What about oil? Have you tired oiling the lock? Maybe it just needs lubricating."

"I did, but I'm happy to do it again for you, ma'am."

"Please. Call me M.J. *Ma'am* is so . . . my mother." Her cringe was barely visible.

"Yes, ma—" He caught himself. "Oil's out in my truck. I'll be right back."

"Fine."

She left the key in the lock and turned to watch him bound down the steps of the wide front porch and lope across the unkempt lawn toward his truck.

It was a warm, muggy night in August, and the fireflies were still active—jumping, frolicking as if at play. She glanced down at the top step where it met the tall white support pillar, where she'd spent hundreds of blissful hours as a child watching them before bedtime, dreaming of fairies and fantastic wonderlands where she reigned as Princess Ariel.

She was almost thirty-three now, and those memories seemed a hundred years old.

So did the paint on the pillars and porch, she ruminated in distaste. Only the ornate cast-iron gate remained of the fence that once encircled the front yard; weeds had choked out what few flowers remained in the beds along the sidewalk. She thought she ought to feel bad that her mother had fallen into such straits at the end of her life, but she didn't—it had been her mother's choice.

There were track marks crisscrossing the front lawn from some monster machine Mr. Brown had loaded up and sent elsewhere to work until he gained cooperation from the house . . . that's what he'd said, *cooperation from the house*, like it was something alive.

She looked away from the yard, and because there was nothing else to do while she waited for Mr. Brown, she reached out and rattled the key in the lock again—and the door sprang open.

"Oh, for . . . Mr. Brown, I have it," she called over her shoulder as she stepped inside. A sigh of aggravation turned to a hacking cough full of dust. Aside from a slightly thicker layer of grime on everything, the place hadn't changed since her last visit a few days after her mother's sudden passing.

The dark wood floors and faded wallpaper in the hall harkened back to a time when fern fronds were in fashion. And while both the front living room and the small parlor on the other side held proof of her mother's attempts at modernizing the décor, the stark white walls had long ago gone grunge brown . . . a not-too-bad basic color, except that everything in both rooms had gone grunge with them.

Yet it was the smell of the place that kept her rooted in the doorway and feeling oddly anxious. A musty smell, of course, as one would expect in a house of this age, but other scents as well . . . her mother's lily perfume, apples and cinnamon . . . and something else . . . baby powder maybe.

"My wife says some things just need a woman's touch. I guess that dang lock is one of them, huh?" Mr. Brown joined her in the vestibule, looking around, nodding his head, his hands on his hips. "I'll get the moving crew back in here first thing Monday morning to remove the items on the list you sent me. I've lined up a good antique dealer for the rest of this stuff. My team can come in Tuesday and start the salvage. If that works for you . . . "

Nodding vaguely, she was still wrapped up in the odors that hadn't faded in her olfactory receptors.

"In fact, I can take those two little tea tables you want shipped to Florida right now. You said to rush them?"

"Mmm, I did, to in-laws from my mother's third marriage." She was staring at a photographed portrait of the three sisters hanging in the hall and speaking absently. "She stole them during the divorce, but I guess she didn't want to take the grudge too far beyond her grave. They've been calling. . . . " She paused. "They all looked so young here."

He nodded noncommittally. "I can drop them off at the postal business center tonight . . . the tables, I mean . . . or first thing Monday morning on my way back here. They'll box 'em up and ship 'em. Insure 'em, too."

"That's fine. Thank you."

He hurried off to fetch a classic eighteenth-century Massachusetts reverse serpentine tilt-top tea table and an American Chippendale from the same era. She ambled down the hall, her high heels clicking in the silence, toward the big kitchen at the back of the house renovated—made bigger and updated—almost fifty years earlier for her aunt Odelia, who'd loved to cook.

The scent of apples and cinnamon grew stronger, thick like a palpable thing. She stopped and turned with the distinct impression she was being watched. "Creepy old house, you'll be whistling a different tune next week, I promise you."

"You talkin' to me, ma'am?" Mr. Brown met her in the hallway coming from the small parlor.

"No." She looked him over. "Why are you out of breath? Are you ill?"

"No, ma'am—"

"M.J."

"But I'm plenty embarrassed to tell you . . . well, it's the damnedest thing, but considering the lock and the windows and all, and what I told you before . . . I guess I just assumed that once we got the door open . . . "

"What is it, Mr. Brown?" She was down to her last drop of patience.

"I can't lift the tables." She stared at him until he finally looked away. "I also can't push them, and the little doily deal and candy dish on the one in the living room won't come off. Queer as snow in July, is all I'm sayin'."

"No, what you're saying makes even less sense than that." She stepped around him, heading for the living room. "It makes no sense at all."

She strode up to the mahogany claw-and-ball-foot tea table where the scent of baby powder tickled her nose and all but made her sneeze. Taking the faded old crochet doily in one hand and the small crystal bowl in the other, she lifted them off the table . . . rather *tried* to lift them off, but they wouldn't budge. They wanted to, she could feel a tiny bit of give, but it was as if something was holding them in place. She pried up the edges of the doily to see if some idiot had glued them to the table.

"Is there a light in here?" The sun had yet to set, but it was dark and gloomy in the house.

"Power's off, but I've got a flashlight out in my truck."

And he was out the door. M.J. could sense his trail of relief and didn't blame him. She hadn't been able to shake the sensation of being watched, but it didn't feel . . . well, it didn't feel threatening, like being watched by a stalker or someone who meant her harm might. It didn't make the hairs on the back of her neck stand up or call on her instinctive alarm to run. Still, it wasn't entirely comfortable, so she whispered out loud, "It's rude to stare at people, especially if they're not allowed to stare back."

"There, you see? I told you she'd catch on quickly." It was her mother's voice coming from behind her. Spinning around, she was in time to see her materialize, tall and young and beautiful, before the boxed-in fireplace. "Hello, darling, sorry to cause you all this trouble, but who knew that crossing over to the Other Side was going to be such a royal pain in the ass?"

TWO

"You knew it, you ninny," came another voice from the doorway where Aunt Odelia, short and plumpish with pink cheeks and wild curly blond hair—and much, much younger than M.J. remembered her—was entering the room from the hall, drawing with her the wafting aroma of fresh-baked apple pies. "Imogene and I told you before you died. We said, 'Crossing over to the Other Side is a royal pain in the ass' . . . unless you know what you're looking for."

"Which none of us do," said a third voice, again behind M.J., who turned to see her aunt Imogene *sitting* on the Chippendale tea table, doily and candy dish in her lap. "And now you've got this dear girl trying to remove things from the house and planning to tear the place down when you know perfectly well she can't until we leave."

"How old are you?" M.J. asked of Imogene, whom she'd only seen in pictures as a sad, dour-looking woman.

Her aunt smiled and wrinkled her nose in a cute, impish way. "As you're seeing me now, you mean? In my late twenties, I think. I was a looker, wasn't I?"

"And now you're a ghost. The three of you are ghosts."

They all seemed to think about the term and weighed it against the way they felt.

"That's such a generic term, don't you think?" her mother asked, looking as she always did—expecting better of M.J. "What about specter or apparition?"

"I'm fond of ghoul myself." Odelia giggled.

"There's a list of things you could call us, dear, but the facts are these: our bodies are no longer alive, and the rest of who we were can't leave this house until we find what we lost here." Imogene had a plain way of speaking, which M.J. liked.

"Which is?"

"Well, that's just it." Odelia giggled again. "We have no idea. If we knew what we were looking for, we could have turned this place inside out eons ago, found it, and moved on. We need your help."

"Mine?" She felt the blood drain from her face and sweat pop out on her forehead. "No way. First off, I don't have the time for this, and secondly, I don't think I believe in ghosts . . . or whatever you prefer to call yourselves. I'm leaving."

"Sorry." Mr. Brown rushed into the room, huffing for breath, with a wide-beam emergency flashlight in his hand. "Never fails that when you want something it's always on the bottom. Here ya go."

Stymied for a second, M.J. took the flashlight and aimed it at the tea table . . . and the aunt thereon.

"Tell me what you see, Mr. Brown."

"The table you want me to send to someone in Florida."

"Wait a second, wait a second." Odelia called out, rushing toward her sister—with steps, not floating as one expected of a ghost. "I love being in the spotlight. Shine it on me, dear."

"Anything else, Mr. Brown?"

"The thingy and the dish on top?" He cast her a sidelong glance and looked back. "And a lot of dust."

"Really, darling, do you think we're going to let just any-one see us?" her mother asked. "In this particular state of disarray?"

"Did you hear that, Mr. Brown?"

"What's that?"

M.J. sighed and shook her head. "Let's just get the table and get out of here."

They both stepped up to the table. The closer M.J. got, the stronger Odelia's scent became, until she wanted apple pie so bad her salivary glands overflowed.

"Please move aside," she said to Odelia, and Mr. Brown sidestepped a few inches to be directly across from her.

Taking the edge of the table in four places they tried to lift it. It didn't even quiver.

"What do you think you're doing?" she asked Imogene, her voice cross and frustrated.

"Trying to move the table," Mr. Brown snapped back.

"I'm sitting as hard as I can," Imogene replied with a grimace and a grunt.

"I want this table."

"I get that. But it seems to be stuck to the floor."

"Not you—" She stopped herself. If not him, who? "Okay. Fine. Have it your way. Mr. Brown, you were right. The house is clearly possessed or whatever you want to call it, but I'm a firm believer that where there's a will, there's a way." She adjusted her purse strap on her shoulder and her heels marched a snappy tattoo toward the front door. "So come Monday morning I want this place loaded with dynamite and blown off the face of the earth."

The next morning, Saturday, a reluctant M.J. once again made the trip from Alexandria to Johnnie's Bend.

Mr. Brown had whittled a fine point to the fact that the harder they fought against the house, the more likely they would be to draw attention to its peculiarity, which would then draw peculiar people who would in turn, no doubt, provide her with any number of peculiar situations far worse than having a house that refused to fall down. He hadn't had to stab her with it; she got the point—the last thing she needed was more peculiar.

Furthermore, given a little time and distance to cool off and gather her thoughts, she found she had a few questions, such as:

"If you can lock us out of the house, why didn't you lock us in last night?" she asked her mother and aunts as they congregated in the kitchen to watch Odelia make pies. "You said you needed my help, and I wasn't planning to ever come back here. Why'd you let me leave?"

In the sunny kitchen they were considerably more . . . nimbus than they had been the night before in the gloomy shadows of the evening. In the light of day the house took on a fascinating *second life*—the only way she could describe it—one hovering over the other so that while the three of them sat at the kitchen table together, M.J. sat at one as solid and real as she was while her mother and Aunt Imogene lounged in chairs across from her that were as hazy and transparent as they were.

The same was true of Odelia, who worked happily rolling out crusts on a butcher board that was now a ceramic countertop and baking in an oven that was in the same place in the kitchen but larger and from a different era.

"Goodness." Imogene laughed. "We let you leave because if you have even a single drop of our blood in your veins, then you would have been mad enough to chew nails and spit rivets if we'd locked you in. Better to let you go and let your natural curiosity bring you back." She held her hands out as if it were as clear as she was.

"I told them you could be quite stubborn, Mari—"

"Don't say it."

"It's your name."

"I prefer M.J."

Her mother played with one of the diamond rings on her fingers. There were four of them, one from each of her marriages. She sighed. "Well, anyway, I'm gratified to see you're learning to flex a little, darling."

"Flex? Are you kidding? Living with you, I flexed like a freaking Slinky, Mother. It always had to be your way. Did you know about these two before you died? Is that why you refused to sell and move to a retirement community?"

"I refused to sell because this was always my home—except when I didn't live here, of course. After Papa passed, Odelia lived here because she had nowhere else to go. And you and I came to visit from time to time—"

"Between marriages."

"Well, where does one go when one's heart has been shattered, first by death and then by unfaithfulness and greed and neglect? One goes home, of course, to where she has always been loved and sheltered and protected from the harsh realities of the world."

With a fond, sisterly smirk, Imogene chuckled. "I don't suppose it'll surprise you to hear that your mother wanted to be Sandra Dee when she was a teen."

Her mother gasped. "*Early* teen."

Odelia giggled. "She really wanted to be Elizabeth Taylor, but Papa nearly had a stroke when she told him."

"Why? Hasn't she always been considered one of the all-time greats . . . as an actress, I mean? Her personal life aside?"

"Oh, it wouldn't have mattered if it was Meryl Streep or Sally Field. Acting was not what he considered an acceptable profession for a woman." Odelia made the comment casually, her hands on her hips, looking around the kitchen in confusion. She snatched up a small wicker basket with an exasperated "My stars," and headed for the back door.

"Where's she going?"

The sisters were unconcerned. Her mother answered. "She wants more apples."

Okay, first off, M.J. had no idea the ghosts could leave the house. And secondly, not only were the pies as phantom as everything else involved with the three sisters . . . aside from the aroma . . . but where the hell in the backyard was Odelia getting apples?

"Wait a second." She jumped up from her table and reached the back door in time to see Odelia passing through a five-foot wooden fence on the far end of the yard as if it weren't there. "Odelia. Wait. Where are you going? Odelia?"

She heard her happy, chubby aunt giggle from a distance greater than the neighbor's backyard. "Not to worry, dear, I won't be long."

"But where are you going?"

"To my orchard. Papa planted it just for me. There are several different kinds of apple trees, cherry trees, peach trees, and pear trees." She paused, her voice echoing. "The peach tree doesn't bear much fruit, but it tries. Don't you, you sweet old thing?"

M.J. jumped as high as she could to peek over the fence to see which tree she was talking to . . . though there didn't seem to be any trees there at all. "Odelia. How far away from the house did he plant the trees? Where are you?"

"Oh dear, Imogene is better with feet and yards than I am, but it's a ways," she called back. "Flies, you know."

"Flies?"

"They come for the ripe fruit if I don't get to it first. If the trees were too close to the house . . . oh my, Papa would be so angry. They're pesky, you know. Summer flies. And it's like he always said, I can certainly use the exercise. The hard part is hauling all the fruit back to the house."

Papa, Hobart Hedbo, was beginning to sound like someone M.J. was glad she'd never had the chance to meet. "I can smell your apple pies, you know."

"Really?"

She remembered Odelia as a sweet, kind, older woman. She died of breast cancer in her late fifties before M.J. had a real chance to get to know her. . . .

Well, that wasn't exactly true, she realized, shifting her weight uncomfortably. She could have gotten to know Odelia had she been a different sort of youngster, she supposed. But then, who thinks farther than the tip of their nose when they're young?

"They smell delicious, Aunt Odelia."

"Secret recipe. I have a million of them. I wanted to be a great chef, you know."

"What, like Martha Stewart and Rachael Ray?"

Odelia scoffed. "Our Lady of the Ladle. There's never been another like her."

"Who?"

"Julia Child. She didn't *just* cook. She *studied* cooking. She *knew* food. She wasn't simply a television personality who knew how to cook. She was a larger-than-life chef. An American culinary icon."

M.J. smiled, enjoying her good-natured aunt's show of vehemence.

"I wanted to study at Le Cordon Bleu or even the CIA."

"The what?"

"CIA. The Culinary Institute of America in New York." Her voice was getting closer; she was coming back. "Or even Kendall College in Chicago, but no. Papa said if I wanted to go to college, I could become a teacher or a nurse. If I wanted to study history or anthropology, he could help me get a job in a museum or a library, maybe. Those would be acceptable professions. But all great chefs are men, he'd say, and he wouldn't waste his money to get me cooking classes when he could pay Mrs. Wheimer to teach me. . . . She was our cook then. He said even Betty Crocker was made up and named after William Crocker, one of the company directors at the time."

She stepped back through the fence suddenly, startling her niece, her arms around the wicker basket that was now full of hazy-looking apples.

"So what did you do?" M.J. asked, giving the little ghost a moment to catch her breath, struggling with the impulse to take the heavy basket from her. It was a short struggle. Feeling ridiculous, she reached for the apples, and Odelia gave them up gladly. She held her arms out in a circle as Odelia had, knowing full well that they'd pass straight through the basket if she didn't.

"Oh, I cried. I cried and cried, hoping Papa would change his mind, but he never did. Eventually, I let Mrs. Wheimer teach me what she could. Imogene and Adeline bought me all of Julia's cookbooks . . . and of course as every fine chef is wont to do, I did a great deal of experimenting on my own while I waited—" She caught herself and looked ashamed.

"Waited for what, Odelia?"

She leaned in so close, M.J. could almost spit apple juice, then whispered, "For Papa to die." She stepped back, aghast. "I've never said that out loud before. My stars. You must think I'm just a terrible person. Oh my."

"No, no. I don't. Really. I understand completely. I do."

"I don't!" An angry male voice from the other side of the fence was quickly reinforced with the scowling face of a man as he peered over the fence at her. "What the hell's the matter with you? Are you nuts?"

Three

"What?"

He glanced down at her bowed arms, and she immediately dropped them to her sides.

"My apples! Now they'll all have bruises," Odelia exclaimed, falling to her knees to gather them up from around M.J.'s feet.

"Are you rehearsing for a play or something?" the man asked, giving her a better explanation than *nuts*—not that it was any of his business in the first place.

Unless he was standing on something, she gauged him at close to six feet, his dark hair clipped short and neat; the lack of fashionable facial hair a plus in her book. But it was the way his eyes flashed from angry to intrigued that popped her defenses in place.

"Why should I tell you?"

"Because my six-year-old son heard you talking to yourself, and now he thinks you're able to speak to the ghosts that he thinks live in that old house." He frowned again. "Come to think of it, what are you doing over there? I didn't know the place was for sale."

"It's not, and I don't have to explain anything to you." She hesitated. "Sorry about your little boy though. I didn't mean to upset him."

The tough-soft paradox of her nature fascinated him. He shook his head. "He wasn't upset. I was. He's been obsessed with the ghosts since we moved in here two years ago. At least once or twice a week he'll come in and tell me one walked across the yard looking for apples. I come out, there's nothing here. I explain there's no such thing as ghosts, distract him with other things like the doctor told me to, and he's right back at it the next week. At least today he had someone else back here besides the ghost."

Odelia giggled at her feet. "That's my little friend, Jimmy. Sweet boy."

M.J. glowered down at her aunt as she got to her feet and picked up her basket of apples.

"Like I said, I'm sorry about that." She turned to go inside with Odelia.

"Ryan Doyle," he said with a friendly smile, extending his arm over the fence to his elbow.

She turned back and glanced first at his smile and his out-stretched hand, then at the unruly gone-to-seed-and-weed flower-erbed below and decided just to wave a hand from where she was. "Hi. M. J. Biderman."

"M.J?" he said and she watched in trepidation as a slow, sexy smile spread across his face. "M.J. . . . Maribelle Joy."

Now in reflex mode, her molars ground against each other, and she growled as she stomped her right foot in disgust. She stared at him as if he were a hideous six-headed snake. "How do you know that?"

"That's your name, isn't it?" He laughed, the light in his eyes dancing. "Your mother told me. She said you were a little touchy about it."

"Ridiculous names are the Hedbo curse." She didn't need to, of course, but she automatically held the screen door open for Odelia because her arms were full.

"And you married Biderman?" His eyes continued to twin-kle with delight.

"No." She grimaced at him, not wanting to enjoy the fact that he was enjoying himself at her expense. But her name was ludicrous. How could anyone hear it and not laugh? "I was born a Calvert. My father died. *My mother* married Larry Biderman, who adopted me before she divorced him and mar-ried Michael Moore, who I refused to let adopt me because he already had four kids and it was the only way for me to stand apart from them until my mother finally dumped him for Jonathan Shaw, who insisted I call him Uncle Jon instead of Dad because it made him feel old. I was in my early twenties by then anyway, so"—she shrugged—"I just stuck with Biderman."

"Well, it's not a moniker I'll forget anytime soon."

She simply nodded, simpered, and followed her aunt into the house.

"Mother, how could you?" she asked before the door was closed completely. "Is nothing sacred to you? Telling family secrets to perfect strangers . . . Who else have you told?"

"Oh posh, your name is not a family secret, darling." She waved diamond-encrusted fingers in the air. "It comes from the Latin Mabel, meaning *lovable*, as both your father and I believed you to be the moment we laid eyes on you." She threw her arms out wide. "And you filled us with such *joy*. What else could we name you but Maribelle Joy?"

"Jane, Susan, Linda . . . Mabel?"

Her mother laughed. Even Imogene and Odelia wore indulgent smiles.

"You would have hated Mabel much more than Maribelle, darling, trust me. Besides, you looked like a Maribelle Joy as a child. A little fairy named Maribelle Joy, with your soft brown curls and your big green eyes and you were so perfect . . . *everything* was so perfect. It was the happiest time of my life. Just you, me, and your daddy."

Adeline sighed contentedly, and a look of happiness and . . . peace settled in the fine slopes and planes of a face that had always been beautiful and animated but now radiated with an inner glow and verve M.J. couldn't recall seeing before.

"But then Daddy died in the accident, and I could never quite live up to your expectations, could I? Instead of the perky, cheerleader-type daughter you wanted, you got a shy, awkward math nerd."

"I just wanted you to have some fun, darling."

"You paid my stepbrother to take me to my prom."

"He told you?"

"I guessed, and you just confirmed."

"Ow. She gotcha," Odelia muttered as she sorted out bruised apples.

"That's not fair." Adeline looked indignant. "And it would have been wrong to miss your own prom, sweetheart."

"It's more wrong to meddle in my life simply because it doesn't meet with your standards, Mother." Also, Adeline hadn't denied M.J.'s original statement—that she'd never once lived up to her mother's expectations. Despite the fact that she'd known this for most of her life, it hurt. A lot. "I have a headache. I'm going for a walk."

She could hear the sisters chattering as she snatched up her purse and left through the front door.

She walked down the hill into the town of Johnnie's Bend, noting how far *up* the hill the town had spread in the past few years. Hedbo Street, named after the man and the house, had been rezoned for commercial use and was now an oddly appealing mix of older homes and new businesses of every kind.

She didn't expect to recognize anyone; she hadn't lived in Johnnie's Bend for years and hadn't attended school there as a child for more than a few months or a single academic year between her mother's marriages. So it was a surprise to her when halfway through the club sandwich she ordered at King's Café, she heard her name ring out loud and clear.

"Maribelle Joy!"

She flinched and began to slide deeper into the shadow of her booth before she saw who was calling her and decided to stand her ground. She shook her head at Ryan Doyle, refusing to answer to that name, and picked up another triangle of the first food she'd eaten all day—it was going a long way to curing her headache.

He waved and patted the shoulders of other people he knew as he made his way across the room to her table. With laughter still ringing in his voice, he tried to cajole her.

"Ah, come on, don't be mad. It was out of my mouth before I could stop it. Tell you what—we came in for hot fudge sundaes. Let us buy you one."

"We?"

"My son, Jimmy." He half turned and, sure enough, standing behind him was a small boy with shaggy black hair and wide, almond-shaped brown eyes that looked much too clever and much too old to belong to someone his age. He had on a multicolored striped T-shirt and denim shorts and his feet—

below bone-thin legs with bandaged knees—were encased in red sneakers with no socks. She thought it ironic that she knew three ghosts who didn't make her as anxious as this one little boy did. "Jimmy, this is the lady you heard talking this morning. Ms. Biderman. I told you she wasn't a ghost."

Jimmy narrowed his eyes and studied her assiduously as his father urged him into the booth and to move farther down the bench so he could follow.

"Mind if we join you?"

She gave him a do-I-really-have-a-choice look and he grinned at her—no.

"Okay, so the burning question on our minds is"—he wagged his hand between him and his son—"what happened to the cool backhoe?"

"The . . . oh, Mr. Brown's machine . . . Well, he decided not to use it after all. Or at least not right now. We're going to try to recycle what we can from the house first. Go Green." She chanted the slogan lamely. The kid was still watching her. What went on in a head that small? "He tells me there's a use for everything—even asphalt roofing is reused for hot-mix paving, and people will pay big money for some of the fine carpentry inside the house."

"So you're not even tempted to keep the old place."

"No." Her answer was too quick and too sharp. "I mean, I have no emotional attachment to the place. A few memories from my childhood, maybe, but it was more my mother's touchstone than mine. A place she loved and came back to when she needed to feel safe. I don't have those sorts of feelings for the place." She lowered her eyes from Ryan's intense gaze to Jimmy's—time for *first contact*? "And next summer you'll have a Smoothie Hut in your own backyard. How about that?"

He tipped his head to one side and considered his answer. Suddenly his enormous brown eyes began to fill with tears, and his chin quivered. M.J. was so appalled he might as well have been growing extra appendages.

"What will happen to them?" he whimpered. "If you tear down their house and put up a Smoothie Hut, where will they go? Can they stay at the Smoothie Hut?"

In general, M.J. made a rule of not playing stupid, but in this case it felt . . . well, smart.

"Hey, champ." Ryan put his arm around his son and tried to

soothe him. "What's all this? Don't you want a Smoothie Hut next door?"

"No," he wailed and turned his face into his father's chest.

"Ah. You're not worried that we won't be having hot fudge sundaes anymore, are you? Cuz you know I can't live for more than a week without one, right?"

"No." He sniffed and lifted his tear-stained face toward Ryan. "I'm worried about my friends, Dad. Where will they go?"

"My guess is they'll be coming to our house, hoping to get free smoothies out of me." He chucked good-naturedly and glanced at M.J. as he smoothed dark hair from his son's face. "I'll have to get a second job—"

"Not those friends!" The boy was distraught now. "The ladies, Dad, the ladies who live in the house. Where will they go?" Once again he launched himself at his father's chest. And the sisters thought Adeline was dramatic. "Where will they go if she smashes down their house? Tell her to don't do it, Dad."

Casually, as if this had nothing to do with her, M.J. picked up another triangle of her club sandwich and resumed her lunch.

It didn't matter how he'd come to know there was more than one ghost in the house—whether Odelia had told him or if all three of them had been outside the house and talked to him— she thought it was cruel of them to make themselves known to him and couldn't help but wonder if he'd been frightened at first. Terrified, maybe. And yet now he was concerned with their welfare?

Children were a total mystery to her.

To Ryan as well, if the look on his face was any indication.

"Jimbo." Gently, he took the boy by the shoulders and held him away to look at his face. "Is this about those ghosts again?" Jimmy nodded, and M.J. chewed a little faster. Ryan sighed and sent an apologetic look her way. "You see what I mean? I've done everything I can to convince him there are no ghosts in that house. Would you mind giving it a try?"

"Me?" She squirreled her bite of turkey club in her cheek to keep from choking. "But I—"

The expression he gave her was beseeching; he was counting on her to tell the boy the truth. Her gaze gravitated to Jimmy's . . . which was all but daring her to lie . . . because he already knew the truth. Instinctively, she knew this was a deal-breaker with the boy. Tell the truth and become an adult he can respect and trust or lie and become subhuman slime. And this mattered to her, why?

She nodded, looked down at her plate as she replaced her food and gathered her thoughts. Why was this suddenly *her* problem to deal with? Her mother and aunts should never have contacted Jimmy. Of course, once they found what they'd lost in the house and were free to cross over to the Other Side, this would no longer be a problem—for Jimmy or for her. The sisters would be gone, and the house would come down. So, as far as she could tell, her choices were few. She had to help the ghosts find what they had lost, and she needed to convince Jimmy that they had better places to go.

"Well, I don't know that much about ghosts." She saw Ryan's face change in her peripheral vision as she directed herself to the boy. He'd just have to think she was humoring the boy to prove their point . . . well, his point, anyway. "But maybe if you come over tomorrow afternoon, you'll see that that big old house isn't as scary . . . or worth saving . . . as you might think."

"I'm not a-scared of the house . . . or the ladies."

"Good." He was sort of cute in a fuzzy-puppy-on-a-thick-leash sort of way . . . from her side of the table. "Come after lunch and bring a flashlight."

The waitress arrived to take their order.

"Let me guess." She grinned at Jimmy. "Hot fudge sundaes."

"You got it." Ryan ruffled his son's hair. "We'll have our usual plus one more for our friend here."

M.J. waved her hand, shook her head, and made negative noises as she finished chewing and swallowing her last bite of sandwich.

"Actually, would you happen to have any apple pie?"

Four

Her mother held out her hands to stop M.J.'s lecture, then turned them palms-up for understanding.

"How many times must we tell you, darling? Children, until they reach the age of reason, straddle the fence between fantasy and reality and are more susceptible to seeing us whether we want them to or not." She stopped in front of a floor mirror in her room and smoothed her already perfect blond shag of thick, lustrous curls. M.J. noted there was no reflection in the glass. "He came here twice before I died, with his father, who wanted me to convince the boy that Odelia didn't exist. I did my best. I showed him pictures of when she was as old as I was at the time . . . a truly hideous creature, you must remember. Almost as wide as she was tall and the pain from her arthritis permanently written on her face so that she scowled almost constantly. The boy didn't recognize her, of course, but he could smell her pies. The little bugger broke loose from his father and found her in the kitchen. What more could I do?"

"Couldn't she have waited somewhere else until he was gone?"

"It may not have done any good." She walked by the cold fireplace to touch and readjust the pictures that were—and weren't—on the mantel at the time of her death. Lingering over the photo in the center, she caressed the glass with two fingers as she spoke. "We can travel anywhere we want . . . anywhere we've been before, but there are places we, our spirits, are more attracted to than others. It's usually a place where our strongest emotions were felt, a place we loved or a place where the decisions we made affected us most . . . or for some, places where we were murdered."

"You weren't—"

"Gracious no, Maribelle, I would have told you by now." She turned from the mantel to face her daughter, her impatience present but short-lived. "But those are the souls who give us a bad name, you know . . . stuck in the places where they feel only fear and anger until they can find whatever they lost there and pass over to the Other Side. Dreadful, really."

"You mean, find their lives again?" M.J. frowned. She stood and walked to the mantel to inspect the photos thereon. Husbands mostly. The shot in the center was of M.J. at age three, sitting on her father's lap; his dark hair slicked back, his dark eyes wonderfully wicked and dancing happily. Her mother embraced them both from behind—blond and golden, blue eyes twinkling like sun on calm waters.

"Oh no." She smiled. "The loss of your life is, of course, a permanent thing, sweetheart. But the dying part isn't what's important. It's everything that leads up to it. And if you're mostly satisfied with your life—content at the time of your death—then death is simply a part of the package. But murder . . . that's unnatural . . . like suicide. Lots of issues there, let me tell you."

Her mother's tolerance in explaining how being a ghost—or becoming one—worked was uncharacteristic of the edgy, easily irritated mother she was accustomed to. In the past, as a child, M.J. was given adult answers to questions and was expected to look them up or fathom them out on her own . . . As an adult, she found she'd had no interest in her mother's answers at all.

"So someone who's been murdered would be looking for, what? Revenge against the person who killed them? What would they need to find to pass over?"

Her mother's smooth, lovely brow furrowed as she thought of an answer. M.J. watched in silence, recalling a time long ago when she had considered her mother *the most beautiful of all the princesses in the land.*

She heard the words in her head in a deep male whisper and

felt suddenly warm and happy and . . . entrenched in a love so deep and solid it rocked her to the core.

"Maybe revenge," her mother speculated, drawing her back to their conversation. "Haunt the murderer, perhaps, but that still wouldn't get them to the Other Side. They'd have to stay here to do that. No, I would think it would be more about what got them killed in the first place, some sort of explanation . . . forgiveness maybe, or just acceptance of the fact."

"Some way to make peace with it."

Adeline gave a short nod. "Peace. That would be nice." She hesitated. "I can't tell you how frustrating it is to not know what you're looking for."

"We'll figure it out." She, too, nodded, realizing that might have been the nicest thing she'd said to her mother in quite a while. "We used to be a team, remember?"

Adeline took on that same inner glow of tranquillity and delight that M.J. had seen the day before . . . the one in the picture on the mantel. Why, oh why, wasn't she enough to make her mother shine all the time?

"The boy and his father are arriving," Imogene announced, appearing in the room beside her sister. Despite her more youthful appearance, she had the same sad, woeful expression on her face that M.J. had come to associate with her in the past—which hadn't been there the day before.

"Is something wrong, Aunt Imogene? Has something happened?"

She smiled kindly. "No, dear. I'm just having one of my days."

"It's the boy." Adeline put her arm around her sister's shoulders. "Children upset her."

"Oh. Sorry. I didn't know."

"How could you?" Still smiling, she laced her fingers with her sister's and gave her a hug. "But don't concern yourself with me. It's more important to ease the boy's fears, the poor little thing. He must be so confused."

M.J. chuckled as she stepped to the door. "No, actually he's not confused. He's as certain you're here as I am." She turned to look at them. "I can't believe I just said that."

She was halfway down the wide staircase when the door knocker echoed through the lower floor. She looked over the banister to make certain Odelia was out of sight for the time being, then skipped down the last few steps and across the foyer to welcome her guests.

"Hi." She didn't mean to sound so exuberant, but after spending the entire morning with ghosts, real people made her feel . . . well, glad to be alive. "Welcome. Please come in."

Ryan, clearly assuming her high spirits were for his benefit, grinned back and nudged Jimmy. Jimmy drew his left arm out from behind his back and shook a bouquet of cheerful white daisies at her. "Dad says we have to give you these."

She pressed her lips together and took them as solemnly as they were offered. "Thank you, Jimmy, they're beautiful. I . . . You know, there used to be flowers everywhere here when I was a little girl. Inside, outside. The air was sweet with them."

"Now the air smells like apple pies."

She closed the door, her nose sniffing. The scent was there but very faint. "Is that what that is? My aunt Odelia liked to bake. I bet she baked so many apple pies the smell is stuck in the wallpaper."

"Na-uh. It's stuck in the kitchen."

"It is? Well, let's go see why."

He was off like a light, needing no further permission to seek out proof of his ghosts. M.J. and Ryan followed at a sedate pace.

"Thanks for doing this." She could see his prime objective was to put his son's mind at ease; seeing her a clear but solid second. Trying to fool one and lying to the other wasn't how she would normally handle . . . well, any situation involving a father and his young son. But what was normal about ghosts? "I've tried everything I can think of. . . . I'm lost."

"I'm no expert, but I've been told that their imaginations are almost as strong as their sense of reality. I thought if he came over and took a good look around, and if I got a little creative myself, maybe we could work something out." Still, she felt like she was doing something wrong. "I'm not making any promises. Like I said, I'm not a child psychologist or anything. I mean, the last kid I had any contact with was me, and I have to tell you I was not, in general, a happy camper."

He laughed. "So what do you really think about kids?"

"I don't know. I think I could take one in a fair fight if it was small enough, probably, but I tend to group Roswell, the Bermuda Triangle, and kids in the same weird little mystery group." She held the tips of her fingers together to show him.

"But you don't hate kids, right?"

"No. I just don't know any." She looked at him. "Yours seems okay."

He laughed. "Even with the ghost thing?"

She was thoughtful. "Yeah." She especially liked that he didn't back down when he knew he was right . . . which might also be a problem for her. "I like that he's worried about them, where they'll go when the house comes down."

They entered the kitchen to find Jimmy standing near the tiled counter, arms at his sides, his expression mutinous and suspicious. "What'd you do with her?"

Okay, so maybe not a fair fight. "Well, it's not like I killed her, Jimmy. We talked. I told her I had plans for the house and that it was time for her to leave."

"Where'd she go?"

"I don't know. Wherever ghosts go when they're done being ghosts."

"Heaven?"

She needed to think quickly . . . she wasn't a particularly religious person, but she didn't know what he'd been taught. She glanced at Ryan, who was watching and revealing very little.

"I'm going to say yes," she guessed, nodding. "Odelia was a very sweet, very good person. I think she did go to heaven."

"What about the sad one?"

"The sad one?"

"The one who watches me from the upstairs window and cries."

"You've heard her crying?"

"No, but I can tell. I see her tears and then she puts her face in a paper towel or something and her shoulders shake. I can tell she's crying."

Her mother? No, the concept of her mother crying over a child for no reason just didn't fit. But Imogene, who had lost her young son . . . well, watching over Jimmy every day must be a torment for her. M.J. reasserted her resolve to help the three sisters find their way out of the house, and not for the sake of the Smoothie Hut anymore.

"That would have to be my Aunt Imogene. She had a little

boy a long time ago. He got sick and died. But she's gone, too, Jimmy. They're all gone."

"All?" This from Ryan, who was beginning to take on the same dubious air his son had—like he couldn't tell if she was telling the truth or not, but from an entirely different perspective than his son's.

"Jimmy said there were three ladies in the house. My mother and her two sisters were the last true Hedbos to grow up and live in this house. I can't think of anyone else it might be."

"Have you seen these ghosts?" Now he looked like he wished he hadn't asked her to help. Jimmy looked expectant.

"Sure." Stepping between them, she gave a play-along look to the father that the son couldn't see. She reached for a vase for the daisies. "I sat them down yesterday afternoon. I told them Jimmy was concerned about them and that they had to find someplace else to go because the house was coming down. Would you like some coffee? The power's off, so I brought a thermos today." Her laugh was nervous. "After they cremate me all they'll find in my urn are tiny pieces of bone and a few pounds of ground Colombian dark roast."

Ryan chuckled, his qualms put to rest. But Jimmy wasn't buying any of it.

"If they coulda gone to heaven whenever they wanted, why'd they stay here?"

"Good question." She'd have to remember not to underestimate his intelligence—his brain worked just fine despite its small container. "Maybe they needed to find something or do something or . . . or maybe they were just having fun." She nodded. "That's my bet. I think they were just having fun together."

"They can do that in heaven." He looked around, and he was clearly thinking—a notion that alarmed every nerve ending in M.J.'s body. "I think they're lookin' for something." His gaze came around to meet hers, and she felt suddenly pinned to the wall with his directness and honesty. "What are they lookin' for?"

"I don't know." She felt she had no choice but to answer truthfully; she felt mesmerized by his bright, believing eyes. In that moment he could have asked her anything, and she would have told him nothing but the truth. Thankfully, his father chose that instant to move toward her thermos of coffee, and the spell was broken. "But . . . but I'm sure that whatever it was, they've found it and left. They're gone. You can check the whole house if you like. You won't find them."

The boy's whole body twitched with eagerness. He jerked a small flashlight from his back pocket and looked to his father for permission. Ryan smiled at his son and jerked his head at the doorway. "Just don't break anything, okay?"

"Okay," Jimmy called back from halfway down the hall.

And just as they'd planned it, the three sisters passed through the second floor into the kitchen—the last place Jimmy would look for them.

"Oh, it feels so good to have a man in the house again," Odelia chirped happily, putting the pie she'd made earlier into her oven. "Men enjoy food so much more than women do."

"That's not true." Adeline sat at the table observing Ryan and her daughter. "I love food."

Imogene, too, sat at the table to wait out Jimmy's inspection of the house. She held her hands in her lap and considered Ryan. "He's very good with the boy, a good father."

"Here." Ryan handed her one of the two mugs she'd dusted off for the visit. She wasn't sure coffee was what her jangled nerves needed just then but . . . what the heck. She wasn't sure of anything anymore. "This could take a while. Care to sit?"

They made a cozy gathering—the two ghosts, Ryan, and her—seated around the kitchen table; Odelia on a stool cutting apples at the sink.

Ryan shook his head and grinned. "Crazy kid has me thinking I can smell apple pie now. It's amazing how your mind can play tricks on you."

Raising her brows, she nodded and glanced at Odelia, who couldn't stop making pies, even for a brief while, it seemed. "I smell my mother's perfume sometimes."

"You must miss her."

"Surprisingly, I do, though we never did get along very well."

"That's not true." Adeline looked hurt. "We used to get along. Once. I remember that we did."

"Too much alike?" Ryan asked.

"Not enough alike. I was never good enough for her. I never met her high standards."

"That's just plain not true, Maribelle." Her mother stood and began pacing the room. "I adored you. Your father and I both did. You made our life complete."

Ryan shivered. "Man, this place is drafty." Overhead they heard Jimmy calling, his footsteps running from room to room, doors opening and closing. "But I have to tell you, it's hard being a parent. You don't know, and no one tells you, if the decisions you're making are good ones or if you're accidentally turning your kid into the next Jeffrey Dahmer . . . or in my case, Egon Spengler."

"Who?"

"The ghost buster who wore the glasses . . . in the movie? He was my favorite." He sipped his coffee. "Sometimes I almost wish he'd find one, he believes so strongly. I hate having to tell him they don't exist when he's so sure they do." He sighed and deliberately changed the subject. "So what do you do when you're not dealing with ghosts and tearing down old houses?"

"I'm an investment analyst with Wilson and Bows in McLean. What about you? I'm assuming you're not married, but you know what happens when you do that, right?"

"I do." He was watching his fingers play with his mug of coffee but glanced up and smiled at her. "But in this case you're safe. I lost my wife to cancer when Jimmy was nine months old. It took us by surprise, and she went really fast . . . threw everything into a tailspin."

"I'm sorry."

"Thanks. But we figured it out . . . Jimmy and me . . . how to go on without her. I tried a nanny at first, and she was great, but . . . well, when he took his first step, I wasn't there to see it. And she was a stranger I hired from an agency. My folks were too old to be taking on a small child. My dad has heart problems and my mom had her hands full with him. His other grandfather is a bit of a boozer. So I . . . My degree is in computer engineering. I was working as a systems analyst for Blackboard, days and nights, trying to meet deadlines. It was crazy." He sat up straighter in his chair and took another sip of coffee. "I looked up from my computer one afternoon, and I didn't know what I was doing. Why was I working so hard to make a good life for a son I never saw? I tried to quit, but my boss is a good guy. He said if I could keep up, I could try working from home, touch base in the office a couple times a month, and it's worked out great. I got rid of the condo we were cramped up in and bought a house with a yard in a small town where my son feels safe . . . even with the ghosts who live next door." She must have looked strange, because he chuckled. "Ironic, huh? But he really isn't afraid, he says. Worried about them but not afraid."

"Such a sweet boy." Odelia trimmed the crust on her next pie. "Always offers to carry my apples, and I let him until we get to the fence."

"He says he carries apples for one of them." Ryan shook his head. "It's probably too early to tell, but he has such a vivid imagination, I wonder if he'll be a writer or maybe an actor."

M.J. glanced at her mother, who'd always given her the impression that she should marry money and give lawn parties, that her MBA from Columbia and using her brain to make a living were . . . unladylike. "Does it matter to you what he becomes?"

"Not if he's happy. That's all any parent wants—for their child to be healthy and happy and well-adjusted."

Adeline nodded. "Healthy. Happy."

"Well-adjusted?" M.J. asked, looking at her pointedly.

Ryan leaned back in his chair, taken aback. "Well, yeah. I mean, I supposed this ghost thing is pretty weird to you, but he's still just a little guy who likes to pretend—"

"No, I didn't mean—"

"He'll figure it out and realize there's no such thing as ghosts soon enough. But if he doesn't, I guess I can take him to a shrink or something."

"Of course. I didn't mean . . . I'm sorry. That came out wrong." One of the hazards of talking to ghosts with another human in the room. "I'm the last person to be talking about well-adjusted."

"You're not well-adjusted?"

"How well-adjusted can someone named Maribelle be?"

"Oh, for crying out loud." Her mother's exasperation was gratifying.

He laughed. "I'm sorry, but I like it. Especially on you. It suits you."

She stared at him, horrified. "And I thought we were going to be friends."

"Really?" He sat up straight again, his grin wicked and way more than friendly. "I was hoping the same thing. You'll be coming out again next weekend, won't you? Maybe we can have dinner one night . . . or lunch . . . or both."

She opened her mouth to speak, while her brain raced for a good excuse to decline, only to be saved by Jimmy's stomping steps on the stairs. And again, as planned, the sisters rose up through the ceiling so the boy wouldn't see them . . . Imogene didn't even bother to stand.

Five

Their gazes met in anticipation of the future they were momentarily setting aside as they listened to the boy clatter down the hall until he stood in the doorway . . . disgruntled.

"Okay, let's go."

His father hesitated. "Don't you want to come over and thank M.J. for letting you have a look around?"

Nothing but his eyes moved in her direction "Thanks."

"You're welcome." She and Ryan exchanged a look and a shrug and started to stand. They'd both expected more of a reaction from him—but where Ryan was smart enough to let sleeping dogs lie, M.J.'s curiosity got to her. "So? Did you see the ghosts?"

"Nope." He turned on his heel and started walking toward the front door. They followed.

"Are you less worried about them now?"

A pause. "Sure." Even she could tell he was fibbing. He was still a believer, and he was still worried. He opened the door and marched out onto the wide front porch.

"Hey. Wait a second." Ryan sent her an apologetic grimace. "Are you sure there's nothing else you want to say to M.J. before we go?"

Having already thanked her, she and Jimmy formed identical furrows between their brows as they looked at him, then at each other. The boy grew thoughtful.

"School is starting soon. I'm going to be in first grade, and I have a new backpack already. Spider-Man." He jutted out his right arm, hand hyperextended to expose his wrist, which was, if M.J. recalled correctly, from whence Spidey's webbing came. "My teeth are gonna to fall out, but then my big teeth will grow in, and then Dad's gonna to teach me to whistle." He took a breath; his gaze darted away and came back. "That's enough for now."

Reeling a little from the to-and-fro and abrupt halt of his news report, M.J. shook her head as a genuine grin of pleasure creased her face and danced in her eyes.

"Wow. Thank you, Jimmy. I'm glad to know all those things about you."

He gave her a firm nod, as if he'd known she would be, then turned and hopped two footed down the steps.

Looking up at Ryan, she held her hands out at her sides, speechless, but still more amused than she'd been in a long, long time.

"This coming week we'll be buying crayons and Power Rangers underwear. Exciting times at our house." Chuckling, he glanced over her shoulder, then back over his at all the shattered windows along the front of the house. "What's with the windows? Vandals?"

"Ah, no, actually." She pushed her hair from the side of her face and glanced again at the glass. It looked dangerous. Precarious. Shattered glass just waiting to burst into smithereens. Had she been thinking clearly, she never would have let the boy or his father onto the porch or into the house, anywhere near it, despite the fact that she knew it wouldn't come down until the sisters allowed it. "Mr. Brown backed his machine into the house Friday. It must have happened then."

"Did he say it was safe? Should you be wandering around in there alone?" He held out his hand. "Give me your phone."

Even as she reached into her pocket, there were so many things in those four words that confused her—how he knew she was intractable about keeping it on her person instead of in her purse, what he planned to do with it, her willingness to obey. . . .

With the practiced fingers of a computer nerd, he installed

his home and cell phone numbers. "There." He beamed at her. "Now you can call me if you get into trouble over here . . . or anytime you want to talk or just say hello."

She nodded, replacing her phone, head down, her cheeks rounding from an unexpectedly charmed smile. It was simply a neighborly thing to do, yet when was the last time anyone had offered to help her with anything . . . much less to listen when she was lonely?

And why was that? she wondered suddenly, looking up when he withdrew his cell from his pocket. His gaze was warm and encouraging. "Want to give me yours so I can call you for our date next weekend, or are you going to make me work for it?"

Well . . .

"Da-aaad! C'mon." Saved by the boy.

She grinned, backing away from Ryan, the challenge implied. "Have a good week."

He laughed, undaunted. "You, too, Maribelle," he said, then skipped down the steps to join his son. She stood in the doorway and watched them walk away.

"How much do you think a computer person like him would make a year?" Her mother was an educated woman who couldn't even spell *subtle*.

M.J. stepped inside quickly and closed the door. "Mother!" She stood frowning at the sisters, hands on her hips.

"Isn't Jimmy a sweetie pie?" Odelia asked, turning to go back to her pies in the kitchen. "I could just eat him up without a fork."

"Hold it right there, Odelia." She waited for her aunt's attention. "Remember what you promised me. If you want my help, you have to make yourselves scarce when I'm not here. No more apple fetching in the orchard until after Jimmy's gone to bed. No more watching him from the upstairs window, Imogene. Promise me."

"I didn't know he could see me." She looked so sad M.J. wanted to put her arms around her, hold her until the ache in her heart dried up. "I didn't mean to scare him."

"But you don't scare him. Don't you understand? He can see you. He believes you're real. And he feels bad for you."

"Darling," her mother said in a tone she'd heard a thousand times—a once-again-you-haven't-thought-this-through-to-the-end tenor that jangled her nerves and annoyed her because it

Never Too Late to Love

was sometimes true . . . Not always, but often enough to be irritating. "You can see us. You know we're real."

"Yeah, well, I'm an adult. I have a conversational filter that keeps me from broadcasting the fact that I'm in here talking to my ghostly relatives. That kid will tell you anything that floats through his brain."

"Not everything." Her mother smiled wisely. "I don't think he bought our disappearing act."

"He could probably still smell us." Imogene agreed.

"All the more reason for him to not see you from now on. Next weekend I'll bring my laptop and a copy of *The Sixth Sense* so you can see what happens to kids who can see and talk to dead people. People think they're crazy." She bobbed her head. "I don't think Ryan does yet, but I think he's worried."

Her mother grinned and then teased her. "Maybe we should keep him worried for a little while longer. . . . We don't want him to stop coming around, do we?"

M.J. made a face. "Why would I want him to keep coming around? To see you, maybe? Haven't we already been there, done that, with Elvis Parker when I was in high school?"

"We are not going down that road again, Maribelle Joy. I've told you a million times I did nothing"—she waved a vaporous finger at her daughter—"*nothing* to encourage that boy."

"You didn't have to. You'd just walk through the room, and he'd just about fall off his chair watching you leave. He couldn't take his eyes off you."

"That's not my fault."

"You couldn't have locked yourself in the bathroom until he was gone?"

"Certainly. I could have worn a basket over my head, too. Would that have made you happy?"

It was a preposterous question, and one that didn't matter now anyway. But she did hate losing, so she said, "Maybe."

"Listen. I couldn't help being beautiful." Her sisters—both of whom were just as pretty as she in their own way—groaned and turned away. Odelia put a finger in the air and muttered "Pies," then followed her finger down the hall. Imogene simply sighed and started up the stairs. "No, really. It wasn't as easy as you think to look this way."

Now this was *not* a familiar topic of conversation for her mother. Granted, she'd never made any secret of the lengths she'd go to, to keep up her physical appearance, but she'd never actually *bragged* about them . . . or better yet, complained about being *too* beautiful. M.J. was amused. "Inside, we're all weeping for you, Mother."

"No, you're not . . . but if you knew what it was like, you might."

"Ho! Well, lucky for me I have the face only a mother could love."

"Now that's not true either," Adeline scolded. "You were a lovely child, and you've become a beautiful woman . . . except that you don't realize *how* beautiful."

Truly uncomfortable in the spotlight, M.J. made for the stairs with Imogene. She intended to go back to her mother's room and take up where they'd left off when the Doyles arrived. Adeline shook her head and followed.

"After your daddy died you became so . . . quiet . . . confused, I guess. You were so young. I tried my best. I bought you the prettiest, hippest clothes, pushed you to go out and socialize, join clubs, have fun . . . and you fought me constantly. You were always so angry with me for some reason, and you did everything you could to be the very opposite of me . . . despite all our commonalities."

Commonalities? Aside from half her DNA and a weakness for Almond Joy candy bars, she was hard put to list any more *commonalities* between them, but before she could mention this, her mother spoke again.

"And you've done a fine job of it. You've spent your time filling your head with an education and making a living for yourself, a name for yourself . . . isolating yourself with your independence—"

"I'm not iso—"

"And you have no idea how very beautiful you are, so if you ever choose to marry, it might not even occur to you that your husband wants you only because of the way you look beside him. If he cheats on you, you won't automatically assume it's because you've lost your looks. You'll never feel like you have to use your looks alone to get a man to spend time with you because you're lonely . . . or marry because you don't know who you are unless you're somebody's beautiful wife."

By now M.J. had come to a full stop midstep on the staircase, staring at her mother as if she'd never seen her before . . . and maybe she hadn't.

"Is that really how you've always felt?" Her voice was weak in a tight throat. "I didn't . . . I mean, I had no . . . "

She shook her head, not knowing what to say. She'd considered her mother's vanity a failing, an annoying character flaw, not a survival mechanism—and a very sad one at that. Had her mother really been so insecure? So lonely? So lacking an identity that she had to use someone else's—the men she married?

Her mother smiled and raised a hand as if she wanted to touch M.J.'s face, then, knowing neither of them would feel anything, lowered it again, saying, "If old age doesn't give you perfect hindsight, sweetheart, death certainly does. I'm aware of the mistakes I made, and why, and I've accepted them. I can't even regret them if they were partly responsible, even in a roundabout way, for the outstanding woman you've become."

"Are you drunk? Can ghosts get high?"

"Don't be flip. I'm trying to pay you a compliment."

They'd reached Adeline's bedroom at the top of the stairs, and she sailed through the closed door without hesitating, leaving M.J. in the hallway, sputtering in disbelief. Falling back on her heels, she shook her head and wondered if she'd *ever* understand her mother . . . alive or dead.

She glanced down the hall to see Imogene's form, which had preceded them up the stairs, disappear into the room at the far end of the hall. It was a huge room, hers the times she'd come to stay as a child. A room that served as both bedroom—with small, child-sized furniture—and playroom, as her toys weren't to be left about. Later, they replaced the furniture to make it a guest suite. It was also the only room that had windows overlooking the backyard . . . and Ryan's backyard where Jimmy played.

She was tempted to remind Imogene of her promise but held her tongue. Her aunt had given her word, and she had no reason to doubt her.

Besides, she was still dealing with her mother. . . .

"Since when do you pay me compliments?" She opened the door and sailed through her own way. "I can't remember the last time you said anything nice about me or my life without an *if* or a *but* and a negating comment on the end of it."

"Didn't I just call you an outstanding woman?" She waited two beats, denoting the lack of an *if* or a *but*, then grinned playfully. "Some mistakes I do regret, darling."

If that was an apology after all this time . . . well, M.J. was happy to receive it. Happier than she should be probably, considering the source was a ghost of its former being.

"I know what you're thinking." Adeline stepped close and spoke softly. "You're wondering why we couldn't have talked like this when I was alive. It was one of those commonalities I talked about before, I believe. We're both too stubborn and unforgiving. Once the crack in the bond between us started, it just got bigger and wider until neither one of us knew how to bridge the gap and fix it. I think we both wanted to, but we didn't know how."

M.J. sat on the bed. "Do you know what happened? How it started? I mean, underneath it all, we always loved each other, right?"

"Of course." Her mother sat down next to her. She smelled of lilies. "I've thought about it . . . I've gone over every second of the past and . . . I believe it started sometime after your father died, because before that we were so happy together, the three of us."

She thought about it. "You weren't, you know . . . like you said a few minutes ago . . . about being beautiful. You weren't like that with him, were you?"

"Gracious, no." Her tone became dreamy. "Alex was my childhood sweetheart. I loved him before I even knew what beautiful was. And he adored me, always. No matter how I looked. No matter what I said or did—even when he was annoyed with me, I always knew he loved me." She played with the wedding rings on her ring finger, silent for a moment, then she looked at her daughter. "He adored you, too. The three of us were perfect. We waited so long to have you, wanted you so badly. When we were finally blessed, we believed you were the symbol of our love that would live on after we'd grown old together and passed on." She hesitated. "Is it bad, do you think, to be grateful that I wasn't able to have any more children? After your father . . . I never wanted any more. I was afraid I wouldn't love them like I loved you."

M.J. shook her head. "I don't think it's bad." She stared at the pink and gray floral pattern in the rug and wondered what it would have been like to have siblings. Naturally, she'd wondered before . . . wishing for a sister to take some of the social pressure off her or a brother or two to become *Mama's boys* so she could fade into the sidelines altogether. But looking back, it was easy to see she might have smothered with a pillow any other children vying for what little attention her mother had to offer.

"What are you thinking?" Adeline asked. "Did you want brothers and sisters? Sisters especially can be quite comforting at times."

"No, I'm glad you didn't have more children. As you may have noticed over the years, I don't play well with others. There are people at the office who I think are actually a little afraid of me."

Adeline chuckled. "Only because you've become so adept at isolating yourself."

"I'm not iso—"

"If you'd just open yourself up and reach out to other people, you'd see how eager they are to be your friends." She leaned as if to bump shoulders, everything about her lighthearted and mischievous—not at all the way M.J. remembered her. "Like Ryan. He seems very eager to know you."

"Mother."

She stood. It was starting to get dark, and if she wanted to go through more of her mother's things, looking for whatever it was that she'd lost, she needed to keep at it. She had no time for silly ghost games.

"Oh." Adeline sighed wistfully, falling back on the bed like a love-dazed teenager. "I loved falling in love with your father. I even loved *thinking* I was falling in love with the others."

Strange . . . it wasn't what her mother was saying but the way she'd fallen back on the bed that caught M.J.'s attention. She recalled the last time she'd spent the weekend with her mother and how, at not even sixty-five yet, the arthritis in her knees made climbing the stairs a struggle . . . Had she flung herself on the bed like that then, it would have looked a little like watching a turtle on its back.

"How old are you?"

"What?" Adeline lifted her head off the bed.

"Why aren't you an old ghost? You know, the age you were when you died? Why are you young? How old are you as a ghost?"

Her mother sat up easily. "We wondered about that, too. We don't know. Poor Odelia looks older than Imogene and me put together, but she's only the middle child. I'm hoping this is how we look or feel or . . . whatever when we get to the Other Side." Her smile was anxious. "I want your father to recognize me."

"So you were this age when he died?"

"This or close to it, yes, I believe so."

"And Imogene?"

She nodded. "Has to be after Rufus died, she's still so young and weepy."

She tsked in disgust. "Rufus?"

"It's from the Latin for redheaded. And he had the darkest blue eyes I've ever seen." Half her mouth curved up in remembrance, then fell again. "After a few years, Imogene stopped crying and became very bitter and sharp-tongued. Her husband left her finally, and she came back here to live for years and years. I don't know how Odelia stood her. She was a very unhappy woman. Thank God her ghost isn't so bad. She sheds a good many tears, but she's far from mean-spirited . . . no pun intended. She's just very sad, you know?"

"And Odelia? Does she cry?"

"She cooks. Incessantly."

"She was never married."

"As far as I know, she's never loved anyone or anything but her stove."

"How old do you think her ghost looks?"

"Maybe midfifties."

"Did anything significant happen to her during those years?"

"Not that I recall."

Rats. M.J. thought she was going somewhere with the ghost's ages and corresponding events in their lives, but Odelia didn't fit that pattern. It had to be something else. Something they all experienced. Something they all lost. The death of a loved one worked for Imogene and Adeline except, one, it was too obvious, and, again, it didn't include Odelia.

Six

"Maybe we should put off the deconstruction for the time being, Mr. Brown," she said bright and early Monday morning—admitting nothing. "I hadn't been in the house since the day of my mother's funeral, but now that I have, and I've had time to think"—*and to realize what an adolescent snit I've been in most of my life,* she thought to herself—"well, I think there might be a few things from the house that I'd like to keep after all."

"Oh." He sounded disappointed.

"There will still be plenty to recycle and for the consignment shops and all that. I'm thinking mostly family pictures, things no one else would have any interest in."

"You take what you want, Ms. Biderman. I'm glad you're having second thoughts. Do you have boxes, or can I drop a few off at the house for you?"

"Thank you. That would be great. I won't be out again until Saturday. Will they be okay on the porch?"

"Sure thing. I'll fold 'em flat and set a rock on top of them." He paused. "Just, ah, let me know when you'd like me to take another run at the house."

"You know I will, and it won't be long. We have a deadline for the Smoothie Hut deal, and I intend to meet it." Call waiting beeped in her ear and the light on her second line began to blink—she spoke a little faster. "You're still with me on that, right?"

"Absolutely. You tell me when, and I'll clean it out and tear it down in a matter of days . . . five, tops."

She glanced at her computer calendar and noted the narrow time frame. "I'll be in touch, Mr. Brown. Thank you."

She touched her earpiece to disconnect and answer her second line. "Biderman. How can I help you?"

"You can agree to go out with me Saturday night." She recognized his voice immediately—his topic was a big clue, too. She tittered a little inside and, without thinking twice, tossed her pen down on the Longwire file that lay open in front of her. "Are you busy? I can call back and ask again later."

"No. I haven't even finished my second liter of coffee yet. I'm just getting started. I can't believe you remembered where I work."

"I know I should claim the credit, but I'll tell you the truth; I searched for you on the Internet. You are the only Maribelle Joy Biderman in the whole wide world . . . as my son would say."

She sat up straight. "I'm listed on the Internet that way . . . by that name?"

He laughed. "Only in the real official places like birth records, Columbia's list of graduates, and—"

"How'd you know I graduated from Columbia? That's not on the Internet, is it?"

"Company profile says you got your MBA there . . . *and* your mother told me. Every time I saw her, she'd brag about it like there was no one smart enough to be with you."

"And now you want to prove her wrong, huh?"

She didn't need the stunned silence on the other end of the line to realize that what she'd just said . . . what had slipped from her lips so easily, so thoughtlessly, so naturally was exactly the sort of statement she'd been making for years to keep most people at bay; to isolate herself just as her mother said . . . but why?

She liked Ryan. Naturally, he wasn't the first man to ask her out, nor was he the first to ask from someplace other than the more clinical *let's-scratch-our-itch* arena that she generally preferred. . . . No, come to think of it, she didn't prefer it; she simply felt safer and less vulnerable there.

"I'm sorry. I'm . . . That was rude. I—"

"Hey. No. I get it." He laughed good-naturedly. "You're a beautiful, successful woman. You must have guys hitting on you all the time. It's smart to keep your defenses up, but—"

"No. It isn't. And if you're still offering, I'd be pleased to go out with you Saturday night. Very pleased."

She heard the smile in his voice when he said, "Good. I'm glad."

"I'm . . . I'm here late most evenings, but in case Jimmy gets sick or . . . "

"I change my mind?" he finished for her. "It ain't gonna happen, Maribelle Joy. I've wanted time alone with you since I first saw you on the other side of the fence. So, as you were saying . . . barring a catastrophe with my son and the end of the world . . . ?"

Oh yes, she liked him very much. "I was just going to say that this number will patch you through to my cell phone anytime."

She heard him draw a surprised breath and pressed three fingers firmly against her lips to keep from laughing out loud.

"I still don't get your cell number?"

"Maybe you need to work a little harder for it," she said in a remarkably seductive voice that she hadn't even known she owned. She bit down on her lower lip and grinned so hard her face felt stretched beyond endurance. His chuckle made her giggle like an idiot, and for the first time in her life she didn't mind feeling like one.

"Maybe I do. And that's okay. I don't mind working hard for the things I think are worth it."

Exactly four days, twenty-two hours, and seventeen minutes later, she was still smiling when she turned the key in the lock at Hedbo House and felt it give. It was early, barely seven, but she needed every ray of daylight she could get.

"Hello? Anybody home?" Immediately she was assaulted with the scents of apple pies, lilies, and baby powder. She watched the gradual manipulation of light and shadow recon-figure itself until the familiar images of her mother and her two aunts presented themselves before her.

"Good morning, darling. You're very early"—Adeline tipped her head and studied her for a moment—"and very

happy this morning. Has something happened? Have you figured it out?"

"Figured what out?"

"What we've lost?"

"Oh. No. But don't worry, we will. We have two weeks to figure it out and one to tear the house down to meet the Smoothie
Hut contract, and I intend to." She spoke with determination to
all of them, but it was obvious they'd been searching too long to
feel her optimism. "Come on now. Think positive."

Odelia smiled kindly. "I have pies in the oven, dear. May I
think positively in the kitchen?"

She didn't wait for permission, and M.J.'s eyes narrowed
with purpose as she followed her aunt down the hall. Odelia
was as good a place to begin as any.

She looked back over her shoulder before entering the
kitchen to see her mother and Imogene walking up the stairs
to the rooms they felt most comfortable in to await their own
interrogations. Eventually it might prove beneficial to talk to
all of them at the same time, but for now she'd concentrate on
one at a time—looking for common threads in their stories,
similarities of any kind, or something lost that one may have
forgotten but one or both of the other two recall very well.

"Apple pie again? Did you never make any other kind of
pies?"

"Don't you like apple pie?" She took her oven mitts off the
counter and opened the shadowy oven door. "I thought it was
everyone's favorite. I won a bake-off with this recipe and received fifty dollars in the mail when it was published in the
Pillsbury Down Home Fall Favorites Cookbook."

"But Grandfather still wasn't impressed?"

"Oh, but he was. He was thrilled for me. He loved my cooking. He always said he was my biggest fan. He even spon-
sored several annual cooking bees to raise money for the local
schools. But when I kept winning, it started to look like the con-
tests were fixed, even though Papa always refused to be one of
the judges. Eventually it came down to making money for the
schools or keeping me as a contestant, so I stopped participat-
ing." She set the steaming-hot pie on the counter and, admiring
it, sighed. "Papa said it was probably for the best. I was putting
too much stock in winning, getting my hopes up too high on a
dream that could never come true."

"But what about Julia Child? Didn't you ever use her as an example of what you wanted to be?"

"Of course I did." She turned to the pie waiting on the counter behind her and put it in the oven, closing the door silently. "He said the only reason she was who she was, was because she was a freak . . . a freakishly tall woman, with a freakishly odd voice and a similar sense of humor—people are always drawn to the ridiculous. I, on the other hand, was a lovely girl, he'd say, that any young man would be honored to have as a wife, but I was too ordinary to be like Julia Child." Her laugh wasn't amused. "And thank God for that, he'd say."

"What an ass."

"I beg your pardon?" Odelia looked up, startled.

"I'm sorry. I know you loved him, but your father was an ass . . . in my opinion. I think you would have made a wonderful chef. He should have encouraged your dreams."

She smiled her gratitude. "It was a different time, dear. Perhaps it was for the best. It wouldn't have been easy, you know."

"Nothing worth having ever is. But with his encouragement and some of his money and all your talent and a little luck, there's no telling what might have happened."

They stared at one another for a long moment, the truth about hope hanging in the air between them like a bright string of sparkling Christmas lights. In the end it was Odelia who sighed softly and lowered her gaze to the piecrust in front of her. She took up her rolling pin.

Sitting at the table, her chin in her hand, M.J. said, "I wish there was a way to taste your prizewinning pie, Odelia. It looks amazing, and it smells even better."

She just laughed at the compliment and gave her niece a thrilled little grin, then sobered. "But there is a way for you to taste it."

"There is?"

"Yes. The recipe is right over there in that drawer."

M.J. followed the direction in which the rolling pin was pointed, below a set of glass-front cupboards containing dust-covered dishes, bowls, and platters, and opened the middle drawer. It was stuffed to the brim with notebooks and journals, not a page left unfilled. And pressed below were hundreds and hundreds of loose sheets.

"Pesto-Turkey Manicotti." She began to read from the loose

sheets. "Cheesy Mashed Potato Casserole. Devil's Favorite White Chocolate Frosting. Crock Pot Pork with Root Beer Sauce?"

"Oh. I'd forgotten that one. Fabulous. And so easy." Odelia shook her head and began to trim her crust. "I was always going to write two cookbooks. One with simple, fun, easy recipes and another more serious cookbook for real connoisseurs."

Standing with enough evidence for several serious cookbooks in her hands, she asked, "Are these all your own original recipes?"

"Mostly, plus a few classics that I improved on . . . if I do say so myself. Although I'll have you know I wasn't the only one to say so. Everyone I knew thought I was an excellent cook."

"I believe you." She pulled on a red ribbon that marked a page in a royal blue journal. *Odelia's Delight* it read, and below in parentheses, *A Prizewinning Apple Pie*. "So why didn't you? You know, organize these a little and write your cookbook?"

Her aunt looked up, surprised. "I died."

"What?"

"Well, it was always one of those things I was going to get around to doing one day, but then I died." Carefully, she walked her newest creation to the counter nearest the stove to await its turn in the oven. She turned back to M.J. "It's not like the world was going to miss another cookbook, dear."

"But—" She was flabbergasted. "Did your father object to the cookbook?"

"Goodness, no. He was dead before the idea even occurred to me. It's how Julia started, you know." Odelia was looking at something on the floor on the other side of the counter.

M.J. stood watching her, her chest tight with a sadness that came from several directions. She didn't for a second believe that the world would miss another cookbook, but one lousy cookbook could have been Odelia's mark on the world, her declaration of having been present. Unmarried, childless, careerless . . . one stinking little cookbook with her name on it—with her *pride* and pleasure in it—could have made all the difference in the world to her life.

"Land sakes alive, where do all my apples go?" She stooped to pick up her basket, then headed for the back door. "I'd swear those girls are eating them"—she stopped to give her niece an arched brow and a pointed nod—"but we know that can't be."

"Hey. Where are you going? It's daylight. You haven't been gathering apples during the day all week, have you? What about Jimmy? You promised—"

"Jimmy's grandparents came to fetch him for the weekend last night. They frequently do; they're a very tight-knit family." She paused in front of the door. "These are Jimmy's father's people, you understand, and they were very pleased to hear that he has a date tonight."

M.J. was alarmed to feel the heat rising up her neck and into her cheeks. And looking blasé didn't fool Odelia. She giggled. "We were very pleased to hear it, too."

Seven

Did one knock on a ghost's door or simply let oneself in? How much privacy did a ghost expect? M.J. pondered, as she knocked softly on Imogene's door before entering. Not Imogene's bedroom but the room at the end of the hall where she clearly felt the most comfortable—a child's room when M.J. had been growing up, later a guest room during her mother's influence. To Imogene, as she stood calmly among the surreal furnishings superimposed on those more tangible, it was a nursery.

"Come in, Maribelle, and please don't give me any grief about using your proper name." She took the sting out of the command by smiling fondly at her. "We Hedbos take naming our offspring very seriously. For instance, did you know that Imogene comes from the Latin for 'likeness' and that it became my cross to bear because I looked exactly like my father's grandmother . . . *when I was born*!?" She laughed. "Can you imagine what a sad little wizened-up thing one of us was?"

M.J. chuckled. She did indeed like her aunt Imogene. The more she knew her, the more she liked about her . . . and, of course, the more she realized how little she knew her.

"Fair enough." She sat on the end of the bed, which to her aunt was a cedar hope chest that sat at the bottom of an ornately carved crib. "I see now it could have been a lot worse."

"Don't get me wrong. I quite agree with you about the nonsensicality of our names in relation to the times we live in." She sat gracefully in a lovely tall-backed wooden rocking chair that had a knit afghan in muted colors draped over the arms, sagging in the middle to pad the seat and folded in such a way as to allow whoever sat in the chair the ease of pulling it about them if they got cold. "My husband, Andrew, and I had every intention of breaking from the tradition and had planned to name our baby Albert if it was a boy—Teutonic for noble and bright—something he would grow into, you understand."

Maribelle nodded.

"But when he was finally born he . . . my dear, he was born with a whole head of thick red hair. What was I to do? It was clearly an omen, so we named him Rufus Albert, still quite intent on calling him Albert but, well, what can I say? He was Rufus with the bright red roof of hair on his head. Ruffie caught on the first night I breast-fed him, just him and me in the silence, the lights low. . . . " Her voice faded away as she recalled the memory. "Little Ruffie."

After a moment or two she looked up and seemed almost surprised to see M.J. sitting there. "Andrew was so proud to have a son. Delighted. He couldn't wait for him to start walking and talking . . . swinging bats and chasing balls, all those things that fathers look forward to sharing with their sons. Andrew loved to sail, you know."

"I didn't."

Imogene smiled. "He was a Southampton boy growing up, but when we met and married, he was settled in Charleston . . . South Carolina? A beautiful city. I enjoyed living there, but I have to admit, I did get homesick from time to time. The first time I brought Ruffie home I was thrilled to see that my papa had had this room completely redecorated for him . . . his first grandchild, you understand.

"Did you know that when the house was built this was actually two more bedrooms? Apparently, your great-grandfather Horatio didn't want to get caught in a small house with a large family." She laughed softly. "Instead, the opposite happened, and it was our papa who had three healthy, noisy daughters and a nervous, sickly wife on his hands. We each had our own room, of course, but he very cleverly had the wall removed in this space and turned it into our playroom for the sake of our mother's sanity."

M.J. laughed. "At least we know *that* worked. We haven't seen her wandering around looking for the mind she lost."

Imogene's expression was droll. "It's your date. It's affecting your concentration, isn't it?"

Maribelle grinned and bobbed her head. "A little, but I can handle it. I think. Go on. Please. You brought Ruffie home, and grandfather had redecorated the playroom for him. . . . "

"It was the first time I felt like I'd actually done something to please him. I gave him a grandson, a male heir. But now don't get me wrong, I know Papa loved me. He loved all his girls, we were his world. He just . . . well, he had certain notions about women . . . he even thought his notions were fairly progressive. He wanted all of us to be well-educated but only in certain fields and only about certain things. There were only a few specific things he felt women did well, and being a wife and mother was at the top of the list, no matter how well-educated she was."

"And you?"

"I met Andrew when I was in graduate school. I was in Charleston working on my thesis in history. I wanted to teach at the college level, hoping older students would make my teaching feel more consequential, I suppose. Teaching students who wanted to be in my class as opposed to those who had to be when I taught high school."

"I get that. So what was your thesis about?"

"The contribution of slaves to our early development as a nation. At the time I met Andrew I was investigating a man by the name of Robert Smalls who was born into slavery, escaped, and helped write the South Carolina Constitution at the constitutional convention in Charleston in 1868. Later he served in the state legislature in both the House of Representatives and the Senate, and after that he was elected to the United States House of Representatives. A brave, fascinating man." She became thoughtful, glanced away then back at Maribelle. "Naturally, I lost all interest in my thesis the instant I met Andrew. All I wanted then was to marry him, settle down, and have baby after baby after baby.

"The ultimate woman, in my father's eyes. And I must say I felt like the ultimate woman when I brought my son here for Papa to see. I'd given birth to the healthiest, most beautiful baby. . . . I felt like the only woman to ever give life." She laughed a little. "Looking back, my attitude was appalling. And don't for a second think I didn't rub Odelia's and your mother's noses in it. I was insufferable. In fact I—"

She stopped abruptly, looking down at her hands.

"What?"

She shrugged and looked up. "Later . . . after . . . when I was trying to figure out why, I thought maybe it was my pride. Maybe I'd been too proud. Too happy. Too . . . something, and God or Karma or however it works took Ruffie away to teach me a lesson. Humility, or perhaps I wasn't grateful enough. I kept looking for some way to make sense of it, some way to come to terms with the death of my precious baby."

"What happened to him? I don't want to make you sad again, but losing Ruffie is too obvious to be what you're looking for. You'd have figured that one out years ago, but maybe it's something related to it." She paused. "Or maybe it's not. But if you can talk about it, I'll listen."

Imogene shook her head slowly. "I've seen it in my mind's eye a million times, gone over it and over it, and it's never more than a simple accident. A stupid, simple accident that could have happened anywhere, at any time, to anyone. What I don't know is why it happened to me . . . to us.

"It was a beautiful morning in August. Midmorning and they were forecasting a hot afternoon, so we planned to sail all day. I packed a big lunch basket for us. Ruffie was three, and he loved to sail. He was so excited that morning. And . . . and it wasn't his first time on the dock. He knew he couldn't set foot on the boat without his life preserver; he knew there were rules. Andrew was aft working on the rigging. I let go of Ruffie's hand and told him not to move, that I was going to get his life jacket. I set the basket on the deck and opened the bench where we stored the vests. I looked away long enough to pick his out and when I looked up again, he was gone. I immediately panicked and screamed . . . and Andrew, from his angle looked up in time to see him walk off the end of the dock."

I looked away. . . . It wasn't hard to imagine her aunt's horrendous guilt at that moment. *I looked away.* . . . Not a mother, and with basically no understanding of children, she was sure her aunt's burden was massive. *I looked away.* . . .

"Andrew was a hero that day. He was off the boat and into the water before I realized what had happened. He passed my baby's cold, blue little body up to me when I got to the end of the dock. I was useless. I was . . . numb. I . . . " She closed her eyes and put a hand to her throat in an attempt to control herself. She drew in a deep breath. "Andrew screamed at me to go for help. He picked the baby up by his feet and whacked him on the back a couple times before he started blowing in his mouth and doing CPR. I ran for the pay phone at the gate. They . . . they told me to wait for the ambulance so they wouldn't waste time looking for us, so I did. By the time I got back, Andrew was holding our baby in his arms, and they were both crying."

"So he didn't drown?" She was amazed at how relieved she was.

"No, dear, but he did swallow and inhale a great deal of water that day. He had trouble breathing, so of course we took him to the hospital immediately. They treated him with oxygen and gave him antibiotics to ward off pneumonia, and after several days we brought him home good as new. Almost. I mean, we thought he was good as new, but the water had damaged his lungs. He developed severe asthmalike symptoms, and every time he caught a cold, it went straight to his lungs. The year he started school he was hospitalized three times with pneumonia. They wanted him to repeat kindergarten. I wanted to keep him home and get him a tutor, or homeschool him myself, but Andrew said I couldn't keep him in a bubble; I needed to let him live as normal a life as he could. I . . . I believed that was my penance, you see . . . for looking away that day . . . the waiting for the next runny nose, the next sore throat, the next cough; watching him gasp for air during his next brush with death.

"And when it finally happened, I was as relieved for him as I was devastated. He suffered so. My poor, sweet, precious boy."

"How old was he?"

"Just eight. Two weeks after his birthday." She smiled. "He had so much fun at his party. All his friends came. We had a Superman theme. He could hardly sleep the night before."

"And was it because Ruffie was so sick all the time that you didn't have more children, the way you'd planned?"

"Oh no. The miracle of him only increased my desire to have more." She got to her feet, as if suddenly agitated and restless. "Unfortunately, the loss of him gradually drove a wedge between Andrew and me. It was a difficult time for us both."

"I'm so sorry."

"No need. I've come to believe that we create our own fate. I don't think that one day you can have all the luck in the world and the next you haven't any. Once, I admit, I thought God just wanted to see me suffer, but truly, with all the pain in the world, did he really need my pain, too? If he existed at all, which I now doubt, as how could I possibly believe in a God who didn't believe in me? . . . who also refused to give me a second chance to be happy? That's not the kind and loving God I was brought up on." She turned to one of the two large windows that overlooked the overgrown gardens at the rear of the house . . . and Jimmy's backyard. She held her elbows and stood straight and tall and beautiful. "Don't be sorry for me, Maribelle. I didn't realize it at the time, but dying alone was the destiny I chose for myself by taking my son and husband for granted, by assuming I'd always be happy and making so little effort, taking so few steps to ensure it."

"But, Imogene, no one's happiness is guaranteed, no matter how hard you try. It's crazy to blame yourself."

"Who else is there?" she asked, her tone flat and certain.

It was a good question—one philosophers and scholars and people a lot more . . . intellectually profound than she had struggled with since the beginning of time. And somehow she didn't think her own mind-set of *Shit happens . . . deal with it* would be of any comfort to her aunt.

Besides, who was she to judge Imogene? M.J. must have loved her father, but she could barely remember him and couldn't recall feeling the bone-deep pain her mother spoke of when he passed away. She had missed Larry Biderman when her mother divorced him, resented her for it and vowed never to become attached to her mother's husbands again. Even then she'd felt her mother's capacity to love anyone beyond the walls she'd built around herself diminishing. And so, in self-defense, she'd fashioned her own shields to deflect what had seemed like her mother's constant disappointment in her.

But she'd never lost a child. She'd never been abandoned by someone she loved. Her mother's death had been a blow, and something inside her missed her like she might miss a limb . . . but she wondered now how much greater that grief might be if they'd been closer—friends even. She had nothing in her life to compare to Imogene's great love . . . or her great despair.

"We'll figure it out, Imogene. I promise you. We'll figure out what it is you've lost so you can leave all the heartache and regret behind. That is what happens, right? You won't feel this way on the Other Side, will you?"

At first she didn't answer, but just as M.J. was about to repeat the question, she murmured, "I don't know." She turned from the window. "All we're convinced of is that we no longer belong here. And we can't move on because our spirit or soul or essence or whatever it is that made us who we were is no longer whole. We each lost a part of ourselves in this house, and until we know what it is, whatever happens to us next will remain a mystery."

"You don't think the Other Side is a good place to go." She could tell by her aunt's voice.

Imogene shrugged elegantly and turned back to stare out the window. "I don't think it's a place at all. I think it's just the other side of life."

Eight

"Now don't let talking to Imogene set the mood for your date, darling," Adeline told M.J. as she changed from jeans and a sweatshirt to a sweater and slacks for her date a few hours later. M.J. brushed her hair in her mother's dusty mirror as the older woman watched from the middle of the bed. "She got very cynical and morose after little Ruffie died. That and her desperation to have another child finally drove Andrew away for good, so you mustn't judge him too harshly. He did love her, you know."

"Did he blame her for the boy's accident?"

"Never, that I know of. That was all her thinking. But to be fair, I doubt there's a mother in the world who wouldn't feel the same. You feel responsible for everything that happens to your children."

She turned and stood at attention for her mother's approval. "How do I look?"

"Beautiful." Her eyes lowered to the square-shaped diamond that hung from a chain and sparkled like a star from the hollow of her daughter's throat. "Come closer."

Touching the stone that her mother had worn for as long as she could remember, she walked to the bed. "Do you mind if I wear it?"

"Of course not; it pleases me. You know your father gave that to me when you were born."

"I know," she said softly as the doorbell rang below. They looked at one another for a long moment, savoring a connectedness they'd both longed for, intensely, for years. "Is it too late to say I miss you, Mom?"

Adeline smiled through the tears welling in her eyes and shook her head.

"What about I love you?"

"No, my darling, it's never too late to love."

Maribelle Joy Biderman was feeling pretty darn happy with the world in general when she opened the front door to Ryan Doyle—and more specifically, thrilled to see him standing there.

"Hey."

"Hi."

They stood staring and grinning at one another like they each knew a secret the other was unaware of . . . unaware themselves that the excitement they felt was written all over their faces.

"I'd invite you in, but the batteries in my flashlight are weak, and I don't have anything to drink but bottled water."

"That's all right. We have a reservation anyway."

"Oh. Is what I'm wearing going to be okay?"

"You look great." He made *great* sound like . . . *mouthwatering* or . . . *scrumptious.*

She turned to close and lock the door, hoping her face wouldn't crack from the extreme pressure of her smile. She was conscious of the fact that computer geeks who spent so much time alone were notoriously bad dressers and let it speak to her ego that he'd donned navy slacks, a gray sports coat, and a silver-striped oxford shirt for their date—his one concession being the buttons undone at his throat.

"You do, too . . . Look great, I mean. I'm . . . " She took a deep breath. "God, I'm nervous."

A loud, surprised bark of laughter escaped him. "I feel like I haven't been on a date since I was sixteen. I keep wondering what you'll do if I try to hold your hand."

"So you don't date much?" She swallowed the word *either* just in time.

"An occasional blind date I haven't been able to avoid, but since my wife died"—he shrugged—"I haven't really had the desire. Until now." For that one she'd let him hold her hand. She held it palm up between them, and he quickly zippered his fingers with hers. "I brought my car around in case you'd be wearing heels or didn't want to walk, but it's a nice evening, and the restaurant isn't very far. . . . "

"Then let's walk. I enjoyed my walk down to King's last weekend. Johnnie's Bend has grown up so much since I lived here."

There wasn't a single lull in the conversation—not during their walk to the classic Italian restaurant on Main Street with its red and white checked tablecloths and Chianti bottle candlesticks—not throughout their fabulous dinner, which explained why the place was so crowded and reservations were wise—and not for the duration of the short meander they took to the park rather than to the movie theater, where they could continue talking and laughing and teasing during energetic games of miniature golf—her best two out of three.

"No, no. If you don't know how long my beginner's luck is going to last, then I'm quitting while I'm ahead. I'm not stupid, you know."

"Oh, I know that." His fingers slid over hers as he took her club and put both his and hers in the rack at the beginning of the course. "At least be a good sport and agree to let the loser buy you a coffee or a drink. How about dessert? King's is open until eleven, and they have great homemade cobblers."

It tickled her that he was trying so hard to keep their date from ending. She held her hand out, as she had in the beginning, and waited for him to take it, saying, "Can I have a rain check? By the time we walk back to the house and I drive home, it'll be late, and I want to come back early again tomorrow."

"You may have a rain check," he said with great benevolence as he took her hand. But instead of simply holding it, he looped it over the bend in his elbow so they stood closer and walked arm in arm. "And a sun check and a snow check and a wind check and an earthquake check. . . . "

She laughed.

"But tell me what you've been doing in the house. Something I can help you with?"

"No, not really, it's just . . . well, it finally occurred to me that I'm actually the last Hedbo. And while I have no compunctions about tearing the house down and selling the land and the contents, I am having second thoughts about some of the pictures and papers. . . . I found some love notes my father sent to my mother and pictures of my only true blood cousin before he died. There's a whole drawer full of original recipes that belonged to my Aunt Odelia—I'm thinking of finishing her cookbook for her."

"Your favorite aunt?"

"I barely remember her."

"Then why go to all that trouble?"

She shook her head. "*Because* I barely remember her? Does that make any sense?" She thought about her answer. "I told you my father died when I was four, and my mother remarried . . . three more times. I didn't . . . I don't have good sense of family. I don't feel like I ever had one, really. Just about the time I started settling in, my mother would divorce and marry someone new. I'm in touch with Larry Biderman, who cared enough to give me his name and keep track of me for years afterward, and one of my stepsisters from my mother's third marriage, but that's not exactly family, is it?"

"It is, I think, if that's what you've got. People make families with far less. It isn't the legal or blood links you have to people that make them family, it's the bonds you make with your heart that tie a family together."

"That's just it, though. I haven't let many—any people, really—get close enough to me to make those kinds of bonds. And wandering around that old house, learning more about my mother and her sisters—who they were and why they made some of the choices they made . . . well, I'm learning a lot about me, too."

"Like you want to publish a cookbook?"

She laughed. "No. That was one of my aunt Odelia's dreams. I thought . . . I'd hate to die without seeing at least one of my dreams come true, wouldn't you?"

"I would." He studied her face as she watched the sidewalk in front of them. She could feel him preparing to ask about her dreams and decided to cut him off so she wouldn't have to get explicit.

"And don't ask me which dream I want to make come true, because now that I'm thinking about them specifically, it turns out I have several, and I haven't decided between just one or maybe all of them."

Playfully, he made his eyes big. "All of them?"

"I'm a very big dreamer."

"Isn't that a little greedy?"

"As it happens, I'm a lot greedy. You got a problem with that?"

"No, ma'am." He grinned. "Not when it comes to dreams. As a matter of fact, I have a few of my own."

The old streetlights were soft and cozy, protecting them from the night. They made it easy to see the spark in his eyes that made her heart quiver with the knowledge that at least one of his immediate dreams involved her.

Quite a coincidence, really, as her newly revised list of wishes contained his name in several places as well.

It was this coincidence, she supposed, that made actually verbalizing their desires unnecessary when they stopped on the sidewalk in front of Hedbo House and turned to one another. He wanted to kiss her, and her smile gave him permission.

Lifting her face as he lowered his, their lips touched with a sweet, blistering need that both surprised and pleased them. The next kiss was deeper, more familiar, waking and feeding passions like dragons of old, with fire in their breath and wings that carried them to the stars.

"Holy . . . Wow," she gasped, one hand to her throat to calm herself while the other clung to the back of his neck for support. His forehead came to rest on hers, and he murmured a soft, "Yeah."

When they could hold their heads up and breathe and focus their eyes all at the same time, they laughed.

She put her hand in her pocket. "I guess I should get going. Thank you. I had fun tonight."

"Me, too." He turned with her and followed her slow walk to her car, parked at the curb in front of his. He let several long seconds go by. "I don't suppose I could convince you not to drive home tonight."

"There's no electricity and it's cold and I didn't bring any overnight—"

"You wouldn't really need any."

"Oh! You mean . . . you know . . . with you."

He grinned at her fluster, in his eyes a light of wicked delight at her sudden sexual unease. But she was no mouse who would play to his cat. . . .

"Well, I don't know. Could you?"

He looked startled. "Could I what?"

"Convince me not to drive home tonight?"

His grin said that he'd do his best. Hers answered that it wouldn't be difficult.

Okay, so maybe it was foolish to think she could sneak into the house around noon and not have anyone notice—it was like trying to slip dawn past a rooster.

"Ahhhhhh."

"At last."

"Now, don't tease her. We may have something here. Darling, are you in love?"

"Look at her face. Of course she is."

"You can't tell by her face alone. What if he's just really good in bed?"

"Is he?"

"*Maybe,*" she said, tucking her grin into her cheeks to present only a smug smile. "Maybe it's both."

"Oooooooh."

"I knew it. The first time I saw him look at you, I knew."

"And did you tell him about us, dear? Father always put a new face on things. Maybe we need a male perspective. Perhaps a man would know exactly what we're looking for."

"No, Odelia, I didn't tell him." She looked at each lady in turn, feeling her emotional high slip away to one simple truth: she'd lied to Ryan. But if she told him now, he either wouldn't believe her and decide she was delusional or he'd be angry that she lied to him in the first place. No, the best solution was to help her mother and aunts find what they'd lost, quickly, and allow them to pass on to the Other Side—to end Jimmy's fascination with them and to keep their existence as another family secret. "And I don't plan to. We don't need him. We'll work harder at figuring out what you've all lost, and we'll do it ourselves. I promise you. Now, instead of going over the past individually, I think we should spend the afternoon going over it together. You're bound to see each other's lives in a different light, and who knows what you might have forgotten that someone else remembers."

And that's exactly what they did. Even Odelia set aside her pies to sit at the kitchen table and reminisce over story after story from their past. People they knew and events they'd attended. They laughed and were sad and grew boisterous and then silent as they contemplated their lives until sundown, when the room became gloomy and dim and forced M.J. to finally go home.

Nine

"So when did you put your number in my cell phone?" Ryan asked early Monday morning when he called her at work.

"Yesterday when you went down to make coffee."

"Here I thought I was going to be so smart taking it off my caller ID when you called last night to tell me you were home safe."

She laughed. "I figured that's why you wanted me to call, so I just beat you to the punch."

"It wasn't the *only* reason I wanted you to call. I like knowing you're safe. I also like falling asleep with your voice in my ear."

"Me, too." Her voice was warm and cozy.

"I like having you here more."

"Me, too."

They went silent, remembering their night together—dreaming of the next one.

"I put you on speed dial. Cops, poison control, pediatrician, you, Jimmy's school, my parents, my plumber, who also happens to be my best friend . . . "

"I'm flattered." She really was. Picking up her BlackBerry: "I see you're already in my speed dial."

Never Too Late to Love

"Number five," he said in his defense. "In the middle, not too high, not too low, not too presumptive, easy access."

She laughed, and the sound was so strange in the early morning quiet of her office—well, in her office, period—she thought the paint might crack.

"I'll use it tonight."

"I'll be waiting."

Still smiling, she sighed contentedly. She had someone waiting to hear from her—personally, not professionally. Elbows on her desk, chin on her fists, she entertained the notion of grabbing her purse and skipping out for the day until her eyes lowered to the Longwire files in front of her.

Her analysis of their financials was not going well, and her recommendations to Barren Electronics, who very much wanted to buy out Longwire, wasn't going to please anyone—including, most likely, her bosses, who liked keeping their customers happy at all costs.

She settled into her chair to work—putting Ryan on the back burner until she went home and the sisters in the fridge till the weekend.

It rained on Thursday—not unheard of, considering the high humidity in northern Virginia in late summer—but as she'd worn her favorite summer silk suit that day, perhaps she should have taken it as an omen when the light intermittent sprinkles that were called for that day turned out to be a six-hour deluge.

Add to that the urgent call to her boss's office *before* her first cup of office coffee and his anxious frown when she opened his door, and she should have known that her life was about to encounter some very slippery doo-doo.

Well, it was bad enough when he asked if she was ready to present her conclusions on Longwire Industries to the president and board of directors of Barren Electronics—they were eager and anxious and pressuring him for answers. Her deadline was still a few weeks away, but she had her deductions and barely enough time to prepare a PowerPoint presentation before the ten o'clock meeting. She was a professional. She could handle short notice. Her make-me-or-break-me moment was coming . . . and it was, just not in the way she thought.

To say the Barren board, especially the chairman, had a negative response to her due diligence on Longwire was an understatement. They seemed furious that she hadn't been able to manipulate the numbers to make it appear a more favorable acquisition for their stockholders. The chair in particular kept trying to catch her boss's eye to run interference, but he looked as if he was completely oblivious to the situation—giving her plenty of rope to hang herself with, she supposed.

But sometimes it has to be about more than just the job. She'd never cheated on a test, lied about her age, or submitted a false report in her life. And as nervous as she felt—nauseous actually—she knew her findings were accurate and her recommendations were the best for Barren Electronics.

She stood her ground for nearly ninety minutes, giving and regiving her presentation behind a calm facade she was far from feeling, with only the occasional twitching of her fingers to give her away.

When her cell phone began to vibrate on the conference table beside her laptop, she quickly turned it off, using steely determination not to look at the caller ID to demonstrate her commitment to her work to those around her. Five minutes later she was tested again, and she made a mental note to ream her assistant for putting calls through when she was in conference.

But not five minutes after that, she had to admit she was as relieved as she was frustrated when same said assistant stepped into the room.

"I'm sorry to interrupt, but there's a Ryan Doyle on the phone who insists on speaking to you. He says it's an emergency."

"An emergency? For me?" Three meetings, ten phone calls, one date, and one great night of sex, and he was calling her with an emergency? Was she ready for this? Well, that would depend on the emergency, wouldn't it?

No, she decided in the next quarter second, a string of emotions busting loose in her chest. Concern. Happiness. Curiosity. Pride. Fear. An eagerness to respond. The hope of not failing him. It didn't depend on the emergency at all. He was calling for her help, and she'd answer him as best she could. She loved him.

It was that simple.

"Excuse me, please. This'll only take a moment." Her eyes met the assistant's. "Put him through again, please."

Once again, the cell vibrated. She picked it up, turned her back to the board and her boss, and stepped to the long window that overlooked Route 123.

"Ms. Biderman? M.J.?" her employer's voice seemed to come from far off when she turned back to the room. "Is everything all right? Has someone died? You look very pale."

"No. No one died."

"Are you going to be sick?"

"No." She looked around the room until her eyes focused on him. "I'm just going."

"But can't it wait? What about Longwire and Barren Electronics? Your presentation . . . You have a responsibility here."

All the late nights and long weekends over the last nine years flashed through her mind; her ambitious dedication and the fatigue and frustration of having to deal with the Old Boys' Club who seemed hell-bent on proving to women that they can't have it all—and her sudden shame of having believed them.

Or maybe it hadn't been the Old Boys at all. Maybe she'd just been trying so hard *not* to be her own mother that she'd lost sight of all the truly important things in life.

Her laugh was small and ironic. "Wow. You know, I never dreamed I'd be put in the position of having to choose between my job and my life. In fact, until recently I thought my job *was* my life—but it's not." She took a deep breath and several steps toward the door. "Now, I've been over my PowerPoint more than once, and I think it speaks for itself. If you don't want to hear what it's saying, there's nothing more I can do here anyway. So I'm leaving. And if that costs me my promotion"—she sighed and tried to swallow the lump in her throat—"so be it. If it costs me my job . . . well, then that would be a big mistake because . . . I'm honest and I'm good at what I do and . . . the loss would be yours."

She pushed through the conference room door blindly, hoping no one had seen the tears in her eyes. She wanted her job, but she was being driven by a far greater fear than that of losing it: an overwhelming fear of losing the things she hadn't—until recently—even known she believed in.

Faith. Hope. Love.

Ten

She straddled the line between rational and crazed as she drove out of town to Johnnie's Bend—not wanting to waste time getting tickets or causing a pileup on the highway. She was still traveling exactly nine miles over the speed limit when she skidded to a halt in front of Hedbo House.

Ryan was on the porch. He looked frantic.

There was a spark of anxiety for her favorite spring silk suit that fizzled out the moment she opened the car door to get out. Her heels made a nervous clattering noise in the muddy road and across the wet sidewalk as she watched him leap from the porch and join her halfway.

"I called the cops. I knocked on every door in the neighborhood. . . . Everyone's looking for him. I was just going to break a window and go in and look around for him. . . . I just have this gut feeling he's in there. . . . Where else would he go? But . . . hell, I didn't know they even had shatterproof glass when this place was built. And the doors are like granite. They don't build houses like this anymore. But I've looked all around . . . have this sick feeling he got in somehow, through some small space or something, and he's locked inside." He ran a frenzied hand through his hair. "I've called and called, but he doesn't answer . . . or can't answer."

Unable to get a word in edgewise—even if she could think of a word to give—M.J. continued up the walk, separating the keys on her ring until she found the right one for the front door. As usual, the key to the dead bolt worked perfectly, and she'd developed a confidence that the sisters would let her in using the old skeleton key, so she was shocked when it didn't budge.

"Oh God," she muttered—a prayer as panic and dread shot through her like adrenaline. A quick look at Ryan's face, and she knew what she had to do. "I am so very sorry, Ryan. I shouldn't have lied to you."

"About what?"

She shook her head. Better to show than tell.

She started to beat on the door with her fist. "Mother! Open the door. Is Jimmy in there with you? Mother! Please? Let us in."

Another glance up, and she could see the horror and confusion on his face like he couldn't deal with the loss of his son and the loss of her mind at the same time.

"Mother! Please."

"I'm sorry, darling. I tried." Adeline came through the door to join them on the porch. "Odelia tried. But Imogene's been dead longer than both of us. She has the most power."

"What? The longer you're dead, the more powerful you get?"

"What?" asked Ryan.

"Apparently. It seems the longer it takes you to find what you're looking for, the more power you get to help you find it."

"So Imogene is the one holding the house up, because without the house she—"

"What the hell are you talking about?" Ryan grabbed her arm. "What's happening to you?"

Obviously he couldn't see her mother.

"Mother? Would you mind?"

And clearly she didn't, as Ryan's eyes shifted from her face to over her shoulder, they grew larger and larger; his lips parted, and the pulse at the base of his throat began to pound rapidly. Then when Odelia took form behind him and said, "I'm here, too," he jumped three feet and threw his back against the door.

"Holy shit!"

"I know, I know, and I'm sorry. I shouldn't have lied to you, but I didn't think you'd believe me, number one. And number two, I was hoping I could help them leave before Jimmy ended up like that kid in *The Sixth Sense*. Now I see I only made him more curious and more determined to show you they were real and . . . and since she isn't here and I can't get into the house, I'm assuming this has something to do with Imogene."

"Who's Imogene?"

"She's our sister, dear," Odelia told him as Adeline addressed her daughter.

"He found the old coal chute on the side of the house and pried it open with a metal pipe of some kind he'd brought from home. I don't know if she was unaware of it or if she allowed it, but she went down into the cellar to light his way out when he lost his flashlight. He . . . he was excited to see us. I mean, once he'd seen Imogene, there was no point in us remaining a secret, was there?"

"I guess not. But why won't she let us in? Why didn't you send Jimmy home?"

"I thought we were going to. He wasn't afraid. He was laughing and . . . he's a charming child. We're all very fond of him." She saw that this was little comfort to Ryan and went on. "He asked to see some of Ruffie's toys."

"Roofie? You drugged him?" Ryan wasn't afraid anymore. He was enraged.

"No, no. Rufus. Imogene's son, dear." Odelia tried to calm him. "He passed as a child."

"There's a kid ghost in there, too?"

"Oh, no. We're convinced he passed to the Other Side without delay. Children nearly always do, they say."

"They who?"

She giggled and shrugged. "They who make the rules, I suppose."

"So you let Imogene take him upstairs to see the toys." M.J. was feeling sick to her stomach. "Then what happened?"

"We heard Ryan calling for him," Adeline said. "So Odelia and I went upstairs to tell him it was time to go home. But . . . "

"Go on. But what?"

"Imogene was rocking him in the chair, like she used to rock Ruffie when he was sick and couldn't breathe. She ignored us, like she couldn't hear us, when we told her Ryan was calling for him. She started singing to him, softly, but he could still hear us. He opened his eyes . . . he didn't say anything, but we could tell he was frightened and confused."

"Oh for God's sake." Ryan turned to the door and began hammering with his fist. "Jimmy. Hang in there, buddy, I'm coming. Don't be afraid. Daddy's here. I'm coming for you."

"Ryan. Ryan." She dodged his fist even as she tried to catch it with both her hands. "That won't help. She's literally holding the house up. Mr. Brown backed his backhoe into it two weeks ago, and it barely unsettled the dust." She stepped back and looked at them. "But there must be a limit to her powers, right? Do you think she can handle all four of us at once?"

"I should think that I have a good deal of strength, but I've never had the need to test it." Odelia clenched and unclenched her fists experimentally. She turned to the large picture window behind her and, summoning every ounce of concentration she had, dealt it a blow that had the cracked glass wobbling back and forth as if it were made of Jell-O.

"Wow." Ryan's appreciation was short-lived with Jimmy uppermost on his mind. He instructed them not to move when he dashed off the porch, saying he'd be right back as he ran up the street and around the corner.

"She won't hurt him, will she?" M.J. asked the sisters as soon as he was out of earshot. "He's so little and trusting. He must be terrified if she's not letting him loose. . . . I should never have lied to him . . . to either of them. This is all my fault."

"How were you supposed to know he'd break into the house?"

"You were doing what you thought was best, dear."

She sat on the top step in her favorite summer silk suit and put her head in her hands. Her chest felt over-full, and it hurt as if she'd been physically pummeled. It ached to breathe, and it was even more painful when she thought of Jimmy . . . and the hell Ryan must be going through.

It felt like forever but was only a matter of minutes before they heard Ryan's quick steps jogging back toward them. He was carrying a long-handled sledgehammer. His jaw was set with a scary determination that only a parent of an endangered child could muster.

"You take that window," he shouted to Odelia. "I'll work on this one."

"Wait a second." She got to her feet and stepped back onto

the porch. "Mother, you go up and do what you can to distract her. Tell Jimmy his dad's here so he won't worry." Adeline disappeared. "I'll do what I can with the door."

She and Ryan looked to Odelia for a go sign, and after a second or two, she gave the nod. M.J. turned the old key in the lock and jiggled the knob and threw her body against the door, over and over, until her teeth began to rattle. Ryan took swing after power-packed swing at the window on her right, knocking out tiny shards of glass here and there. And Odelia plowed first one fist and then the other above her head against the window on M.J.'s left, causing ripple after ripple in the old, shattered panes.

She finally sagged against the door to catch her breath, and a few minutes later Ryan let the hammer thump on the porch to get his second wind. That's when they heard the high-pitched ringing noise from Odelia's window, like a shrill scream that grew louder and louder until they covered their ears and then suddenly stopped.

Odelia turned her head and looked at them in surprise, and then everything happened at once. There came a fine cracking noise like footsteps on fine ice; Ryan grabbed her arm, turning her away from the window, bent her low over the arm he had around her waist, and covered as much of her body as he could when the window finally exploded, blasting glass in every direction.

"My goodness." Odelia sounded pleased and proud of her efforts, while they unfurled their bodies. Had there been more time, she would have taken a moment to relish the concern in Ryan's eyes as they scanned her head to toe for injuries, but as it was, she set it aside for now with the tiny hope of his forgiveness and turned to follow him through the window.

"My God, Ryan, you're bleeding!" She grabbed the back of his shirt to stop him; it was peppered with dime- to quarter-sized red spots. He jerked away.

"Forget it. I need to get Jimmy."

Calling for an ambulance occurred to her, but it was the last thing they needed at the moment unless Ryan was in serious danger. She grabbed his shirt again. "At least let me look. Jimmy needs his dad, not a corpse and"—this seemed to get through as he held his arms in the air and let her make a full inspection of his upper torso—"I don't know how I'd explain to him that you got shredded and bled to death protecting me from the . . . Oh, here's one. Is that better? The rest seem to be stuck in your shirt. Nothing too deep. Here's another. Okay. Okay?"

"Okay," he said, looking down at her as she passed below his right armpit to stand before him. He lowered his arms, and when his hand came even with her chin, he pinched it gently between his thumb and his fist and tilted her face up to his. "When this is over, we're going to have a long talk about keeping secrets from each other in the future. Okay?"

His expression and tone were unsmiling and stern, and she was thrilled. "Okay."

But she wasn't so elated that she for one second forgot the peril Jimmy was in . . . or how ill-equipped she was to deal with it. She hiked her skirt up high enough to step through the window casing behind Ryan—her heels making the move particularly tricky—and made straight for the stairs once inside.

The door at the end of the hall opened easily. Odelia and Adeline stood to one side of their sister, their expressions empathetic and disapproving at the same time. They looked at M.J. helplessly when she entered and remained silent.

Imogene sat in the high-backed rocker with Jimmy cradled in her arms, the afghan of muted colors pulled up around her shoulders and tucked securely about his young body.

"Jimmy!"

"Dad!" The boy turned his head at his father's voice and started to cry at the sight of him. Ryan started to charge forward . . . then flew out the door and halfway down the hall. Staggering, he got to his feet again and after a second or two started back with the same determined step.

"Wait." She put her hands on his chest and stopped him with her body. "Please. Let me try."

He cast her a look that was hard to decipher but didn't push through her. She dropped her hands and turned to the sisters.

"Imogene," she said softly. The ghost ignored her, pulling Jimmy closer and trying to soothe him instead. She caressed his brow and the outer side of his face. He shivered. "Imogene, he's cold. You need to let him go now so he doesn't get sick. He's frightened. Imogene?"

"His lips are turning blue." Ryan started forward again, and again she stopped him.

"Imogene, I've figured it out. At least . . . I think I have. While I was driving over here . . . I was thinking . . . I think I know what you lost in this house. I think I know what you all lost here because . . . because I've found it." She had Odelia and Adeline's confused attention. "Please. Let Jimmy go so we can talk about it."

Imogene raised her head at last and looked at her—ready to listen but far from willing to let Jimmy go. It was a start. A small one, if the grief and yearning on her face were any indication.

"I know it must feel so *good* to be holding a young boy in your arms again. Like a miracle, maybe . . . if you believed in that sort of thing. But you stopped believing in . . . well, everything, didn't you? At first it was just your ability to mother another child, and then it was your husband and your marriage that you abandoned; then you moved back here and lost your faith in everything else—God, life . . . yourself. I bet in all the time you've been dead you haven't really looked for what you lost because you had no faith that the Other Side even existed—your life was a misery of loneliness, guilt, and pain, so why shouldn't your afterlife be? And yet"—she held up her index finger and stepped closer to Jimmy—"and yet you gave up on living because you had no faith in an afterlife . . . but here you are. Think about it, Imogene. If you were wrong about there being nothing after death, then maybe you're also wrong about there being nowhere better to go from here."

She took a breath and another step toward Jimmy, watched the thoughtful expression on her aunt's face, then walked up next to the chair and placed the palm of her hand on Jimmy's chilly cheek to warm him.

"I'm no theologian . . . I don't know how it works. But I do know that for some things, so many things"—she glanced at Ryan and then down at Jimmy—"and for all the really important things in life, you have to believe and have a little faith and trust. Otherwise, nothing ever changes. You don't change." She slipped her hand through the emptiness of the afghan and took hold of Jimmy's arm. "Let go of Jimmy now. He's not what you need to ease the anguish in your heart."

Jimmy must have felt the tension in the ghost's arms slacken, because he reached up and took M.J.'s other hand, then lowered his feet to the floor and stepped away from the chair. Quickly, she put her body between them and pushed him toward Ryan, but he was reluctant to go. Instead, he peeked around her leg and addressed himself to Imogene.

"When you get to heaven, you can talk to my mom. She's been there a long time, and she'll know what you should do."

She stared at him a moment then gave him a small smile with a smaller nod to go with it.

All the women watched father and son embrace until a queer popping noise finally registered in their minds, and they looked back at one another.

"What is that?"

"Quick, dear, finish telling us what we lost. I believe the house is beginning to falter." Odelia and Adeline stepped closer to Imogene, silently encouraging her to maintain her hold on the house until M.J. was finished.

She turned to Ryan. "Go!"

"Not without you."

"I'll be fine. I'll come as soon as I can, but take Jimmy out of here before one of you gets hurt. Please. They won't let anything happen to me." She smiled in the light of her own newfound faith. "I'll only be a few more minutes. I promise."

Now it was his turn to have faith—in her—and despite the misgivings in his expression, he picked Jimmy up and headed for the stairs.

Still smiling, she turned back to the spirits of her mother and aunts with tears in her eyes. She was going to miss them.

With plaster dust floating down from the ceiling as the house began to tremble slightly, she shook her head at Odelia. "How long did you wait before you gave up all hope of becoming the second Julia Child . . . of being the world-famous chef, Odelia Hedbo?"

The sweet little woman giggled. "My stage name was going to be Heddy. *High Times with Heddy Hedbo.* And instead of *bon appétit!* I'd toast with real wine to my audiences' *health and wealth*! More *H*s, you see."

"And when did you realize your dream might not come true? Before or after your father died?"

Some of the joy drained from her face. "I kept getting older and older, and he kept living longer and longer . . . but Julia didn't appear on *The French Chef* until she was fifty-one."

"So you still had a little hope. And when your father died?"

She slipped a cautious glance at each of her sisters. "I was sad and I missed him very much but . . . but I was excited, too." She spoke rapidly. "I'd waited so long to start the life I wanted. I . . . I decided to start with my cookbook; that's how Julia did it. Hers was a great success, and then some big television executive saw her demonstrating how to make an omelet during an interview, and the rest was history. My cookbook was going to knock their socks off and—" She stopped abruptly.

"Except you didn't finish it."

Odelia shook her head.

"Because you got cancer and died."

She nodded once.

"And was that when you lost the rest of your hope?"

"I knew I'd die before I saw even one of my dreams come true. I'd wasted my entire life waiting and planning for something that would never be." She looked up in sudden understanding. "You're right, dear, I died with no hope at all."

"I'm sorry, Odelia." She was hard put to tell which sister had the sadder story. "I don't know if it'll help, but I thought if it was okay with you, I'd try to make some sense of those recipes in the drawer downstairs. I can't make any promises, of course, but maybe I can get your cookbook published."

"Truly?"

They grinned at one another and nodded.

"My name?"

"Of course."

"Odelia then. Not Heddy."

She heard running footsteps in the hall and turned to see Ryan, alone, coming after her. "I'm almost done. Go back. Please. Jimmy needs you."

"He's fine; he's with a neighbor. And I need you. The southeast corner is crumbling. I want you out now." He grabbed her hand and started to pull.

"Call it *Delicious Delights* by Odelia Hedbo."

"The simple, fun one or the serious one?" M.J. grabbed the doorjamb and held tight.

"Both? Oh my. Then call the fun one *Dandy Delights,* dear girl."

Suddenly, Imogene looked up, shook her head, and smiled—like she had the first day M.J. met her, so beautiful and serene. Throwing off the afghan, she got to her feet and wrapped her arms around Odelia. The sisters hugged and whispered to each other as Adeline stepped away from them and toward her daughter.

"Ryan's right, darling, you should leave now."

"Wait. Wait!" She used her eyes to plead with him. "She's my mother."

"Oh my," Adeline sighed. "I am that, and it's lovely to hear you say so with no remorse in your voice, but you've accomplished all we asked for and more. I believe you and I both know what I lost in this house—"

"What *we* lost in this house, Mother . . . we lost . . . our ability to love. We cut ourselves off from each other and from everyone else around us. You isolated yourself with your beauty just like I isolated myself with my brains—and we both missed out on so much of the joy and happiness we could have shared together. We blew it."

Adeline pressed her lips tight and bobbed her head in an iffy fashion. "Maybe not . . . not completely anyway. What's that old saying about a mistake not being a mistake if a lesson is learned. Have you learned any lessons here, Maribelle Joy?"

Man, she still hated that think-this-through tone of voice. . . .

"I thought we were working on *your* lessons, Mother."

Adeline's smile was amused and heartfelt. "We don't have time for a good argument, darling." She held her arms out to the sides, and M.J. noticed that both she and her sisters were becoming . . . thinner, starting to fade. "If you've learned anything from me, I'd like to hear it. Please."

She took a step forward, she was losing her mother—again. She wanted to fling her arms around her and hold on as she never had before but . . . instead she held a fist over her breaking heart and began to speak.

"I was born of a love so pure and strong it couldn't be replaced or forgotten or destroyed. I am lovable . . . just like you named me. And I know I can love because . . . well, because you've known all along what you lost in this house, but you hung around waiting for me, so we could have this time together and admit to what we were too stubborn to say when we had the chance—that we love one another. You did that for me. And that's what love is . . . caring and doing for others."

She felt Ryan's hand slip around hers, not urgently pulling her away, simply there—caring.

Her mother's smiling expression glowed as it had in every picture she'd seen of her with her father—happy and content. Imogene and Odelia joined her, their features satisfied and carefree. All three were barely visible now.

"Take good care of my daughter, young man."

"Mother!"

The aunts laughed.

"Yes, ma'am, I plan to. I will."

All three ghosts disappeared.

"That's a little creepy." Ryan stepped in front of her and took her other hand. "Are you all right?"

She was about to nod but screamed instead and hurled herself against him when the house shuddered, groaned, and settled into sudden silence. They held each other, heads down, hearts hammering, frozen in fear . . . then gradually started to thaw.

"I . . . I think that's it. The windows, the foundation under the southeast corner, everything she had supported until they could leave." She turned her face to where she'd last seen them. "I'm sorry I lied . . . but I'm going to miss them." She tipped her head back suddenly to look at him. "Is Jimmy okay? Oh God. Come on, you need to be with him. He'll never believe a thing I say after—"

She almost slipped when she came to the end of her arm and he didn't budge. Staggering back, she felt his arms come around her and knew she was safe.

She was half laughing when they came face-to-face, his arms locked around her waist, her hands on his forearms—but he was dead-dog serious.

"I feel we should continue your lessons before we go any further." He had a tone that was even more annoying than her mother's, but she owed him one this time, so . . .

"First, no more lies."

"I promise."

"Even if you don't think I'll believe you, at least let me decide whether or not I think you're nuts." She nodded. His mood was clearing quickly. "Second, don't worry about Jimmy not trusting you. Just be yourself and let him love you." Another nod despite the speculation on her face.

"And thirdly," he brought a hand to her face, caressed her cheek with his palm as he skimmed his fingers through her plaster-filled hair to the back of her head and drew her closer. "I want to reiterate that part of your lesson about you being completely lovable, so pay attention."

And he kissed her.